普通高等学校教材

英国文学教程:阅读与视角

王海燕　编著

武汉理工大学出版社
·武汉·

内 容 提 要

　　本书选取了莎士比亚的《一报还一报》、玛丽·雪莱的《弗兰肯斯坦》、D. H. 劳伦斯的《菊馨》、福斯特的《印度之行》、莱辛的《野草在歌唱》、威廉姆·戈尔丁的《蝇王》、约翰·福尔斯的《法国中尉的女人》和安吉拉·卡特的《与狼为伴》等英国文学史上不同历史时期、不同体裁的八个文本,引导学生从女性主义批评、文学伦理学批评、后殖民主义批评、生态批评、文化研究、后现代主义批评等视角来解读这些文本。

　　本书采用文本细读和理论分析相结合的方式,每个章节包括作家简介、作品简介、文本节选、问题思考、欣赏导读和拓展阅读等六部分,重在引导学生培养文本细读的能力和批判性思维的能力,为学生学习、欣赏和评析英国文学作品提供有益的指导和启示。本书的使用对象主要是高等学校的英语本科生和研究生以及喜欢英国文学的读者。

图书在版编目(CIP)数据

　英国文学教程:阅读与视角/王海燕编著. —武汉:武汉理工大学出版社,2019.8
　ISBN 978-7-5629-6003-4

　Ⅰ.①英… Ⅱ.①王… Ⅲ.①英国文学-文学研究-教材 Ⅳ.①I561.06

　中国版本图书馆 CIP 数据核字(2019)第 169938 号

项目负责人:王兆国　　　　　　　　　　　　　　责任编辑:王兆国
责 任 校 对:雷红娟　　　　　　　　　　　　　　排　　版:芳华时代
出版发行:武汉理工大学出版社(武汉市洪山区珞狮路 122 号　邮编:430070)
　　　　　http://www.wutp.com.cn
经 销 者:各地新华书店
印 刷 者:武汉市金港彩印有限公司
开　　本:710×1000　1/16
印　　张:16
字　　数:408 千字
版　　次:2019 年 8 月第 1 次印刷
印　　次:2019 年 8 月第 1 次印刷
定　　价:49.00 元

前　言

国内英美文学教材的编写多以史为纲,选编为主。本教材的编写有所突破,尝试着将文学文本的细读和文学批评理论结合,以问题为导向,引导学生深入阅读文本,并在文学批评理论的支撑下,学会从不同视角分析和研究文本;同时,强调培养学生的批判性思维能力和文学批评的写作能力。教材具有以下的特点:

首先,文本的选择尽量涵盖英国文学史的每个阶段,让读者可以较为全面地了解英国文学的发展脉络。文本的选择尽量多元化,文本涵盖了戏剧、小说和短篇小说,文本的风格也尽量多元化,让读者全面了解英国文学的成就。

其次,本教材的亮点在于提出问题,引导学生的批判性思维和深入阅读文本的能力。针对每篇文本的十个左右的问题、两个不同的视角、十本左右的拓展阅读文献,都旨在帮助学生培养文学批评素养、提高文学批评的能力,为学生的文学学术论文的写作打下良好的基础,也为读者进行更深入的文学研究提供路径。

本书是武汉理工大学研究生教材基金资助项目,也是研究生《英国文学导读》慕课课程的重要内容。在编写过程中,感谢我的研究生们的辛勤付出。

由于水平和学识有限,纰漏之处难免,敬请读者批评指正。

编者

CONTENTS

Chapter 1

William Shakespeare: Measure for Measure
Feminist Reading and Political Reading

Ⅰ. Introduction to William Shakespeare

William Shakespeare (1564—1616) is widely regarded as the greatest writer and the most preeminent dramatist in the world. His plays have been translated in over 50 languages and performed across the globe.

Unfortunately, the facts about Shakespeare's life are sparse and scattered. Shakespeare was born in 1564 in Stratford-upon-Avon, Warwickshire. His father, John Shakespeare, was a tanner, glover, and town official of Stratford. His mother Mary Arden came from an ancient family. William Shakespeare received primary education in Stratford Grammar School, where he studied mostly Latin literature, in Latin. Shakespeare probably left school at the age of 15, in 1579. There is no record of his attending university. Shakespeare married Anne Hathaway in 1582 and then had three children.

In about 1586, William Shakespeare left for London. Shakespeare started with some trivial work in a theater, which has great significance for his later career. Because of his extraordinary talents, he quickly began a successful career in London as an actor, writer, and part-owner of a playing company called the Lord Chamberlain's Men, later known as the King's Men. Most of his known plays were created between 1589 and 1613, which is said to be 38, including comedies, tragedies, histories and romances. His early plays were primarily comedies and histories, for example, the four greatest comedies, *A Midsummer Night's Dream* (1595), *Merchant of Venice* (1596), *Twelfth Night* (1599), *As You Like It* (1599). He then wrote mainly tragedies until about 1608, including *Hamlet* (1600), *Othello* (1604), *King Lear* (1605), and *Macbeth* (1605), considered four of the finest tragedies in the English language. His history plays include *Henry IV* (1597), *Henry V* (1599), *Henry VI* (1591), *Henry VIII* (1612), *King John* (1596), *Richard II* (1595), and *Richard III* (1591). Besides, he produced 154 sonnets and 2 long narrative poems. His sonnets are also masterpieces in English poetry.

William Shakespeare retired to Stratford around 1613, at age 49, where he died three years later. He is regarded as the greatest writer in the English language and the world's best-known dramatist and often called England's national poet and the "Bard of Avon". Ben Jonson, an excellent playwright, complimented Shakespeare as "not of an age, but for all time".

II. Introduction to the Play

Measure for Measure is a play believed to have been written by William Shakespeare in 1604. It was published in the *First Folio* of 1623, where it was listed as a comedy. Now it's widely considered as a "problem plays", meaning it shifts drastically between comedy and very dark tragedy. And the play's first recorded performance occurred in 1604.

Vincentio, the Duke of Vienna, makes it known that he intends to leave the city on a diplomatic mission. He leaves the government in the hands of a strict judge, Angelo, and appoints Escalus second in command.

Moral corruption is severe in the city due to the duke's lax management. Angelo intends stricter enforcement of laws, who orders the closure of whorehouse and cruel punishment on the moral transgressors. Thus, Claudio, a young gentleman who has got his lover Juliet pregnant, is sentenced to death. Claudio and Juliet love each other. Their marriage is delayed because Juliet's dowry has been held up by her relatives.

Claudio's friend, Lucio, visits Claudio's sister, Isabella, a novice nun, and asks her to intercede with Angelo on Claudio's behalf. Isabella pleads for mercy for Claudio. Over the course of two scenes between Angelo and Isabella, it becomes clear that he lusts after her, and he eventually offers her a deal: Angelo will spare Claudio's life if Isabella yields him her virginity. Isabella refuses. But when she threatens to publicly expose his lust, he tells her that no one will believe her, since his reputation is too austere. Later, Isabella visits her brother in prison and counsels him to prepare himself for death. Claudio desperately pleads with Isabella to satisfy Angelo's desire to save his life, but Isabella refuses.

The Duke, disguised as a friar, stays in the city and intervenes in and controls the action. He arranges a "bed trick", in which Mariana, betrothed to Angelo and forsaken by him because her dowry gets lost in an accident, will take Isabella's place to complete her deal with Angelo. Angelo, after the sexual encounter with Mariana (he is unaware of the substitution), still orders the death of Claudio. So the Duke arranges the "head trick", in which the head of another prisoner is sent in the name of Claudio.

The Duke also arranges Isabella's accusation of Angelo on his day back. In argument and contention, the truth is revealed. The Duke orders Angelo to marry Mariana and sentences him to death. With the plea from Mariana and Isabella, Angelo is forgiven. Two other marriages have also been ordered by the Duke: the marriage between Claudio and Juliet, between Lucio and his whore. Finally, the Duke himself proposes to Isabella.

This play touches upon complex issues and problems, social, moral, religious, and political, such as justice vs. mercy, sin and forgiveness, law and morality, chastity vs charity, benevolence and forgiveness, power and corruption, power and sex, sex and ordering, good and bad governing, which leaves great space for discussion from different perspectives. We mainly focus on the political and feminist reading of this play.

Ⅲ. Excerpt

Excerpt 1

ACT 1, SCENE 3. A monastery.

Enter DUKE VINCENTIO and FRIAR THOMAS

DUKE VINCENTIO
   No, holy father; throw away that thought;
   Believe not that the dribbling dart of love
   Can pierce a complete bosom. Why I desire thee
   To give me secret harbour, hath a purpose

More grave and wrinkled than the aims and ends
Of burning youth.

FRIAR THOMAS

May your grace speak of it?

DUKE VINCENTIO

My holy sir, none better knows than you
How I have ever loved the life removed
And held in idle price to haunt assemblies
Where youth, and cost, a witless bravery keeps.
I have deliver'd to Lord Angelo,
A man of stricture and firm abstinence,
My absolute power and place here in Vienna,
And he supposes me travell'd to Poland;
For so I have strew'd it in the common ear,
And so it is received. Now, pious sir,
You will demand of me why I do this?

FRIAR THOMAS

Gladly, my lord.

DUKE VINCENTIO

We have strict statutes and most biting laws, —
The needful bits and curbs to headstrong weeds, —
Which for this fourteen years we have let slip;
Even like an o'ergrown lion in a cave,
That goes not out to prey. Now, as fond fathers,
Having bound up the threatening twigs of birch,
Only to stick it in their children's sight
For terror, not to use, in time the rod
Becomes more mock'd than fear'd; so our decrees,
Dead to infliction, to themselves are dead;
And liberty plucks justice by the nose;
The baby beats the nurse, and quite athwart
Goes all decorum.

FRIAR THOMAS

It rested in your grace

To unloose this tied-up justice when you pleased:

And it in you more dreadful would have seem'd

Than in Lord Angelo.

DUKE VINCENTIO

I do fear, too dreadful:

Sith'twas my fault to give the people scope,

'Twould be my tyranny to strike and gall them

For what I bid them do: for we bid this be done,

When evil deeds have their permissive pass

And not the punishment. Therefore indeed, my father,

I have on Angelo imposed the office;

Who may, in the ambush of my name, strike home,

And yet my nature never in the fight

To do in slander. And to behold his sway,

I will, as'twere a brother of your order,

Visit both prince and people: therefore, I pr'ythee,

Supply me with the habit and instruct me

How I may formally in person bear me

Like a true friar. More reasons for this action

At our more leisure shall I render you;

Only, this one: Lord Angelo is precise;

Stands at a guard with envy; scarce confesses

That his blood flows, or that his appetite

Is more to bread than stone: hence shall we see,

If power change purpose, what our seemers be.

Exeunt

Excerpt 2

ACT 2, SCENE 4. A room in ANGELO's house.

Enter ANGELO

ANGELO

When I would pray and think, I think and pray

To several subjects. Heaven hath my empty words;
Whilst my invention, hearing not my tongue,
Anchors on Isabel: Heaven in my mouth,
As if I did but only chew his name;
And in my heart the strong and swelling evil
Of my conception. The state whereon I studied
Is like a good thing, being often read,
Grown sear'd and tedious; yea, my gravity,
Wherein—let no man hear me—I take pride,
Could I with boot change for an idle plume,
Which the air beats for vain. O place! O form!
How often dost thou with thy case, thy habit,
Wrench awe from fools and tie the wiser souls
To thy false seeming! Blood, thou art blood:
Let's write good angel on the devil's horn:
'Tis not the devil's crest.

Enter a Servant

How now! who's there?

Servant

One Isabel, a sister, desires access to you.

ANGELO

Teach her the way.

Exit Servant

O heavens!
Why does my blood thus muster to my heart,
Making both it unable for itself,
And dispossessing all my other parts
Of necessary fitness?
So play the foolish throngs with one that swoons;
Come all to help him, and so stop the air
By which he should revive: and even so
The general, subject to a well-wished king,

Quit their own part, and in obsequious fondness

Crowd to his presence, where their untaught love

Must needs appear offence.

Enter ISABELLA

How now, fair maid?

ISABELLA

I am come to know your pleasure.

ANGELO

That you might know it, would much better please me

Than to demand what'tis. Your brother cannot live.

ISABELLA

Even so. Heaven keep your honour!

ANGELO

Yet may he live awhile; and, it may be,

As long as you or I

yet he must die.

ISABELLA

Under your sentence?

ANGELO

Yea.

ISABELLA

When, I beseech you? that in his reprieve,

Longer or shorter, he may be so fitted

That his soul sicken not.

ANGELO

Ha! fie, these filthy vices! It were as good

To pardon him that hath from nature stolen

A man already made, as to remit

Their saucy sweetness that do coin heaven's image

In stamps that are forbid: 'tis all as easy

Falsely to take away a life true made

As to put metal in restrained means

To make a false one.

ISABELLA

'Tis set down so in heaven, but not in earth.

ANGELO

Say you so? then I shall pose you quickly.

Which had you rather, that the most just law

Now took your brother's life; or, to redeem him,

Give up your body to such sweet uncleanness

As she that he hath stain'd?

ISABELLA

Sir, believe this,

I had rather give my body than my soul.

ANGELO

I talk not of your soul: our compell'd sins

Stand more for number than for accompt.

ISABELLA

How say you?

ANGELO

Nay, I'll not warrant that; for I can speak

Against the thing I say. Answer to this:

I, now the voice of the recorded law,

Pronounce a sentence on your brother's life:

Might there not be a charity in sin

To save this brother's life?

ISABELLA

Please you to do't,

I'll take it as a peril to my soul,

It is no sin at all, but charity.

ANGELO

Pleased you to do't at peril of your soul,

Were equal poise of sin and charity.

ISABELLA

> That I do beg his life, if it be sin,
>
> Heaven let me bear it! you granting of my suit,
>
> If that be sin, I'll make it my morn prayer
>
> To have it added to the faults of mine,
>
> And nothing of your answer.

ANGELO

> Nay, but hear me.
>
> Your sense pursues not mine: either you are ignorant,
>
> Or seem so craftily; and that's not good.

ISABELLA

> Let me be ignorant, and in nothing good,
>
> But graciously to know I am no better.

ANGELO

> Thus wisdom wishes to appear most bright
>
> When it doth tax itself: as these black masks
>
> Proclaim an enshield beauty ten times louder
>
> Than beauty could, display'd. But mark me;
>
> To be received plain, I'll speak more gross:
>
> Your brother is to die.

ISABELLA

> So.

ANGELO

> And his offence is so, as it appears,
>
> Accountant to the law upon that pain.

ISABELLA

> True.

ANGELO

> Admit no other way to save his life,—
>
> As I subscribe not that, nor any other,
>
> But, in the loss of question,—that you, his sister,
>
> Finding yourself desired of such a person,

Whose credit with the judge, or own great place,
Could fetch your brother from the manacles
Of the all-building law; and that there were
No earthly mean to save him, but that either
You must lay down the treasures of your body
To this supposed, or else to let him suffer;
What would you do?

ISABELLA

As much for my poor brother as myself:
That is, were I under the terms of death,
The impression of keen whips I'd wear as rubies,
And strip myself to death, as to a bed
That longing have been sick for, ere I'd yield
My body up to shame.

ANGELO

Then must your brother die.

ISABELLA

And'twere the cheaper way:
Better it were a brother died at once
Than that a sister, by redeeming him,
Should die for ever.

ANGELO

Were not you then as cruel as the sentence
That you have slandered so?

ISABELLA

Ignominy in ransom and free pardon
Are of two houses: lawful mercy
Is nothing kin to foul redemption.

ANGELO

You seem'd of late to make the law a tyrant;
And rather proved the sliding of your brother
A merriment than a vice.

ISABELLA

O, pardon me, my lord; it oft falls out,

To have what we would have, we speak not what we mean:

I something do excuse the thing I hate,

For his advantage that I dearly love.

ANGELO

We are all frail.

ISABELLA

Else let my brother die,

If not a fedary, but only he

Owe and succeed thy weakness.

ANGELO

Nay, women are frail too.

ISABELLA

Ay, as the glasses where they view themselves;

Which are as easy broke as they make forms.

Women! Help Heaven! men their creation mar

In profiting by them. Nay, call us ten times frail;

For we are soft as our complexions are,

And credulous to false prints.

ANGELO

I think it well:

And from this testimony of your own sex,—

Since I suppose we are made to be no stronger

Than faults may shake our frames,—let me be bold;

I do arrest your words. Be that you are,

That is, a woman; if you be more, you're none;

If you be one, as you are well express'd

By all external warrants, show it now,

By putting on the destined livery.

ISABELLA

I have no tongue but one: gentle, my lord,

Let me entreat you speak the former language.

ANGELO

Plainly conceive, I love you.

ISABELLA

My brother did love Juliet,

And you tell me that he shall die for it.

ANGELO

He shall not, Isabel, if you give me love.

ISABELLA

I know your virtue hath a licence in't,

Which seems a little fouler than it is,

To pluck on others.

ANGELO

Believe me, on mine honour,

My words express my purpose.

ISABELLA

Ha! little honour to be much believed,

And most pernicious purpose! Seeming, seeming!

I will proclaim thee, Angelo; look for't:

Sign me a present pardon for my brother,

Or with an outstretch'd throat I'll tell the world aloud

What man thou art.

ANGELO

Who will believe thee, Isabel?

My unsoil'd name, the austereness of my life,

My vouch against you, and my place i' the state,

Will so your accusation overweigh,

That you shall stifle in your own report

And smell of calumny. I have begun,

And now I give my sensual race the rein:

Fit thy consent to my sharp appetite;

Lay by all nicety and prolixious blushes,

That banish what they sue for; redeem thy brother

By yielding up thy body to my will;

Or else he must not only die the death,

But thy unkindness shall his death draw out

To lingering sufferance. Answer me to-morrow,

Or, by the affection that now guides me most,

I'll prove a tyrant to him. As for you,

Say what you can, my false o'erweighs your true.

Exit

ISABELLA

To whom should I complain? Did I tell this,

Who would believe me? O perilous mouths,

That bear in them one and the self-same tongue,

Either of condemnation or approof!

Bidding the law make court'sy to their will:

Hooking both right and wrong to the appetite,

To follow as it draws! I'll to my brother:

Though he hath fallen by prompture of the blood,

Yet hath he in him such a mind of honour.

That, had he twenty heads to tender down

On twenty bloody blocks, he'd yield them up,

Before his sister should her body stoop

To such abhorr'd pollution.

Then, Isabel, live chaste, and, brother, die:

More than our brother is our chastity.

I'll tell him yet of Angelo's request,

And fit his mind to death, for his soul's rest.

Exit

Excerpt 3

ACT 5, SCENE 1. The city gate.

MARIANA veiled, ISABELLA, and FRIAR PETER, at their stand.
Enter DUKE VINCENTIO, VARRIUS, Lords, ANGELO, ESCALUS,
LUCIO, Provost, Officers, and Citizens, at several doors

DUKE VINCENTIO

My very worthy cousin, fairly met;—

Our old and faithful friend, we are glad to see you.

ANGELO ESCALUS

Happy return be to your royal grace!

DUKE VINCENTIO

Many and hearty thankings to you both.

We have made inquiry of you; and we hear

Such goodness of your justice, that our soul

Cannot but yield you forth to public thanks,

Forerunning more requital.

ANGELO

You make my bonds still greater.

DUKE VINCENTIO

O, your desert speaks loud; and I should wrong it,

To lock it in the wards of covert bosom,

When it deserves, with characters of brass,

A forted residence 'gainst the tooth of time

And razure of oblivion. Give me your hand,

And let the subject see, to make them know

That outward courtesies would fain proclaim

Favours that keep within. Come, Escalus,

You must walk by us on our other hand;

And good supporters are you.

FRIAR PETER and ISABELLA come forward

FRIAR PETER

Now is your time: speak loud and kneel before him.

ISABELLA

Justice, O royal duke! Vail your regard

Upon a wrong'd, I would fain have said, a maid!

O worthy prince, dishonour not your eye

By throwing it on any other object

Till you have heard me in my true complaint

And given me justice, justice, justice, justice!

DUKE VINCENTIO

Relate your wrongs; In what? By whom? Be brief.

Here is Lord Angelo shall give you justice:

Reveal yourself to him.

ISABELLA

O worthy duke,

You bid me seek redemption of the devil:

Hear me yourself; for that which I must speak

Must either punish me, not being believed,

Or wring redress from you. Hear me, O hear me, here!

ANGELO

My lord, her wits, I fear me, are not firm:

She hath been a suitor to me for her brother

Cut off by course of justice.

ISABELLA

By course of justice!

ANGELO

And she will speak most bitterly and strange.

ISABELLA

Most strange, but yet most truly, will I speak:

That Angelo's forsworn; is it not strange?

That Angelo's a murderer; is't not strange?

That Angelo is an adulterous thief,

An hypocrite, a virgin-violator;

Is it not strange and strange?

DUKE VINCENTIO

Nay, it is ten times strange.

ISABELLA

It is not truer he is Angelo

Than this is all as true as it is strange:

Nay, it is ten times true; for truth is truth
To the end of reckoning.

DUKE VINCENTIO

Away with her! Poor soul,
She speaks this in the infirmity of sense.

ISABELLA

O prince, I conjure thee, as thou believ'st
There is another comfort than this world,
That thou neglect me not, with that opinion
That I am touch'd with madness! Make not impossible
That which but seems unlike; 'tis not impossible
But one, the wicked'st caitiff on the ground,
May seem as shy, as grave, as just, as absolute
As Angelo; even so may Angelo,
In all his dressings, characts, titles, forms,
Be an arch-villain; believe it, royal prince:
If he be less, he's nothing; but he's more,
Had I more name for badness.

DUKE VINCENTIO

By mine honesty,
If she be mad, as I believe no other,
Her madness hath the oddest frame of sense,
Such a dependency of thing on thing,
As e'er I heard in madness.

ISABELLA

O gracious duke,
Harp not on that, nor do not banish reason
For inequality; but let your reason serve
To make the truth appear where it seems hid,
And hide the false seems true.

DUKE VINCENTIO

Many that are not mad
Have, sure, more lack of reason. What would you say?

ISABELLA

> I am the sister of one Claudio,
> Condemn'd upon the act of fornication
> To lose his head; condemn'd by Angelo:
> I, in probation of a sisterhood,
> Was sent to by my brother; one Lucio
> As then the messenger,—

LUCIO

> That's I, an't like your grace:
> I came to her from Claudio, and desired her
> To try her gracious fortune with Lord Angelo
> For her poor brother's pardon.

ISABELLA

> That's he indeed.

DUKE VINCENTIO

> You were not bid to speak.

LUCIO

> No, my good lord;
> Nor wish'd to hold my peace.

DUKE VINCENTIO

> I wish you now, then;
> Pray you, take note of it: and when you have
> A business for yourself, pray heaven you then
> Be perfect.

LUCIO

> I warrant your honour.

DUKE VINCENTIO

> The warrant's for yourself; take heed to't.

ISABELLA

> This gentleman told somewhat of my tale.

LUCIO

> Right.

DUKE VINCENTIO

It may be right; but you are in the wrong

To speak before your time. Proceed.

ISABELLA

I went

To this pernicious caitiff deputy.

DUKE VINCENTIO

That's somewhat madly spoken.

ISABELLA

Pardon it;

The phrase is to the matter.

DUKE VINCENTIO

Mended again. The matter; proceed.

ISABELLA

In brief, to set the needless process by,

How I persuaded, how I pray'd, and kneel'd,

How he refell'd me, and how I replied,—

For this was of much length,—the vile conclusion

I now begin with grief and shame to utter:

He would not, but by gift of my chaste body

To his concupiscible intemperate lust,

Release my brother; and, after much debatement,

My sisterly remorse confutes mine honour,

And I did yield to him. But the next morn betimes,

His purpose surfeiting, he sends a warrant

For my poor brother's head.

DUKE VINCENTIO

This is most likely!

ISABELLA

O, that it were as like as it is true!

DUKE VINCENTIO

By heaven, fond wretch, thou know'st not what thou speak'st,

Or else thou art suborn'd against his honour

In hateful practise. First, his integrity

Stands without blemish. Next, it imports no reason

That with such vehemency he should pursue

Faults proper to himself: if he had so offended,

He would have weigh'd thy brother by himself

And not have cut him off. Some one hath set you on:

Confess the truth, and say by whose advice

Thou cam'st here to complain.

ISABELLA

And is this all?

Then, O you blessed ministers above,

Keep me in patience, and with ripen'd time

Unfold the evil which is here wrapt up

In countenance! Heaven shield your grace from woe,

As I, thus wrong'd, hence unbelieved go!

DUKE VINCENTIO

I know you'd fain be gone. An officer!

To prison with her! Shall we thus permit

A blasting and a scandalous breath to fall

On him so near us? This needs must be a practise.

Who knew of your intent and coming hither?

ISABELLA

One that I would were here, Friar Lodowick.

DUKE VINCENTIO

A ghostly father, belike. Who knows that Lodowick?

LUCIO

My lord, I know him; 'tis a meddling friar;

I do not like the man: had he been lay, my lord

For certain words he spake against your grace

In your retirement, I had swinged him soundly.

DUKE VINCENTIO

Words against me? This is a good friar, belike!

And to set on this wretched woman here

Against our substitute! Let this friar be found.

LUCIO

But yesternight, my lord, she and that friar,

I saw them at the prison: a saucy friar,

A very scurvy fellow.

FRIAR PETER

Blessed be your royal grace!

I have stood by, my lord, and I have heard

Your royal ear abused. First, hath this woman

Most wrongfully accused your substitute,

Who is as free from touch or soil with her

As she from one ungot.

DUKE VINCENTIO

We did believe no less.

Know you that Friar Lodowick that she speaks of?

FRIAR PETER

I know him for a man divine and holy;

Not scurvy, nor a temporary meddler,

As he's reported by this gentleman;

And, on my trust, a man that never yet

Did, as he vouches, misreport your grace.

LUCIO

My lord, most villanously; believe it.

FRIAR PETER

Well, he in time may come to clear himself;

But at this instant he is sick, my lord,

Of a strange fever. Upon his mere request,

Being come to knowledge that there was complaint

Intended 'gainst Lord Angelo, came I hither,

To speak, as from his mouth, what he doth know

Is true and false; and what he with his oath

And all probation will make up full clear,

Whensoever he's convented. First, for this woman,

To justify this worthy nobleman,

So vulgarly and personally accused,

Her shall you hear disproved to her eyes,

Till she herself confess it.

DUKE VINCENTIO

Good friar, let's hear it.

ISABELLA is carried off guarded; and MARIANA comes forward

Do you not smile at this, Lord Angelo?

O heaven, the vanity of wretched fools!

Give us some seats. Come, cousin Angelo;

In this I'll be impartial; be you judge

Of your own cause. Is this the witness, friar?

First, let her show her face, and after speak.

MARIANA

Pardon, my lord; I will not show my face

Until my husband bid me.

DUKE VINCENTIO

What, are you married?

MARIANA

No, my lord.

DUKE VINCENTIO

Are you a maid?

MARIANA

No, my lord.

DUKE VINCENTIO

A widow, then?

MARIANA

Neither, my lord.

DUKE VINCENTIO

Why, you are nothing then: neither maid, widow, nor wife?

LUCIO

My lord, she may be a punk; for many of them are
neither maid, widow, nor wife.

DUKE VINCENTIO

Silence that fellow: I would he had some cause
To prattle for himself.

LUCIO

Well, my lord.

MARIANA

My lord; I do confess I ne'er was married;
And I confess besides I am no maid:
I have known my husband; yet my husband
Knows not that ever he knew me.

LUCIO

He was drunk then, my lord: it can be no better.

DUKE VINCENTIO

For the benefit of silence, would thou wert so too!

LUCIO

Well, my lord.

DUKE VINCENTIO

This is no witness for Lord Angelo.

MARIANA

Now I come to't, my lord
She that accuses him of fornication,
In self-same manner doth accuse my husband,
And charges him my lord, with such a time
When I'll depose I had him in mine arms
With all the effect of love.

ANGELO

Charges she more than me?

MARIANA

Not that I know.

DUKE VINCENTIO

No? you say your husband.

MARIANA

Why, just, my lord, and that is Angelo,

Who thinks he knows that he ne'er knew my body,

But knows he thinks that he knows Isabel's.

ANGELO

This is a strange abuse. Let's see thy face.

MARIANA

My husband bids me; now I will unmask.

Unveiling

This is that face, thou cruel Angelo,

Which once thou sworest was worth the looking on;

This is the hand which, with a vow'd contract,

Was fast belock'd in thine; this is the body

That took away the match from Isabel,

And did supply thee at thy garden-house

In her imagined person.

DUKE VINCENTIO

Know you this woman?

LUCIO

Carnally, she says.

DUKE VINCENTIO

Sirrah, no more!

LUCIO

Enough, my lord.

ANGELO

My lord, I must confess I know this woman:

And five years since there was some speech of marriage

Betwixt myself and her; which was broke off,

Partly for that her promised proportions

Came short of composition, but in chief

For that her reputation was disvalued

In levity: since which time of five years

I never spake with her, saw her, nor heard from her,

Upon my faith and honour.

MARIANA

Noble prince,

As there comes light from heaven and words from breath,

As there is sense in truth and truth in virtue,

I am affianced this man's wife as strongly

As words could make up vows: and, my good lord,

But Tuesday night last gone in's garden-house

He knew me as a wife. As this is true,

Let me in safety raise me from my knees,

Or else for ever be confixed here,

A marble monument!

ANGELO

I did but smile till now:

Now, good my lord, give me the scope of justice

My patience here is touch'd. I do perceive

These poor informal women are no more

But instruments of some more mightier member

That sets them on: let me have way, my lord,

To find this practise out.

DUKE VINCENTIO

Ay, with my heart

And punish them to your height of pleasure.

Thou foolish friar, and thou pernicious woman,

Compact with her that's gone, think'st thou thy oaths,

Though they would swear down each particular saint,

Were testimonies against his worth and credit

That's seal'd in approbation? You, Lord Escalus,

Sit with my cousin; lend him your kind pains

To find out this abuse, whence'tis derived.

There is another friar that set them on;

Let him be sent for.

. . . . .

DUKE VINCENTIO

[To ESCALUS] What you have spoke I pardon: sit you down:

We'll borrow place of him.

To ANGELO

Sir, by your leave.

Hast thou or word, or wit, or impudence,

That yet can do thee office? If thou hast,

Rely upon it till my tale be heard,

And hold no longer out.

ANGELO

O my dread lord,

I should be guiltier than my guiltiness,

To think I can be undiscernible,

When I perceive your grace, like power divine,

Hath look'd upon my passes. Then, good prince,

No longer session hold upon my shame,

But let my trial be mine own confession:

Immediate sentence then and sequent death

Is all the grace I beg.

DUKE VINCENTIO

Come hither, Mariana.

Say, wast thou e'er contracted to this woman?

ANGELO

I was, my lord.

DUKE VINCENTIO

Go, take her hence, and marry her instantly.

Do you the office, friar; which consummate,

Return him here again. Go with him, Provost.

Exeunt ANGELO, MARIANA, FRIAR PETER and Provost

ESCALUS

My lord, I am more amazed at his dishonour

Than at the strangeness of it.

DUKE VINCENTIO

Come hither, Isabel.

Your friar is now your prince. As I was then

Advertising and holy to your business,

Not changing heart with habit, I am still

Attorney'd at your service.

ISABELLA

O, give me pardon,

That I, your vassal, have employ'd and pain'd

Your unknown sovereignty!

DUKE VINCENTIO

You are pardon'd, Isabel.

And now, dear maid, be you as free to us.

Your brother's death, I know, sits at your heart;

And you may marvel why I obscured myself,

Labouring to save his life, and would not rather

Make rash remonstrance of my hidden power

Than let him so be lost. O most kind maid,

It was the swift celerity of his death,

Which I did think with slower foot came on,

That brain'd my purpose. But, peace be with him!

That life is better life, past fearing death,

Than that which lives to fear: make it your comfort,

So happy is your brother.

ISABELLA

I do, my lord.

Re-enter ANGELO, MARIANA, FRIAR PETER, and Provost

DUKE VINCENTIO

> For this new-married man approaching here,
> Whose salt imagination yet hath wrong'd
> Your well defended honour, you must pardon
> For Mariana's sake: but as he adjudged your brother,—
> Being criminal, in double violation
> Of sacred chastity and of promise-breach
> Thereon dependent, for your brother's life,—
> The very mercy of the law cries out
> Most audible, even from his proper tongue,
> 'An Angelo for Claudio, death for death!'
> Haste still pays haste, and leisure answers leisure;
> Like doth quit like, and measure still for measure.
> Then, Angelo, thy fault's thus manifested;
> Which, though thou wouldst deny, denies thee vantage.
> We do condemn thee to the very block
> Where Claudio stoop'd to death, and with like haste.
> Away with him!

MARIANA

> O my most gracious lord,
> I hope you will not mock me with a husband!

DUKE VINCENTIO

> It is your husband mock'd you with a husband.
> Consenting to the safeguard of your honour,
> I thought your marriage fit; else imputation,
> For that he knew you, might reproach your life
> And choke your good to come; for his possessions,
> Although by confiscation they are ours,
> We do instate and widow you withal,
> To buy you a better husband.

MARIANA

> O my dear lord,
> I crave no other, nor no better man.

DUKE VINCENTIO

Never crave him; we are definitive.

MARIANA

Gentle my liege,—

Kneeling

DUKE VINCENTIO

You do but lose your labour.
Away with him to death!

To LUCIO

Now, sir, to you.

MARIANA

O my good lord! Sweet Isabel, take my part;
Lend me your knees, and all my life to come
I'll lend you all my life to do you service.

DUKE VINCENTIO

Against all sense you do importune her:
Should she kneel down in mercy of this fact,
Her brother's ghost his paved bed would break,
And take her hence in horror.

MARIANA

Isabel,
Sweet Isabel, do yet but kneel by me;
Hold up your hands, say nothing; I'll speak all.
They say, best men are moulded out of faults;
And, for the most, become much more the better
For being a little bad: so may my husband.
O Isabel, will you not lend a knee?

DUKE VINCENTIO

He dies for Claudio's death.

ISABELLA

Most bounteous sir,

Kneeling

Look, if it please you, on this man condemn'd,
As if my brother lived: I partly think
A due sincerity govern'd his deeds,
Till he did look on me: since it is so,
Let him not die. My brother had but justice,
In that he did the thing for which he died:
For Angelo,
His act did not o'ertake his bad intent,
And must be buried but as an intent
That perish'd by the way: thoughts are no subjects;
Intents but merely thoughts.

MARIANA

Merely, my lord.

DUKE VINCENTIO

Your suit's unprofitable; stand up, I say.
I have bethought me of another fault.
Provost, how came it Claudio was beheaded
At an unusual hour?

Provost

It was commanded so.

DUKE VINCENTIO

Had you a special warrant for the deed?

Provost

No, my good lord; it was by private message.

DUKE VINCENTIO

For which I do discharge you of your office:
Give up your keys.

Provost

Pardon me, noble lord:
I thought it was a fault, but knew it not;
Yet did repent me, after more advice;

For testimony whereof, one in the prison,

That should by private order else have died,

I have reserved alive.

DUKE VINCENTIO

What's he?

Provost

His name is Barnardine.

DUKE VINCENTIO

I would thou hadst done so by Claudio.

Go fetch him hither; let me look upon him.

Exit Provost

ESCALUS

I am sorry, one so learned and so wise

As you, Lord Angelo, have still appear'd,

Should slip so grossly, both in the heat of blood.

And lack of temper'd judgment afterward.

ANGELO

I am sorry that such sorrow I procure:

And so deep sticks it in my penitent heart

That I crave death more willingly than mercy;

'Tis my deserving, and I do entreat it.

Re-enter Provost, with BARNARDINE, CLAUDIO muffled, and JULIET

DUKE VINCENTIO

Which is that Barnardine?

Provost

This, my lord.

DUKE VINCENTIO

There was a friar told me of this man.

Sirrah, thou art said to have a stubborn soul.

That apprehends no further than this world,

And squar'st thy life according. Thou'rt condemn'd:
But, for those earthly faults, I quit them all;
And pray thee take this mercy to provide
For better times to come. Friar, advise him;
I leave him to your hand. What muffled fellow's that?

Provost

This is another prisoner that I saved.
Who should have died when Claudio lost his head;
As like almost to Claudio as himself.

Unmuffles CLAUDIO

DUKE VINCENTIO

[To ISABELLA] If he be like your brother, for his sake
Is he pardon'd; and, for your lovely sake,
Give me your hand and say you will be mine.
He is my brother too: but fitter time for that.
By this Lord Angelo perceives he's safe;
Methinks I see a quickening in his eye.
Well, Angelo, your evil quits you well:
Look that you love your wife; her worth worth yours.
I find an apt remission in myself;
And yet here's one in place I cannot pardon.

To LUCIO

You, sirrah, that knew me for a fool, a coward,
One all of luxury, an ass, a madman;
Wherein have I so deserved of you,
That you extol me thus?

LUCIO

Faith, my lord. I spoke it but according to the
trick. If you will hang me for it, you may; but I
had rather it would please you I might be whipped.

DUKE VINCENTIO

Whipp'd first, sir, and hanged after.

Proclaim it, provost, round about the city.
Is any woman wrong'd by this lewd fellow,
As I have heard him swear himself there's one
Whom he begot with child, let her appear,
And he shall marry her: the nuptial finish'd,
Let him be whipp'd and hang'd.

LUCIO

I beseech your highness, do not marry me to a whore.
Your highness said even now, I made you a duke:
good my lord, do not recompense me in making me a cuckold.

DUKE VINCENTIO

Upon mine honour, thou shalt marry her.
Thy slanders I forgive; and therewithal
Remit thy other forfeits. Take him to prison;
And see our pleasure herein executed.

LUCIO

Marrying a punk, my lord, is pressing to death,
whipping, and hanging.

DUKE VINCENTIO

Slandering a prince deserves it.

Exit Officers with LUCIO

She, Claudio, that you wrong'd, look you restore.
Joy to you, Mariana! Love her, Angelo:
I have confess'd her and I know her virtue.
Thanks, good friend Escalus, for thy much goodness:
There's more behind that is more gratulate.
Thanks, provost, for thy care and secrecy:
We shill employ thee in a worthier place.
Forgive him, Angelo, that brought you home
The head of Ragozine for Claudio's:
The offence pardons itself. Dear Isabel,
I have a motion much imports your good;
Whereto if you'll a willing ear incline,

What's mine is yours and what is yours is mine.

So, bring us to our palace; where we'll show

What's yet behind, that's meet you all should know.

Exeunt

Ⅳ. Questions For Thinking

1. Isabella can have sex with Angelo and save her brother's life, or she can remain a virgin and watch her brother die. How do we understand her choice?
2. Why does Isabella herself refuse to have sexual relation with Angelo, but agree to persuade Mariana into the "bed trick"?
3. At the play's end, when the Duke proposes to Isabella, Isabella remains completely silent (5. 1). Do you think Isabella will accept or reject Duke's proposal? Why?
4. Does Isabella function as a symbol of femininity? Why or why not?
5. Why does Mariana go along with the "bed trick"? Does she really love Angelo and want to win him back? Does she want to get back at Angelo?
6. Comment on other female images in the play, Juliet, Mrs. Overdone and other prostitutes.
7. Compare two rulers in the play: Angelo and the Duke. Do you think the Duke a good ruler? Does Shakespeare seem to think the Duke a good ruler?
8. How do you understand the crisis of the state? Does the play think morality can or should be regulated by the government?
9. Do you think moral transgression can lead to political corruption?
10. What does Angelo's behavior to Isabella and Mariana suggest about the relationship between gender and power?

Ⅴ. Guidance of Appreciation

Since its publication and public performance, the play *Measure for Measure* has attracted the attention of both readers as well as critics. The research into this play is fruitful in its quantity and quality. The themes of mercy vs justice, the images of Angelo, the Duke and Isabella, the arrangements of the plot have been explored. However, a feminist reading of this play is worth trying.

In this play, there are four major female characters, Isabella, Mariana, Juliet and Mistress. Overdone. Among them, Isabella is a nun even not willing to sacrifice her virginity to save her brother's life. Mrs. Overdone is a prostitute. Juliet is forced to separate from her beloved fiancé because of her unwed pregnancy. And Mariana is abandoned by her fiancé because she has lost her dowries. The portrayal of these characters has received much criticism.

All these four female characters are passive in their life, without any control of their life and fate. At the beginning of the play, Isabella stands on the threshold of a nunnery, ready to submit herself to the strict order of the Rule. Why does Isabella make such a choice? Critics have assumed several reasons: the lack of dowry and her retreat from the corrupt "Viennese marriage market" that objectifies women as "commodities". No matter for what reason, she makes her own choice. However, she soon gets involved and has to face the difficult choice between her virginity and her brother's life. In this hard choice between chastity and charity, she believes that her chastity is more valuable to her brother's life. In doing so, she is criticized for being an uptight ice-maiden. To complicate matters, Shakespeare introduces another ambiguous matter at the play's end. When the Duke proposes to her, Isabella remains completely silent (5. 1). Isabella has to face another difficult choice between devoting herself to God and to the Duke. Isabella is speechless because she has no way to reject the Duke. Some may consider it a happy ending when Isabella becomes the wife of the town's leader, particularly since she has saved her brother's life. But at the same time this situation reinforces her loss of sexual independence. Her marriage to the Duke confirms her virtue while denying her independence.

Mariana is another pathetic female image. She is Angelo's fiancée but deserted by him after the loss of dowries. However, when Isabella persuades her into the "bed trick", she accepts with pleasure. She gives her virginity to her unmarried husband but doesn't get his love. That is to say, she is just a tool, and her destiny is controlled by others. Although Angelo discards her and does not love her, in the end, she still begs the Duke to forgive Angelo and is willing to marry him. Are all these things out of love? Does Mariana really love Angelo? So she did all these to win him back. Or we think it twice, since she is engaged to Angelo, it is difficult for her to find another husband. As she is taught, she can only have one husband and keep her virginity to her husband. Although she finally gets married to Angelo, they probably will not be happy. Mariana is the object while Angelo is the subject and the center.

Juliet is the only female in this play who has found her beloved man. But because of the premarital sex, her fiancé is sentenced to death. These two young people love each other but cannot have a happy ending, why is it? The social ethic forbids premarital sex while prostitutes can make a living by selling themselves. Angelo hates Claudio's behavior but he himself wants to occupy Isabella illegally as well. It seems that everyone has two different standards towards women and women's bodies. At the end of the play, Juliet and Claudio can have a happy ending. Is this a victory of female rebellion? All in all, feminism is a good way to interpret those female images in this play.

American feminist writer, Kate Millett, once said in her *Sexual Politics* that a female is born but a woman is created, showing society's influence on women. Is Mrs. Overdone bound to be a prostitute? I bet not. Her name "Mistress Overdone" suggests that she is just the passive receiver of male's sexual desire. Her body involves economic profits. On one hand, males despise prostitutes for their flippancy; on the other hand, they are happy to play with them. Obviously, prostitutes have no status and they are just vent tools of men. They even don't have names in this play. They are voiceless and live in the margin of society. From Mistress. Overdone and other prostitutes, we could learn that men and women are far away from being equal.

Moreover, like many of Shakespeare's plays, *Measure for Measure* ends with four marriages, Angelo and Maria, the Duke and Isabella, Claudio and Juliet, and Lucio and unknown prostitute. But if we explore the essence of these marriages, we can find that all the marriages are arranged by the duke, and he is employing the power of Father. Angelo shows no affection to Maria; Lucio makes no disguise of his dislike towards for his match; and Isabella remains silent and indifferent to his proposal. Marriage is not an expression for ensuring mutual love and cooperation but a tool for displaying the monarch's authority. It is ironical that the marriage between Claudio and Julietta, the only one based on mutual love and mutual consent is severely condemned as sinful.

The political reading of the play can start from the question "why does the Duke leave the city?" The Duke declares that he leaves on a diplomatic mission. He also mentions that the state is faced with serious problems of morality decline and lax law, for which he himself should be responsible. However, he doesn't want to undertake the due obligations. Instead, he leaves them to Angelo, who, after takes the power, immediately orders the close down of brothels and death sentence of moral transgressor Claudio. In this sense, the whole play seems to focus on moral issues so someone thinks it is a moral play. But if we go further, we can find more under the cover of moral issues. We can consider at least three points: the crisis of the state, the corruption of Angelo, and the conflict between the Duke and Angelo.

First, the state is not only faced with moral problems, but also diplomatic, social, economic and political crises. The mention of the talk of the Duke with other Dukes against the King of Hungary implies the possibility of war. The decline of morality not only corrupts males' bodies and minds, but also influences the stability of the state and economic downturn. The law is poorly implemented, leading to many social problems. Angelo's fame becomes more and more impressive, and may even overshadow him, which is unacceptable to the Duke.

Second, the corruption of Angelo is not only moral degeneration. When he sentences Claudio to death for the crime of "fornication" and then turns around and propositions an apprentice nun, by using his power, it has turned into political corruption. We can go further to discuss the relationship between power and sex.

Third, the conflict between the Duke and Angelo can be understood from the perspective of two ways of governing a state. We cannot forget that the play *Measure for Measure* was written at the time of a major political turning point in history when James I's ascension to the throne. So questions such as who is to rule, what is the nature of that rule, What is the relation between ruler and law, remain on the agenda of English life. So *Measure for Measure*, from its first moment, announces itself "of government, the properties to unfold" (*Measure for Measure*, Act I)

Ⅵ. **Further Reading**

1. Cooper, Tarnya. Searching for Shakespeare[M]. London : National Portrait Gallery, 2006.
2. Halper, Louise. *Measure For Measure*: Law, Prerogative, Subversion[J]. Cardozo Studies in Law and Literature , Vol. 13, No. 2 (Fall 2001): 221-264.

3. Lascelles, Mary. Shakespeare's *Measure for measure* [M]. London : Bloomsbury Academic, 2013.

4. Schanzer, Ernest. The problem plays of Shakespeare: a study of Julius Caesar, Measure for measure, Antony and Cleopatra [M]. New York : Routledge, Taylor & Francis Group, 2005.

5. Wood, Nigel & Peter Corbin. Measure for Measure [M]. Bristol, PA : Open University Press, 1996.

6. (美)阿兰·布鲁姆(Allan Bloom). 莎士比亚的政治 [M]. 南京：江苏人民出版社, 2009.

7. 陆谷孙. 莎士比亚研究十讲 [M]. 上海：复旦大学出版社, 2005.

8. 彭磊. 莎士比亚戏剧与政治哲学 [M]. 北京：华夏出版社, 2011.

9. 张冲. 莎士比亚专题研究 [M]. 上海：上海外语教育出版社, 2004.

10. 张冲. 视觉时代的莎士比亚：莎士比亚电影研究 [M]. 北京：北京大学出版社, 2009.

Chapter 2

Marry Shelley: *Frankenstein*
Psychoanalysis and Identity

I. Introduction to Marry Shelley

Mary Shelley (1797—1851) is an English novelist and short story writer. She is best remembered as the author of *Frankenstein: or, The Modern Prometheus* (1818) and the wife of Percy Bysshe Shelley, a famous Romantic poet. The word "Frankenstein" has become a synonym for monster.

Mary Wollstonecraft Godwin was born on Aug. 30, 1797, in London. Mary was the only daughter of "two persons of distinguished literary celebrity". Her mother Mary Wollstonecraft was an early advocate of educational and social equality for women in the 1880s, and the author to the book *Vindication of the Rights of Woman* (1792). Her father William Godwin was the most influential political thinker at that time and the author to the book *Enquiry Concerning Political Justice*.

Eleven days after her birth, Mary's mother Wollstonecraft died of puerperal fever. William Goldwin married to Mary Jane Clairmont in 1801, who brought her own two children into the family. Mary Godwin never got along with her stepmother. Mary Godwin was educated at home by her father. She also got the early education of literature in her father's house where a number of distinguished guests often visited, including Samuel Taylor Coleridge and William Wordsworth. She also educated herself by making great use of her father's extensive library.

Mary started writing at a young age and published her first book at the age of ten. In 1812, Mary went to Scotland and stayed there for sixteen months.

There she was introduced to Scottish traditions and legends and was encouraged to write stories.

In 1814, Mary Shelley began a romance with Percy Bysshe Shelley, one of her father's political followers and the Romantic poet. Percy Shelley was already married at that time. In July, 1814, the couple eloped to European continent accompanied by Mary's step-sister Claire. They married in late 1816, after the suicide of Percy Shelley's first wife, Harriet.

In 1816, together with Lord Byron, John William Polidori, and Claire Clairmont, the couple spent a summer near Geneva, Switzerland. During this time, Mary started her novel *Frankenstein*. In 1817, she published a travelogue of their escape to Europe, *History of a Six Weeks' Tour*. In 1818, *Frankenstein, or the Modern Prometheus* was published in France anonymously.

In 1822, Percy Bysshe Shelley drowned when his sailing boat sank during a storm near Viareggio. During the eight years of their staying together, they were often on the move, in England, France, Italy, and elsewhere. Between 1815 and 1819, Mary lost three of her four children. She also suffered from the suicides of Fanny Imlay, her half sister and Harriet Shelley, Percy Bysshe Shelley's wife.

In 1823, Mary Shelley returned to England. She died in 1851 when she was 53. She devoted her later life to the upbringing of her son, compiling her husband's works and her own writing.

The major works of Mary Shelley include: *History of a Six Weeks' Tour* (1817), *Frankenstein* (1818), *Mathila* (1819), *Valperga* (1823), *The Last Man* (1826), *The Fortunes of Perkin Warbeck* (1830), *Lodore* (1835), and *Falkner* (1837).

II. Introduction to the Novel

Mary Shelley started working on the novel *Frankenstein* in 1816. In 1818, *Frankestein; or, The Modern Prometheus* was published anonymously in France. The novel was republished in 1831 with Mary Shelley's name as the author and "Author's Introduction" as a preface. In the preface, Mary Shelley introduced the origin of the novel. In 1816, when stayed in Geneva, she, Percy Bysshe Shelley, Byron and William Polidori, after reading ghost stories together, agreed each to write a horror story. On June 15, Mary Shelley had a nightmare in which she saw "the pale student of unhallowed arts kneeling beside the thing he had put together". This nightmare leads to the composition of *Frankenstein*. The novel *Frankenstein* combines multiple types of elements, such as elements of Gothic novel, the Romantic Movement, and science fiction.

The novel *Frankenstein: or, The Modern Prometheus* takes place in the late 1700s in various parts of Europe, especially Switzerland and Germany, and in the Arctic. It tells the story of Victor Frankenstein, a young scientist from Geneva, who creates a grotesque creature out of a scientific experiment. Abandoned at the birth, the Creature, in his searching for his father, finds himself rejected by Victor and mankind in general. So the Creature seeks its revenge through murder and terror and turns himself into a Monster.

Written in the form of a frame story, the novel consists of three major parts: Captain Robert Walton's letters to his sister Margaret Walton Saville, Victor Frankenstein's narrative infused with the Creature's narrative, and Captain Walton's concluding frame narrative.

In first part, Walton recounts to his sister of his dangerous journey to the North Pole, and of his encounter with Victor Frankenstein.

In second part, Victor first recalls his blissful childhood in Geneva, where he grew up with Elizabeth Lavenza, who was adopted by his family. Later, Victor enters the university of Ingolstadt to study natural philosophy and chemistry. There, he is inspired by the desire to discover the secret of life and devotes several years to the research. As a result, on one stormy night, Victor completes his creation and brings to life a new creation, which horrifies him with its awful appearance. So he runs away.

In his narration, Monster (Victor's creation) admits to the murder of William, Victor's brother. He curses Victor for his careless creation, and later desertion which leaves him in loneliness. The monster begs Victor to create a mate for him. Victor refuses at first, and later agrees. However, horrified by the possible consequences of his work, Victor destroys his new creation. The monster vows revenge.

The monster then kills Henry Clerval, Victor's best friend, and Elizabath, Victor's wife on their wedding night. Victor vows to revenge and starts his journey of finding the monster.

The novel ends with Walton's letters, in which he finishes the story. Victor, gets ill and dies shortly thereafter. The monster weeps over Victor, and asserts that now that his creator has died, he too can end his suffering. The monster then departs for the northernmost ice to die.

Since its publication, the novel *Frankenstein* has impacted the literary world and common readers deeply. But the reviews of the novel are diverse between the two extremes of fascination and revulsion. Walter Scott praises that "the work impresses us with a high idea of the author's original genius and happy power of expression", while John Wilson Croker finds the novel despicable, and suggests "the head or heart of the author be the most diseased". In the context of modern technology, the novel is gaining new currency.

Frankenstein has been translated into many languages and adapted into many genres and forms. Continuations and retellings persist in print. Frankenstein and his creature have become a pervasive image of modern world.

Ⅲ. Excerpt

CHAPTER 5

IT was on a dreary night of November, that I beheld the accomplishment of my toils. With an anxiety that almost amounted to agony, I collected the instruments of life around me, that I might infuse a spark of being into the lifeless thing that lay at my feet. It was already one in the morning; the rain pattered dismally against the panes, and my candle was nearly burnt out, when, by the glimmer of the half-extinguished light, I saw the dull yellow eye of the creature open; it breathed hard, and a convulsive motion agitated its limbs.

How can I describe my emotions at this catastrophe, or how delineate the wretch whom with such infinite pains and care I had endeavoured to form? His limbs were in proportion, and I had selected his features as beautiful. Beautiful! —Great God! His yellow skin scarcely covered the work of muscles and arteries beneath; his hair was of a lustrous black, and flowing; his teeth of a pearly whiteness; but these luxuriances only formed a more horrid contrast with his watery eyes, that seemed almost of the same colour as the dun white sockets in which they were set, his shrivelled complexion and straight black lips.

The different accidents of life are not so changeable as the feelings of human nature. I had worked hard for nearly two years, for the sole purpose of infusing life into an inanimate body. For this I had deprived myself of rest and health. I had desired it with an ardour that far exceeded moderation; but now that I had finished, the beauty of the dream vanished, and breathless horror and disgust filled my heart. Unable to endure the aspect of the being I had created, I rushed out of the room, and continued a long time traversing my bedchamber, unable to compose my mind to sleep. At length lassitude succeeded to the tumult I had before endured; and I threw myself on the bed in my clothes, endeavouring to seek a few moments of forgetfulness. But it was in vain; I slept, indeed, but I was disturbed by the wildest dreams. I thought I saw Elizabeth, in the bloom of health, walking in the streets of Ingolstadt. Delighted and surprised, I embraced her, but as I imprinted the first kiss on her lips, they became livid with the hue of death; her features appeared to change, and I thought that I held the corpse of my dead mother in my arms; a shroud enveloped her form, and I saw the graveworms crawling in the folds of the flannel. I started from my sleep with horror; a cold dew covered my forehead, my teeth chattered, and every limb became convulsed; when, by the dim and yellow light of the moon, as it forced its way through the window shutters, I beheld the wretch—the miserable monster whom I had created. He held up the curtain of the bed; and his eyes, if eyes they may be called, were fixed on me. His jaws opened, and he muttered some inarticulate sounds, while a grin wrinkled his cheeks. He might have spoken, but I did not hear; one hand was stretched out, seemingly to detain me, but I escaped, and rushed down stairs. I took refuge in the courtyard belonging to the house which I inhabited; where I remained during the rest of the night, walking up and down in the greatest agitation, listening attentively, catching and fearing each sound as if it were to announce the approach of the demoniacal corpse to which I had so miserably given life.

Oh! no mortal could support the horror of that countenance. A mummy again endued with animation could not be so hideous as that wretch. I had gazed on him while unfinished; he was ugly then; but when those muscles and joints were rendered capable of motion, it became a thing such as even Dante could not have conceived.

I passed the night wretchedly. Sometimes my pulse beat so quickly and hardly that I felt the palpitation of every artery; at others, I nearly sank to the ground through languor and extreme weakness. Mingled with this horror, I felt the bitterness of disappointment; dreams that had been my food and pleasant rest for so long a space were now become a hell to me; and the change was so rapid, the overthrow so complete!

Morning, dismal and wet, at length dawned, and discovered to my sleepless and aching eyes the church of Ingolstadt, its white steeple and clock, which indicated the sixth hour. The porter opened the gates of the court, which had that night been my asylum, and I issued into the streets, pacing them with quick steps, as if I sought to avoid the wretch whom I feared every turning of the street would present to my view. I did not dare return to the apartment which I inhabited, but felt impelled to hurry on, although drenched by the rain which poured from a black and comfortless sky.

I continued walking in this manner for some time, endeavouring by bodily exercise to ease the load that weighed upon my mind. I traversed the streets, without any clear conception of where I was or what I was doing. My heart palpitated in the sickness of fear, and I hurried on with irregular steps, not daring to look about me:

Like one who, on a lonely road,

Doth walk in fear and dread,

And, having once turned round, walks on,

And turns no more his head;

Because he knows a frightful fiend

Doth close behind him tread.

[Coleridge's "Ancient Mariner."]

CHAPTER 10

I spent the following day roaming through the valley. I stood beside the sources of the Arveiron, which take their rise in a glacier, that with slow pace is advancing down from the summit of the hills, to barricade the valley. The abrupt sides of vast mountains were before me; the icy wall of the glacier overhung me; a few shattered pines were scattered around; and the solemn silence of this glorious presence-chamber of imperial nature was broken only by the brawling waves or the fall of some vast fragment, the thunder sound of the avalanche or the cracking, reverberated along the mountains, of the accumulated ice, which, through the silent working of immutable laws, was ever and anon rent and torn, as if it had been but a plaything in their hands. These sublime and magnificent scenes afforded me the greatest consolation that I was capable of receiving. They elevated me from all littleness of feeling, and although they did not remove my grief, they subdued and tranquillized it. In some degree, also, they diverted my mind from the thoughts over which it had brooded for the last month. I retired to rest at night; my slumbers, as it were, waited on and ministered to by the assemblance of grand shapes which I had contemplated during the day. They congregated round me; the unstained snowy mountaintop, the glittering pinnacle, the pine woods, and ragged bare ravine, the eagle, soaring amidst the clouds —they all gathered round me and bade me be at peace.

Where had they fled when the next morning I awoke? All of soul-inspiriting fled with sleep, and dark melancholy clouded every thought. The rain was pouring in torrents, and thick mists hid the summits of the mountains, so that I even saw not the faces of those mighty friends. Still I would penetrate their misty veil and seek them in their cloudy retreats. What were rain and storm to me? My mule was brought to the door, and I resolved to ascend to the summit of Montanvert. I remembered the effect that the view of the tremendous and ever-moving glacier had produced upon my mind when I first saw it. It had then filled me with a sublime ecstasy, that gave wings to the soul, and allowed it to soar from the obscure world to light and joy. The sight of the awful and majestic in nature had indeed always the effect of solemnizing my mind and causing me to forget the passing cares of life. I determined to go without a guide, for I was well acquainted with the path, and the presence of another would destroy the solitary grandeur of the scene.

The ascent is precipitous, but the path is cut into continual and short windings, which enable you to surmount the perpendicularity of the mountain. It is a scene terrifically desolate. In a thousand spots the traces of the winter avalanche may be perceived, where trees lie broken and strewed on the ground, some entirely destroyed, others bent, leaning upon the jutting rocks of the mountain or transversely upon other trees. The path, as you ascend higher, is intersected by ravines of snow, down which stones continually roll from above; one of them is particularly dangerous, as the slightest sound, such as even speaking in a loud voice, produces a concussion of air sufficient to draw destruction upon the head of the speaker. The pines are not tall or luxuriant, but they are sombre and add an air of severity to the scene. I looked on the valley beneath; vast mists were rising from the rivers which ran through it and curling in thick wreaths around the opposite mountains, whose summits were hid in the uniform clouds, while rain poured from the dark sky and added to the melancholy impression I received from the objects around me. Alas! Why does man boast of sensibilities superior to those apparent in the brute; it only renders them more necessary beings. If our impulses were confined to hunger, thirst, and desire, we might be nearly free; but now we are moved by every wind that blows and a chance word or scene that that word may convey to us.

We rest; a dream has power to poison sleep.

We rise; one wand'ring thought pollutes the day.

We feel, conceive, or reason; laugh or weep,

Embrace fond woe, or cast our cares away;

It is the same: for, be it joy or sorrow,

The path of its departure still is free.

Man's yesterday may ne'er be like his morrow;

Nought may endure but mutability!

It was nearly noon when I arrived at the top of the ascent. For some time I sat upon the rock that overlooks the sea of ice. A mist covered both that and the surrounding mountains. Presently a breeze dissipated the cloud, and I descended upon the glacier. The surface is very uneven, rising like the waves of a troubled sea, descending low, and interspersed by rifts that sink deep. The field of ice is almost a league in width, but I spent nearly two hours in crossing it. The opposite mountain is a bare perpendicular rock. From the side where I now stood Montanvert was exactly opposite, at the distance of a league; and above it rose Mont Blanc, in awful majesty. I remained in a recess of the rock, gazing on this wonderful and stupendous scene. The sea, or rather the vast river of ice, wound among its dependent mountains, whose aerial summits hung over its recesses. Their icy and glittering peaks shone in the sunlight over the clouds. My heart, which was before sorrowful, now swelled with something like joy; I exclaimed, "Wandering spirits, if indeed ye wander, and do not rest in your narrow beds, allow me this faint happiness, or take me, as your companion, away from the joys of life."

As I said this, I suddenly beheld the figure of a man, at some distance, advancing towards me with superhuman speed. He bounded over the crevices in the ice, among which I had walked with caution; his stature, also, as he approached, seemed to exceed that of man. I was troubled: a mist came over my eyes, and I felt a faintness seize me; but I was quickly restored by the cold gale of the mountains. I perceived, as the shape came nearer (sight tremendous and abhorred!) that it was the wretch whom I had created. I trembled with rage and horror, resolving to wait his approach and then close with him in mortal combat. He approached; his countenance bespoke bitter anguish, combined with disdain and malignity, while its unearthly ugliness rendered it almost too horrible for human eyes. But I scarcely observed this; rage and hatred had at first deprived me of utterance, and I recovered only to overwhelm him with words expressive of furious detestation and contempt.

"Devil," I exclaimed, "do you dare approach me? and do not you fear the fierce vengeance of my arm wreaked on your miserable head? Begone, vile insect! or rather, stay, that I may trample you to dust! and, oh! that I could, with the extinction of your miserable existence, restore those victims whom you have so diabolically murdered!"

"I expected this reception," said the daemon. "All men hate the wretched; how, then, must I be hated, who am miserable beyond all living things! Yet you, my creator, detest and spurn me, thy creature, to whom thou art bound by ties only dissoluble by the annihilation of one of us. You purpose to kill me. How dare you sport thus with life? Do your duty towards me, and I will do mine towards you and the rest of mankind. If you will comply with my conditions, I will leave them and you at peace; but if you refuse, I will glut the maw of death, until it be satiated with the blood of your remaining friends. "

"Abhorred monster! fiend that thou art! the tortures of hell are too mild a vengeance for thy crimes. Wretched devil! you reproach me with your creation; come on, then, that I may extinguish the spark which I so negligently bestowed. "

My rage was without bounds; I sprang on him, impelled by all the feelings which can arm one being against the existence of another.

He easily eluded me and said—

"Be calm! I entreat you to hear me, before you give vent to your hatred on my devoted head. Have I not suffered enough, that you seek to increase my misery? Life, although it may only be an accumulation of anguish, is dear to me, and I will defend it. Remember, thou hast made me more powerful than thyself; my height is superior to thine; my joints more supple. But I will not be tempted to set myself in opposition to thee. I am thy creature, and I will be even mild and docile to my natural lord and king if thou wilt also perform thy part, the which thou owest me. Oh, Frankenstein, be not equitable to every other and trample upon me alone, to whom thy justice, and even thy clemency and affection, is most due. Remember, that I am thy creature; I ought to be thy Adam, but I am rather the fallen angel, whom thou drivest from joy for no misdeed. Every where I see bliss, from which I alone am irrevocably excluded. I was benevolent and good; misery made me a fiend. Make me happy, and I shall again be virtuous. "

"Begone! I will not hear you. There can be no community between you and me; we are enemies. Begone, or let us try our strength in a fight, in which one must fall. "

"How can I move thee? Will no entreaties cause thee to turn a favourable eye upon thy creature, who implores thy goodness and compassion? Believe me, Frankenstein: I was benevolent; my soul glowed with love and humanity; but am I not alone, miserably alone? You, my creator, abhor me; what hope can I gather from your fellow-creatures, who owe me nothing? they spurn and hate me. The desert mountains and dreary glaciers are my refuge. I have wandered here many days; the caves of ice, which I only do not fear, are a dwelling to me, and the only one which man does not grudge. These bleak skies I hail, for they are kinder to me than your fellow-beings. If the multitude of mankind knew of my existence, they would do as you do, and arm themselves for my destruction. Shall I not then hate them who abhor me? I will keep no terms with my enemies. I am miserable, and they shall share my wretchedness. Yet it is in your power to recompense me, and deliver them from an evil which it only remains for you to make so great, that not only you and your family, but thousands of others, shall be swallowed up in the whirlwinds of its rage. Let your compassion be moved, and do not disdain me. Listen to my tale: when you have heard that, abandon or commiserate me, as you shall judge that I deserve. But hear me. The guilty are allowed, by human laws, bloody as they are, to speak in their own defence before they are condemned. Listen to me, Frankenstein. You accuse me of murder, and yet you would, with a satisfied conscience, destroy your own creature. Oh, praise the eternal justice of man! Yet I ask you not to spare me: listen to me, and then, if you can, and if you will, destroy the work of your hands. "

"Why do you call to my remembrance," I rejoined, "circumstances, of which I shudder to reflect, that I have been the miserable origin and author? Cursed be the day, abhorred devil, in which you first saw light! Cursed (although I curse myself) be the hands that formed you! You have made me wretched beyond expression. You have left me no power to consider whether I am just to you, or not. Begone! relieve me from the sight of your detested form. "

"Thus I relieve thee, my creator," he said, and placed his hated hands before my eyes, which I flung from me with violence; "thus I take from thee a sight which you abhor. Still thou canst listen to me, and grant me thy compassion. By the virtues that I once possessed, I demand this from you. Hear my tale; it is long and strange, and the temperature of this place is not fitting to your fine sensations; come to the hut upon the mountain. The sun is yet high in the heavens; before it descends to hide itself behind your snowy precipices, and illuminate another world, you will have heard my story, and can decide. On you it rests, whether I quit forever the neighbourhood of man, and lead a harmless life, or become the scourge of your fellow creatures, and the author of your own speedy ruin. "

As he said this, he led the way across the ice: I followed. My heart was full, and I did not answer him; but as I proceeded, I weighed the various arguments that he had used, and determined at least to listen to his tale. I was partly urged by curiosity, and compassion confirmed my resolution. I had hitherto supposed him to be the murderer of my brother, and I eagerly sought a confirmation or denial of this opinion. For the first time, also, I felt what the duties of a creator towards his creature were, and that I ought to render him happy before I complained of his wickedness. These motives urged me to comply with his demand. We crossed the ice, therefore, and ascended the opposite rock. The air was cold, and the rain again began to descend: we entered the hut, the fiend with an air of exultation, I with a heavy heart, and depressed spirits. But I consented to listen, and, seating myself by the fire which my odious companion had lighted, he thus began his tale.

CHAPTER 11

"It is with considerable difficulty that I remember the original era of my being: all the events of that period appear confused and indistinct. A strange multiplicity of sensations seized me, and I saw, felt, heard, and smelt at the same time; and it was, indeed, a long time before I learned to distinguish between the operations of my various senses. By degrees, I remember, a stronger light pressed upon my nerves, so that I was obliged to shut my eyes.

Darkness then came over me and troubled me, but hardly had I felt this when, by opening my eyes, as I now suppose, the light poured in upon me again. I walked and, I believe, descended, but I presently found a great alteration in my sensations. Before, dark and opaque bodies had surrounded me, impervious to my touch or sight; but I now found that I could wander on at liberty, with no obstacles which I could not either surmount or avoid. The light became more and more oppressive to me, and the heat wearying me as I walked, I sought a place where I could receive shade. This was the forest near Ingolstadt; and here I lay by the side of a brook resting from my fatigue, until I felt tormented by hunger and thirst. This roused me from my nearly dormant state, and I ate some berries which I found hanging on the trees or lying on the ground. I slaked my thirst at the brook, and then lying down, was overcome by sleep.

"It was dark when I awoke; I felt cold also, and half frightened, as it were, instinctively, finding myself so desolate. Before I had quitted your apartment, on a sensation of cold, I had covered myself with some clothes, but these were insufficient to secure me from the dews of night. I was a poor, helpless, miserable wretch; I knew, and could distinguish, nothing; but feeling pain invade me on all sides, I sat down and wept.

"Soon a gentle light stole over the heavens and gave me a sensation of pleasure. I started up and beheld a radiant form rise from among the trees. [The moon] I gazed with a kind of wonder. It moved slowly, but it enlightened my path, and I again went out in search of berries. I was still cold when under one of the trees I found a huge cloak, with which I covered myself, and sat down upon the ground. No distinct ideas occupied my mind; all was confused. I felt light, and hunger, and thirst, and darkness; innumerable sounds rang in my ears, and on all sides various scents saluted me; the only object that I could distinguish was the bright moon, and I fixed my eyes on that with pleasure.

"Several changes of day and night passed, and the orb of night had greatly lessened, when I began to distinguish my sensations from each other. I gradually saw plainly the clear stream that supplied me with drink and the trees that shaded me with their foliage. I was delighted when I first discovered that a pleasant sound, which often saluted my ears, proceeded from the throats of the little winged animals who had often intercepted the light from my eyes. I began also to observe, with greater accuracy, the forms that surrounded me and to perceive the boundaries of the radiant roof of light which canopied me. Sometimes I tried to imitate the pleasant songs of the birds but was unable. Sometimes I wished to express my sensations in my own mode, but the uncouth and inarticulate sounds which broke from me frightened me into silence again.

"The moon had disappeared from the night, and again, with a lessened form, showed itself, while I still remained in the forest. My sensations had by this time become distinct, and my mind received every day additional ideas. My eyes became accustomed to the light and to perceive objects in their right forms; I distinguished the insect from the herb, and by degrees, one herb from another. I found that the sparrow uttered none but harsh notes, whilst those of the blackbird and thrush were sweet and enticing.

"One day, when I was oppressed by cold, I found a fire which had been left by some wandering beggars, and was overcome with delight at the warmth I experienced from it. In my joy I thrust my hand into the live embers, but quickly drew it out again with a cry of pain. How strange, I thought, that the same cause should produce such opposite effects! I examined the materials of the fire, and to my joy found it to be composed of wood. I quickly collected some branches, but they were wet and would not burn. I was pained at this and sat still watching the operation of the fire. The wet wood which I had placed near the heat dried and itself became inflamed. I reflected on this, and by touching the various branches, I discovered the cause and busied myself in collecting a great quantity of wood, that I might dry it and have a plentiful supply of fire. When night came on and brought sleep with it, I was in the greatest fear lest my fire should be extinguished. I covered it carefully with dry wood and leaves and placed wet branches upon it; and then, spreading my cloak, I lay on the ground and sank into sleep.

"It was morning when I awoke, and my first care was to visit the fire. I uncovered it, and a gentle breeze quickly fanned it into a flame. I observed this also and contrived a fan of branches, which roused the embers when they were nearly extinguished. When night came again I found, with pleasure, that the fire gave light as well as heat; and that the discovery of this element was useful to me in my food, for I found some of the offals that the travellers had left had been roasted, and tasted much more savoury than the berries I gathered from the trees. I tried, therefore, to dress my food in the same manner, placing it on the live embers. I found that the berries were spoiled by this operation, and the nuts and roots much improved.

"Food, however, became scarce, and I often spent the whole day searching in vain for a few acorns to assuage the pangs of hunger. When I found this, I resolved to quit the place that I had hitherto inhabited, to seek for one where the few wants I experienced would be more easily satisfied. In this emigration, I exceedingly lamented the loss of the fire which I had obtained through accident and knew not how to reproduce it. I gave several hours to the serious consideration of this difficulty, but I was obliged to relinquish all attempt to supply it, and wrapping myself up in my cloak, I struck across the wood towards the setting sun. I passed three days in these rambles and at length discovered the open country. A great fall of snow had taken place the night before, and the fields were of one uniform white; the appearance was disconsolate, and I found my feet chilled by the cold damp substance that covered the ground.

"It was about seven in the morning, and I longed to obtain food and shelter; at length I perceived a small hut, on a rising ground, which had doubtless been built for the convenience of some shepherd. This was a new sight to me, and I examined the structure with great curiosity. Finding the door open, I entered. An old man sat in it, near a fire, over which he was preparing his breakfast. He turned on hearing a noise, and perceiving me, shrieked loudly, and quitting the hut, ran across the fields with a speed of which his debilitated form hardly appeared capable. His appearance, different from any I had ever before seen, and his flight somewhat surprised me. But I was enchanted by the appearance of the hut; here the snow and rain could not penetrate; the ground was dry; and it presented to me then as exquisite and divine a retreat as Pandemonium appeared to the demons of hell after their sufferings in the lake of fire. I greedily devoured the remnants of the shepherd's breakfast, which consisted of bread, cheese, milk, and wine; the latter, however, I did not like. Then, overcome by fatigue, I lay down among some straw and fell asleep.

"It was noon when I awoke, and allured by the warmth of the sun, which shone brightly on the white ground, I determined to recommence my travels; and, depositing the remains of the peasant's breakfast in a wallet I found, I proceeded across the fields for several hours, until at sunset I arrived at a village. How miraculous did this appear! The huts, the neater cottages, and stately houses engaged my admiration by turns. The vegetables in the gardens, the milk and cheese that I saw placed at the windows of some of the cottages, allured my appetite. One of the best of these I entered, but I had hardly placed my foot within the door before the children shrieked, and one of the women fainted. The whole village was roused; some fled, some attacked me, until, grievously bruised by stones and many other kinds of missile weapons, I escaped to the open country and fearfully took refuge in a low hovel, quite bare, and making a wretched appearance after the palaces I had beheld in the village. This hovel, however, joined a cottage of a neat and pleasant appearance, but after my late dearly bought experience, I dared not enter it. My place of refuge was constructed of wood, but so low that I could with difficulty sit upright in it. No wood, however, was placed on the earth, which formed the floor, but it was dry; and although the wind entered it by innumerable chinks, I found it an agreeable asylum from the snow and rain.

"Here, then, I retreated and lay down happy to have found a shelter, however miserable, from the inclemency of the season, and still more from the barbarity of man. As soon as morning dawned I crept from my kennel, that I might view the adjacent cottage and discover if I could remain in the habitation I had found. It was situated against the back of the cottage and surrounded on the sides which were exposed by a pig sty and a clear pool of water. One part was open, and by that I had crept in; but now I covered every crevice by which I might be perceived with stones and wood, yet in such a manner that I might move them on occasion to pass out; all the light I enjoyed came through the sty, and that was sufficient for me.

"Having thus arranged my dwelling and carpeted it with clean straw, I retired, for I saw the figure of a man at a distance, and I remembered too well my treatment the night before to trust myself in his power. I had first, however, provided for my sustenance for that day by a loaf of coarse bread, which I purloined, and a cup with which I could drink more conveniently than from my hand of the pure water which flowed by my retreat. The floor was a little raised, so that it was kept perfectly dry, and by its vicinity to the chimney of the cottage it was tolerably warm.

"Being thus provided, I resolved to reside in this hovel until something should occur which might alter my determination. It was indeed a paradise compared to the bleak forest, my former residence, the rain-dropping branches, and dank earth. I ate my breakfast with pleasure and was about to remove a plank to procure myself a little water when I heard a step, and looking through a small chink, I beheld a young creature, with a pail on her head, passing before my hovel. The girl was young and of gentle demeanour, unlike what I have since found cottagers and farmhouse servants to be. Yet she was meanly dressed, a coarse blue petticoat and a linen jacket being her only garb; her fair hair was plaited but not adorned: she looked patient yet sad. I lost sight of her, and in about a quarter of an hour she returned bearing the pail, which was now partly filled with milk. As she walked along, seemingly incommoded by the burden, a young man met her, whose countenance expressed a deeper despondence. Uttering a few sounds with an air of melancholy, he took the pail from her head and bore it to the cottage himself. She followed, and they disappeared. Presently I saw the young man again, with some tools in his hand, cross the field behind the cottage; and the girl was also busied, sometimes in the house and sometimes in the yard. "On examining my dwelling, I found that one of the windows of the cottage had formerly occupied a part of it, but the panes had been filled up with wood. In one of these was a small and almost imperceptible chink through which the eye could just penetrate. Through this crevice a small room was visible, whitewashed and clean but very bare of furniture. In one corner, near a small fire, sat an old man, leaning his head on his hands in a disconsolate attitude. The young girl was occupied in arranging the cottage; but presently she took something out of a drawer, which employed her hands, and she sat down beside the old man, who, taking up an instrument, began to play and to produce sounds sweeter than the voice of the thrush or the nightingale. It was a lovely sight, even to me, poor wretch who had never beheld aught beautiful before. The silver hair and benevolent countenance of the aged cottager won my reverence, while the gentle manners of the girl enticed my love. He played a sweet mournful air which I perceived drew tears from the eyes of his amiable companion, of which the old man took no notice, until she sobbed audibly; he then pronounced a few sounds, and the fair creature, leaving her work, knelt at his feet. He raised her and smiled with such kindness and affection that I felt sensations of a peculiar and overpowering nature; they were a mixture of pain and pleasure, such as I had never before experienced, either from hunger or cold, warmth or food; and I withdrew from the window, unable to bear these emotions.

"Soon after this the young man returned, bearing on his shoulders a load of wood. The girl met him at the door, helped to relieve him of his burden, and taking some of the fuel into the cottage, placed it on the fire; then she and the youth went apart into a nook of the cottage, and he showed her a large loaf and a piece of cheese. She seemed pleased and went into the garden for some roots and plants, which she placed in water, and then upon the fire. She afterwards continued her work, whilst the young man went into the garden and appeared busily employed in digging and pulling up roots. After he had been employed thus about an hour, the young woman joined him and they entered the cottage together.

"The old man had, in the meantime, been pensive, but on the appearance of his companions he assumed a more cheerful air, and they sat down to eat. The meal was quickly dispatched. The young woman was again occupied in arranging the cottage, the old man walked before the cottage in the sun for a few minutes, leaning on the arm of the youth. Nothing could exceed in beauty the contrast between these two excellent creatures. One was old, with silver hairs and a countenance beaming with benevolence and love; the younger was slight and graceful in his figure, and his features were moulded with the finest symmetry, yet his eyes and attitude expressed the utmost sadness and despondency. The old man returned to the cottage, and the youth, with tools different from those he had used in the morning, directed his steps across the fields.

"Night quickly shut in, but to my extreme wonder, I found that the cottagers had a means of prolonging light by the use of tapers, and was delighted to find that the setting of the sun did not put an end to the pleasure I experienced in watching my human neighbours. In the evening the young girl and her companion were employed in various occupations which I did not understand; and the old man again took up the instrument which produced the divine sounds that had enchanted me in the morning. So soon as he had finished, the youth began, not to play, but to utter sounds that were monotonous, and neither resembling the harmony of the old man's instrument nor the songs of the birds; I since found that he read aloud, but at that time I knew nothing of the science of words or letters.

"The family, after having been thus occupied for a short time, extinguished their lights and retired, as I conjectured, to rest."

CHAPTER 16

"Cursed, cursed creator! Why did I live? Why, in that instant, did I not extinguish the spark of existence which you had so wantonly bestowed? I know not; despair had not yet taken possession of me; my feelings were those of rage and revenge. I could with pleasure have destroyed the cottage and its inhabitants and have glutted myself with their shrieks and misery.

"When night came I quitted my retreat and wandered in the wood; and now, no longer restrained by the fear of discovery, I gave vent to my anguish in fearful howlings. I was like a wild beast that had broken the toils, destroying the objects that obstructed me and ranging through the wood with a staglike swiftness. Oh! What a miserable night I passed! The cold stars shone in mockery, and the bare trees waved their branches above me; now and then the sweet voice of a bird burst forth amidst the universal stillness. All, save I, were at rest or in enjoyment; I, like the arch-fiend, bore a hell within me, and finding myself unsympathized with, wished to tear up the trees, spread havoc and destruction around me, and then to have sat down and enjoyed the ruin.

"But this was a luxury of sensation that could not endure; I became fatigued with excess of bodily exertion and sank on the damp grass in the sick impotence of despair. There was none among the myriads of men that existed who would pity or assist me; and should I feel kindness towards my enemies? No; from that moment I declared everlasting war against the species, and more than all, against him who had formed me and sent me forth to this insupportable misery.

"The sun rose; I heard the voices of men and knew that it was impossible to return to my retreat during that day. Accordingly I hid myself in some thick underwood, determining to devote the ensuing hours to reflection on my situation.

"The pleasant sunshine and the pure air of day restored me to some degree of tranquillity; and when I considered what had passed at the cottage, I could not help believing that I had been too hasty in my conclusions. I had certainly acted imprudently. It was apparent that my conversation had interested the father in my behalf, and I was a fool in having exposed my person to the horror of his children. I ought to have familiarized the old De Lacey to me, and by degrees to have discovered myself to the rest of his family, when they should have been prepared for my approach. But I did not believe my errors to be irretrievable, and after much consideration I resolved to return to the cottage, seek the old man, and by my representations win him to my party.

"These thoughts calmed me, and in the afternoon I sank into a profound sleep; but the fever of my blood did not allow me to be visited by peaceful dreams. The horrible scene of the preceding day was forever acting before my eyes; the females were flying and the enraged Felix tearing me from his father's feet. I awoke exhausted, and finding that it was already night, I crept forth from my hiding-place, and went in search of food.

"When my hunger was appeased, I directed my steps towards the well-known path that conducted to the cottage. All there was at peace. I crept into my hovel and remained in silent expectation of the accustomed hour when the family arose. That hour passed, the sun mounted high in the heavens, but the cottagers did not appear. I trembled violently, apprehending some dreadful misfortune. The inside of the cottage was dark, and I heard no motion; I cannot describe the agony of this suspense.

"Presently two countrymen passed by, but pausing near the cottage, they entered into conversation, using violent gesticulations; but I did not understand what they said, as they spoke the language of the country, which differed from that of my protectors. Soon after, however, Felix approached with another man; I was surprised, as I knew that he had not quitted the cottage that morning, and waited anxiously to discover from his discourse the meaning of these unusual appearances.

"'Do you consider,' said his companion to him, 'that you will be obliged to pay three months' rent and to lose the produce of your garden? I do not wish to take any unfair advantage, and I beg therefore that you will take some days to consider of your determination.'

"'It is utterly useless,' replied Felix; 'we can never again inhabit your cottage. The life of my father is in the greatest danger, owing to the dreadful circumstance that I have related. My wife and my sister will never recover from their horror. I entreat you not to reason with me any more. Take possession of your tenement and let me fly from this place.'

"Felix trembled violently as he said this. He and his companion entered the cottage, in which they remained for a few minutes, and then departed. I never saw any of the family of De Lacey more.

"I continued for the remainder of the day in my hovel in a state of utter and stupid despair. My protectors had departed and had broken the only link that held me to the world. For the first time the feelings of revenge and hatred filled my bosom, and I did not strive to control them, but allowing myself to be borne away by the stream, I bent my mind towards injury and death. When I thought of my friends, of the mild voice of De Lacey, the gentle eyes of Agatha, and the exquisite beauty of the Arabian, these thoughts vanished and a gush of tears somewhat soothed me. But again when I reflected that they had spurned and deserted me, anger returned, a rage of anger, and unable to injure anything human, I turned my fury towards inanimate objects. As night advanced I placed a variety of combustibles around the cottage, and after having destroyed every vestige of cultivation in the garden, I waited with forced impatience until the moon had sunk to commence my operations.

"As the night advanced, a fierce wind arose from the woods and quickly dispersed the clouds that had loitered in the heavens; the blast tore along like a mighty avalanche and produced a kind of insanity in my spirits that burst all bounds of reason and reflection. I lighted the dry branch of a tree and danced with fury around the devoted cottage, my eyes still fixed on the western horizon, the edge of which the moon nearly touched. A part of its orb was at length hid, and I waved my brand; it sank, and with a loud scream I fired the straw, and heath, and bushes, which I had collected. The wind fanned the fire, and the cottage was quickly enveloped by the flames, which clung to it and licked it with their forked and destroying tongues.

"As soon as I was convinced that no assistance could save any part of the habitation, I quitted the scene and sought for refuge in the woods.

"And now, with the world before me, whither should I bend my steps? I resolved to fly far from the scene of my misfortunes; but to me, hated and despised, every country must be equally horrible. At length the thought of you crossed my mind. I learned from your papers that you were my father, my creator; and to whom could I apply with more fitness than to him who had given me life? Among the lessons that Felix had bestowed upon Safie, geography had not been omitted; I had learned from these the relative situations of the different countries of the earth. You had mentioned Geneva as the name of your native town, and towards this place I resolved to proceed.

"But how was I to direct myself? I knew that I must travel in a southwesterly direction to reach my destination, but the sun was my only guide. I did not know the names of the towns that I was to pass through, nor could I ask information from a single human being; but I did not despair. From you only could I hope for succour, although towards you I felt no sentiment but that of hatred. Unfeeling, heartless creator! You had endowed me with perceptions and passions and then cast me abroad an object for the scorn and horror of mankind.

But on you only had I any claim for pity and redress, and from you I determined to seek that justice which I vainly attempted to gain from any other being that wore the human form.

"My travels were long and the sufferings I endured intense. It was late in autumn when I quitted the district where I had so long resided. I travelled only at night, fearful of encountering the visage of a human being. Nature decayed around me, and the sun became heatless; rain and snow poured around me; mighty rivers were frozen; the surface of the earth was hard and chill, and bare, and I found no shelter. Oh, earth! How often did I imprecate curses on the cause of my being! The mildness of my nature had fled, and all within me was turned to gall and bitterness. The nearer I approached to your habitation, the more deeply did I feel the spirit of revenge enkindled in my heart. Snow fell, and the waters were hardened, but I rested not. A few incidents now and then directed me, and I possessed a map of the country; but I often wandered wide from my path. The agony of my feelings allowed me no respite; no incident occurred from which my rage and misery could not extract its food; but a circumstance that happened when I arrived on the confines of Switzerland, when the sun had recovered its warmth and the earth again began to look green, confirmed in an especial manner the bitterness and horror of my feelings.

"I generally rested during the day and travelled only when I was secured by night from the view of man. One morning, however, finding that my path lay through a deep wood, I ventured to continue my journey after the sun had risen; the day, which was one of the first of spring, cheered even me by the loveliness of its sunshine and the balminess of the air. I felt emotions of gentleness and pleasure, that had long appeared dead, revive within me. Half surprised by the novelty of these sensations, I allowed myself to be borne away by them, and forgetting my solitude and deformity, dared to be happy. Soft tears again bedewed my cheeks, and I even raised my humid eyes with thankfulness towards the blessed sun, which bestowed such joy upon me.

"I continued to wind among the paths of the wood, until I came to its boundary, which was skirted by a deep and rapid river, into which many of the trees bent their branches, now budding with the fresh spring. Here I paused, not exactly knowing what path to pursue, when I heard the sound of voices, that induced me to conceal myself under the shade of a cypress. I was scarcely hid when a young girl came running towards the spot where I was concealed, laughing, as if she ran from someone in sport. She continued her course along the precipitous sides of the river, when suddenly her foot slipped, and she fell into the rapid stream. I rushed from my hiding-place and with extreme labour, from the force of the current, saved her and dragged her to shore. She was senseless, and I endeavoured by every means in my power to restore animation, when I was suddenly interrupted by the approach of a rustic, who was probably the person from whom she had playfully fled. On seeing me, he darted towards me, and tearing the girl from my arms, hastened towards the deeper parts of the wood. I followed speedily, I hardly knew why; but when the man saw me draw near, he aimed a gun, which he carried, at my body and fired. I sank to the ground, and my injurer, with increased swiftness, escaped into the wood.

"This was then the reward of my benevolence! I had saved a human being from destruction, and as a recompense I now writhed under the miserable pain of a wound which shattered the flesh and bone. The feelings of kindness and gentleness which I had entertained but a few moments before gave place to hellish rage and gnashing of teeth. Inflamed by pain, I vowed eternal hatred and vengeance to all mankind. But the agony of my wound overcame me; my pulses paused, and I fainted.

"For some weeks I led a miserable life in the woods, endeavouring to cure the wound which I had received. The ball had entered my shoulder, and I knew not whether it had remained there or passed through; at any rate I had no means of extracting it. My sufferings were augmented also by the oppressive sense of the injustice and ingratitude of their infliction. My daily vows rose for revenge — a deep and deadly revenge, such as would alone compensate for the outrages and anguish I had endured.

"After some weeks my wound healed, and I continued my journey. The labours I endured were no longer to be alleviated by the bright sun or gentle breezes of spring; all joy was but a mockery which insulted my desolate state and made me feel more painfully that I was not made for the enjoyment of pleasure.

"But my toils now drew near a close, and in two months from this time I reached the environs of Geneva.

"It was evening when I arrived, and I retired to a hiding-place among the fields that surround it to meditate in what manner I should apply to you. I was oppressed by fatigue and hunger and far too unhappy to enjoy the gentle breezes of evening or the prospect of the sun setting behind the stupendous mountains of

Jura.

　　"At this time a slight sleep relieved me from the pain of reflection, which was disturbed by the approach of a beautiful child, who came running into the recess I had chosen, with all the sportiveness of infancy. Suddenly, as I gazed on him, an idea seized me that this little creature was unprejudiced and had lived too short a time to have imbibed a horror of deformity. If, therefore, I could seize him and educate him as my companion and friend, I should not be so desolate in this peopled earth.

　　"Urged by this impulse, I seized on the boy as he passed and drew him towards me. As soon as he beheld my form, he placed his hands before his eyes and uttered a shrill scream; I drew his hand forcibly from his face and said, 'Child, what is the meaning of this? I do not intend to hurt you; listen to me.'

　　"He struggled violently. 'Let me go,' he cried; 'monster! Ugly wretch! You wish to eat me and tear me to pieces. You are an ogre. Let me go, or I will tell my papa.'

　　"'Boy, you will never see your father again; you must come with me.'

　　"'Hideous monster! Let me go. My papa is a syndic —he is M. Frankenstein —he will punish you. You dare not keep me.'

　　"'Frankenstein! you belong then to my enemy —to him towards whom I have sworn eternal revenge; you shall be my first victim.'

　　"The child still struggled and loaded me with epithets which carried despair to my heart; I grasped his throat to silence him, and in a moment he lay dead at my feet.

　　"I gazed on my victim, and my heart swelled with exultation and hellish triumph; clapping my hands, I exclaimed, 'I too can create desolation; my enemy is not invulnerable; this death will carry despair to him, and a thousand other miseries shall torment and destroy him.'

　　"As I fixed my eyes on the child, I saw something glittering on his breast. I took it; it was a portrait of a most lovely woman. In spite of my malignity, it softened and attracted me. For a few moments I gazed with delight on her dark eyes, fringed by deep lashes, and her lovely lips; but presently my rage returned; I remembered that I was forever deprived of the delights that such beautiful creatures could bestow and that she whose resemblance I contemplated would, in regarding me, have changed that air of divine benignity to one expressive of disgust and affright.

"Can you wonder that such thoughts transported me with rage? I only wonder that at that moment, instead of venting my sensations in exclamations and agony, I did not rush among mankind and perish in the attempt to destroy them.

"While l was overcome by these feelings, I left the spot where I had committed the murder, and seeking a more secluded hiding-place, I entered a barn which had appeared to me to be empty. A woman was sleeping on some straw; she was young, not indeed so beautiful as her whose portrait I held, but of an agreeable aspect and blooming in the loveliness of youth and health. Here, I thought, is one of those whose joy-imparting smiles are bestowed on all but me. And then I bent over her and whispered, 'Awake, fairest, thy lover is near —he who would give his life but to obtain one look of affection from thine eyes; my beloved, awake!'

"The sleeper stirred; a thrill of terror ran through me. Should she indeed awake, and see me, and curse me, and denounce the murderer? Thus would she assuredly act if her darkened eyes opened and she beheld me. The thought was madness; it stirred the fiend within me —not I, but she, shall suffer; the murder I have committed because I am forever robbed of all that she could give me, she shall atone. The crime had its source in her; be hers the punishment! Thanks to the lessons of Felix and the sanguinary laws of man, I had learned now to work mischief. I bent over her and placed the portrait securely in one of the folds of her dress. She moved again, and I fled.

"For some days I haunted the spot where these scenes had taken place, sometimes wishing to see you, sometimes resolved to quit the world and its miseries forever. At length I wandered towards these mountains, and have ranged through their immense recesses, consumed by a burning passion which you alone can gratify. We may not part until you have promised to comply with my requisition. I am alone and miserable; man will not associate with me; but one as deformed and horrible as myself would not deny herself to me. My companion must be of the same species and have the same defects. This being you must create."

CHAPTER 20

I sat one evening in my laboratory; the sun had set, and the moon was just rising from the sea; I had not sufficient light for my employment, and I remained idle, in a pause of consideration of whether I should leave my labour for the night or hasten its conclusion by an unremitting attention to it. As I sat, a train of reflection occurred to me which led me to consider the effects of what I was now doing. Three years before, I was engaged in the same manner and had created a fiend whose unparalleled barbarity had desolated my heart and filled it forever with the bitterest remorse. I was now about to form another being of whose dispositions I was alike ignorant; she might become ten thousand times more malignant than her mate and delight, for its own sake, in murder and wretchedness. He had sworn to quit the neighbourhood of man and hide himself in deserts, but she had not; and she, who in all probability was to become a thinking and reasoning animal, might refuse to comply with a compact made before her creation. They might even hate each other; the creature who already lived loathed his own deformity, and might he not conceive a greater abhorrence for it when it came before his eyes in the female form? She also might turn with disgust from him to the superior beauty of man; she might quit him, and he be again alone, exasperated by the fresh provocation of being deserted by one of his own species. Even if they were to leave Europe and inhabit the deserts of the new world, yet one of the first results of those sympathies for which the daemon thirsted would be children, and a race of devils would be propagated upon the earth who might make the very existence of the species of man a condition precarious and full of terror. Had I right, for my own benefit, to inflict this curse upon everlasting generations? I had before been moved by the sophisms of the being I had created; I had been struck senseless by his fiendish threats; but now, for the first time, the wickedness of my promise burst upon me; I shuddered to think that future ages might curse me as their pest, whose selfishness had not hesitated to buy its own peace at the price, perhaps, of the existence of the whole human race.

I trembled and my heart failed within me, when, on looking up, I saw by the light of the moon the daemon at the casement. A ghastly grin wrinkled his lips as he gazed on me, where I sat fulfilling the task which he had allotted to me. Yes, he had followed me in my travels; he had loitered in forests, hid himself in caves, or taken refuge in wide and desert heaths; and he now came to mark my progress and claim the fulfillment of my promise.

As I looked on him, his countenance expressed the utmost extent of malice and treachery. I thought with a sensation of madness on my promise of creating another like to him, and trembling with passion, tore to pieces the thing on which I was engaged. The wretch saw me destroy the creature on whose future existence he depended for happiness, and with a howl of devilish despair and revenge, withdrew.

I left the room, and locking the door, made a solemn vow in my own heart never to resume my labours; and then, with trembling steps, I sought my own apartment. I was alone; none were near me to dissipate the gloom and relieve me from the sickening oppression of the most terrible reveries.

Several hours passed, and I remained near my window gazing on the sea; it was almost motionless, for the winds were hushed, and all nature reposed under the eye of the quiet moon. A few fishing vessels alone specked the water, and now and then the gentle breeze wafted the sound of voices as the fishermen called to one another. I felt the silence, although I was hardly conscious of its extreme profundity, until my ear was suddenly arrested by the paddling of oars near the shore, and a person landed close to my house.

In a few minutes after, I heard the creaking of my door, as if some one endeavoured to open it softly. I trembled from head to foot; I felt a presentiment of who it was and wished to rouse one of the peasants who dwelt in a cottage not far from mine; but I was overcome by the sensation of helplessness, so often felt in frightful dreams, when you in vain endeavour to fly from an impending danger, and was rooted to the spot. Presently I heard the sound of footsteps along the passage; the door opened, and the wretch whom I dreaded appeared.

Shutting the door, he approached me and said in a smothered voice, "You have destroyed the work which you began; what is it that you intend? Do you dare to break your promise? I have endured toil and misery; I left Switzerland with you; I crept along the shores of the Rhine, among its willow islands and over the summits of its hills. I have dwelt many months in the heaths of England and among the deserts of Scotland. I have endured incalculable fatigue, and cold, and hunger; do you dare destroy my hopes?"

"Begone! I do break my promise; never will I create another like yourself, equal in deformity and wickedness. "

"Slave, I before reasoned with you, but you have proved yourself unworthy of my condescension. Remember that I have power; you believe yourself miserable, but I can make you so wretched that the light of day will be hateful to you. You are my creator, but I am your master; obey!"

"The hour of my irresolution is past, and the period of your power is arrived. Your threats cannot move me to do an act of wickedness; but they confirm me in a determination of not creating you a companion in vice. Shall I, in cool blood, set loose upon the earth a daemon whose delight is in death and wretchedness? Begone! I am firm, and your words will only exasperate my rage."

The monster saw my determination in my face and gnashed his teeth in the impotence of anger. "Shall each man," cried he, "find a wife for his bosom, and each beast have his mate, and I be alone? I had feelings of affection, and they were requited by detestation and scorn. Man! You may hate, but beware! Your hours will pass in dread and misery, and soon the bolt will fall which must ravish from you your happiness forever. Are you to be happy while I grovel in the intensity of my wretchedness? You can blast my other passions, but revenge remains —revenge, henceforth dearer than light or food! I may die, but first you, my tyrant and tormentor, shall curse the sun that gazes on your misery. Beware, for I am fearless and therefore powerful. I will watch with the wiliness of a snake, that I may sting with its venom. Man, you shall repent of the injuries you inflict."

"Devil, cease; and do not poison the air with these sounds of malice. I have declared my resolution to you, and I am no coward to bend beneath words. Leave me; I am inexorable."

"It is well. I go; but remember, I shall be with you on your wedding-night."

I started forward and exclaimed, "Villain! Before you sign my death-warrant, be sure that you are yourself safe."

I would have seized him, but he eluded me and quitted the house with precipitation. In a few moments I saw him in his boat, which shot across the waters with an arrowy swiftness and was soon lost amidst the waves.

All was again silent, but his words rang in my ears. I burned with rage to pursue the murderer of my peace and precipitate him into the ocean. I walked up and down my room hastily and perturbed, while my imagination conjured up a thousand images to torment and sting me. Why had I not followed him and closed with him in mortal strife? But I had suffered him to depart, and he had directed his course towards the mainland. I shuddered to think who might be the next victim sacrificed to his insatiate revenge. And then I thought again of his words —"*I will be with you on your wedding-night.*" That, then, was the period fixed for the fulfillment of my destiny. In that hour I should die and at once satisfy and extinguish his malice. The prospect did not move me to fear; yet when I thought of my beloved Elizabeth, of her tears and endless sorrow, when she should find her lover so barbarously snatched from her, tears, the first I had shed for many months, streamed from my eyes, and I resolved not to fall before my enemy without a bitter struggle.

The night passed away, and the sun rose from the ocean; my feelings became calmer, if it may be called calmness when the violence of rage sinks into the depths of despair. I left the house, the horrid scene of the last night's contention, and walked on the beach of the sea, which I almost regarded as an insuperable barrier between me and my fellow creatures; nay, a wish that such should prove the fact stole across me.

I desired that I might pass my life on that barren rock, wearily, it is true, but uninterrupted by any sudden shock of misery. If I returned, it was to be sacrificed or to see those whom I most loved die under the grasp of a daemon whom I had myself created.

I walked about the isle like a restless spectre, separated from all it loved and miserable in the separation. When it became noon, and the sun rose higher, I lay down on the grass and was overpowered by a deep sleep. I had been awake the whole of the preceding night, my nerves were agitated, and my eyes inflamed by watching and misery. The sleep into which I now sank refreshed me; and when I awoke, I again felt as if I belonged to a race of human beings like myself, and I began to reflect upon what had passed with greater composure; yet still the words of the fiend rang in my ears like a death-knell; they appeared like a dream, yet distinct and oppressive as a reality.

The sun had far descended, and I still sat on the shore, satisfying my appetite, which had become ravenous, with an oaten cake, when I saw a fishing-boat land close to me, and one of the men brought me a packet; it contained letters from Geneva, and one from Clerval entreating me to join him. He said that he was wearing away his time fruitlessly where he was, that letters from the friends he had formed in London desired his return to complete the negotiation they had entered into for his Indian enterprise. He could not any longer delay his departure; but as his journey to London might be followed, even sooner than he now conjectured, by his longer voyage, he entreated me to bestow as much of my society on him as I could spare. He besought me, therefore, to leave my solitary isle and to meet him at Perth, that we might proceed southwards together. This letter in a degree recalled me to life, and I determined to quit my island at the expiration of two days. Yet, before I departed, there was a task to perform, on which I shuddered to reflect; I must pack up my chemical instruments, and for that purpose I must enter the room which had been the scene of my odious work, and I must handle those utensils the sight of which was sickening to me. The next morning, at daybreak, I summoned sufficient courage and unlocked the door of my laboratory. The remains of the half-finished creature, whom I had destroyed, lay scattered on the floor, and I almost felt as if I had mangled the living flesh of a human being. I paused to collect myself and then entered the chamber. With trembling hand I conveyed the instruments out of the room, but I reflected that I ought not to leave the relics of my work to excite the horror and suspicion of the peasants; and I accordingly put them into a basket, with a great quantity of stones, and laying them up, determined to throw them into the sea that very night; and in the meantime I sat upon the beach, employed in cleaning and arranging my chemical apparatus.

Nothing could be more complete than the alteration that had taken place in my feelings since the night of the appearance of the daemon. I had before regarded my promise with a gloomy despair as a thing that, with whatever consequences, must be fulfilled; but I now felt as if a film had been taken from before my eyes and that I for the first time saw clearly. The idea of renewing my labours did not for one instant occur to me; the threat I had heard weighed on my thoughts, but I did not reflect that a voluntary act of mine could avert it. I had resolved in my own mind that to create another like the fiend I had first made would be an act of the basest and most atrocious selfishness, and I banished from my mind every thought that could lead to a different conclusion.

Ⅳ. Questions for Thinking

1. Use psychoanalytical theory to explain the image of the Monster.
2. Mary Shelley mentions that a nightmare leads to the composition of this novel. Explain the relation between the nightmare and the Monster. How is the Monster related to the psyche of Mary Shelley?
3. The monster is nameless. How does this namelessness suggest his crisis of identity?

4. The monster is often mistakenly referred to as Frankenstein, the name of his creator. What do you think causes this mistake among readers?

5. How does the Monster try to form his identity and concept of self? In his identity construction, what refuses him to identify himself as a human? What leads him to a monster?

6. Comment on the images of women in the novel: Elizabeth, Safie, Agatha, Caroline, Justine, and Mrs. Moritz. Discuss the gender roles women are expected to play.

7. Does Shelley's perspective on gender roles seem progressive for her time? Mary Shelley's mother, Mary Wollstonecraft, was the author of the strongly feminist book *A Vindication of the Rights of Woman*. Do you think Mary Shelley a feminist or not?

8. Discuss the subtitle of the novel? Whom does the modern Prometheus refer to?

9. From the perspective of eco-criticism, discuss Victor's and the monster's relationships with nature. What place humankind should take within the cosmos? How far can we go in tampering with Nature?

10. Discuss from the perspective of ethical literary criticism, the following point: every child needs "mothering" in order to become "human"; all parents love their children unconditionally; children who are "deformed" physically or mentally should be isolated from society.

11. Discuss how the new creation challenges the traditional ethical principles. Discuss the monster's ethical choice.

12. Do you think a scientist has a right, or even a duty, to conduct scientific experiments that may lead to outcomes that some believe are immoral or unethical? For example, does a scientist have a right to clone a human being?

V. Guidance for Appreciation

"Frankenstein is a great work because we can read what we will from it. It has the resilience, the elasticity and the power of a myth. Writers and critics have, since Mary's death, uncovered more ways of interpreting it than the young author can ever have dreamed of" (Seymour 172). The statement by Seymour suggests that *Frankenstien* is a rich ore for literary studies and criticism.

　　The themes of the novel have been explored, including appearance vs reality, nature vs nurture, fate vs free will, education, knowledge, love, duty, revenge, prejudice, family, exploration, monstrosity, etc. Male characters, including Victor Frankenstein, the Monster, Robert Walton, Henry Clerval, and female characters Elizabeth, Safie, Agatha, Caroline, Justine, and Mrs. Moritz are studied by critics. Symbols of light, darkness, fire, and Biblical symbols of Adam and Satan have been analyzed.

The novel has also been studied and analyzed by employing different literary theories, such as feminism, psychoanalysis ethical literary criticism, ecocriticism, post-colonial theory, cultural studies, queer theory, and disability studies etc.

At the first reading, readers may not consider Frankenstein a novel much concerned with gender issues, since the dominant characters in the novels are males, female characters exist only in the background, suffering passively and most of the time remaining speechless. They are generally pure, innocent, kind, but powerless and passive. Caroline Beaufort is a self-sacrificing mother who dies taking care of her adopted daughter; Justine is executed for murder, despite her innocence; the creation of the female monster is aborted by Victor; Elizabeth waits, impatiently but helplessly, for Victor to return to her, and she is eventually murdered by the monster. Males in the novel speak for females and even usurp the most important gender role of females—birth.

But critics point out that Mary Shelley focuses on male characters to exam the vices and follies of the men. Shelley tries to demonstrate that males may not be as superior to females as they may expect. Moreover, Shelley also demonstrates that the disastrous results may occur when they try to create life with only male entities.

Feminist critics also link the composition of novels with female experience of giving birth to babies. "Frankenstein is a 'birth myth' that reveals the 'revulsion against newborn life, and the drama of guilt, dread, and flight surrounding birth and its consequences'"(Ellen Moers). The composition of the novel is a release of Mary Shelley's sense of guilt, stress and anxiety. Some feminist critics like Mary Poovey even go further to declare that "the narrative strategy of *Frankenstein*, like the symbolic presentation of the monster, enables Shelley to express and efface herself at the same time and thus, at least partially, to satisfy her conflicting desires for self-assertion and social acceptance. " (qtd. Schor 48)

The novel *Frankenstein* attracts many psychoanalytical criticism. The mental aspects of main character Victor and the Creation are one of the focus of research. The homosexual tendencies of Victor, Oedipus Complex (Victor's dream in which Elizabeth turned into his dead mother), and Victor's narcissism have been studied by using Freudian theory. The conflict of Victor's id, ego and superego is another aspect of research. The psychoanalysis of Victor's dreams in the novel also helps us better understand his complex.

Another focus of psychoanalytical criticism is try to link the novel text with the psyche of the author. Mary Shelley's nightmare on June 16, 1816 gave birth to the story of a monster. What has the monster to do with Shelley's nightmare? Why does Mary Shelley, then a girl of eighteen year old, dream such a nightmare that she transforms into the novel?

Anthony F. Badalamenti after studying the parallels between the novel text and the life of Mary Shelley, points out that "Mary Shelley's novel *Frankenstein; or, the Modern Prometheus* is presented here as her encoded image of unconscious emotions too painful for her waking personality to deal with", and that "her innovative image of man-made life is taken as emerging from the confrontation of her hopes for secure love with painful events in her life with Percy Shelley".

First, the novel is a catharsis for Mary Shelley. The pains in Mary Shelley's life find a way into the novel. The motherless characters in the novel Victor, monster, Felix, Agatha, and Safie are a reflection of Shelley's loss of mother when she was an infant and the leave of her nurse Louisa. So themes of being alone and being abandoned run through the whole novel. Moreover, Mary is under the great stress of being the daughter of two prestigious writers. Her love with Percy Bysshe Shelley adds more stress on her. Their extramarital relationship, her father's disapproval of this relation, the financial problem after their elope, and the suicide of Shelley's wife are pressure too much for a girl of eighteen-year-old. The greatest stress comes when she loses her first daughter. So Victor's feeling of regret, fear and anxiety in the novel may be Mary's encoded expression of pressure and stress in reality. The author's inescapable pain found an opportunity for creative and alternative expression in novel. Mary's longing for secure love might be illustrated in Frankenstein's regretting for creating the Creature and hoping for a peaceful life.

Critic Marc A. Rubenstein in his essay centers mainly on motherhood in the novel and in Mary Shelley's life. By examining Mary Shelley's loss of mother, her understanding of her mother and her feminist ideas, the problematic relationship between her mother and father, her own problematic relationship with Percy Bysshe Shelley and her loss of her baby, Rubenstein points out that "Frankenstein, for all its exclusion of women, is—among other things a parable of motherhood". Theme of searching for mother runs through the novel. "The pursuit of a coherent maternal identity was expressed and served by the unique structural organization of the novel. The 'search for the mother' was not merely the expression of a longing. It was also an effort in the direction of self-definition, particularly in terms of sexuality." Writing a novel is like a pregnancy of a baby. The feared experience of giving birth to a baby is reflected in the relative safety of authorship.

Another perspective to approach the novel *Frankenstein* is the discussion of identity. Identity, "how we define who we are", is one of the most fundamental and central conceptions concerning human experience. "I can think of no other concept that is so central to the human experience, or one that infuses so many interpretations and actions, than the notion of identity"(Whetten 17).

The analysis of identity crisis of the Creation and his identity pursuit can help the reader gain more insight into the novel. The Creature, after his birth, is abandoned by his creator, so he is left into the confusion of his identity. "Who was I? What was I? Whence did I come? What was my destination? These questions continually recurred, but I was unable to solve them" (125). As a creature born of an unnatural birth, and abandoned by his creator, how should he define himself? Is he a man or a monster? It is rather hard and even impossible for him to categorize himself to any certain kind of category. According to the Creation's narration part, he has tried to construct his identity. The Creation spends the most of his life in searching for his "father", the creator Frankenstein, questing for knowledge and attempting connections and community with other people. He tries to identify himself as a man and integrate into society.

However, the Creation's individual pursuit and endless efforts to acquire human language, read classic books as well as obtain a sense of belonging are proved to be fruitless. In the end, the Creation turns out to be a failure and an outcast after all. Through characterizing the Creation, the author Mary Shelley tries to attack the original standard of defining two pairs of antonyms, one pair of "beauty" and "ugliness" and another pair of "good" and "evil". His ethical dilemma and choice also raise questions for the modern society.

Ⅵ. **Further Reading**

1. Badalamenti, Anthony F. Why did Mary Shelley Write Frankenstein? [J]. Journal of Religion and Health, 2006, Vol. 45, No. 3: 419-439.

2. Bloom, Horald. Mary Shelley[M]. New York: Infobase Publishing, 2008.

3. Higgins, David Minden. Frankenstein: Character Studies [M]. London: Continuum, 2008.

4. Horton, Robert. Frankenstein[M]. London: Wallflower Press, 2014.

5. Moers, Ellen. Literary Women[M]. Garden City: Doubleday, 1976.

6. Schor, Esther. The Cambridge Companion to Mary Shelley[M]. Cambridge: Cambridge University Press, 2003.

7. 郝田虎.《失乐园》《弗兰肯斯坦》和《机械姬》中的科学普罗米修斯主义[J]. 外国文学,2019 (01): 3-14.

8. 苏耕新. 浮士德迟来的成长与弗兰肯斯坦早到的觉醒[J]. 外国文学,2017(1): 111-119.

9. 张鑫. 出版体制、阅读伦理与《弗兰肯斯坦》的经典化之路[J]. 外国文学研究, 2011(4):74-81.

10. 朱岩岩. 女性主义批评的"母矿"——《弗兰肯斯坦》的国外女性主义批评研究 [J]. 国外文学, 2015(4): 48-54+154.

Chapter 3

E.M. Forster: A Passage to India
Postcolonialism and Cultural Reading

Ⅰ. Introduction to E. M. Forster

Edward Morgan Forster(1879—1970) is an acknowledged British novelist, essayist, and social and literary critic. His mastery in literature made him nominated for the Nobel Prize in Literature 16 times.

Edward Morgan Forster was born on January 1, 1879 in London into an Anglo-Irish and Welsh middle-class family. He is the only child of Edward Morgan Forster, an architect. His father died when he was less than two years old, so his childhood and much of his adult life were influenced by his mother and his aunts.

In 1890, Forster entered a preparatory school in Eastbourne, Sussex, to receive primary education. From 1897 to 1901, he stayed at King's College, Cambridge, where he first read classics and then history.

After graduation from the King's College, he took a year-long tour to Italy and Greece with his mother where he gained a great number of materials for his two novels, *Where Angels Fear to Tread* (1905), *A Room with a View* (1908) , and his short fiction such as "The Story of a Panic" and "The Eternal Moment".

After returning to England, he began giving a weekly Latin class at the Working Men's College, devoting his spare time to writing. His first published story, "Albergo Empedocle", appeared in 1903, followed by *Where Angels Fear to Tread* (1905), *The Longest Journey* (1907), *A Room with a View* (1908), *Howards End* (1910). *Howards End* is a great success both critically and commercially. It had been reprinted four times that year.

From October, 1912 to April, 1913, E. M. Forster made his first visit to India. From March 1921 to January 1922, he returned to India and worked as the private secretary to the Maharaja of Dewas. These two visits to India bring about the composition of his masterpiece *A Passage to India*.

After 1924, Forster turned from fiction and short story writing to nonfiction, articles, essays, broadcasts, biographies, which established him an international reputation as one of the most prominent, authoritative, and engaging public intellectuals of his day. In 1934, Forster was elected the first President of the National Council for Civil Liberties, forerunner of the modern day Liberty organization. In June, 1935, Forster addressed International Writers' Congress in Paris. During World War II, he made regular anti-Nazi talks on BBC. In 1946, Forster was elected to an Honorary Fellowship of King's College, Cambridge. In 1947 and 1949, he made two lecture tours to USA. He died on June 7, 1970 at the age of 90.

With a literary career over fifty years, E. M Forster has produced 6 novels, *Where Angels Fear to Tread* (1905), *The Longest Journey* (1907), *A Room with a View* (1908), *Howards End* (1910), *A Passage to India* (1924), and *Maurice* (published posthumously in 1971). His short story collections include *The Celestial Omnibus (and other stories)* (1911), *The Eternal Moment and other stories* (1928), *Collected Short Stories* (1947), *The Life to Come and other stories* (1972). *Aspects of the Novel* (1927), *The Feminine Note in Literature* (posthumous) (2001), and *The Creator as Critic and Other Writings* are collections of his literary criticism.

"Connection" is a major theme in most of his novels, in which Forster emphasizes on the the need for connection between different races, classes, sexes, and sides of the individual self. His masterpiece *A Passage to India* ponders on the possibility of a connection between an Englishman and an Indian in the colonial context, which offers us a good text to study from the perspectives of postcolonialism and cultural studies.

Ⅱ. Introduction to the Novel

E. M. Forster's *A Passage to India*, published in 1924, is set against the background of the British Raj and the Indian independence movement in the 1920s. The story develops mainly around four characters, Dr. Aziz, a Muslin

Indian doctor, Cyril Fielding, an English humanist, Mrs. Moore, and Miss Adela Quested. The whole novel is divided into three parts: "Mosque", "Caves" and "Temple".

Part 1 "Mosque" opens with a panoramic view of the fictional city of Chandrapore, India. The garden-like British buildings are set in great contrast to the muddy city of Chandrapore. Dr. Aziz, an Indian Muslim, lives alone after the death of his wife, and sees his three children at his mother-in-law's house often. Aziz is called away from dinner with his friends by his superior at the hospital, Major Callendar. On the way home, he goes to the local mosque, where he meets Mrs. Moore, an Englishwoman who has recently arrived to visit her son, Ronny Heaslop, with his love interest, Adela Quested. After the mosque, Mrs. Moore arrives at the club of Englishmen, where they enjoy English style of life and where no Indians are allowed to enter. Adela expresses in the conversation that she would like to see the real India, so Mr. Turton offers to set up a Bridge Party. At the Bridge Party, the Indian guests stand at one side of the tennis lawn while the English stand at the other. Communication and connection seem impossible between them. Mr. Fielding, the principal of the local Government College, invites Adela to a tea party where she might meet more Indians. Adela meets Dr. Aziz at the party, who invites her and Mrs. Moore to visit the Marabar Caves.

Part 2 "Caves" starts with their journey to the Marabar Caves. At the train station, Fielding and Godbole arrive too late to catch the train, so Aziz, Adela, Mrs. Moore, and the rest of their party proceed to the Marabar Caves. In the first cave, Mrs. Moore is terrified by the echo within the cave, so she refuses to go into the second cave. Adela enters the second cave distracted, when she suddenly realizes that she doesn't love Ronny. Aziz goes into another cave. When Aziz comes out to find Adela, he finds that Adela has already left in a motorcar for Chandrapore. When Aziz and Fielding return to Chandrapore, Aziz is arrested and sent to the prison because Adela reports that she has been sexually assaulted in one of the Marabar Caves. In order to prove the innocence of Aziz, Fielding first goes to Mr. McBryde, superintendent of police. He also defends Aziz in the club, which offends other Englishmen. Mrs. Moore, believing the innocence of Aziz, refuses to testify at the trial and decides to leave India. On the day of the trial, Indians gather outside the courtroom to support Aziz. When giving witness, Adela admits that she has made a mistake, that Aziz never followed her. She withdraws all the charges, and Aziz is released. Adela breaks her marriage engagement with Ronny and returns England.

Part 3, "Temple," is set two years later in Hindu city of Mau, where now Aziz lives and works as physician to the Rajah. On the night of celebrating the birth of the god Krishna, Aziz meets with Godbole, who informs him that Golding has arrived in India. Finally, Aziz and Golding do meet each other, but they both realize that there will be no true friendship between the two peoples before India gets complete independence.

Ⅲ. Excerpt

CHAPTER 1

Except for the Marabar Caves and they are twenty miles off the city of Chandrapore presents nothing extraordinary. Edged rather than washed by the river Ganges, it trails for a couple of miles along the bank, scarcely distinguishable from the rubbish it deposits so freely. There are no bathing-steps on the river front, as the Ganges happens not to be holy here; indeed there is no river front and bazaars shut out the wide and shifting panorama of the stream. The streets are mean, the temples ineffective and though a few fine houses exist they are hidden away in gardens or down alleys whose filth deters all but the invited guest. Chandrapore was never large or beautiful, but two hundred years ago it lay on the road between Upper India, then imperial and the sea and the fine houses date from that period. The zest for decoration neither continued in the eighteenth century, nor was it ever democratic. There is no painting and scarcely any carving in the bazaars. The very wood seems made of mud, the inhabitants of mud moving. So abased, so monotonous is everything that meets the eye, that when the Ganges comes down it might be expected to wash the excrescence back into the soil. Houses do fall, people are drowned and left rotting, but the general outline of the town persists, swelling here, shrinking there, like some low but indestructible form of life.

Inland, the prospect alters. There is an oval Maidan and a long sallow hospital. Houses belonging to Furasians stand on the high ground by the railway station. Beyond the railway which runs parallel to the river the land sinks, then rises again rather steeply. On the second rise is laid out the little civil station and viewed hence Chandrapore appears to be a totally different place. It is a city of gardens. It is no city, but a forest sparsely scattered with huts. It is a tropical pleasance washed by a noble river. The toddy palms and neem trees and mangoes and pepul that were hidden behind the bazaars now become visible and in their turn hide the bazaars. They rise from the gardens where ancient tanks nourish them; they burst out of stifling purlieus and unconsidered temples. Seeking light and air and endowed with more strength than man or his works, they soar above the lower deposit to greet one another with branches and beckoning leaves and to build a city for the birds. Especially after the rains do they screen what passes below, but at all times, even when scorched or leafless, they glorify the city to the English people who inhabit the rise, so that new-corners cannot believe it to be as meager as it is described and have to be driven down to acquire disillusionment. As for the civil station itself, it provokes no emotion. It charms not; neither does it repel. It is sensibly planned, with a red-brick club on its brow and farther back a grocer's and a cemetery and the bungalows are disposed along roads that intersect at right angles. It has nothing hideous in it and only the view is beautiful; it shares nothing with the city except the overarching sky.

The sky too has its changes, but they are less marked than those of the vegetation and the river. Clouds map it tip at times, but it is normally a dome of blending tints and the main tint blue. By day the blue will pale down into white where it touches the white of the land, after sunset it has a new circumference orange, melting upwards into tenderest purple. But the core of blue persists and so it is by night. Then the stars hang like lamps from the immense vault. The distance between the vault and them is as nothing to the distance behind them and that farther distance, though beyond color, last freed itself from blue.

The sky settles everything not only climates and seasons but when the earth shall be beautiful. By herself she can do little only feeble outbursts of flowers. But when the sky chooses, glory can rain into the Chandrapore bazaars or a benediction pass from horizon to horizon. The sky can do this because it is so strong and so enormous. Strength comes from the sun, infused in it daily; size from the prostrate earth. No mountains infringe on the curve. League after league the earth lies flat, heaves a little, is flat again. Only in the south, where a group of fists and fingers are thrust up through the soil, is the endless expanse interrupted. These fists and fingers are the Marabar Hills, containing the extraordinary caves.

CHAPTER 2

He had always liked this mosque. It was gracious and the arrangement pleased him. The courtyard entered through a ruined gate contained an ablution tank of fresh clear water, which was always in motion, being indeed part of a conduit that supplied the city. The courtyard was paved with broken slabs. The covered part of the mosque was deeper than is usual; its effect was that of an English parish church whose side has been taken out. Where he sat, he looked into three arcades whose darkness was illuminated by a small hanging lamp and by the moon. The front in full moonlight had the appearance of marble and the ninety-nine names of God on the frieze stood out black, as the frieze stood out white against the sky. The contest between this dualism and the contention of shadows within pleased Aziz and he tried to symbolize the whole into some truth of religion or love. A mosque by winning his approval let loose his imagination. The temple of another creed, Hindu, Christian, or Greek, would have bored him and failed to awaken his sense of beauty. Here was Islam, his own country, more than a Faith, more than a battle-cry, more, much more... Islam, an attitude towards life both exquisite and durable, where his body and his thoughts found their home.

His seat was the low wall that bounded the courtyard on the left. The ground fell away beneath him towards the city; visible as a blur of trees and in the stillness he heard many small sounds. On the right, over in the club, the English community contributed an amateur orchestra. Elsewhere some Hindus were drumming he knew they were Hindus, because the rhythm was uncongenial to him and others were bewailing a corpse he knew who's, having certified it in the afternoon. There were owls, the Punjab mail... and flowers smelt deliciously in the station-master's garden. But the mosque that alone signified and he returned to it from the complex appeal of the night and decked it with meanings the builder had never intended. Some day he too would build a mosque, smaller than this but in perfect taste, so that all who passed by should experience the happiness he felt now. And near it, under a low dome, should be his tomb, with a Persian inscription:

Alas, without me for thousands of years

The Rose will blossom and the Spring will bloom,

But those who have secretly understood my heart

They will approach and visit the grave where I lie.

He had seen the quatrain on the tomb of a Deccan king and regarded it as profound philosophy he always held pathos to be profound. The secret understanding of the heart! He repeated the phrase with tears in his eyes and as he did so one of the pillars of the mosque seemed to quiver. It swayed in the gloom and detached itself. Belief in ghosts ran in his blood, but he sat firm. Another pillar moved, a third and then an Englishwoman stepped out into the moonlight. Suddenly he was furiously angry and shouted: "Madam! Madam! Madam!"

"Oh! Oh!" the woman gasped.

"Madam, this is a mosque, you have no right here at all; you should have taken off your shoes; this is a holy place for Moslems. "

"I have taken them off. "

"You have?"

"I left them at the entrance. "

"Then I ask your pardon. "

Still startled, the woman moved out, keeping the ablution-tank between them. He called after her, "I am truly sorry for speaking. "

"Yes, I was right, was I not? If I remove my shoes, I am allowed?"

"Of course, but so few ladies take the trouble, especially if thinking no one is there to see. "

"That makes no difference. God is here. "

"Madam!"

"Please let me go. "

"Oh, can I do you some service now or at any time?"

"No, thank you, really none good night. "

"May I know your name?"

She was now in the shadow of the gateway, so that he could not see her face, but she saw his and she said with a change of voice, "Mrs. Moore. "

"Mrs. " Advancing, he found that she was old. A fabric bigger than the mosque fell to pieces and he did not know whether he was glad or sorry. She was older than Hamidullah Begum, with a red face and white hair. Her voice had deceived him.

"Mrs. Moore, I am afraid I startled you. I shall tell my community our friends about you. That God is here-very good, very fine indeed. I think you are newly arrived in India. ”

“Yes how did you know?”

“By the way you address me. No, but can I call you a carriage?”

“I have only come from the club. They are doing a play that I have seen in London and it was so hot. ”

“What was the name of the play?”

“Cousin Kate. ”

“I think you ought not to walk at night alone, Mrs. Moore. There are bad characters about and leopards may come across from the Marabar Hills. Snakes also. ”

She exclaimed; she had forgotten the snakes.

“For example, a six-spot beetle,” he continued. “You pick it up, it bites, you die. ”

“But you walk about yourself. ”

“Oh, I am used to it. ”

“Used to snakes?”

They both laughed. “I’m a doctor,” he said. “Snakes don’t dare bite me. ” They sat down side by side in the entrance and slipped on their evening shoes. “Please may I ask you a question now? Why do you come to India at this time of year, just as the cold weather is ending?”

“I intended to start earlier, but there was an unavoidable delay. ”

“It will soon be so unhealthy for you! And why ever do you come to Chandrapore?”

“To visit my son. He is the City Magistrate here. ”

“Oh no, excuse me, that is quite impossible. Our City Magistrate’s name is Mr. Heaslop. I know him intimately. ”

“He’s my son all the same,” she said, smiling.

“But, Mrs. Moore, how can he be?”

“I was married twice. ”

“Yes, now I see and your first husband died. ”

“He did and so did my second husband. ”

“Then we are in the same box,” he said cryptically. “Then is the City Magistrate the entire of your family now?”

“No, there are the younger ones Ralph and Stella in England. ”

“And the gentleman here is he Ralph and Stella’s half-brother?”

"Quite right. "

"Mrs. Moore, this is all extremely strange, because like you I have also two sons and a daughter. Is not this the same box with a vengeance?"

"What are their names? Not also Ronny, Ralph and Stella, surely?"

The suggestion delighted him. "No, indeed. How funny it sounds! Their names are quite different and will surprise you. Listen, please. I am about to tell you my children's names. The first is called Ahmed, the second is called Karim, the third she is the eldest Jamila. Three children are enough. Do not you agree with me?"

"I do. "

They were both silent for a little, thinking of their respective families. She sighed and rose to go.

"Would you care to see over the Minto Hospital one morning?" he enquired. "I have nothing else to offer at Chandrapore. "

"Thank you, I have seen it already, or I should have liked to come with you very much. "

"I suppose the Civil Surgeon took you. "

"Yes and Mrs. Callendar. "

His voice altered. "Ah! A very charming lady. "

"Possibly, when one knows her better. "

"What? What? You didn't like her?"

"She was certainly intending to be kind, but I did not find her exactly charming. "

He burst out with: "She has just taken my tonga without my permission do you call that being charming? and Major Callendar interrupts me night after night from where I am dining with my friends and I go at once, breaking tip a most pleasant entertainment and he is not there and not even a message. Is this charming, pray? But what does it matter? I can do nothing and he knows it. I am just a subordinate, my time is of no value, the verandah is good enough for an Indian, yes, yes, let him stand and Mrs. Callendar takes my carriage and cuts me dead . . ." She listened.

He was excited partly by his wrongs, but much more by the knowledge that someone sympathized with them. It was this that led him to repeat, exaggerate and contradict. She had proved her sympathy by criticizing her fellow countrywoman to him, but even earlier he had known. The flame that not even beauty can nourish was springing up and though his words were querulous his heart began to glow secretly. Presently it burst into speech.

"You understand me, you know what others feel. Oh, if others resembled you!"

Rather surprised, she replied: "I don't think I understand people very well. I only know whether I like or dislike them."

"Then you are an Oriental."

She accepted his escort back to the club and said at the gate that she wished she was a member, so that she could have asked him in.

"Indians are not allowed into the Chandrapore Club even as guests," he said simply. He did not expatiate on his wrongs now, being happy. As he strolled downhill beneath the lovely moon and again saw the lovely mosque, he seemed to own the land as much as anyone owned it. What did it matter if a few flabby Hindus had preceded him there and a few chilly English succeeded?

CHAPTER 14

. . .

A Marabar cave had been horrid as far as Mrs. Moore was concerned, for she had nearly fainted in it and had some difficulty in preventing herself from saying so as soon as she got into the air again. It was natural enough: she had always suffered from faintness and the cave had become too full, because all their retinue followed them. Crammed with villagers and servants, the circular chamber began to smell. She lost Aziz and Adela in the dark, didn't know who touched her couldn't breathe and some vile naked thing struck her face and settled on her mouth like a pad. She tried to regain the entrance tunnel, but an influx of villagers swept her back. She hit her head. For an instant she went mad, hitting and gasping like a fanatic. For not only did the crush and stench alarm her; there was also a terrifying echo.

Professor Godbole had never mentioned an echo; it never impressed him, perhaps. There are some exquisite echoes in India; there is the whisper round the dome at Bijapur; there are the long, solid sentences that voyage through the air at Mandu and return unbroken to their creator. The echo in a Marabar cave is not like these, it is entirely devoid of distinction. Whatever is said, the same monotonous noise replies and quivers up and down the walls until it is absorbed into the roof. "Bourn" is the sound as far as the human alphabet can express it, or "bou-oum," or "ou-boum," utterly dull. Hope, politeness, the blowing of a nose, the squeak of a boot, all produce "bourn." Even the striking of a match starts a little worm coiling, which is too small to complete a circle but is eternally watchful. And if several people talk at once, an overlapping howling noise begins, echoes generate echoes and the cave is stuffed with a snake composed of small snakes, which writhe independently.

After Mrs. Moore all the others poured out. She had given the signal for the reflux. Aziz and Adela both emerged smiling and she did not want him to think his treat was a failure, so smiled too. As each person emerged she looked for a villain, but none was there and she realized that she had been among the mildest individuals, whose only desire was to honor her and that the naked pad was a poor little baby, astride its mother's hip. Nothing evil had been in the cave, but she had not enjoyed herself; no, she had not enjoyed herself and she decided not to visit a second one.

"Did you see the reflection of his match rather pretty?" asked Adela.

"I forget . . ."

"But he says this isn't a good cave, the best are on the Kawa Dol."

"I don't think I shall go on to there. I dislike climbing."

"Very well, let's sit down again in the shade until breakfast's ready."

"Ah, but that'll disappoint him so; he has taken such trouble. You should go on; you don't mind."

"Perhaps I ought to," said the girl, indifferent to what she did, but desirous of being amiable.

The servants, etc., were scrambling back to the camp, pursued by grave censures from Mohammed Latif. Aziz came to help the guests over the rocks. He was at the summit of his powers, vigorous and humble, too sure of himself to resent criticism and he was sincerely pleased when he heard they were altering his plans. "Certainly, Miss Quested, so you and I will go together and leave Mrs. Moore here and we will not be long, yet we will not hurry, because we know that will be her wish."

"Quite right. I'm sorry not to come too, but I'm a poor walker."

"Dear Mrs. Moore, what does anything matter so long as you are my guests? I am very glad you are not coming, which sounds strange, but you are treating me with true frankness, as a friend."

"Yes, I am your friend," she said, laying her hand on his sleeve and thinking, despite her fatigue, how very charming, how very good, he was and how deeply she desired his happiness. "So may I make another suggestion? Don' t let so many people come with you this time. I think you may find it more convenient. "

"Exactly, exactly," he cried and, rushing to the other extreme, forbade all except one guide to accompany Miss Quested and him to the Kawa Dol. "Is that all right?" he enquired.

"Quite right, now enjoy yourselves and when you come back tell me all about it. " And she sank into the deck-chair.

If they reached the big pocket of caves, they would be away nearly an hour. She took out her writingpad and began, "Dear Stella, Dear Ralph," then stopped and looked at the queer valley and their feeble invasion of it. Even the elephant had become a nobody. Her eye rose from it to the entrance tunnel. No, she did not wish to repeat that experience. The more she thought over it, the more disagreeable and frightening it became. She minded it much more now than at the time. The crush and the smells she could forget, but the echo began in some indescribable way to undermine her hold on life. Coming at a moment when she chanced to be fatigued, it had managed to murmur, "Pathos, piety, courage they exist, but are identical and so is filth. Everything exists, nothing has value. " If one had spoken vileness in that place, or quoted lofty poetry, the comment would have been the same "out bourn. " If one had spoken with the tongues of angels and pleaded for all the unhappiness and misunderstanding in the world, past, present and to come, for all the misery men must undergo whatever their opinion and position and however much they dodge or bluff it would amount to the same, the serpent would descend and return to the ceiling. Devils are of the North and poems can be written about them, but no one could romanticize the Marabar because it robbed infinity and eternity of their vastness, the only quality that accommodates them to mankind.

She tried to go on with her letter, reminding herself that she was only an elderly woman who had got up too early in the morning and journeyed too far, that the despair creeping over her was merely her despair, her personal weakness and that even if she got a sunstroke and went mad the rest of the world would go on. But suddenly, at the edge of her mind, Religion appeared, poor little talkative Christianity and she knew that all its divine words from "Let there be Light" to "It is finished" only amounted to "bourn. " Then she was terrified over an area larger than usual; the universe, never comprehensible to her intellect, offered no repose to her soul, the mood of the last two months took definite form at last and she realized that she didn't want to write to her children, didn't want to communicate with anyone, not even with God. She sat motionless with horror and, when old Mohammed Latif came up to her, thought he would notice a difference. For a time she thought, "I am going to be ill," to comfort herself, then she surrendered to the vision. She lost all interest, even in Aziz and the affectionate and sincere words that she had spoken to him seemed no longer hers but the airs.

CHAPTER 24

. . .

"Ronny—"

"Yes, old girl?"

"Isn't it all queer."

"I'm afraid it's very upsetting for you."

"Not the least. I don't mind it."

"Well, that's good."

She had spoken more naturally and healthily than usual. Bending into the middle of her friends, she said: "Don't worry about me, I'm much better than I was; I don't feel the least faint; I shall be all right, and thank you all, thank you, thank you for your kindness." She had to shout her gratitude, for the chant, Esmiss Esmoor, went on.

Suddenly it stopped. It was as if the prayer had been heard and the relics exhibited. "I apologize for my colleague," said Mr. Amritrao, rather to everyone's surprise. "He is an intimate friend of our client, and his feelings have carried him away."

"Mr. Mahmoud Ali will have to apologize in person," the Magistrate said.

"Exactly, sir, he must. But we had just learnt that Mrs. Moore had important evidence which she desired to give. She was hurried out of the country by her son before she could give it; and this unhinged Mr. Mahmoud Ali—coming as it does upon an attempt to intimidate our only other European witness, Mr. Fielding. Mr. Mahmoud Ali would have said nothing had not Mrs. Moore been claimed as a witness by the police." He sat down.

"An extraneous element is being introduced into the case," said the

Magistrate. " I must repeat that as a witness Mrs. Moore does not exist. Neither you, Mr. Amritrao, nor, Mr. McBryde, you, have any right to surmise what that lady would have said. She is not here, and consequently she can say nothing. "

"Well, I withdraw my reference," said the Superintendent wearily. "I would have done so fifteen minutes ago if I had been given the chance. She is not of the least importance to me. "

"I have already withdrawn it for the defence. " He added with forensic humour: "Perhaps you can persuade the gentlemen outside to withdraw it too," for the refrain in the street continued.

"I am afraid my powers do not extend so far," said Das, smiling.

So peace was restored, and when Adela came to give her evidence the atmosphere was quieter than it had been since the beginning of the trial. Experts were not surprised. There is no stay in your native. He blazes up over a minor point, and has nothing left for the crisis. What be seeks is a grievance, and this he had found in the supposed abduction of an old lady. He would now be less aggrieved when Aziz was deported.

But the crisis was still to come.

Adela had always meant to tell the truth and nothing but the truth, and she had rehearsed this as a difficult task—difficult, because her disaster in the cave was connected, though by a thread, with another part of her life, her engagement to Ronny. She had thought of love just before she went in, and had innocently asked Aziz what marriage was like, and she supposed that her question had roused evil in him. To recount this would have been incredibly painful, it was the one point she wanted to keep obscure; she was willing to give details that would have distressed other girls, but this story of her private failure she dared not allude to, and she dreaded being examined in public in case something came out. But as soon as she rose to reply, and heard the sound of her own voice, she feared not even that. A new and unknown sensation protected her, like magnificent armour. She didn't think what had happened or even remember in the ordinary way of memory, but she returned to the Marabar Hills, and spoke from them across a sort of darkness to Mr. McBryde. The fatal day recurred, in every detail, but now she was of it and not of it at the same time, and this double relation gave it indescribable splendour. Why had she thought the expedition "dull "? Now the sun rose again, the elephant waited, the pale masses of the rock flowed round her and presented the first cave; she entered, and a match was reflected in the polished walls—all beautiful and significant, though she had been blind to it at the time. Questions were asked, aiid to each she found the exact reply; yes, she had noticed the "Tank of the Dagger," but not known its name; yes, Mrs. Moore had been tired after the first cave and sat in the shadow of a great rock, near the dried-up mud. Smoothly the voice in the distance proceeded, leading along the paths of truth, and the airs from the punkah behind her wafted her on. . . .

"... the prisoner and the guide took you on to the Kawa Dol, no one else being present?"

"The most wonderfully shaped of those hills. Yes." As she spoke, she created the Kawa Dol, saw the niches up the curve of the stone, and felt the heat strike her face. And something caused her to add: "No one else was present to my knowledge. We appeared to be alone."

"Very well, there is a ledge half-way up the hill, or broken ground rather, with caves scattered near the beginning of a nullah."

"I know where you mean."

"You went alone into one of those caves?"

"That is quite correct."

"And the prisoner followed you."

"Now we've got'im," from the Major.

She was silent. The court, the place of question, awaited her reply. But she could not give it until Aziz entered the place of answer.

"The prisoner followed you, didn't he?" he repeated in the monotonous tones that they both used; they were employing agreed words throughout, so that this part of the proceedings held no surprises.

"May I have half a minute before I reply to that, Mr. McBryde?"

"Certainly."

Her vision was of several caves. She saw herself in one, and she was also outside it, watching its entrance, for Aziz to pass in. She failed to locate him. It was the doubt that had often visited her, but solid and attractive, like the hills, "I am not—" Speech was more difficult than vision. "I am not quite sure."

"I beg your pardon?" said the Superintendent of Police.

"I cannot be sure . . ."

"I didn't catch that answer." He looked scared, his mouth shut with a snap. "You are on that landing, or whatever we term it, and you have entered a cave. I suggest to you that the prisoner followed you."

She shook her head.

"What do you mean, please?"

"No," she said in a flat, unattractive voice. Slight noises began in various parts of the room, but no one yet understood what was occurring except Fielding. He saw that she was going to have a nervous breakdown and that his friend was saved.

"What is that, what are you saying? Speak up, please." The Magistrate bent forward.

"I'm afraid I have made a mistake."

"What nature of mistake?"

"Dr. Aziz never followed me into the cave."

The Superintendent slammed down his papers, then picked them up and said calmly: "Now, Miss Quested, let us go on. I will read you the words of the deposition which you signed two hours later in my bungalow."

"Excuse me, Mr. McBryde, you cannot go on. I am speaking to the witness myself. And the public will be silent. If it continues to talk, I have the court cleared. Miss Quested, address your remarks to me, who am the Magistrate in charge of the case, and realize their extreme gravity. "Remember you speak on oath, Miss Quested."

"Dr. Aziz never—"

"I stop these proceedings on medical grounds," cried the Major on a word from Turton, and all the English rose from their chairs at once, large white figures behind which the little magistrate was hidden. The Indians rose too, hundreds of things went on at once, so that afterwards each person gave a different account of the catastrophe.

"You withdraw the charge? Answer me," shrieked the representative of Justice.

Something that she did not understand took hold of the girl and pulled her through. Though the vision was over, and she had returned to the insipidity of the world, she remembered what she had learnt. Atonement and confession— they could wait. It was in hard prosaic tones that she said, "I withdraw everything."

"Enough—sit down. Mr. McBryde, do you wish to continue in the face of this?"

The Superintendent gazed at his witness as if she was a broken machine, and said, "Are you mad?"

"Don't question her, sir; you have no longer the right."

"Give me time to consider"

"Sahib, you will have to withdraw; this becomes a scandal," boomed the Nawab Bahadur suddenly from the back of the court.

"He shall not," shouted Mrs. Turton against the gathering tumult. "Call the other witnesses; we're none of us safe" Ronny tried to check her, and she gave him an irritable blow, then screamed insults at Adela.

The Superintendent moved to the support of his friends, saying nonchalantly to the Magistrate as he did so, "Right, I withdraw."

Mr. Das rose, nearly dead with the strain. He had controlled the case, just controlled it. He had shown that an Indian can preside. To those who could hear him he said, "The prisoner is released without one stain on his character; the question of costs will be decided elsewhere."

And then the flimsy framework of the court broke up, the shouts of derision and rage culminated, people screamed and cursed, kissed one another and wept passionately. Here were the English, whom their servants protected; there Aziz fainted in Hamidullah's arms. Victory on this side, defeat on that—complete for one moment was the antithesis. Then life returned to its complexities, person after person struggled out of the room to their various purposes, and before long no one remained on the scene of the fantasy but the beautiful naked god. Unaware that anything unusual had occurred, he continued to pull the cord of his punkah, to gaze at the empty dais and the overturned special chairs, and rhythmically to agitate the clouds of descending dust.

CHAPTER 30

Another local consequence of the trial was a Hindu-Moslem entente. Loud protestations of amity were exchanged by prominent citizens and there went with them a genuine desire for a good understanding. Aziz, when he was at the hospital one day, received a visit from rather a sympathetic figure: Mr. Das. The magistrate sought two favours from him: a remedy for shingles and a poem for his brother-in-law's new monthly magazine. He accorded both.

"My dear Das, why, when you tried to send me to prison, should I try to send Mr. Bhattacharya a poem? Eh? That is naturally entirely a joke. I will write him the best I can, but I thought your magazine was for Hindus. "

"It is not for Hindus, but Indians generally," he said timidly.

"There is no such person in existence as the general Indian. "

"There was not, but there may be when you have written a poem. You are our hero; the whole city is behind you, irrespective of creed. "

"I know, but will it last?"

"I fear not," said Das, who had much mental clearness. "And for that reason, if I may say so, do not introduce too many Persian expressions into the poem, and not too much about the bulbul. "

"Half a sec'" said Aziz, biting his pencil. He was writing out a prescription. "Here you are.... Is not this better than a poem?"

"Happy the man who can compose both. "

"You are full of compliments to-day. "

"I know you bear me a grudge for trying that case," said the other, stretching out his hand impulsively. "You are so kind and friendly, but always I detect irony beneath your manner. "

"No, no, what nonsense! " protested Aziz. They shook hands, in a half-embrace that typified the entente. Between people of distant climes there is always the possibility of romance, but the various branches of Indians know too much about each other to surmount the unknowable easily. The approach is prosaic. "Excellent," said Aziz, patting a stout shoulder and thinking, "I wish they did not remind me of cow-dung"; Das thought, "Some Moslems are very violent. " They smiled wistfully, each spying the thought in the other's heart, and Das, the more articulate, said: "Excuse my mistakes, realize my limitations. Life is not easy as we know it on the earth. "

"Oh, well, about this poem. How did you hear I sometimes scribbled?" he asked, much pleased, and a good deal moved for literature had always been a solace to him, something that the ugliness of facts could not spoil.

"Professor Godbole often mentioned it, before his departure for Mau. "

"How did he hear?"

"He too was a poet; do you not divine each other?"

Flattered by the invitation, he got to work that evening. The feel of the pen between his fingers generated bulbuls at once. His poem was again about the decay of Islam and the brevity of love; as sad and sweet as he could contrive, but not nourished by personal experience and of no interest to these excellent Hindus. Feeling dissatisfied, he rushed to the other extreme and wrote a satire, which was too libellous to print. He could only express pathos or venom, though most of his life had no concern with either. He loved poetry—science was merely an acquisition, which he laid aside when unobserved like his European dress—and this evening he longed to compose a new song which should be acclaimed by multitudes and even sung in the fields. In what language shall it be written? And what shall it announce? He vowed to see more of Indians who were not Mohammedans, and never to look backward. It is the only healthy course. Of what help, in this latitude and hour, are the glories of Cordova and Samarcand? They have gone, and while we lament them the English occupy Delhi and exclude us from East Africa. Islam itself, though true, throws cross-lights over the path to freedom. The song of the future must transcend creed.

The poem for Mr. Bhattacharya never got written, but it had an effect. It led him towards the vague and bulky figure of a mother-land. He was without natural affection for the land of his birth, but the Marabar Hills drove him to it. Half closing his eyes, he attempted to love India. She must imitate Japan. Not until she is a nation will her sons be treated with respect. He grew harder and less approachable. The English, whom he had laughed at or ignored, persecuted him everywhere; they had even thrown nets over his dreams. "My great mistake has been taking our rulers as a joke," he said to Hamidullah next day; who replied with a sigh: "It is far the wisest way to take them, but not possible in the long run. Sooner or later a disaster such as yours occurs, and reveals their secret thoughts about our character. If God himself descended from heaven into their club and said you were innocent, they would disbelieve him. Now you see why Mahmoud Ali and self waste so much time over intrigues and associate with creatures like Ram Chand."

"I cannot endure committees. I shall go right away."

"Where to? Turtons and Burtons, all are the same."

"But not in an Indian state."

"I believe the Politicals are obliged to have better manners. It amounts to no more."

"I do want to get away from British India, even to a poor job. I think I could write poetry there. I wish I had lived in Babur's time and fought and written for him. Gone, gone, and not even any use to say 'Gone, gone,' for it weakens us while we say it. We need a king, Hamidullah; it would make our lives easier. As it is, we must try to appreciate these quaint Hindus. My notion now is to try for some post as doctor in one of their states. "

"Oh, that is going much too far. "

"It is not going as far as Mr. Ram Chand. "

"But the money, the money, they will never pay an adequate salary, those savage Rajas. "

"I shall never be rich anywhere, it is outside my character. "

"If you had been sensible and made Miss Quested pay"

"I chose not to. Discussion of the past is useless," he said, with sudden sharpness of tone. "I have allowed her to keep her fortune and buy herself a husband in England, for which it will be very necessary. Don't mention the matter again. "

"Very well, but your life must continue a poor man's; no holidays in Kashmir for you yet, you must stick to your profession and rise to a highly paid post, not retire to a jungle-state and write poems. Educate your children, read the latest scientific periodicals, compel European doctors to respect you. Accept the consequences of your own actions like a man. "

Aziz winked at him slowly and said: "We are not in the law courts. There are many ways of being a man; mine is to express what is deepest in my heart. "

"To such a remark there is certainly no reply," said Hamidullah, moved. Recovering himself and smiling, he said: "Have you heard this naughty rumour that Mohammed Latif has got hold of?"

"Which?"

"When Miss Quested stopped in the College, Fielding used to visit her ... rather too late in the evening, the servants say. "

"A pleasant change for her if he did," said Aziz, making a curious face.

"But you understand my meaning!"

The young man winked again and said: "Just! Still, your meaning doesn't help me out of my difficulties. I am determined to leave Chandrapore. The problem is, for where? I am determined to write poetry. The problem is, about what? You give me no assistance. " Then, surprising both Hamidullah and himself, he had an explosion of nerves. "But who does give me assistance? No one is my friend. All are traitors, even my own children. I have had enough of friends. "

"I was going to suggest we go behind the purdah, but your three treacherous children are there, so you will not want to."

"I am sorry, it is ever since I was in prison my temper is strange; take me, forgive me."

"Nureddin's mother is visiting my wife now. That is all right, I think."

"They come before me separately, but not so far together. You had better prepare them for the united shock of my face."

"No, let us surprise them without warning, far too much nonsense still goes on among our ladies. They pretended at the time of your trial they would give up purdah! Indeed, those of them who can write composed a document to that effect, and now it ends in humbug. You know how deeply they all respect Fielding, but not one of them has seen him. My wife says she will, but always when he calls there is some excuse—she is not feeling well, she is ashamed of the room, she has no nice sweets to offer him, only Elephants' Ears, and if I say Elephants' Ears are Mr. Fielding's favourite sweet, she replies that he will know how badly hers are made, so she cannot see him on their account. For fifteen years, my dear boy, have I argued with my begum, for fifteen years, and never gained a point, yet the missionaries inform us our women are down-trodden. If you want a subject for a poem, take this: The Indian lady as she is and not as she is supposed to be."

CHAPTER 37

Friends again, yet aware that they could meet no more, Aziz and Fielding went for their last ride in the Mau jungles. The floods had abated and the Rajah was officially dead, so the Guest House party was departing next morning, as decorum required. What with the mourning and the festival, the visit was a failure. Fielding had scarcely seen Godbole, who promised every day to show him over the King-Emperor George Fifth High School, his main objective, but always made some excuse. This afternoon Aziz let out what had happened: the King-Emperor had been converted into a granary and the Minister of Education did not like to admit this to his former Principal. The school had been opened only last year by the Agent to the Governor-General and it still flourished on paper; he hoped to start it again before its absence was remarked and to collect its scholars before they produced children of their own. Fielding laughed at the tangle and waste of energy, but he did not travel as lightly as in the past; education was a continuous concern to him, because his income and the comfort of his family depended on it. He knew that few Indians think education good in itself and he deplored this now on the widest grounds. He began to say something heavy on the subject of Native States, but the friendliness of Aziz distracted him. This reconciliation was a success, anyhow. After the funny shipwreck there had been no more nonsense or bitterness and they went back laughingly to their old relationship as if nothing had happened. Now they rode between jolly bushes and rocks. Presently the ground opened into full sunlight and they saw a grassy slope bright with butterflies, also a cobra, which crawled across doing nothing in particular and disappeared among some custard apple trees. There were round white clouds in the sky and white pools on the earth; the hills in the distance were purple. The scene was as parklike as England, but did not cease being queer. They drew rein, to give the cobra elbow-room and Aziz produced a letter that he wanted to send to Miss Quested. A charming letter. He wanted to thank his old enemy for her fine behavior two years back: perfectly plain was it now that she had behaved well. "As I fell into our largest Mau tank under circumstances our other friends will relate, I thought how brave Miss Quested was and decided to tell her so, despite my imperfect English. Through you I am happy here with my children instead of in a prison, of that I make no doubt. My children shall be taught to speak of you with the greatest affection and respect."

"Miss Quested will be greatly pleased. I am glad you have seen her courage at last."

"I want to do kind actions all-round and wipe out the wretched business of the Marabar for ever. I have been so disgracefully hasty, thinking you meant to get hold of my money: as bad a mistake as the cave itself."

"Aziz, I wish you would talk to my wife. She too believes that the Marabar is wiped out."

"How so?"

"I don't know, perhaps she might tell you, she won't tell me. She has ideas I don't share indeed, when I'm away from her I think them ridiculous. When I'm with her, I suppose because I'm fond of her, I feel different, I feel half dead and half blind. My wife's after something. You and I and Miss Quested are, roughly speaking, not after anything. We jog on as decently as we can, you a little in front a laudable little party. But my wife is not with us."

"What are you meaning? Is Stella not faithful to you, Cyril? This fills me with great concern. "

Fielding hesitated. He was not quite happy about his marriage. He was passionate physically again the final flare-up before the clinkers of middle age and he knew that his wife did not love him as much as he loved her and he was ashamed of pestering her. But during the visit to Mau the situation had improved. There seemed a link between them at last that link outside either participant that is necessary to every relationship. In the language of theology, their union had been blessed. He could assure Aziz that Stella was not only faithful to him, but likely to become more so; and trying to express what was not clear to himself, he added dully that different people had different points of view. "If you won't talk about the Marabar to Stella, why won't you talk to Ralph? He is a wise boy really. And (same metaphor) he rides a little behind her, though with her. "

"Tell him also, I have nothing to say to him, but he is indeed a wise boy and has always one Indian friend. I partly love him because he brought me back to you to say good-bye. For this is good-bye, Cyril, though to think about it will spoil our ride and make us sad. "

"No, we won't think about it. " He too felt that this was their last free intercourse. All the stupid misunderstandings had been cleared up, but socially they had no meeting-place. He had thrown in his lot with Anglo India by marrying a countrywoman and he was acquiring some of its limitations and already felt surprise at his own past heroism. Would lie today defy all his people for the sake of a stray Indian? Aziz was a memento, a trophy, they were proud of each other, yet they must inevitably part. And, anxious to make what he could of this last afternoon, he forced himself to speak intimately about his wife, the person most dear to him. He said: "From her point of view, Man has been a success. It calmed her both of them suffer from restlessness. She found something soothing, some solution of her queer troubles here. " After a silence myriad of kisses around them as the earth drew the water in; he continued: "Do you know anything about this Krishna business?"

"My dear chap, officially they call it Gokul Ashtami. All the States offices are closed, but how else should it concern you and me?"

"Gokul is the village where Krishna was born well; more or less born, for there's the same hovering between it and another village as between Bethlehem and Nazareth. What I want to discover is its spiritual side, if it has one. "

"It is useless discussing Hindus with me. Living with them teaches me no more. When I think I annoy them, I do not. When I think I don't annoy them, I do Perhaps they will sack me for tumbling on to their dolls' house; on the other hand, perhaps they will double my salary. Time will prove. Why so curious about them?"

"It's difficult to explain. I never really understood or liked them, except an occasional scrap of Godbole. Does the old fellow still say 'Come, come?'""Oh, presumably. "

Fielding sighed, opened his lips, shut them, then said with a little laugh, "I can't explain, because it isn't in words at all, but why do my wife and her brother like Hinduism, though they take no interest in its forms? They won't talk to me about this. They know I think a certain side of their lives is a mistake and are shy. That's why I wish you would talk to them, for at all events you're Oriental. "

Aziz refused to reply. He didn't want to meet Stella and Ralph again, knew they didn't want to meet him, was incurious about their secrets and felt good old Cyril to be a bit clumsy. Something not a sight, but a sound flitted past him and caused him to re-read his letter to Miss Quested. Hadn't lie wanted to say something else to her? Taking out his pen, he added: "For my own part, I shall henceforth connect you with the name that is very sacred in my mind, namely, Mrs. Moore. " When lie had finished, the mirror of the scenery was shattered, the meadow disintegrated into butterflies. A poem about Mecca the Kaaba of Union the thorn bushes where pilgrims die before they have seen the Friend they flitted next; he thought of his wife; and then the whole semi-mystic, semi-sensuous overturn, so characteristic of his spiritual life, came to end like a landslip and rested in its due place and he found himself riding in the jungle with his dear Cyril.

"Oh, shut up," he said. "Don't spoil our last hour with foolish questions. Leave Krishna alone and talk about something sensible. "

They did. All the way back to Mau they wrangled about politics. Each had hardened since Chandrapore and a good knock about proved enjoyable. They trusted each other, although they were going to part, perhaps because they were going to part. Fielding had "no further use for politeness," he said, meaning that the British Empire really can't be abolished because it's rude. Aziz retorted, "Very well and we have no use for you," and glared at him with abstract hate.

Fielding said: "Away from us, Indians go to seed at once. Look at the King Emperor High School! Look at you, forgetting your medicine and going back to charms. Look at your poems.""Jolly good poems, I'm getting published Bombay side.""Yes and what do they say? Free our women and India will be free. Try it, my lad. Free your own lady in the first place and see who'll wash Ahmed, Karim and Jemila's faces. A nice situation!"

Aziz grew more excited. He rose in his stirrups and pulled at his horse's head in the hope it would rear. Then he should feel in a battle. He cried: "Clear out, all you Turtons and Burtons. We wanted to know you ten years back now it's too late. If we see you and sit on your committees, it's for political reasons, don't you make any mistake." His horse did rear. "Clear out, clear out, I say. Why are we put to so much suffering? We used to blame you, now we blame ourselves, we grow wiser. Until England is in difficulties we keep silent, but in the next European war aha, aha! Then is our time." He paused and the scenery, though it smiled, fell like a gravestone on any human hope. They cantered past a temple to Hanuman God so loved the world that he took monkey's flesh upon him and past a Saivite temple, which invited to lust, but under the semblance of eternity, it's obscenities bearing no relation to those of our flesh and blood. They splashed through butterflies and frogs; great trees with leaves like plates rose among the brushwood. The divisions of daily life were returning, the shrine had almost shut.

"Who do you want instead of the English? The Japanese?" jeered Fielding, drawing rein.

"No, the Afghans. My own ancestors."

"Oh, your Hindu friends will like that, won't they?"

"It will be arranged a conference of Oriental statesmen."

"It will indeed be arranged."

"Old story of 'We will rob every man and rape every woman from Peshawar to Calcutta,' I suppose, which you get some nobody to repeat and then quote every week in the Pioneer in order to frighten us into retaining you! We know!" Still he couldn't quite fit in Afghans at Mau and, finding he was in a corner, made his horse rear again until he remembered that he had, or ought to have, a mother-land. Then he shouted: "India shall be a nation! No foreigners of any sort! Hindu and Moslem and Sikh and all shall be one! Hurrah! Hurrah for India! Hurrah! Hurrah!"

India a nation! What an apotheosis! Last corner to the drab nineteenth-century sisterhood! Waddling in at this hour of the world to take her seat! She, whose only peer was the Holy Roman Empire, she shall rank with Guatemala and Belgium perhaps! Fielding mocked again. And Aziz in an awful rage danced this way and that, not knowing what to do and cried: "Down with the English anyhow. That's certain. Clear out, you fellows, double quick, I say. We may hate one another, but we hate you most. If I don't make you go, Ahmed will, Karim will, if it's fifty-five hundred years we shall get rid of you, yes, we shall drive every blasted Englishman into the sea and then " he rode against him furiously "and then," he concluded, half kissing him, "you and I shall be friends. "

"Why can't we be friends now?" said the other, holding him affectionately. "It's what I want. It's what you want. "

But the horses didn't want it they swerved apart; the earth didn't want it, sending up rocks through which riders must pass single file; the temples, the tank, the jail, the palace, the birds, the carrion, the Guest House, that came into view as they issued from the gap and saw Mau beneath: they didn't want it, they said in their hundred voices, "No, not yet," and the sky said, "No, not there. "

Ⅳ. Questions for Thinking

1. Adela and Mrs. Moore hope to know the real India, but what prevents them from achieving their goal?

2. Examine the friendship between Aziz and Fielding. What do you think it possible for an Englishman and an Indian to be friends, within the context of British colonialism? Consider the ending of this novel. What does the author suggest about the relationship between them?

3. Discuss Forster's depiction of the British in Chandrapore. Discuss Forster's depiction of the Indian community. Does Forster present the Indians in a more favorable light than the British? How successful do you think the novel is in its critique of "Orientalist" stereotypes? Do you think the novel still clings to some of these racial stereotypes when it depicts Indian characters?

4. Discuss the symbols Forster chooses to represent India. Do these symbols reveal the stereotypical impressions the westerners hold?

5. How does the novel elaborate the cultural hypocrisies of the British in India?

6. Discuss the identity construction of Aziz in the racial and cultural conflicts.

7. What is the role of nature in *A Passage to India*?

8. How does the author develop the theme of "Culture clash"?

9. Why does the author keep what happen in the Maraba cave an indeterminacy?

10. What is the author's opinion on the conflicts between religions of Islam, Hinduism and Christianity?

V. Guidance for Appreciation

"*A Passage to India* is the most controversial of Forster's novels. The majority of critics regard it as his finest work, yet no consensus has emerged about its meanings, partly because the book has proven highly responsive to so many approaches. Despite literary criticism's changing focal points over the decades, from politics and spirituality through to ethnicity and sexuality, it has always kept *A Passage to India* firmly in its sights because Forster's novel offers fertile ground for the broadest range of analytical and theoretical perspectives" (Bradshaw,188). Just as Bradshaw's statement suggests, the novel *A Passage to India* is a rich ore for literary criticism.

The novel mainly discusses the complex encounter between East and West, trying to answer the question put forward at the beginning of the novel whether British and Indians can be friends when India is the colony of England. It regarded as a good text for the analysis of postcolonialism and cultural studies.

The conventional reading of *A Passage to India* emphasizes Forster's criticism of British imperialism. In this novel, he criticizes the Euro-centrism of the Englishmen who hold "white man's burden" ideology, believing in their superiority of their Anglo-European culture to that of the colonized, and their obligation of staying in and governing India. The arrogance is best represented by Mrs. Callendar who declares that "The kindest thing one can do to a native is to let him die" (p. 27). In the novel, Forster explores the emotional and moral shortcomings of England's upper classes. During the Bridge Party, the colonizers' inhuman attitude towards the colonized Indians reflects their snobbery. Forster wants to convey the message that the abnormal relationship is based on the inequitable political, economic and cultural backgrounds, which are supported by the imperialistic power. The ending where the land physically separates Aziz and Fielding shows the author's message that imperialism will not work in India because resistance against it is inevitable. Moreover, the novel differs from other narrations about India at that time as it places its focus on Indian characters, culture, and religion, as well as on friendships between Britons and Indians. This is the reason why some Indian critics hail *A Passage to India* as an emblem of British understanding of the Indian, and the first "successful" representation of Indian life.

However, this traditional understanding has been challenged by critics by employing postcolonial theories. Through a reassessment of Forster's politics, they point out his limitations in viewing India, Indians and Indian culture. In the novel, India looms as unfathomable, undefinable, or, to use E. M. Forster's expression: a mystery and a muddle. This is a land beyond all order and all comprehension. The Indian culture is represented as incomprehensible, erotic, and mysterious. Edward Said points that Forster's depiction of India as "unapprehendable" is an act of evasion rather than understanding, as "he exoticises and mystifies the nation, rather than engaging and elucidating". Said finds that "Forster's India is so affectionately personal and remorselessly metaphysical that his view of India as a nation contending for sovereignty with Britain is not politically very serious, or even respectful". Indian critics like Chaudhuri and Naik insist that the representation of Hindus and Muslims in the novel is oversimplified, which reducing the political conflicts and cultural apartheid into personalized relationship between Aziz and Fielding.

The title of the novel comes from the poem "A Passage to India" by the great American poet Walt Whitman. In his poem, Whitman expresses an optimistic view on international connection, implying the infinite possibilities of human relationship. On the contrary, *A Passage to India* expresses a negative view by declaring that "No, not yet," "No, not there" (316) In the novel, though the four major characters Mrs. Moore, Adela Quested, Dr. Aziz and Fielding all express the strong wishes for cross-cultural communication, their efforts fail.

Several cultural encounters have been discussed in the novel. The first in the Mosque between Aziz and Mrs. Moore might be a good start. However, the departure and death of Mrs. Moore indicate the disillusionment of a connection. The Bridge Party only makes both Englishmen and Indians realize the huge gap between, just as Mrs. Turton says, "Why they come at all I don't know. They hate it as much as we do" (61). In Maraba Caves, Mrs. Moore, Adela and Aziz all experience cultural shocks which shatter their temporary connection. "*A Passage to India* demonstrates the inconvenience and ungainliness of cross-cultural exchange by an expression of the continual disappointment and bafflement such an exchange generates"(Tayeb, 53).

Similarly, the instances of cross-cultural friendship in *A Passage to India* also end in a calamitous breach or a painful rupture. The friendships between Aziz and Mrs. Moore, Aziz and Adela, and Aziz and Fielding are fruitless. As the ending of the novel suggests, "All stupid misunderstandings had been cleared up, but socially they had no meeting-place" (312). To Forster, "India is the site of gorgeous variety, on which the indecipherability of cultural difference and the implausibility of colonial exchange are enacted"(Tayeb, 54).

In the novel, Aziz develops from a detached, politically unaffected Indian to a zealous insurgent against British rule, and a nationalist-oriented thinker. Tao Jiajun believes that Aziz's identity construction as a nationalist undergoes three stages: the impact on his national identity when he goes to Europe to pursue modern knowledge, his identity crisis in the colonial, cultural and racial conflicts, and the formation of his identity as a nationalist. The knowledge of modern medicine and philosophy lifts him out of ignorance and establish modern consciousness, which leads to his double consciousness: modern and tradition. The double consciousness and his awkward situation in India causes Aziz's identity dilemma. He is despised and marginalized by the English colonizers due to his ethnic identity. But at the same time, his westernized manner and modern consciousness also make him dislocated in the indigenous culture. Due to the spiritual and cultural homelessness caused by the interstice of the two warring cultures, Aziz undergoes uneasiness, agony and despair to maintain his own secure identity which is distorted by colonialism. Therefore, he becomes hyper-sensitive and suspicious. His identity construction undergoes the conflicts between different races and different cultures. In the conflicts, his servility declines and rebellion increases. He finally gains his identity as a nationalist.

Ⅵ. Further Reading

1. Bradshaw, David. The Cambridge Companion to E. M. Forster[M]. Cambridge: Cambridge UP, 2007.

2. Cavaliero, Glen. A Reading of E. M. Forster[M]. Houndmills: the Macmilian Press Ltd, 1986.

3. Childs, Peter, ed. A Routledge Literary sourcebook on E. M. Forster's *A Passage to India*[M]. London: Routledge, 2002.

4. Christensen, Timothy. Bearing the White Man's Burden: Misrecognition and Cultural Difference in E. M. Forster's "A Passage to India"[J]. NOVEL: A Forum on Fiction, 2006, Vol. 39, (2): 155-178.

5. Gardner, Philip. Ed. E. M. Forster: Critical Heritage[M]. London: Routledge, 2002.

6. Shaheen, Mohammad. E. M. Forster and the Politics of Imperialism [M]. Houndmills: the Macmilian Press Ltd, 2004.

7. Tayeb, Lamia. The Inscription of Cultural Bafflement in E. M. Forster's "A Passage to India"[J]. Interdisciplinary Literary Studies, 2004, Vol. 6, (1): 37-59.

8. 李宵垅，李建波. 帝国主义语境中的个人关系——《印度之行》新解[J]. 当代外国文学, 2014 (4): 93-100.

9. 石海峻. 混沌与蛇:《印度之行》[J]. 外国文学评论, 1996(2):63-68.

10. 陶家俊. 文化身份的嬗变——E. M. 福斯特小说和思想研究[M]. 北京:中国社会科学出版社, 2003.

Chapter 4

D.H. Lawrence: Odour of Chrysanthemums Ecocriticism and Feminism

I. Introduction to the Author

David Herbert Lawrence (1885—1930) is regarded as one of the most influential and controversial British novelists of the 20th century, whose artistic accomplishment and literary talent have been recognized and affirmed by many critics. His prolific output includes novels, short stories, poems, plays, literary criticism, travel books, translations, and paintings.

David Herbert Lawrence was born on September 11, 1885 in the midlands mining village of Eastwood Nottinghamshire, which becomes one of the major settings of his stories. His father Arthur John Lawrence was an illiterate coal miner at the nearby Brinsley Colliery, and his mother Lydia Lawrence a failed school teacher. The friction between his parents and the poverty of the family haunted his childhood and gave him a strong feeling of insecurity during his earliest years. Between September 1898 and July 1901, he received formal education in Nottingham High School. After graduation, he worked as a clerk in a surgical appliance factory. In1902, Lawrence became a pupil-teacher at the British School in Eastwood. In 1904 he got a chance to attend the Pupil-Teacher Centre in Ilkeston, where he developed his artistic interests. During this period, Lawrence started writing and composed his first poems. In 1906, he went to study at Nottingham University College, and obtained a teaching certificate in 1908. He then took a teaching post at an elementary school in the London suburb of Croydon. He continued his writing of poems and also tried stories. In 1909, five poems were published in *English Review*. He also started his Eastwood stories, one of which is the short story "Odour of Chrysanthemums".

In March 1912, Lawrence met Frieda von Richthofen, a German noblewoman and the wife of a professor at Nottingham University, with whom he was to share the rest of his life. They left for Metz and Germany, and later settled at Gargnano, Italy. The two years of 1913 and 1914 are important for Lawrence to establish his reputation as a writer. He published *Sons and Lovers* in 1913 and short story collection *The Prussian Officer and Other Stories* in 1914. During WW I , Lawrence and Frieda were trapped in England for Frieda's German origins and Lawrence's political views. *The Rainbow* (1915) was suppressed after an investigation into its alleged obscenity in 1915.

After WW I , Lawrence and his wife went to Italy, working on *The Lost Girl* (1920), *Aaron's Rod* (1922), and *Mr. Noon* (later published in 1984). In 1921 the Lawrences started their long journey around the world. They first went to the United States, then Ceylon, Australia, Mexico and back to the United States, then Italy and at last France. He died of tuberculosis at Vence, France at the age of 44.

All his own life experiences have provided the direct material for artistic creation and thus have laid a solid foundation for his established literary career. D. H. Lawrence is best known for his novels, including *The White Peacock* (1911), *The Trespasser* (1912), *Sons and Lovers* (1913), *The Rainbow* (1915), *Women in Love* (1920), *The Lost Girl* (1920), *Aaron's Rod* (1922), *Kangaroo* (1923), *The Boy in the Bush* (1924), *The Plumed Serpent* (1926), *Lady Chatterley's Lover* (1928), and *The Escaped Cock* (1929). His major short-story collections are *The Prussian Officer and Other Stories* (1914), *The Horse Dealer's Daughter* (1922), *The Rocking-Horse Winner* (1926), *Mother and Daughter* (1929), and *Love Among the Haystacks and other stories* (1930). Lawrence has also published poetry collections, plays, non-fiction books, travel books and translations.

Ⅱ. Introduction to the Short Story

The short story "Odour of Chrysanthemums" (1909) is rightly considered to be among Lawrence's finest tales. It was first published in *English Review* in 1909. Later, D. H. Lawrence revised it and collected in the short story collection *The Prussian Officer and Other Stories* (1914).

Lawrence drew the plot of the story directly from his Uncle James, who died in a mining accident at Brinsley Colliery in 1880. The story, as Lawrence put it, "full of childhood's atmosphere". The tensions and conflicts between the Bates reflect those between Lawrence' parents.

The short story "Odour of Chrysanthemums" opens with the description of the scene of England's coal country at dusk. A locomotive engine comes chugging along the tracks, carrying coal miners home and disturbing the peace. Elizabeth Bates, the main character, appears and calls her son John to go back home. Elizabeth's father comes for a visit and tells Elizabeth that it is time he remarried. He also informs her that her husband, Walter, has gone on another drinking binge and was heard bragging in the local pub about how much he was going to spend. When he leaves, Elizabeth prepares for the dinner and waits for her husband to come home. As time goes by, Walter does not appear, so Elizabeth suspects that he has gone to the pub to drink, as he usually does. Elizabeth grows increasingly anxious and angry. After she puts her children to bed, Elizabeth goes out for her husband. She goes to Mrs. Rigley, who informs her that he last saw Walter at the coal pit, finishing a job. He also offers to go to the pub, but Walter is not there.

Elizabeth returns and waits, when suddenly her mother-in-law enters the cottage, crying hysterically that Walter has been in a serious accident. Soon a miner comes in with the news that Walter has been dead for hours, smothered after a cave-in.

The climax comes at the end of the story with the bringing in of the collier's body, the washing of the corpse by the wife and the collier's mother, and the wife's realization of the years of estrangement between her husband and herself. Throughout the whole tragic story, the author gives a full expression of his dissatisfaction about the industrial civilization and also shows profound concern about people's alienation and estrangement.

III. Excerpt

I.

The small locomotive engine, Number 4, came clanking, stumbling down from Selston—with seven full waggons. It appeared round the corner with loud threats of speed, but the colt that it startled from among the gorse, which still flickered indistinctly in the raw afternoon, outdistanced it at a canter. A woman, walking up the railway line to Underwood, drew back into the hedge, held her basket aside, and watched the footplate of the engine advancing. The trucks thumped heavily past, one by one, with slow inevitable movement, as she stood insignificantly trapped between the jolting black waggons and the hedge; then they curved away towards the coppice where the withered oak leaves dropped noiselessly, while the birds, pulling at the scarlet hips beside the track, made off into the dusk that had already crept into the spinney. In the open, the smoke from the engine sank and cleaved to the rough grass. The fields were dreary and forsaken, and in the marshy strip that led to the whimsey, a reedy pit-pond, the fowls had already abandoned their run among the alders, to roost in the tarred fowl-house. The pit-bank loomed up beyond the pond, flames like red sores licking its ashy sides, in the afternoon's stagnant light. Just beyond rose the tapering chimneys and the clumsy black head-stocks of Brinsley Colliery. The two wheels were spinning fast up against the sky, and the winding-engine rapped out its little spasms. The miners were being turned up.

The engine whistled as it came into the wide bay of railway lines beside the colliery, where rows of trucks stood in harbour.

Miners, single, trailing and in groups, passed like shadows diverging home. At the edge of the ribbed level of sidings squat a low cottage, three steps down from the cinder track. A large bony vine clutched at the house, as if to claw down the tiled roof. Round the bricked yard grew a few wintry primroses. Beyond, the long garden sloped down to a bush-covered brook course. There were some twiggy apple trees, winter-crack trees, and ragged cabbages. Beside the path hung dishevelled pink chrysanthemums, like pink cloths hung on bushes. A woman came stooping out of the felt-covered fowl-house, half-way down the garden. She closed and padlocked the door, then drew herself erect, having brushed some bits from her white apron.

She was a tall woman of imperious mien, handsome, with definite black eyebrows. Her smooth black hair was parted exactly. For a few moments she stood steadily watching the miners as they passed along the railway; then she turned towards the brook course. Her face was calm and set, her mouth was closed with disillusionment. After a moment she called:

"John!" There was no answer. She waited, and then said distinctly:

"Where are you?"

"Here!" replied a child's sulky voice from among the bushes. The woman looked piercingly through the dusk.

"Are you at that brook?" she asked sternly.

For answer the child showed himself before the raspberry-canes that rose like whips. He was a small, sturdy boy of five. He stood quite still, defiantly.

"Oh!" said the mother, conciliated. "I thought you were down at that wet brook—and you remember what I told you—"

The boy did not move or answer.

"Come, come on in," she said more gently, "it's getting dark. There's your grandfather's engine coming down the line!"

The lad advanced slowly, with resentful, taciturn movement. He was dressed in trousers and waistcoat of cloth that was too thick and hard for the size of the garments. They were evidently cut down from a man's clothes.

As they went slowly towards the house he tore at the ragged wisps of chrysanthemums and dropped the petals in handfuls along the path.

"Don't do that—it does look nasty," said his mother. He refrained, and she, suddenly pitiful, broke off a twig with three or four wan flowers and held them against her face. When mother and son reached the yard her hand hesitated, and instead of laying the flower aside, she pushed it in her apron-band. The mother and son stood at the foot of the three steps looking across the bay of lines at the passing home of the miners. The trundle of the small train was imminent. Suddenly the engine loomed past the house and came to a stop opposite the gate.

The engine-driver, a short man with round grey beard, leaned out of the cab high above the woman.

"Have you got a cup of tea?" he said in a cheery, hearty fashion.

It was her father. She went in, saying she would mash. Directly, she returned.

"I didn't come to see you on Sunday," began the little grey-bearded man.

"I didn't expect you," said his daughter.

The engine-driver winced; then, reassuming his cheery, airy manner, he said:

"Oh, have you heard then? Well, and what do you think—?"

"I think it is soon enough," she replied.

At her brief censure the little man made an impatient gesture, and said coaxingly, yet with dangerous coldness:

"Well, what's a man to do? It's no sort of life for a man of my years, to sit at my own hearth like a stranger. And if I'm going to marry again it may as well be soon as late—what does it matter to anybody?"

The woman did not reply, but turned and went into the house. The man in the engine-cab stood assertive, till she returned with a cup of tea and a piece of bread and butter on a plate. She went up the steps and stood near the footplate of the hissing engine.

"You needn't 'a' brought me bread an' butter," said her father. "But a cup of tea"—he sipped appreciatively—"it's very nice." He sipped for a moment or two, then: "I hear as Walter's got another bout on," he said.

"When hasn't he?" said the woman bitterly.

"I heered tell of him in the 'Lord Nelson' braggin' as he was going to spend that b—afore he went: half a sovereign that was."

"When?" asked the woman.

"A' Sat'day night—I know that's true."

"Very likely," she laughed bitterly. "He gives me twenty-three shillings."

"Aye, it's a nice thing, when a man can do nothing with his money but make a beast of himself!" said the grey-whiskered man. The woman turned her head away. Her father swallowed the last of his tea and handed her the cup.

"Aye," he sighed, wiping his mouth. "It's a settler, it is—"

He put his hand on the lever. The little engine strained and groaned, and the train rumbled towards the crossing. The woman again looked across the metals. Darkness was settling over the spaces of the railway and trucks: the miners, in grey sombre groups, were still passing home. The winding-engine pulsed hurriedly, with brief pauses. Elizabeth Bates looked at the dreary flow of men, then she went indoors. Her husband did not come.

The kitchen was small and full of firelight; red coals piled glowing up the chimney mouth. All the life of the room seemed in the white, warm hearth and the steel fender reflecting the red fire. The cloth was laid for tea; cups glinted in the shadows. At the back, where the lowest stairs protruded into the room, the boy sat struggling with a knife and a piece of whitewood. He was almost hidden in the shadow. It was half-past four. They had but to await the father's coming to begin tea. As the mother watched her son's sullen little struggle with the wood, she saw herself in his silence and pertinacity; she saw the father in her child's indifference to all but himself. She seemed to be occupied by her husband. He had probably gone past his home, slunk past his own door, to drink before he came in, while his dinner spoiled and wasted in waiting. She glanced at the clock, then took the potatoes to strain them in the yard. The garden and fields beyond the brook were closed in uncertain darkness. When she rose with the saucepan, leaving the drain steaming into the night behind her, she saw the yellow lamps were lit along the high road that went up the hill away beyond the space of the railway lines and the field.

Then again she watched the men trooping home, fewer now and fewer.

Indoors the fire was sinking and the room was dark red. The woman put her saucepan on the hob, and set a batter pudding near the mouth of the oven. Then she stood unmoving. Directly, gratefully, came quick young steps to the door. Someone hung on the latch a moment, then a little girl entered and began pulling off her outdoor things, dragging a mass of curls, just ripening from gold to brown, over her eyes with her hat.

Her mother chid her for coming late from school, and said she would have to keep her at home the dark winter days.

"Why, mother, it's hardly a bit dark yet. The lamp's not lighted, and my father's not home."

"No, he isn't. But it's a quarter to five! Did you see anything of him?"

The child became serious. She looked at her mother with large, wistful blue eyes.

"No, mother, I've never seen him. Why? Has he come up an' gone past, to Old Brinsley? He hasn't, mother, 'cos I never saw him."

"He'd watch that," said the mother bitterly, "he'd take care as you didn't see him. But you may depend upon it, he's seated in the 'Prince o' Wales'. He wouldn't be this late."

The girl looked at her mother piteously.

"Let's have our teas, mother, should we?" said she.

The mother called John to table. She opened the door once more and looked out across the darkness of the lines. All was deserted: she could not hear the winding-engines.

"Perhaps," she said to herself, "he's stopped to get some ripping done."

They sat down to tea. John, at the end of the table near the door, was almost lost in the darkness. Their faces were hidden from each other. The girl crouched against the fender slowly moving a thick piece of bread before the fire. The lad, his face a dusky mark on the shadow, sat watching her who was transfigured in the red glow.

"I do think it's beautiful to look in the fire," said the child.

"Do you?" said her mother. "Why?"

"It's so red, and full of little caves—and it feels so nice, and you can fair smell it."

"It'll want mending directly," replied her mother, "and then if your father comes he'll carry on and say there never is a fire when a man comes home sweating from the pit. —A public-house is always warm enough."

There was silence till the boy said complainingly: "Make haste, our Annie."

"Well, I am doing! I can't make the fire do it no faster, can I?"

"She keeps wafflin' it about so's to make 'er slow," grumbled the boy.

"Don't have such an evil imagination, child," replied the mother.

Soon the room was busy in the darkness with the crisp sound of crunching. The mother ate very little. She drank her tea determinedly, and sat thinking. When she rose her anger was evident in the stern unbending of her head. She looked at the pudding in the fender, and broke out:

"It is a scandalous thing as a man can't even come home to his dinner! If it's crozzled up to a cinder I don't see why I should care. Past his very door he goes to get to a public-house, and here I sit with his dinner waiting for him—"

She went out. As she dropped piece after piece of coal on the red fire, the shadows fell on the walls, till the room was almost in total darkness.

"I canna see," grumbled the invisible John. In spite of herself, the mother laughed.

"You know the way to your mouth," she said. She set the dustpan outside the door. When she came again like a shadow on the hearth, the lad repeated, complaining sulkily:

"I canna see."

"Good gracious!" cried the mother irritably, "you're as bad as your father if it's a bit dusk!"

Nevertheless she took a paper spill from a sheaf on the mantelpiece and proceeded to light the lamp that hung from the ceiling in the middle of the room. As she reached up, her figure displayed itself just rounding with maternity.

"Oh, mother—!" exclaimed the girl.

"What?" said the woman, suspended in the act of putting the lamp glass over the flame. The copper reflector shone handsomely on her, as she stood with uplifted arm, turning to face her daughter.

"You've got a flower in your apron!" said the child, in a little rapture at this unusual event.

"Goodness me!" exclaimed the woman, relieved. "One would think the house was afire." She replaced the glass and waited a moment before turning up the wick. A pale shadow was seen floating vaguely on the floor.

"Let me smell!" said the child, still rapturously, coming forward and putting her face to her mother's waist.

"Go along, silly!" said the mother, turning up the lamp. The light revealed their suspense so that the woman felt it almost unbearable. Annie was still bending at her waist. Irritably, the mother took the flowers out from her apron-band.

"Oh, mother—don't take them out!" Annie cried, catching her hand and trying to replace the sprig.

"Such nonsense!" said the mother, turning away. The child put the pale chrysanthemums to her lips, murmuring:

"Don't they smell beautiful!"

Her mother gave a short laugh.

"No," she said, "not to me. It was chrysanthemums when I married him, and chrysanthemums when you were born, and the first time they ever brought him home drunk, he'd got brown chrysanthemums in his button-hole."

She looked at the children. Their eyes and their parted lips were wondering. The mother sat rocking in silence for some time. Then she looked at the clock.

"Twenty minutes to six!" In a tone of fine bitter carelessness she continued: "Eh, he'll not come now till they bring him. There he'll stick! But he needn't come rolling in here in his pit-dirt, for I won't wash him. He can lie on the floor—Eh, what a fool I've been, what a fool! And this is what I came here for, to this dirty hole, rats and all, for him to slink past his very door. Twice last week—he's begun now-"

She silenced herself, and rose to clear the table.

While for an hour or more the children played, subduedly intent, fertile of imagination, united in fear of the mothers wrath, and in dread of their fathers home-coming, Mrs Bates sat in her rocking-chair making a 'singlet' of thick cream-coloured flannel, which gave a dull wounded sound as she tore off the grey edge. She worked at her sewing with energy, listening to the children, and her anger wearied itself, lay down to rest, opening its eyes from time to time and steadily watching, its ears raised to listen. Sometimes even her anger quailed and shrank, and the mother suspended her sewing, tracing the footsteps that thudded along the sleepers outside; she would lift her head sharply to bid the children 'hush', but she recovered herself in time, and the footsteps went past the gate, and the children were not flung out of their playing world.

But at last Annie sighed, and gave in. She glanced at her waggon of slippers, and loathed the game. She turned plaintively to her mother.

"Mother!"—but she was inarticulate.

John crept out like a frog from under the sofa. His mother glanced up.

"Yes," she said, "just look at those shirt-sleeves!"

The boy held them out to survey them, saying nothing. Then somebody called in a hoarse voice away down the line, and suspense bristled in the room, till two people had gone by outside, talking.

"It is time for bed," said the mother.

"My father hasn't come," wailed Annie plaintively. But her mother was primed with courage.

"Never mind. They'll bring him when he does come—like a log." She meant there would be no scene. "And he may sleep on the floor till he wakes himself. I know he'll not go to work tomorrow after this!"

The children had their hands and faces wiped with a flannel. They were very quiet. When they had put on their nightdresses, they said their prayers, the boy mumbling. The mother looked down at them, at the brown silken bush of intertwining curls in the nape of the girl's neck, at the little black head of the lad, and her heart burst with anger at their father who caused all three such distress. The children hid their faces in her skirts for comfort.

When Mrs Bates came down, the room was strangely empty, with a tension of expectancy. She took up her sewing and stitched for some time without raising her head. Meantime her anger was tinged with fear.

II

The clock struck eight and she rose suddenly, dropping her sewing on her chair. She went to the stairfoot door, opened it, listening. Then she went out, locking the door behind her.

Something scuffled in the yard, and she started, though she knew it was only the rats with which the place was overrun. The night was very dark. In the great bay of railway lines, bulked with trucks, there was no trace of light, only away back she could see a few yellow lamps at the pit-top, and the red smear of the burning pit-bank on the night. She hurried along the edge of the track, then, crossing the converging lines, came to the stile by the white gates, whence she emerged on the road. Then the fear which had led her shrank. People were walking up to New Brinsley; she saw the lights in the houses; twenty yards further on were the broad windows of the 'Prince of Wales', very warm and bright, and the loud voices of men could be heard distinctly. What a fool she had been to imagine that anything had happened to him! He was merely drinking over there at the 'Prince of Wales'. She faltered. She had never yet been to fetch him, and she never would go. So she continued her walk towards the long straggling line of houses, standing blank on the highway. She entered a passage between the dwellings.

"Mr Rigley? —Yes! Did you want him? No, he's not in at this minute."

The raw-boned woman leaned forward from her dark scullery and peered at the other, upon whom fell a dim light through the blind of the kitchen window.

"Is it Mrs Bates?" she asked in a tone tinged with respect.

"Yes. I wondered if your Master was at home. Mine hasn't come yet."

"'Asn't 'e! Oh, Jack's been 'ome an 'ad 'is dinner an' gone out. E's just gone for 'alf an hour afore bedtime. Did you call at the 'Prince of Wales'?"

"No—"

"No, you didn't like—! It's not very nice." The other woman was indulgent. There was an awkward pause. "Jack never said nothink about—about your Mester," she said.

"No! —I expect he's stuck in there!"

Elizabeth Bates said this bitterly, and with recklessness. She knew that the woman across the yard was standing at her door listening, but she did not care. As she turned:

"Stop a minute! I'll just go an' ask Jack if e' knows anythink," said Mrs Rigley.

"Oh, no—I wouldn't like to put—!"

"Yes, I will, if you'll just step inside an' see as th' childer doesn't come downstairs and set theirselves afire. "

Elizabeth Bates, murmuring a remonstrance, stepped inside. The other woman apologized for the state of the room.

The kitchen needed apology. There were little frocks and trousers and childish undergarments on the squab and on the floor, and a litter of playthings everywhere. On the black American cloth of the table were pieces of bread and cake, crusts, slops, and a teapot with cold tea.

"Eh, ours is just as bad," said Elizabeth Bates, looking at the woman, not at the house. Mrs Rigley put a shawl over her head and hurried out, saying:

"I shanna be a minute. "

The other sat, noting with faint disapproval the general untidiness of the room. Then she fell to counting the shoes of various sizes scattered over the floor. There were twelve. She sighed and said to herself, "No wonder!"— glancing at the litter. There came the scratching of two pairs of feet on the yard, and the Rigleys entered. Elizabeth Bates rose. Rigley was a big man, with very large bones. His head looked particularly bony. Across his temple was a blue scar, caused by a wound got in the pit, a wound in which the coal-dust remained blue like tattooing.

"'Asna 'e come whoam yit?" asked the man, without any form of greeting, but with deference and sympathy. "I couldna say wheer he is—'e's non ower theer!"—he jerked his head to signify the 'Prince of Wales'.

"'E's 'appen gone up to th' 'Yew'," said Mrs Rigley.

There was another pause. Rigley had evidently something to get off his mind:

"Ah left'im finishin' a stint," he began. "Loose-all 'ad bin gone about ten minutes when we com'n away, an' I shouted, 'Are ter comin', Walt?' an' 'e said, 'Go on, Ah shanna be but a'ef a minnit,' so we com'n ter th' bottom, me an' Bowers, thinkin' as 'e wor just behint, an' 'ud come up i' th' next bantle—"

He stood perplexed, as if answering a charge of deserting his mate. Elizabeth Bates, now again certain of disaster, hastened to reassure him:

"I expect 'e's gone up to th' 'Yew Tree', as you say. It's not the first time. I've fretted myself into a fever before now. He'll come home when they carry him. "

"Ay, isn't it too bad!" deplored the other woman.

"I'll just step up to Dick's an' see if 'e istheer," offered the man, afraid of appearing alarmed, afraid of taking liberties.

"Oh, I wouldn't think of bothering you that far," said Elizabeth Bates, with emphasis, but he knew she was glad of his offer.

As they stumbled up the entry, Elizabeth Bates heard Rigley's wife run across the yard and open her neighbour's door. At this, suddenly all the blood in her body seemed to switch away from her heart.

"Mind!" warned Rigley. "Ah've said many a time as Ah'd fill up them ruts in this entry, sumb'dy 'll be breakin' their legs yit."

She recovered herself and walked quickly along with the miner.

"I don't like leaving the children in bed, and nobody in the house," she said.

"No, you dunna!" he replied courteously. They were soon at the gate of the cottage.

"Well, I shanna be many minnits. Dunna you be frettin' now, 'e'll be all right," said the butty.

"Thank you very much, Mr Rigley," she replied.

"You're welcome!" he stammered, moving away. "I shanna be many minnits."

The house was quiet. Elizabeth Bates took off her hat and shawl, and rolled back the rug. When she had finished, she sat down. It was a few minutes past nine. She was startled by the rapid chuff of the winding-engine at the pit, and the sharp whirr of the brakes on the rope as it descended. Again she felt the painful sweep of her blood, and she put her hand to her side, saying aloud, "Good gracious! —it's only the nine o'clock deputy going down," rebuking herself.

She sat still, listening. Half an hour of this, and she was wearied out.

"What am I working myself up like this for?" she said pitiably to herself, "I s'll only be doing myself some damage."

She took out her sewing again.

At a quarter to ten there were footsteps. One person! She watched for the door to open. It was an elderly woman, in a black bonnet and a black woollen shawl—his mother. She was about sixty years old, pale, with blue eyes, and her face all wrinkled and lamentable. She shut the door and turned to her daughterinlaw peevishly.

"Eh, Lizzie, whatever shall we do, whatever shall we do!" she cried.

Elizabeth drew back a little, sharply.

"What is it, mother?" she said.

The elder woman seated herself on the sofa.

"I don't know, child, I can't tell you!"—she shook her head slowly.
Elizabeth sat watching her, anxious and vexed.

"I don't know," replied the grandmother, sighing very deeply. "There's no
end to my troubles, there isn't. The things I've gone through, I'm sure it's
enough—!" She wept without wiping her eyes, the tears running.

"But, mother," interrupted Elizabeth, "what do you mean? What is it?"

The grandmother slowly wiped her eyes. The fountains of her tears were
stopped by Elizabeth's directness. She wiped her eyes slowly.

"Poor child! Eh, you poor thing!" she moaned. "I don't know what we're
going to do, I don't—and you as you are—it's a thing, it is indeed!"

Elizabeth waited.

Is he dead? she asked, and at the words her heart swung violently, though
she felt a slight flush of shame at the ultimate extravagance of the question. Her
words sufficiently frightened the old lady, almost brought her to herself.

"Don't say so, Elizabeth! We'll hope it's not as bad as that; no, may the
Lord spare us that, Elizabeth. Jack Rigley came just as I was sittin' down to a
glass afore going to bed, an' 'e said, "'Appen you'll go down th' line, Mrs
Bates. Walt's had an accident. 'Appen you'll go an' sit wi' 'er till we can get
him home.' I hadn't time to ask him a word afore he was gone. An' I put my
bonnet on an' come straight down, Lizzie. I thought to myself, 'Eh, that poor
blessed child, if anybody should come an' tell her of a sudden, there's no
knowin' what'll 'appen to 'er. 'You mustn't let it upset you, Lizzie—or you
know what to expect. How long is it, six months—or is it five, Lizzie? Ay!"—
the old woman shook her head—"time slips on, it slips on! Ay!"

Elizabeth's thoughts were busy elsewhere. If he was killed—would she be
able to manage on the little pension and what she could earn? —she counted up
rapidly. If he was hurt—they wouldn't take him to the hospital—how tiresome
he would be to nurse! —but perhaps she'd be able to get him away from the
drink and his hateful ways. She would—while he was ill. The tears offered to
come to her eyes at the picture. But what sentimental luxury was this she was

beginning? —She turned to consider the children. At any rate she was absolutely necessary for them. They were her business.

"Ay!" repeated the old woman, "it seems but a week or two since he brought me his first wages. Ay—he was a good lad, Elizabeth, he was, in his way. I don't know why he got to be such a trouble, I don't. He was a happy lad at home, only full of spirits. But there's no mistake he's been a handful of trouble, he has! I hope the Lord'll spare him to mend his ways. I hope so, I hope so. You've had a sight o' trouble with him, Elizabeth, you have indeed. But he was a jolly enough lad wi' me, he was, I can assure you. I don't know how it is ..."

The old woman continued to muse aloud, a monotonous irritating sound, while Elizabeth thought concentratedly, startled once, when she heard the winding-engine chuff quickly, and the brakes skirr with a shriek. Then she heard the engine more slowly, and the brakes made no sound. The old woman did not notice. Elizabeth waited in suspense. The mother-in-law talked, with lapses into silence.

"But he wasn't your son, Lizzie, an' it makes a difference. Whatever he was, I remember him when he was little, an' I learned to understand him and to make allowances. You've got to make allowances for them—"

It was half-past ten, and the old woman was saying: "But it's trouble from beginning to end; you're never too old for trouble, never too old for that—" when the gate banged back, and there were heavy feet on the steps.

"I'll go, Lizzie, let me go," cried the old woman, rising. But Elizabeth was at the door. It was a man in pit-clothes.

"They're bringin' 'im, Missis," he said. Elizabeth's heart halted a moment. Then it surged on again, almost suffocating her.

"Is he—is it bad?" she asked.

The man turned away, looking at the darkness:

"The doctor says 'e'd been dead hours. 'E saw 'im i' th' lamp-cabin."

The old woman, who stood just behind Elizabeth, dropped into a chair, and folded her hands, crying: "Oh, my boy, my boy!"

"Hush!" said Elizabeth, with a sharp twitch of a frown. "Be still, mother, don't waken th' children; I wouldn't have them down for anything!"

The old woman moaned softly, rocking herself. The man was drawing away. Elizabeth took a step forward.

"How was it?" she asked.

"Well, I couldn't say for sure," the man replied, very ill at ease. "'E wor finishin' a stint an' th' butties 'ad gone, an' a lot o'stuff come down atop 'n 'im. "

"And crushed him?" cried the widow, with a shudder.

"No," said the man, "it fell at th' back of 'im. 'E wor under th' face, an' it niver touched 'im. It shut 'im in. It seems 'e wor smothered. "

Elizabeth shrank back. She heard the old woman behind her cry:

"What? —what did 'e say it was?"

The man replied, more loudly: "'E wor smothered!"

Then the old woman wailed aloud, and this relieved Elizabeth.

"Oh, mother," she said, putting her hand on the old woman, "don't waken th' children, don't waken th' children. "

She wept a little, unknowing, while the old mother rocked herself and moaned. Elizabeth remembered that they were bringing him home, and she must be ready. "They'll lay him in the parlour," she said to herself, standing a moment pale and perplexed.

Then she lighted a candle and went into the tiny room. The air was cold and damp, but she could not make a fire, there was no fireplace. She set down the candle and looked round. The candle-light glittered on the lustre-glasses, on the two vases that held some of the pink chrysanthemums, and on the dark mahogany. There was a cold, deathly smell of chrysanthemums in the room. Elizabeth stood looking at the flowers. She turned away, and calculated whether there would be room to lay him on the floor, between the couch and the chiffonier. She pushed the chairs aside. There would be room to lay him down and to step round him. Then she fetched the old red tablecloth, and another old cloth, spreading them down to save her bit of carpet. She shivered on leaving the parlour; so, from the dresser-drawer she took a clean shirt and put it at the fire to air. All the time her mother-in-law was rocking herself in the chair and moaning.

"You'll have to move from there, mother," said Elizabeth. "They'll be bringing him in. Come in the rocker. "

The old mother rose mechanically, and seated herself by the fire, continuing to lament. Elizabeth went into the pantry for another candle, and there, in the little penthouse under the naked tiles, she heard them coming. She stood still in the pantry doorway, listening. She heard them pass the end of the house, and come awkwardly down the three steps, a jumble of shuffling footsteps and muttering voices. The old woman was silent. The men were in the yard.

Then Elizabeth heard Matthews, the manager of the pit, say: "You go in first, Jim. Mind!"

The door came open, and the two women saw a collier backing into the room, holding one end of a stretcher, on which they could see the nailed pit-boots of the dead man. The two carriers halted, the man at the head stooping to the lintel of the door.

"Wheer will you have him?" asked the manager, a short, white-bearded man.

Elizabeth roused herself and came from the pantry carrying the unlighted candle.

"In the parlour," she said.

"In there, Jim!" pointed the manager, and the carriers backed round into the tiny room. The coat with which they had covered the body fell off as they awkwardly turned through the two doorways, and the women saw their man, naked to the waist, lying stripped for work. The old woman began to moan in a low voice of horror.

"Lay th' stretcher at th' side," snapped the manager, "an' put 'im on th' cloths. Mind now, mind! Look you now—!"

One of the men had knocked off a vase of chrysanthemums. He stared awkwardly, then they set down the stretcher. Elizabeth did not look at her husband. As soon as she could get in the room, she went and picked up the broken vase and the flowers.

"Wait a minute!" she said.

The three men waited in silence while she mopped up the water with a duster.

"Eh, what a job, what a job, to be sure!" the manager was saying, rubbing his brow with trouble and perplexity. "Never knew such a thing in my life, never! He'd no business to ha' been left. I never knew such a thing in my life! Fell over him clean as a whistle, an' shut him in. Not four foot of space, there wasn't—yet it scarce bruised him."

He looked down at the dead man, lying prone, half naked, all grimed with coal-dust.

"'Sphyxiated,' the doctor said. It is the most terrible job I've ever known. Seems as if it was done o' purpose. Clean over him, an' shut'im in, like a mouse-trap"—he made a sharp, descending gesture with his hand.

The colliers standing by jerked aside their heads in hopeless comment.

The horror of the thing bristled upon them all.

Then they heard the girl's voice upstairs calling shrilly: "Mother, mother— who is it? Mother, who is it?"

Elizabeth hurried to the foot of the stairs and opened the door:

"Go to sleep!" she commanded sharply. "What are you shouting about? Go to sleep at once—there's nothing—"

Then she began to mount the stairs. They could hear her on the boards, and on the plaster floor of the little bedroom. They could hear her distinctly:

"What's the matter now? —what's the matter with you, silly thing?"—her voice was much agitated, with an unreal gentleness.

"I thought it was some men come," said the plaintive voice of the child. "Has he come?"

"Yes, they've brought him. There's nothing to make a fuss about. Go to sleep now, like a good child. "

They could hear her voice in the bedroom, they waited whilst she covered the children under the bedclothes.

"Is he drunk?" asked the girl, timidly, faintly.

"No! No—he's not! He—he's asleep. "

"Is he asleep downstairs?"

"Yes—and don't make a noise. "

There was silence for a moment, then the men heard the frightened child again:

"What's that noise?"

"It's nothing, I tell you, what are you bothering for?"

The noise was the grandmother moaning. She was oblivious of everything, sitting on her chair rocking and moaning. The manager put his hand on her arm and bade her "Sh—sh!!"

The old woman opened her eyes and looked at him. She was shocked by this interruption, and seemed to wonder.

"What time is it?"—the plaintive thin voice of the child, sinking back unhappily into sleep, asked this last question.

"Ten o'clock," answered the mother more softly. Then she must have bent down and kissed the children.

Matthews beckoned to the men to come away. They put on their caps and took up the stretcher. Stepping over the body, they tiptoed out of the house. None of them spoke till they were far from the wakeful children.

When Elizabeth came down she found her mother alone on the parlour floor, leaning over the dead man, the tears dropping on him.

"We must lay him out," the wife said. She put on the kettle, then returning knelt at the feet, and began to unfasten the knotted leather laces. The room was clammy and dim with only one candle, so that she had to bend her face almost to the floor. At last she got off the heavy boots and put them away.

"You must help me now," she whispered to the old woman. Together they stripped the man.

When they arose, saw him lying in the nave dignity of death, the women stood arrested in fear and respect. For a few moments they remained still, looking down, the old mother whimpering. Elizabeth felt countermanded. She saw him, how utterly inviolable he lay in himself. She had nothing to do with him. She could not accept it. Stooping, she laid her hand on him, in claim. He was still warm, for the mine was hot where he had died. His mother had his face between her hands, and was murmuring incoherently. The old tears fell in succession as drops from wet leaves; the mother was not weeping, merely her tears flowed. Elizabeth embraced the body of her husband, with cheek and lips. She seemed to be listening, inquiring, trying to get some connection. But she could not. She was driven away. He was impregnable.

She rose, went into the kitchen, where she poured warm water into a bowl, brought soap and flannel and a soft towel.

"I must wash him," she said.

Then the old mother rose stiffly, and watched Elizabeth as she carefully washed his face, carefully brushing the big blond moustache from his mouth with the flannel.

She was afraid with a bottomless fear, so she ministered to him. The old woman, jealous, said:

"Let me wipe him!"—and she kneeled on the other side drying slowly as Elizabeth washed, her big black bonnet sometimes brushing the dark head of her daughter. They worked thus in silence for a long time. They never forgot it was death, and the touch of the man's dead body gave them strange emotions, different in each of the women; a great dread possessed them both, the mother felt the lie was given to her womb, she was denied; the wife felt the utter isolation of the human soul, the child within her was a weight apart from her.

At last it was finished. He was a man of handsome body, and his face showed no traces of drink. He was blonde, full-fleshed, with fine limbs. But he was dead.

"Bless him," whispered his mother, looking always at his face, and speaking out of sheer terror. "Dear lad—bless him!" She spoke in a faint, sibilant ecstasy of fear and mother love.

Elizabeth sank down again to the floor, and put her face against his neck, and trembled and shuddered. But she had to draw away again. He was dead, and her living flesh had no place against his. A great dread and weariness held her: she was so unavailing. Her life was gone like this.

"White as milk he is, clear as a twelve-month baby, bless him, the darling!" the old mother murmured to herself. "Not a mark on him, clear and clean and white, beautiful as ever a child was made," she murmured with pride. Elizabeth kept her face hidden.

"He went peaceful, Lizzie—peaceful as sleep. Isn't he beautiful, the lamb? Ay—he must ha' made his peace, Lizzie. 'Appen he made it all right, Lizzie, shut in there. He'd have time. He wouldn't look like this if he hadn't made his peace. The lamb, the dear lamb. Eh, but he had a hearty laugh. I loved to hear it. He had the heartiest laugh, Lizzie, as a lad—"

Elizabeth looked up. The man's mouth was fallen back, slightly open under the cover of the moustache. The eyes, half shut, did not show glazed in the obscurity. Life with its smoky burning gone from him, had left him apart and utterly alien to her. And she knew what a stranger he was to her. In her womb was ice of fear, because of this separate stranger with whom she had been living as one flesh. Was this what it all meant—utter, intact separateness, obscured by heat of living? In dread she turned her face away. The fact was too deadly. There had been nothing between them, and yet they had come together, exchanging their nakedness repeatedly. Each time he had taken her, they had been two isolated beings, far apart as now. He was no more responsible than she. The child was like ice in her womb. For as she looked at the dead man, her mind, cold and detached, said clearly: "Who am I? What have I been doing? I have been fighting a husband who did not exist. He existed all the time. What wrong have I done? What was that I have been living with? There lies the reality, this man. "—And her soul died in her for fear: she knew she had never seen him, he had never seen her, they had met in the dark and had fought in the dark, not knowing whom they met nor whom they fought. And now she saw, and turned silent in seeing. For she had been wrong. She had said he was something he was not; she had felt familiar with him. Whereas he was apart all the while, living as she never lived, feeling as she never felt.

In fear and shame she looked at his naked body, that she had known falsely. And he was the father of her children. Her soul was torn from her body and stood apart. She looked at his naked body and was ashamed, as if she had denied it. After all, it was itself. It seemed awful to her. She looked at his face, and she turned her own face to the wall. For his look was other than hers, his way was not her way. She had denied him what he was—she saw it now. She had refused him as himself. —And this had been her life, and his life. —She was grateful to death, which restored the truth. And she knew she was not dead.

And all the while her heart was bursting with grief and pity for him. What had he suffered? What stretch of horror for this helpless man! She was rigid with agony. She had not been able to help him. He had been cruelly injured, this naked man, this other being, and she could make no reparation. There were the children—but the children belonged to life. This dead man had nothing to do with them. He and she were only channels through which life had flowed to issue in the children. She was a mother—but how awful she knew it now to have been a wife. And he, dead now, how awful he must have felt it to be a husband. She felt that in the next world he would be a stranger to her. If they met there, in the beyond, they would only be ashamed of what had been before. The children had come, for some mysterious reason, out of both of them. But the children did not unite them. Now he was dead, she knew how eternally he was apart from her, how eternally he had nothing more to do with her. She saw this episode of her life closed. They had denied each other in life. Now he had withdrawn. An anguish came over her. It was finished then: it had become hopeless between them long before he died. Yet he had been her husband. But how little! —

"Have you got his shirt, 'Lizabeth?"

Elizabeth turned without answering, though she strove to weep and behave as her mother-inlaw expected. But she could not, she was silenced. She went into the kitchen and returned with the garment.

"It is aired," she said, grasping the cotton shirt here and there to try. She was almost ashamed to handle him; what right had she or anyone to lay hands on him; but her touch was humble on his body. It was hard work to clothe him. He was so heavy and inert. A terrible dread gripped her all the while: that he could be so heavy and utterly inert, unresponsive, apart. The horror of the distance between them was almost too much for her—it was so infinite a gap she must look across.

At last it was finished. They covered him with a sheet and left him lying, with his face bound. And she fastened the door of the little parlour, lest the children should see what was lying there. Then, with peace sunk heavy on her heart, she went about making tidy the kitchen. She knew she submitted to life, which was her immediate master. But from death, her ultimate master, she winced with fear and shame.

Ⅳ. Questions for Thinking

1. Make a comparison and contrast between Elizabeth and Walter's mother? And why doesn't she get a name? Comment their images as women.
2. In "Odour of Chrysanthemums," Walter's death touches off a big epiphany for Elizabeth. What is her understanding about the essence of the relationship between her and her husband?
3. How do we understand Elizabeth's being so practical?
4. Wife and husband relationships are one of the major themes in the short story. How does the author elaborate this theme?
5. Is Elizabeth a victim of gender discrimination? Why or why not?
6. Consider the cultural context—the coal mining town, and discuss women's position therein.
7. At what points in the story are chrysanthemums mentioned? What are the symbolic meanings of chrysanthemums?
8. Discuss Lawrence's view and description of nature. Read the first three paragraphs of the short story, discuss the relationship between man and nature.
9. The author uses many images of the nature and industry. What are they?
10. At what points in the story are chrysanthemums mentioned? What significant

change or emotional "fact" do they reference each time?

Ⅴ. Guidance for Appreciation

The midlands mining area in Nottinghamshire, where D. H. Lawrence was born and brought up, and where most of his stories are set, was undergoing great changes from a traditional county based largely on agriculture to one engaged more firmly in industrialism, especially with the development of coal mines. Pastoral landscape was interrupted and traditional lifestyle was challenged. The industrialization greatly changed the landscape and also the relationship between man and nature, which is one of the major themes of the short story.

At the very beginning of the short story "Odour of Chrysanthemums", the conflict the between machines and nature is revealed. A locomotive engine, the representative of industrialization, comes "clanking, stumbling down from Selston with seven full waggons". The loud noise, the slow but inevitable movement, and the smoke from the engine intrude and interrupt the landscape, by startling animals (the colt, birds and fowls), withering plants (gorse, oak leaves, and grass), and trapping man (Elizabeth), turning fields dreary and forsaken. The description emphasizes the contrast between the mechanical world and the natural surroundings. The noise of the siren and clanking of the locomotive engine contrast the noiseless dropping of withered oak leaves. The inevitable movement of engine contrasts the still and lifeless surroundings. Elizabeth is trapped between the waggons (machines) and hedge (nature) and has no way out.

In the development of the plot, Lawrence uses different symbols to elaborate the great impact of industrialization on man and nature. The locomotive engine, the symbol of industrialization, becomes an inescapable part of people's life. It can be heard all over the town and has replaced the publicly chiming clock bell as the primary means to summon human beings to activities. It takes workers to their underground mines, completely changing their pastoral life style. The narrow and dark underground mine confines men and separate them from other natural elements of animals and plants, and alienate them from their wives and children. The harsh working condition gradually destroys their health even takes their lives away. Machines completely change the relationship between man and nature, when man is reduced to slavery of machinery.

On the other hand, garden and flowers (especially chrysanthemums), the representatives of nature, are dreary and forsaken, losing their vitality. Elizabeth's garden only contains "some twiggy apple trees, winter-crack trees, and ragged cabbages... and dishevelled pink chrysanthemums". The garden symbolizes man's alienation from nature.

Chrysanthemums, the major symbol in the short story, are endowed with more profound meanings. Chrysanthemums are associated with the cycle of birth, marriage, defeat, drunkenness and death. Chrysanthemums in different colors (including wan, pink and brown etc.) have been mentioned 6 times in the story, implying the ever-changing relationship between Elizabeth and Walter from sweet happiness to unutterable heartbreak. At first, chrysanthemums are associated with happiness, since "It was chrysanthemums when I married him, and chrysanthemums when you were born". Gradually, chrysanthemums turn disheveled, wan, giving cold, deathly smell, with no sign of vitality, but only staleness, paralysis, death and decay.

It is near the ending of the tale that the chrysanthemums are mentioned again when the husband's corpse is brought back home by others. "The candle-light glittered on the luster-glasses, on the two vases that held some of the pink chrysanthemums, and on the dark mahogany. There was a cold, deathly smell of chrysanthemums in the room." The whole room is brimmed over with unconquerable horror and terror. An overwhelming sense of dread and weariness tightly grips Elizabeth because of the everlasting separateness of her husband. The pink chrysanthemums in the room are giving off a cold and deathly smell. The author applies the color "pink" to describe the flowers in order to echo "the disheveled pink chrysanthemums" in the bleak and desolate field at the beginning of the story. As a result, the pink chrysanthemums are not only associated with the dreary and forsaken scenery, but also with the husband's death in the pit, both resulting from the industrialization.

Industrialization has not only brought tremendous destruction and devastation to nature but also have corrupted man's emotional life and dried up the springs of human vitality, and exerted dehumanizing effect on human relationship, especially between man and woman, between husband and wife.

Readers may at first blame Walter for the failure of their marriage, who cannot fulfil his gender roles as a husband and father. He is almost absent from family life. After work, he drinks in the pub, putting the family into poverty. He is considered irresponsible, neglecting his wife and children.

The description of Elizabeth is also different from traditional women. From appearance, she is "tall woman of imperious mien", which indicates that she is not obedient or passive. On the contrary, she has a domineering and authoritative look. She is stern with her children. Different from other women in the neighborhood, she cares little and is indifferent to her husband. Through her talking and her manner, readers can find her sense of superiority to her illiterate husband and neighbors. Before her children, she doesn't show much respect to her husband. She vocalizes her sadness and grief at having married a drunkard, which influences children's view of their father. Readers may also be shocked at her indifference. Near the end of the story, when she gets the news that her husband might hurt or die, she doesn't worry about him. Instead, she wonders if the pension will be enough to support her and her children.

When confronted with Walter's corpse, Elizabeth and her mother-in-law act quite differently. Walter's mother, described variously as an "old woman," "grandmother," "elder woman," and "old lady," "had his face between her hands, and was murmuring incoherently. The old tears fell in succession as drops from wet leaves; the mother was not weeping, merely her tears flowed." She keeps murmuring about her son as a good and handsome boy. At the same time, Elizabeth remains so calm and collected although she strives to weep or behave as her mother-in-law might expect. Elizabeth "seemed to be listening, inquiring, trying to get some connection. But she could not. She was driven away. He was impregnable". The sensation of Walter's mother contrasts Elizabeth's rationality. The only physical contact between husband and wife comes at the end when the husband died. And this contact makes Elizabeth realize the gap and distance between her and her husband. It seems that on his death, Elizabeth first discovers the beauty of his body. "He was a man of handsome body, and his face showed no traces of drink. He was blond, full fleshed, with fine limbs. But he was dead." Death removes the dirt and smoke on his face (the effect of machines) and returns him to his original appearance. Elizabeth finds that she has never known her husband. "There had been nothing between them, and yet they had come together, exchange their nakedness repeatedly. Each time he had taken her, they had been two isolated beings, far apart as now." Through this we can see that, the physical contact between husband and wife does not bring any emotional bond. "Death does not separate them, as they were already separate." The alienation is the inescapable result of industrialization since it has destroyed the traditional economy and traditional family life.

As mentioned above, D. H. Lawrence takes the event of the story from his uncle. More than it, the relationship between the husband and wife is an actual portrayal of that of his parents. As a frail and delicate child, Lawrence sympathized with the struggles his mother who endured in her unhappy marriage. As a result, many of the female characters in Lawrence's fiction mirror his mother: sensitive women who are shackled to coarse husbands and suffer from the difficulties of supporting a family in the harsh labor conditions of the day. Lawrence's mother spent many nights lamenting her choices in life, particularly her marriage to a man who made the village pub his primary after-work destination rather than the family home. Lawrence always believed that his mother was the victim of the unhappy marriage. Many years later, especially after the death of his mother, Lawrence himself came to think that his portrayal of his father had been lacking in justice, giving too much weight to his mother's self-righteous condemnation.

In many of his works, D. H. Lawrence expresses his critique of industrialization. To him modern world (money, industrialism) seemed to have corrupted man's emotional life. And he wishes an ideal society of ecology—back to nature, and back to human nature: human beings all returning to nature from modernized cities, they all trying to pursue happiness free from modern civilization.

Ⅵ. Further Reading

1. Beer, John. D. H. Lawrence: Nature, Narrative, Art, Identity [M]. Basingstoke: Palgrave Macmillan, 2014.
2. Booth, Howard J. ed. New D. H. Lawrence[M]. Manchester: Manchester University Press, 2009.
3. Cowan, James C. D. H. Lawrence: Self and Sexuality[M]. Columbus: Ohio State University Press, 2002.
4. Fernihough, Anne. The Cambridge Companion to D. H. Lawrence[M]. Cambridge: Cambridge University Press, 2001.
5. Harrison, Andrew. The Life of D. H. Lawrence: A Critical Biography[M].

Chichester：John Wiley & sons，Ltd，2016.

6. Preston，Peter. Working with Lawrence：Texts，Places，Contexts［M］. Nottingham：Critical，Cultural and Communications Press，2011.

7. 宋阳.《菊馨》中的矿区空间建构与生命哲学思想[J]. 牡丹江大学学报，2017 (5)：57-59.

8. 汪志勤. 劳伦斯中短篇小说多视角研究[M]. 上海：东方出版中心，2010.

9. 张玮玮. D. H. 劳伦斯文学批评中的生态意识研究[J]. 文艺争鸣，2014(8)：165-169.

10. 庄文泉. 文学地理学批评视野下劳伦斯长篇小说研究[M]. 北京：中国社会科学出版社，2017.

Chapter 5

John Fowles: The French Lieutenant's Woman
Postmodernism and Feminism

I. Introduction to the Author

John Robert Fowles (1926—2005), an English novelist and essayist, is regarded as one of the greatest writers in the 20th century. His prominence in literary world rests on his unique and creative narrative techniques and his influence on other writers.

John Robert Fowles was born on March 31, 1926, in a small town in the county of Essex, about 40 miles from London. His father Robert John Fowles was a tobacco importer. The small town is oppressively conformist and his family life is intensely conventional.

From 1939 to 1944, Fowles stayed at Bedford School, a boarding school. In 1944, he enrolled at Edinburgh University. In 1945, he began his military service as a lieutenant at Dartmoor, where he stayed for two years. He never went to the battlefield. In 1947, Fowles entered New College, Oxford, where he studied both French and German. During his stay in university, Fowles developed great interest in French existentialism. In particular he was attracted and influenced by Albert Camus and Jean-Paul Sartre, whose writings corresponded with his own ideas about conformity and the will of the individual. He received a degree in French in 1950. After graduation, he tried several teaching jobs first in France, then in Greece and finally in London, where he ultimately served as the department head.

Fowles began to write when he was in Greece. His first novel, *The Collector*, published in 1963, was an immediate success and best-seller. Since then, he was devoted to writing and continued to be a prominent novelist. *The Aristos*, his second work, appeared in 1964. One year later, *The Magus*, a traditional quest story was published with enduring interest.

In 1968, Fowles moved to Lyme Regis, a place frequently appeared in his works and where he spent the rest of his life. His third novel *The French Lieutenant's Woman*, appearing in 1969, earned him the Silver Pen Award and W. H. Smith Award for his most outstanding contributions to English literature. He was also appointed as curator of the Lyme Regis Museum in 1979, a position he filled for a decade. John Fowles died on November 5, 2005.

As a productive writer, John Fowles has published seven novels, *The Collector* (1963), *The Magus* (1964), *The French Lieutenant's Woman* (1969), *The Ebony Tower*, *Daniel Martin* (1977), *Mantissa* (1982), and *A Maggot* (1985). His collections of poems, nonfiction and essays include *Poems by John Fowles* (1973), *The Tree* (1979), *A Short History of Lyme Regis* (1982), *Wormholes - Essays and Occasional Writings* (1998).

II. Introduction to the Novel

The French Lieutenant's Woman was published in 1967, with an immediate success both commercially and academically. It has remained in *New York Times* and *Times* bestseller lists for more than a year. In 2005, *Time* magazine chose the novel as one of the 100 best English-language novels published between 1923 and 2005. It is by far Fowles' most successful novel, bringing him W. H. Smith prize in 1970 and the silver PEN Award in 1969.

With bold and novel writings, Fowles depicts a nineteenth-century romantic love story with typical Victorian characters, situations, and even dialogues, infusing strong modern sense into historical writing, launching a fierce attack towards social constraints in Victorian era, and conveying his belief in freedom.

The novel was set in Lyme Regis, an old-fashioned small southwestern town. Charles Smithson, a 32-year-old paleontologist from an aristocratic family, comes to Lyme Regis to visit his fiancee Ernestina Freeman, a conventional heiress of a wealthy merchant. Ernestina stays with her aunt Tranter. During their visit to the Cobb at Lyme Regis, Charles and Ernestina first encounter Sarah Woodruff, a fallen woman known also as "The French Lieutenant's Wife" and "Tragedy". Her story of being deserted after an affair with a French naval officer is an open secret in the small town. Sarah is employed by Mrs. Poulteney as a secretary. Mrs. Poultney is an elderly widow, obsessed with her own deed of salvation.

They keep on coming across each other when Charles is searching for fossils and Sarah is walking by the coast. During these meetings, Sarah tells Charles of her story with the French Lieutenant, and asks for his emotional and social support. Charles also finds himself develop mixed feelings to Sarah.

Sarah is later fired by Mrs. Poulteney, so she sends Charles a letter to seek help. The two meet, embrace and kiss. Charles is struggling not to go further in their relationship, convincing and supporting Sarah to leave Lyme. With his money, Sarah settles into her new life in Exeter and gives her address to Charles.

During this time, Charles gets the news that he may lose his place as heir to his elderly uncle. Charles then goes to see Ernestina's father to tell him of the disinheritance. Ernestina's father offers a larger dowry, and a business position, but Charles declines. John Fowles then presents his first ending: Charles returns to Lyme without stopping for a visit to Sarah, and marries Ernestina.

Then the author offers the second and third ending. Charles stops in Exeter to visit Sarah. The moment he sees Sarah he becomes sexually aroused and afterwards he realizes that Sarah has lied about her affair with French lieutenant: she is a virgin, or was. Charles is racked by guilt toward Ernestina and her father, and anger toward Sarah. After long self-examination and torture, Charles finds what he wants is Sarah. Charles confesses to Ernestina and ends the engagement. However, Sarah is nowhere to find. In grief, Charles leaves England to travel in Europe and America.

Two years later, Charles finds Sarah in an artist's house and proposes to her, while she refuses and indicates that she wouldn't marry anybody. Charles begins to furiously accuse her of tormenting him. Nevertheless, when Sarah brings a little girl whom he realizes is his daughter, they embrace with each other. This ending suggests that a reunion between Sarah and Charles is possible.

The narrator re-appears outside the house and turns back his pocket watch by fifteen minutes. Fowles presents the third ending. Sarah refuses Charles and Charles leaves the house, intending to return to the United States.

Ⅲ. Excerpt

CHAPTER 8

> There rolls the deep where grew the tree, O earth, what changes hast thou seen!
>   There where the long street roars, hath been
> The stillness of the central sea.
> The hills are shadows, and they flow From form to form, and nothing stands;
>   They melt like mist, the solid lands,
> Like clouds they shape themselves and go.
> —Tennyson, In Memoriam (1850)

> But if you wish at once to do nothing and be respect—able nowadays, the best pretext is to be at work on some profound study . . .
> —Leslie Stephen, Sketches from Cambridge (1865)

Sam's had not been the only dark face in Lyme that morning. Ernestina had woken in a mood that the brilliant promise of the day only aggravated. The ill was familiar; but it was out of the question that she should inflict its consequences upon Charles. And so, when he called dutifully at ten o'clock at Aunt Tranter's house, he found himself greeted only by that lady: Ernestina had passed a slightly disturbed night, and wished to rest. Might he not return that afternoon to take tea, when no doubt she would be recovered?

Charles's solicitous inquiries—should the doctor not be called? —being politely answered in the negative, he took his leave. And having commanded Sam to buy what flowers he could and to take them to the charming invalid's house, with the permission and advice to proffer a blossom or two of his own to the young lady so hostile to soot, for which light duty he might take the day as his reward (not all Victorian employers were directly responsible for communism), Charles faced his own free hours.

His choice was easy; he would of course have gone wherever Ernestina's health had required him to, but it must be confessed that the fact that it was Lyme Regis had made his pre-marital obligations delightfully easy to support. Stonebarrow, Black Ven, Ware Cliffs—these names may mean very little to you.

But Lyme is situated in the center of one of the rare outcrops of a stone known as blue lias. To the mere landscape enthusiast this stone is not attractive. An exceedingly gloomy gray in color, a petrified mud in texture, it is a good deal more forbidding than it is picturesque. It is also treacherous, since its strata are brittle and have a tendency to slide, with the consequence that this little stretch of twelve miles or so of blue lias coast has lost more land to the sea in the course of history than almost any other in England. But its highly fossiliferous nature and its mobility make it a Mecca for the British paleontologist. These last hundred years or more the commonest animal on its shores has been man—wielding a geologist's hammer.

Charles had already visited what was perhaps the most famous shop in the Lyme of those days—the Old Fossil Shop, founded by the remarkable Mary Anning, a woman without formal education but with a genius for discovering good—and on many occasions then unclassified—specimens. She was the first person to see the bones of *Ichthyosaurus platyodon*; and one of the meanest disgraces of British paleontology is that although many scientists of the day gratefully used her finds to establish their own reputation, not one native type bears the specific *anningii*. To this distinguished local memory Charles had paid his homage—and his cash, for various ammonites and *Isocrina* he coveted for the cabinets that walled his study in London. However, he had one disappointment, for he was at that time specializing in a branch of which the Old Fossil Shop had few examples for sale.

This was the echinoderm, or petrified sea urchin. They are sometimes called tests (from the Latin *testa*, a tile or earthen pot); by Americans, sand dollars. Tests vary in shape, though they are always perfectly symmetrical; and they share a pattern of delicately burred striations. Quite apart from their scientific value (a vertical series taken from Beachy Head in the early 1860s was one of the first practical confirmations of the theory of evolution) they are very beautiful little objects; and they have the added charm that they are always difficult to find. You may search for days and not come on one; and a morning in which you find two or three is indeed a morning to remember. Perhaps, as a man with time to fill, a born amateur, this is unconsciously what attracted Charles to them; he had scientific reasons, of course, and with fellow hobbyists he would say indignantly that the *Echinodermia* had been "shamefully neglected," a familiar justification for spending too much time in too small a field. But whatever his motives he had fixed his heart on tests.

Now tests do not come out of the blue lias, but out of the superimposed strata of flint; and the fossil-shop keeper had advised him that it was the area west of the town where he would do best to search, and not necessarily on the shore. Some half-hour after he had called on Aunt Tranter, Charles was once again at the Cobb.

The great mole was far from isolated that day. There were fishermen tarring, mending their nets, tinkering with crab and lobster pots. There were better-class people, early visitors, local residents, strolling beside the still swelling but now mild sea. Of the woman who stared, Charles noted, there was no sign. But he did not give her—or the Cobb—a second thought and set out, with a quick and elastic step very different from his usual languid town stroll, along the beach under Ware Cleeves for his destination.

He would have made you smile, for he was carefully equipped for his role. He wore stout nailed boots and canvas gaiters that rose to encase Norfolk breeches of heavy flannel. There was a tight and absurdly long coat to match; a canvas wideawake hat of an indeterminate beige; a massive ash-plant, which he had bought on his way to the Cobb; and a voluminous rucksack, from which you might have shaken out an already heavy array of hammers, wrappings, notebooks, pillboxes, adzes and heaven knows what else. Nothing is more incomprehensible to us than the methodicality of the Victorians; one sees it best (at its most ludicrous) in the advice so liberally handed out to travelers in the early editions of Baedeker. Where, one wonders, can any pleasure have been left? How, in the case of Charles, can he not have seen that light clothes would have been more comfortable? That a hat was not necessary? That stout nailed boots on a boulder-strewn beach are as suitable as ice skates?

Well, we laugh. But perhaps there is something admirable in this dissociation between what is most comfortable and what is most recommended. We meet here, once again, this bone of contention between the two centuries: is duty* to drive us, or not? If we take this obsession with dressing the part, with

---

* I had better here, as a reminder that mid-Victorian (unlike modern) agnosticism and atheism were related strictly to theological dogma, quote George Eliot's famous epigram: "God is inconceivable, immortality is unbelievable, but duty is peremptory and absolute." And all the more peremptory, one might add, in the presence of such a terrible dual lapse of faith.

being prepared for every eventuality, as mere stupidity, blindness to the empirical, we make, I think, a grave—or rather a frivolous—mistake about our ancestors; because it was men not unlike Charles, and as overdressed and overequipped as he was that day, who laid the foundations of all our modern science. Their folly in that direction was no more than a symptom of their seriousness in a much more important one. They sensed that current accounts of the world were inadequate; that they had allowed their windows on reality to become smeared by convention, religion, social stagnation; they knew, in short, that they had things to discover, and that the discovery was of the utmost importance to the future of man. We think (unless we live in a research laboratory) that we have nothing to discover, and the only things of the utmost importance to us concern the present of man. So much the better for us? Perhaps. But we are not the ones who will finally judge.

So I should not have been too inclined to laugh that day when Charles, as he hammered and bent and examined his way along the shore, tried for the tenth time to span too wide a gap between boulders and slipped ignominiously on his back. Not that Charles much minded slipping, for the day was beautiful, the liassic fossils were plentiful and he soon found himself completely alone.

The sea sparkled, curlews cried. A flock of oyster catchers, black and white and coral-red, flew on ahead of him, harbingers of his passage. Here there came seductive rock pools, and dreadful heresies drifted across the poor fellow's brain—would it not be more fun, no, no, more scientifically valuable, to take up marine biology? Perhaps to give up London, to live in Lyme ... but Ernestina would never allow that. There even came, I am happy to record, a thoroughly human moment in which Charles looked cautiously round, assured his complete solitude and then carefully removed his stout boots, gaiters and stockings. A schoolboy moment, and he tried to remember a line from Homer that would make it a classical moment, but was distracted by the necessity of catching a small crab that scuttled where the gigantic subaqueous shadow fell on its vigilant stalked eyes.

Just as you may despise Charles for his overburden of apparatus, you perhaps despise him for his lack of specialization. But you must remember that natural history had not then the pejorative sense it has today of a flight from reality—and only too often into sentiment. Charles was a quite competent ornithologist and botanist into the bargain. It might perhaps have been better had he shut his eyes to all but the fossil sea urchins or devoted his life to the distribution of algae, if scientific progress is what we are talking about; but think of Darwin, of *The Voyage of the Beagle*. *The Origin of Species* is a triumph of generalization, not specialization; and even if you could prove to me that the latter would have been better for Charles the ungifted scientist, I should still maintain the former was better for Charles the human being. It is not that amateurs can afford to dabble everywhere; they ought to dabble everywhere, and damn the scientific prigs who try to shut them up in some narrow *oubliette*.

Charles called himself a Darwinist, and yet he had not really understood Darwin. But then, nor had Darwin himself. What that genius had upset was the Linnaean *Scala Naturae*, the ladder of nature, whose great keystone, as essential to it as the divinity of Christ to theology, was nulla species nova: a new species cannot enter the world. This principle explains the Linnaean obsession with classifying and naming, with fossilizing the existent. We can see it now as a foredoomed attempt to stabilize and fix what is in reality a continuous flux, and it seems highly appropriate that Linnaeus himself finally went mad; he knew he was in a labyrinth, but not that it was one whose walls and passages were eternally changing. Even Darwin never quite shook off the Swedish fetters, and Charles can hardly be blamed for the thoughts that went through his mind as he gazed up at the lias strata in the cliffs above him.

He knew that *nulla species nova* was rubbish; yet he saw in the strata an immensely reassuring orderliness in existence. He might perhaps have seen a very contemporary social symbolism in the way these gray-blue ledges were crumbling; but what he did see was a kind of edificiality of time, in which inexorable laws (therefore beneficently divine, for who could argue that order was not the highest human good?) very conveniently arranged themselves for the survival of the fittest and best, *exemplia gratia* Charles Smithson, this fine spring day, alone, eager and inquiring, understanding, accepting, noting and grateful. What was lacking, of course, was the corollary of the collapse of the ladder of nature: that if new species *can* come into being, old species very often have to make way for them. Personal extinction Charles was aware of—no Victorian could not be. But general extinction was as absent a concept from his mind that day as the smallest cloud from the sky above him; and even though, when he finally resumed his stockings and gaiters and boots, he soon held a very concrete example of it in his hand.

It was a very fine fragment of lias with ammonite impressions, exquisitely clear, microcosms of macrocosms, whirled galaxies that Catherine-wheeled their way across ten inches of rock. Having duly inscribed a label with the date and place of finding, he once again hopscotched out of science—this time, into love. He determined to give it to Ernestina when he returned. It was pretty enough for her to like; and after all, very soon it would come back to him, with her. Even better, the increased weight on his back made it a labor, as well as a gift. Duty, agreeable conformity to the epoch's current, raised its stern head.

And so did the awareness that he had wandered more slowly than he meant. He unbuttoned his coat and took out his silver half hunter. Two o'clock! He looked sharply back then, and saw the waves lapping the foot of a point a mile away. He was in no danger of being cut off, since he could see a steep but safe path just ahead of him which led up the cliff to the dense woods above. But he could not return along the shore. His destination had indeed been this path, but he had meant to walk quickly to it, and then up to the levels where the flint strata emerged. As a punishment to himself for his dilatoriness he took the path much too fast, and had to sit a minute to recover, sweating copiously under the abominable flannel. But he heard a little stream nearby and quenched his thirst; wetted his handkerchief and patted his face; and then he began to look around him.

CHAPTER 13

For the drift of the Maker is dark, an Isis hid by the veil ⋯
—Tennyson, Maud (1855)

I do not know. This story I am telling is all imagination. These characters I create never existed outside my own mind. If I have pretended until now to know my characters' minds and innermost thoughts, it is because I am writing in (just as I have assumed some of the vocabulary and "voice" of) a convention universally accepted at the time of my story: that the novelist stands next to God. He may not know all, yet he tries to pretend that he does. But I live in the age of Alain Robbe-Grillet and Roland Barthes; if this is a novel, it cannot be a novel in the modern sense of the word.

So perhaps I am writing a transposed autobiography; perhaps I now live in one of the houses I have brought into the fiction; perhaps Charles is myself disguised. Perhaps it is only a game. Modern women like Sarah exist, and I have never understood them. Or perhaps I am trying to pass off a concealed book of essays on you. Instead of chapter headings, perhaps I should have written "On the Horizontality of Existence," "The Illusions of Progress," "The History of the Novel Form," "The Aetiology of Freedom," "Some Forgotten Aspects of the Victorian Age" ... what you will.

Perhaps you suppose that a novelist has only to pull the right strings and his puppets will behave in a lifelike manner; and produce on request a thorough analysis of their motives and intentions. Certainly I intended at this stage (*Chap. Thirteen—unfolding of Sarah's true state of mind*) to tell all—or all that matters. But I find myself suddenly like a man in the sharp spring night, watching from the lawn beneath that dim upper window in Marlborough House; I know in the context of my book's reality that Sarah would never have brushed away her tears and leaned down and delivered a chapter of revelation. She would instantly have turned, had she seen me there just as the old moon rose, and disappeared into the interior shadows.

But I am a novelist, not a man in a garden—I can follow her where I like? But possibility is not permissibility. Husbands could often murder their wives— and the reverse—and get away with it. But they don't.

You may think novelists always have fixed plans to which they work, so that the future predicted by Chapter One is always inexorably the actuality of Chapter Thirteen. But novelists write for countless different reasons: for money, for fame, for reviewers, for parents, for friends, for loved ones; for vanity, for pride, for curiosity, for amusement: as skilled furniture makers enjoy making furniture, as drunkards like drinking, as judges like judging, as Sicilians like emptying a shotgun into an enemy's back. I could fill a book with reasons, and they would all be true, though not true of all. Only one same reason is shared by all of us: we wish to create worlds as real as, but other than the world that is. Or was. This is why we cannot plan. We know a world is an organism, not a machine. We also know that a genuinely created world must be independent of its creator; a planned world (a world that fully reveals its planning) is a dead world. It is only when our characters and events begin to disobey us that they begin to live. When Charles left Sarah on her cliff edge, I ordered him to walk straight back to Lyme Regis. But he did not; he gratuitously turned and went down to the Dairy.

Oh, but you say, come on—what I really mean is that the idea crossed my mind as I wrote that it might be more clever to have him stop and drink milk ... and meet Sarah again. That is certainly one explanation of what happened; but I can only report—and I am the most reliable witness—that the idea seemed to me to come clearly from Charles, not myself. It is not only that he has begun to gain an autonomy; I must respect it, and disrespect all my quasi-divine plans for him, if I wish him to be real.

In other words, to be free myself, I must give him, and Tina, and Sarah, even the abominable Mrs. Poulteney, their freedom as well. There is only one good definition of God: the freedom that allows other freedoms to exist. And I must conform to that definition.

The novelist is still a god, since he creates (and not even the most aleatory avant-garde modern novel has managed to extirpate its author completely); what has changed is that we are no longer the gods of the Victorian image, omniscient and decreeing; but in the new theological image, with freedom our first principle, not authority.

I have disgracefully broken the illusion? No. My characters still exist, and in a reality no less, or no more, real than the one I have just broken. Fiction is woven into all, as a Greek observed some two and a half thousand years ago. I find this new reality (or unreality) more valid; and I would have you share my own sense that I do not fully control these creatures of my mind, any more than you control—however hard you try, however much of a latterday Mrs. Poulteney you may be—your children, colleagues, friends, or even yourself.

But this is preposterous? A character is either "real" or "imaginary"? If you think that, *hypocrite lecteur*, I can only smile. You do not even think of your own past as quite real; you dress it up, you gild it or blacken it, censor it, tinker with it ... fictionalize it, in a word, and put it away on a shelf—your book, your romanced autobiography. We are all in flight from the real reality. That is a basic definition of *Homo sapiens*.

So if you think all this unlucky (but it *is* Chapter Thirteen) digression has nothing to do with your Time, Progress, Society, Evolution and all those other capitalized ghosts in the night that are rattling their chains behind the scenes of this book ... I will not argue. But I shall suspect you.

I report, then, only the outward facts: that Sarah cried in the darkness, but did not kill herself; that she continued, in spite of the express prohibition, to haunt Ware Commons. In a way, therefore, she had indeed jumped; and was living in a kind of long fall, since sooner or later the news must inevitably come to Mrs. Poulteney of the sinner's compounding of her sin. It is true Sarah went less often to the woods than she had become accustomed to, a deprivation at first made easy for her by the wetness of the weather those following two weeks. It is true also that she took some minimal precautions of a military kind. The cart track eventually ran out into a small lane, little better than a superior cart track itself, which curved down a broad combe called Ware Valley until it joined, on the outskirts of Lyme, the main carriage road to Sidmouth and Exeter. There was a small scatter of respectable houses in Ware Valley, and it was therefore a seemly place to walk. Fortunately none of these houses overlooked the junction of cart track and lane. Once there, Sarah had merely to look round to see if she was alone. One day she set out with the intention of walking into the woods. But as in the lane she came to the track to the Dairy she saw two people come round a higher bend. She walked straight on towards them, and once round the bend, watched to make sure that the couple did not themselves take the Dairy track; then retraced her footsteps and entered her sanctuary unobserved.

She risked meeting other promenaders on the track itself; and might always have risked the dairyman and his family's eyes. But this latter danger she avoided by discovering for herself that one of the inviting paths into the bracken above the track led round, out of sight of the Dairy, onto the path through the woods. This path she had invariably taken, until that afternoon when she recklessly—as we can now realize—emerged in full view of the two men.

The reason was simple. She had overslept, and she knew she was late for her reading. Mrs. Poulteney was to dine at Lady Cotton's that evening; and the usual hour had been put forward to allow her to prepare for what was always in essence, if not appearance, a thunderous clash of two brontosauri; with black velvet taking the place of iron cartilage, and quotations from the Bible the angry raging teeth; but no less dour and relentless a battle.

Also, Charles's down-staring face had shocked her; she felt the speed of her fall accelerate; when the cruel ground rushes up, when the fall is from such a height, what use are precautions?

CHAPTER 22

I too have felt the load I bore

In a too strong emotion's sway;
I too have wished, no woman more,
This starting, feverish heart, away.

I too have longed for trenchant force
And will like a dividing spear;
Have praised the keen, unscrupulous course,
Which knows no doubt, which feels no fear.
But in the world I learnt, what there
Thou too will surely one day prove,
That will, that energy, though rare,
And yet far, far less rare than love.
—Matthew Arnold, "A Farewell" (1853)

Charles's thoughts on his own eventual way back to Lyme were all variations on that agelessly popular male theme: "You've been playing with fire, my boy." But it was precisely that theme, by which I mean that the tenor of his thoughts matched the verbal tenor of the statement. He had been very foolish, but his folly had not been visited on him. He had run an absurd risk; and escaped unscathed. And so now, as the great stone claw of the Cobb came into sight far below, he felt exhilarated.

And how should he have blamed himself very deeply? From the outset his motives had been the purest; he had cured her of her madness; and if something impure had for a moment threatened to infiltrate his defenses, it had been but mint sauce to the wholesome lamb. He would be to blame, of course, if he did not now remove himself, and for good, from the fire. That, he would take very good care to do. After all, he was not a moth infatuated by a candle; he was a highly intelligent being, one of the fittest, and endowed with total free will. If he had not been sure of that latter safeguard, would he ever have risked himself in such dangerous waters? I am mixing metaphors—but that was how Charles's mind worked.

And so, leaning on free will quite as much as on his ashplant, he descended the hill to the town. All sympathetic physical feelings towards the girl he would henceforth rigorously suppress, by free will. Any further solicitation of a private meeting he would adamantly discountenance, by free will. All administration of his interest should be passed to Aunt Tranter, by free will. And he was therefore permitted, obliged rather, to continue to keep Ernestina in the dark, by the same free will. By the time he came in sight of the White Lion, he had free-willed himself most convincingly into a state of self-congratulation ... and one in which he could look at Sarah as an object of his past.

A remarkable young woman, a remarkable young woman. And baffling. He decided that that was—had been, rather—her attraction: her unpredictability. He did not realize that she had two qualities as typical of the English as his own admixture of irony and convention. I speak of passion and imagination. The first quality Charles perhaps began dimly to perceive; the second he did not. He could not, for those two qualities of Sarah's were banned by the epoch, equated in the first case with sensuality and in the second with the merely fanciful. This dismissive double equation was Charles's greatest defect—and here he stands truly for his age.

There was still deception in the flesh, or Ernestina, to be faced. But Charles, when he arrived at his hotel, found that family had come to his aid.

A telegram awaited him. It was from his uncle at Winsyatt. His presence was urgently requested "for most important reasons." I am afraid Charles smiled as soon as he read it; he very nearly kissed the orange envelope. It removed him from any immediate further embarrassment; from the need for further lies of omission. It was most marvelously convenient. He made inquiries ... there was a train early the next morning from Exeter, then the nearest station to Lyme, which meant that he had a good pretext for leaving at once and staying there overnight. He gave orders for the fastest trap in Lyme to be procured. He would drive himself. He felt inclined to make such an urgent rush of it as to let a note to Aunt Tranter's suffice. But that would have been too cowardly. So telegram in hand, he walked up the street.

The good lady herself was full of concern, since telegrams for her meant bad news. Ernestina, less superstitious, was plainly vexed. She thought it "too bad" of Uncle Robert to act the grand vizir in this way. She was sure it was nothing; a whim, an old man's caprice, worse—an envy of young love.

She had, of course, earlier visited Winsyatt, accompanied by her parents; and she had not fallen for Sir Robert. Perhaps it was because she felt herself under inspection; or because the uncle had sufficient generations of squirearchy behind him to possess, by middle-class London standards, really rather bad manners—though a kinder critic might have said agreeably eccentric ones; perhaps because she considered the house such an old barn, so dreadfully old-fashioned in its furnishings and hangings and pictures; because the said uncle so doted on Charles and Charles was so provokingly nephew-ish in return that Ernestina began to feel positively jealous; but above all, because she was frightened.

Neighboring ladies had been summoned to meet her. It was all very well knowing her father could buy up all their respective fathers and husbands lock, stock and barrel; she felt herself looked down on (though she was simply envied) and snubbed in various subtle ways. Nor did she much relish the prospect of eventually living at Winsyatt, though it allowed her to dream of one way at least in which part of her vast marriage portion should be spent exactly as she insisted—in a comprehensive replacement of all those absurd scrolly wooden chairs (Carolean and almost priceless), gloomy cup-boards (Tudor), moth-eaten tapestries (Gobelins), and dull paintings (including two Claudes and a Tintoretto) that did not meet her approval.

Her distaste for the uncle she had not dared to communicate to Charles; and her other objections she hinted at with more humor than sarcasm. I do not think she is to be blamed. Like so many daughters of rich parents, before and since, she had been given no talent except that of conventional good taste ... that is, she knew how to spend a great deal of money in dressmakers', milliners' and furniture shops. That was her province; and since it was her only real one, she did not like it encroached upon.

The urgent Charles put up with her muted disapproval and pretty poutings, and assured her that he would fly back with as much speed as he went. He had in fact a fairly good idea what his uncle wanted him so abruptly for; the matter had been tentatively broached when he was there with Tina and her parents ... most tentatively since his uncle was a shy man. It was the possibility that Charles and his bride might share Winsyatt with him—they could "fit up" the east whig. Charles knew his uncle did not mean merely that they should come and stay there on occasion, but that Charles should settle down and start learning the business of running the estate. Now this appealed to him no more than it would have, had he realized, to Ernestina. He knew it would be a poor arrangement, that his uncle would alternate between doting and disapproving ... and that Ernestina needed educating into Winsyatt by a less trammeled early marriage. But his uncle had hinted privately to him at something beyond this: that Winsyatt was too large for a lonely old man, that he didn't know if he wouldn't be happier in a smaller place. There was no shortage of suitable smaller places in the environs ... indeed, some figured on the Winsyatt rent roll. There was one such, an Elizabethan manor house in the village of Winsyatt, almost in view of the great house.

Charles guessed now that the old man was feeling selfish; and that he was called to Winsyatt to be offered either the manor house or the great house. Either would be agreeable. It did not much matter to him which it should be, provided his uncle was out of the way. He felt certain that the old bachelor could now be maneuvered into either house, that he was like a nervous rider who had come to a jump and wanted to be led over it.

Accordingly, at the end of the brief trio in Broad Street, Charles asked for a few words alone with Ernestina; and as soon as Aunt Tranter had retired, he told her what he suspected.

"But why should he have not discussed it sooner?"

"Dearest, I'm afraid that is Uncle Bob to the life. But tell me what I am to say."

"Which should you prefer?"

"Whichever you choose. Neither, if needs be. Though he would be hurt..."

Ernestina uttered a discreet curse against rich uncles. But a vision of herself, Lady Smithson in a Winsyatt appointed to her taste, did cross her mind, perhaps because she was in Aunt Tranter's not very spacious back parlor. After all, a title needs a setting. And if the horrid old man were safely from under the same roof ... and he was old. And dear Charles. And her parents, to whom she owed ...

"This house in the village—is it not the one we passed in the carriage?"

"Yes, you remember, it had all those picturesque old gables—"

"Picturesque to look at from the outside."

"Of course it would have to be done up."

"What did you call it?"

"The villagers call it the Little House. But only by comparison. It's many years since I was in it, but I fancy it is a good deal larger than it looks."

"I know those old houses. Dozens of wretched little rooms. I think the Elizabethans were all dwarfs."

He smiled (though he might have done better to correct her curious notion of Tudor architecture), and put his arm round her shoulders. "Then Winsyatt itself?"

She gave him a straight little look under her arched eye-brows.

"Do you wish it?"

"You know what it is to me."

"I may have my way with new decorations?"

"You may raze it to the ground and erect a second Crystal Palace, for all I care."

"Charles! Be serious!"

She pulled away. But he soon received a kiss of forgiveness, and went on his way with a light heart. For her part, Ernestina went upstairs and drew out her copious armory of catalogues.

CHAPTER 45

And ah for a man to arise in me, That the man I am may cease to be!
—Tennyson, Maud (1855)

And now, having brought this fiction to a thoroughly traditional ending, I had better explain that although all I have described in the last two chapters happened, it did not happen quite in the way you may have been led to believe.

I said earlier that we are all poets, though not many of us write poetry; and so are we all novelists, that is, we have a habit of writing fictional futures for ourselves, although perhaps today we incline more to put ourselves into a film. We screen in our minds hypotheses about how we might behave, about what might happen to us; and these novelistic or cinematic hypotheses often have very much more effect on how we actually do behave, when the real future becomes the present, than we generally allow.

Charles was no exception; and the last few pages you have read are not what happened, but what he spent the hours between London and Exeter imagining might happen. To be sure he did not think in quite the detailed and coherent narrative manner I have employed; nor would I swear that he followed Mrs. Poulteney's postmortal career in quite such interesting detail. But he certainly wished her to the Devil, so it comes to almost the same thing.

Above all he felt himself coming to the end of a story; and to an end he did not like. If you noticed in those last two chapters an abruptness, a lack of consonance, a betrayal of Charles's deeper potentiality and a small matter of his being given a life span of very nearly a century and a quarter; if you entertained a suspicion, not uncommon in literature, that the writer's breath has given out and he has rather arbitrarily ended the race while he feels he's still winning, then do not blame me; because all these feelings, or reflections of them, were very present in Charles's own mind. The book of his existence, so it seemed to him, was about to come to a distinctly shabby close.

And the "I," that entity who found such slickly specious reasons for consigning Sarah to the shadows of oblivion, was not myself; it was merely the personification of a certain massive indifference in things—too hostile for Charles to think of as "God"—that had set its malevolent inertia on the Ernestina side of the scales; that seemed an inexorable onward direction as fixed as that of the train which drew Charles along.

I was not cheating when I said that Charles had decided, in London that day after his escapade, to go through with his marriage; that was his official decision, just as it had once been his official decision (reaction might be a more accurate word) to go into Holy Orders. Where I have cheated was in analyzing the effect that three-word letter continued to have on him. It tormented him, it obsessed him, it confused him. The more he thought about it the more Sarah-like that sending of the address—and nothing more—appeared. It was perfectly in key with all her other behavior, and to be described only by oxymoron; luring-receding, subtle-simple, proud-begging, defending-accusing. The Victorian was a prolix age; and unaccustomed to the Delphic.

But above all it seemed to set Charles a choice; and while one part of him hated having to choose, we come near the secret of his state on that journey west when we know that another part of him felt intolerably excited by the proximity of the moment of choice. He had not the benefit of existentialist terminology; but what he felt was really a very clear case of the anxiety of freedom—that is, the realization that one is free and the realization that being free is a situation of terror.

So let us kick Sam out of his hypothetical future and back into his Exeter present. He goes to his master's compartment when the train stops.

"Are we stayin' the night, sir?"

Charles stares at him a moment, a decision still to make, and looks over his head at the overcast sky.

"I fancy it will rain. We'll put up at the Ship. "

And so Sam, a thousand unpossessed pounds richer, stood a few minutes later with his master outside the station, watching the loading of Charles's impedimenta on to the roof of a tired fly. Charles showed a decided restlessness. The portmanteau was at last tied down, and all waited on him.

"I think, Sam, after that confounded train journey, I will stretch my legs. Do you go on with the baggage. "

Sam's heart sank.

"With respeck, Mr. Charles, I wouldn't. Not with them rainclouds up there about to break. "

"A little rain won't hurt me. "

Sam swallowed, bowed.

"Yes, Mr. Charles. Shall I give horders for dinner?"

"Yes ... that is ... I'll see when I come in. I may attend Evensong at the Cathedral. "

Charles set off up the hill towards the city. Sam watched him gloomily on his way for a little while, then turned to the cabby.

"Eh—'eard of Hendicott's Family 'Otel?"

"Aye. "

"Know where it is?"

"Aye. "

"Well, you dolly me up to the Ship double quick and you may 'ear somethink to your hadvantage, my man. "

And with a suitable aplomb Sam got into the carriage. It very soon overtook Charles, who walked with a flagrant slowness, as if taking the air. But as soon as it had gone out of sight he quickened his pace.

Sam had plenty of experience of dealing with sleepy provincial inns. The luggage was unloaded, the best available rooms chosen, a fire lit, nightwear laid out with other necessities—and all in seven minutes. Then he strode sharply out into the street, where the cabby still waited. A short further journey took place. From inside Sam looked cautiously round, then descended and paid off his driver.

"First left you'll find 'un, sir. "

"Thank you, my man. 'Ere's a couple o' browns for you. " And with this disgracefully mean tip (even for Exeter) Sam tipped his bowler over his eyes and melted away into the dusk. Halfway down the street he was in, and facing the one the cabby had indicated, stood a Methodist Chapel, with imposing columns under its pediment. Behind one of these the embryo detective installed himself. It was now nearly night, come early under a gray-black sky.

Sam did not have to wait long. His heart leaped as a tall figure came into sight. Evidently at a loss the figure addressed himself to a small boy. The boy promptly led the way to the corner below Sam's viewpoint, and pointed, a gesture that earned him, to judge by his grin, rather more than twopence.

Charles's back receded. Then he stopped and looked up. He retraced a few steps back towards Sam. Then as if impatient with himself he turned again and entered one of the houses. Sam slipped from behind his pillar and ran down the steps and across to the street in which Endicott's Family stood. He waited a while on the corner. But Charles did not reappear. Sam became bolder and lounged casually along the warehouse wall that faced the row of houses. He came to where he could see the hallway of the hotel. It was empty. Several rooms had lights. Some fifteen minutes passed and it began to rain.

Sam bit his nails for a while, in furious thought. Then he began to walk quickly away.

CHAPTER 46

As yet, when all is thought and said, The heart still overrules the head;
Still what we hope we must believe,
And what is given us receive;
Must still believe, for still we hope
That in a world of larger scope,
What here is faithfully begun
Will be completed, not undone.
My child, we still must think, when we
That ampler life together see,
Some true results will yet appear
Of what we are, together, here.
—A. H. Clough, Poem (1849)

Charles hesitated in the shabby hall, then knocked on the door of a room that was ajar and from which light came. He was bade enter, and so found himself face to face with the proprietress. Much quicker than he summed her up, she summed him: a fifteen-shillinger beyond mistake. Therefore she smiled gratefully.

"A room, sir?"

"No. I ... that is, I wish to speak with one of your ... a Miss Woodruff?" Mrs. Endicott's smile abruptly gave way to a long face. Charles's heart dropped. "She is not...?"

"Oh the poor young lady, sir, she was a-coming downstairs the day before yesterday morning and she slipped, sir. She's turned her ankle something horrible. Swole up big as a marrow. I wanted to ask the doctor, sir, but she won't hear of it. 'Tis true a turned ankle mends itself. And physicians come very expensive."

Charles looked at the end of his cane. "Then I cannot see her."

"Oh bless me, you can go up, sir. 'Twill raise her spirits. You'll be some relative, I daresay?"

"I have to see her ... on a business matter."

Mrs. Endicott's respect deepened. "Ah ... a gentleman of the law?"

Charles hesitated, then said, "Yes."

"Then you must go up, sir."

"I think ... would you please send to ask if my visit were not better put off till she is recovered?"

He felt very much at a loss. He remembered Varguennes; sin was to meet in privacy. He had come merely to inquire; had hoped for a downstairs sitting room—somewhere both intimate and public. The old woman hesitated, then cast a quick eye at a certain open box beside her rolltop desk and apparently decided that even lawyers can be thieves—a possibility few who have had to meet their fees would dispute. Without moving and with a surprising violence she called for one Betty Anne.

Betty Anne appeared and was sent off with a visiting card. She seemed gone some time, during which Charles had to repel a number of inquisitive attempts to discover his errand. At last Betty Anne came back: he was prayed to go up. He followed the plump maid's back to the top floor and was shown the scene of the accident. The stairs were certainly steep; and in those days, when they could rarely see their own feet, women were always falling: it was a commonplace of domestic life.

They came to a door at the end of a mournful corridor. Charles, his heart beating far faster than even the three flights of steep stairs had warranted, was brusquely announced.

"The gennelmun, miss."

He stepped into the room. Sarah was seated by the fire in a chair facing the door, her feet on a stool, with both them and her legs covered by a red Welsh blanket. The green merino shawl was round her shoulders, but could not quite hide the fact that she was in a long-sleeved nightgown. Her hair was loose and fell over her green shoulders. She seemed to him much smaller—and agonizingly shy. She did not smile, but looked down at her hands—only, as he first came in, one swift look up, like a frightened penitent, sure of his anger, before she bowed her head again. He stood with his hat in one hand, his stick and gloves in the other.

"I was passing through Exeter."

Her head bowed a fraction deeper in a mingled understanding and shame.

"Had I not better go at once and fetch a doctor?"

She spoke into her lap. "Please not. He would only advise me to do what I am already doing."

He could not take his eyes from her—to see her so pinioned, so invalid (though her cheeks were a deep pink), helpless. And after that eternal indigo dress—the green shawl, the never before fully revealed richness of that hair. A faint cedary smell of liniment crept into Charles's nostrils.

"You are not in pain?"

She shook her head. "To do such a thing ... I cannot understand how I should be so foolish."

"At any rate be thankful that it did not happen in the Undercliff."

"Yes."

She seemed hopelessly abashed by his presence. He glanced round the small room. A newly made-up fire burned in the grate. There were some tired stems of narcissus in a Toby jug on the mantelpiece. But the meanness of the furnishing was painfully obvious, and an added embarrassment. On the ceiling were blackened patches—fumes from the oil lamp; like so many spectral relics of countless drab past occupants of the room.

"Perhaps I should ... "

"No. Please. Sit down. Forgive me. I ... I did not expect... "

He placed his things on the chest of drawers, then sat at the only other, a wooden chair by the table, across the room from her. How should she expect, in spite of her letter, what he had himself so firmly ruled out of the question? He sought for some excuse.

"You have communicated your address to Mrs. Tranter?"

She shook her head. Silence. Charles stared at the carpet.

"Only to myself?"

Again her head bowed. He nodded gravely, as if he had guessed as much. And then there was more silence. An angry flurry of rain spattered against the panes of the window behind her.

Charles said, "That is what I have come to discuss."

She waited, but he did not go on. Again his eyes were fixed on her. The nightgown buttoned high at the neck and at her wrists. Its whiteness shimmered rose in the firelight, for the lamp on the table beside him was not turned up very high. And her hair, already enhanced by the green shawl, was ravishingly alive where the firelight touched it; as if all her mystery, this most intimate self, was exposed before him: proud and submissive, bound and unbound, his slave and his equal. He knew why he had come: it was to see her again. Seeing her was the need; like an intolerable thirst that had to be assuaged.

He forced himself to look away. But his eyes lighted on the two naked marble nymphs above the fireplace: they too took rose in the warm light reflected from the red blanket. They did not help. And Sarah made a little movement. He had to look back to her.

She had raised her hand quickly to her bowed head. Her fingers brushed something away from her cheek, then came to rest on her throat.

"My dear Miss Woodruff, pray don't cry... I should not have not come... I meant not to..."

But she shook her head with a sudden vehemence. He gave her time to recover. And it was while she made little dabbing motions with a handkerchief that he was overcome with a violent sexual desire; a lust a thousand times greater than anything he had felt in the prostitute's room. Her defenseless weeping was perhaps the breach through which the knowledge sprang—but suddenly he comprehended why her face haunted him, why he felt this terrible need to see her again: it was to possess her, to melt into her, to burn, to burn to ashes on that body and in those eyes. To postpone such desire for a week, a month, a year, several years even, that can be done. But for eternity is when the iron bites.

Her next words, to explain her tears, were barely audible.

"I thought never to see you again."

He could not tell her how close she had come to his own truth. She looked up at him and he as quickly looked down. Those same mysterious syncopal symptoms as in the barn swept over him. His heart raced, his hand trembled. He knew if he looked into those eyes he was lost. As if to ban them, he shut his own.

The silence was terrible then, as tense as a bridge about to break, a tower to fall; unendurable in its emotion, its truth bursting to be spoken. Then suddenly there was a little cascade of coals from the fire. Most fell inside the low guard, but one or two bounced off and onto the edge of the blanket that covered Sarah's legs. She jerked it hastily away as Charles knelt quickly and seized the small shovel from the brass bucket. The coals on the carpet were quickly replaced. But the blanket smoldered. He snatched it away from her and throwing it on the ground hastily stamped out the sparks. A smell of singed wool filled the room. One of Sarah's legs still rested on the stool, but she had put the other to the ground. Both feet were bare. He looked down at the blanket, made sure with one or two slaps of his hand that it no longer smoldered, then turned and placed it across her legs once more. He was bent close, his eyes on the arranging. And then, as if by an instinctive gesture, yet one she half dared to calculate, her hand reached shyly out and rested on his. He knew she was looking up at him. He could not move his hand, and suddenly he could not keep his eyes from hers.

There was gratitude in them, and all the old sadness, and a strange concern, as if she knew she was hurting him; but above all she was waiting. Infinitely timid, yet waiting. If there had been the faintest smile on her lips, perhaps he would have remembered Dr. Grogan's theory; but this was a face that seemed almost self-surprised, as lost as himself. How long they looked into each other's eyes he did not know. It seemed an eternity, though in reality it was no more than three or four seconds. Their hands acted first. By some mysterious communion, the fingers interlaced. Then Charles fell on one knee and strained her passionately to him. Their mouths met with a wild violence that shocked both; made her avert her lips. He covered her cheeks, her eyes, with kisses. His hand at last touched that hair, caressed it, felt the small head through its softness, as the thin-clad body was felt against his arms and breast. Suddenly he buried his face in her neck.

"We must not... we must not... this is madness."

But her arms came round him and pressed his head closer. He did not move. He felt borne on wings of fire, hurtling, but in such tender air, like a child at last let free from school, a prisoner in a green field, a hawk rising. He raised his head and looked at her: an almost savage fierceness. Then they kissed again. But he pressed against her with such force that the chair rolled back a little. He felt her flinch with pain as the bandaged foot fell from the stool. He looked back to it, then at her face, her closed eyes. She turned her head away against the back of the chair, almost as if he repelled her; but her bosom seemed to arch imperceptibly towards him and her hands gripped his convulsively. He glanced at the door behind her; then stood and in two strides was at it.

The bedroom was not lit except by the dusk light and the faint street lamps opposite. But he saw the gray bed, the washstand. Sarah stood awkwardly from the chair, supporting herself against its back, the injured foot lifted from the ground, one end of the shawl fallen from her shoulders. Each reflected the intensity in each other's eyes, the flood, the being swept before it. She seemed to half step, half fall towards him. He sprang forward and caught her in his arms and embraced her. The shawl fell. No more than a layer of flannel lay between him and her nakedness. He strained that body into his, straining his mouth upon hers, with all the hunger of a long frustration—not merely sexual, for a whole ungovernable torrent of things banned, romance, adventure, sin, madness, animality, all these coursed wildly through him.

Her head lay back in his arms, as if she had fainted, when he finally raised his lips from her mouth. He swept her up and carried her through to the bedroom. She lay where he threw her across the bed, half swooned, one arm flung back. He seized her other hand and kissed it feverishly; it caressed his face. He pulled himself away and ran back into the other room. He began to undress wildly, tearing off his clothes as if someone was drowning and he was on the bank. A button from his frock coat flew off and rolled into a corner, but he did not even look to see where it went. His waistcoat was torn off, his boots, his socks, his trousers and undertrousers ... his pearl tie pin, his cravat. He cast a glance at the outer door, and went to twist the key in its lock. Then, wearing only his long-tailed shirt, he went barelegged into the bedroom.

She had moved a little, since she now lay with her head on the pillow, though still on top of the bed, her face twisted sideways and hidden from his sight by a dark fan of hair. He stood over her a moment, his member erect and thrusting out his shirt. Then he raised his left knee onto the narrow bed and fell on her, raining burning kisses on her mouth, her eyes, her throat. But the passive yet acquiescent body pressed beneath him, the naked feet that touched his own ... he could not wait. Raising himself a little, he drew up her nightgown. Her legs parted. With a frantic brutality, as he felt his ejaculation about to burst, he found the place and thrust. Her body flinched again, as it had when her foot fell from the stool. He conquered that instinctive constriction, and her arms flung round him as if she would bind him to her for that eternity he could not dream without her. He began to ejaculate at once.

"Oh my dearest. My dearest. My sweetest angel ... Sarah, Sarah ... oh Sarah."

A few moments later he lay still. Precisely ninety seconds had passed since he had left her to look into the bedroom.

CHAPTER 61

Evolution is simply the process by which chance (the random mutations in the nucleic acid helix caused by natural radiation) cooperates with natural law to create living forms better and better adapted to survive.
—Martin Gardner, The Ambidextrous Universe (1967)

True piety is acting what one knows.
—Matthew Arnold, Notebooks (1868)

It is a time-proven rule of the novelist's craft never to introduce any but very minor new characters at the end of a book. I hope Lalage may be forgiven; but the extremely important-looking person that has, during the last scene, been leaning against the parapet of the embankment across the way from 16 Cheyne Walk, the residence of Mr. Dante Gabriel Rossetti (who took—and died of—chloral, by the way, not opium) may seem at first sight to represent a gross breach of the rule. I did not want to introduce him; but since he is the sort of man who cannot bear to be left out of the limelight, the kind of man who travels first class or not at all, for whom the first is the only pronoun, who in short has first things on the brain, and since I am the kind of man who refuses to intervene in nature (even the worst), he has got himself in—or as he would put it, has got himself in as he really is. I shall not labor the implication that he was previously got in as he really wasn't, and is therefore not truly a new character at all; but rest assured that this personage is, in spite of appearances, a very minor figure— as minimal, in fact, as a gamma-ray particle.

As he really is···, and his true colors are not pleasant ones. The once full, patriarchal beard of the railway compartment has been trimmed down to something rather foppish and Frenchified. There is about the clothes, in the lavishly embroidered summer waistcoat, in the three rings on the fingers, the panatella in its amber holder, the malachite-headed cane, a distinct touch of the flashy. He looks very much as if he has given up preaching and gone in for grand opera; and done much better at the latter than the former. There is, in short, more than a touch of the successful impresario about him.

And now, as he negligently supports himself on the para-pet, he squeezes the tip of his nose lightly between the knuckles of his beringed first and middle fingers. One has the impression he can hardly contain his amusement. He is staring back towards Mr. Rossetti's house; and with an almost proprietory air, as if it is some new theater he has just bought and is pretty confident he can fill. In this he has not changed: he very evidently regards the world as his to possess and use as he likes.

But now he straightens. This flanerie in Chelsea has been a pleasant interlude, but more important business awaits him. He takes out his watch—a Breguet—and selects a small key from a vast number on a second gold chain. He makes a small adjustment to the time. It seems—though unusual in an instrument from the bench of the greatest of watchmakers—that he was running a quarter of an hour fast. It is doubly strange, for there is no visible clock by which he could have discovered the error in his own timepiece. But the reason may be guessed. He is meanly providing himself with an excuse for being late at his next appointment. A certain kind of tycoon cannot bear to seem at fault over even the most trivial matters.

He beckons peremptorily with his cane towards an open landau that waits some hundred yards away. It trots smartly up to the curb beside him. The footman springs down and opens the door. The impresario mounts, sits, leans expansively back against the crimson leather, dismisses the monogrammed rug the footman offers towards his legs. The footman catches the door to, bows, then rejoins his fellow servant on the box. An instruction is called out, the coachman touches his cockaded hat with his whip handle.

And the equipage draws briskly away.

"No. It is as I say. You have not only planted the dagger in my breast, you have delighted in twisting it." She stood now staring at Charles, as if against her will, but hypnotized, the defiant criminal awaiting sentence. He pronounced it. "A day will come when you shall be called to account for what you have done to me. And if there is justice in heaven—your punishment shall outlast eternity!"

He hesitated one last second; his face was like the poised-crumbling walls of a dam, so vast was the weight of anathema pressing to roar down. But as suddenly as she had looked guilty, he ground his jaws shut, turned on his heel and marched towards the door.

"Mr. Smithson!"

He took a step or two more; stopped, threw her a look back over his shoulder; and then with the violence of a determined unforgivingness, stared at the foot of the door in front of him. He heard the light rustle of her clothes. She stood just behind him.

"Is this not proof of what I said just now? That we had better never to have set eyes on each other again?"

"Your logic assumes that I knew your real nature. I did not."

"Are you sure?"

"I thought your mistress in Lyme a selfish and bigoted woman. I now perceive she was a saint compared to her companion."

"And I should not be selfish if I said, knowing I cannot love you as a wife must, you may marry me?"

Charles gave her a freezing look. "There was a time when you spoke of me as your last resource. As your one remain-ing hope in life. Our situations are now reversed. You have no time for me. Very well. But don't try to defend yourself. It can only add malice to an already sufficient injury."

It had been in his mind all through: his most powerful, though also his most despicable, argument. And as he said it, he could not hide his trembling, his being at the end of his tether, at least as regards his feeling of outrage. He threw her one last tortured look, then forced himself onward to open the door.

"Mr. Smithson!"

Again. And now he felt her hand on his arm. A second time he stood arrested, hating that hand, his weakness in letting it paralyze him. It was as if she were trying to tell him something she could not say in words. No more, perhaps, than a gesture of regret, of apology. Yet if it had been that, her hand would surely have fallen as soon as it touched him; and this not only psychologically, but physically detained him. Very slowly he brought his head round and looked at her; and to his shock saw that there was in her eyes, if not about her lips, a suggestion of a smile, a ghost of that one he had received before, so strangely, when they were nearly surprised by Sam and Mary. Was it irony, a telling him not to take life so seriously? A last gloating over his misery? But there again, as he probed her with his own distressed and totally humorless eyes, her hand should surely have dropped. Yet still he felt its pressure on his arm; as if she were saying, look, can you not see, a solution exists?

It came upon him. He looked down to her hand, and then up to the face again. Slowly, as if in answer, her cheeks were suffused with red, and the smile drained from her eyes. Her hand fell to her side. And they remained staring at each other as if their clothes had suddenly dropped away and left them facing each other in nakedness; but to him far less a sexual nakedness than a clinical one, one in which the hidden cancer stood revealed in all its loathsome reality. He sought her eyes for some evidence of her real intentions, and found only a spirit prepared to sacrifice everything but itself—ready to surrender truth, feeling, perhaps even all womanly modesty in order to save its own integrity. And there, in that possible eventual sacrifice, he was for a moment tempted. He could see a fear behind the now clear knowledge that she had made a false move; and that to accept her offer of a Platonic —and even if one day more intimate, never consecrated—friendship would be to hurt her most.

But he no sooner saw that than he saw the reality of such an arrangement— how he would become the secret butt of this corrupt house, the starched soupirant, the pet donkey. He saw his own true superiority to her: which was not of birth or education, not of intelligence, not of sex, but of an ability to give that was also an inability to compromise. She could give only to possess; and to possess him—whether because he was what he was, whether because possession was so imperative in her that it had to be constantly renewed, could never be satisfied by one conquest only, whether ... but he could not, and would never, know—to possess him was not enough.

And he saw finally that she knew he would refuse. From the first she had manipulated him. She would do so to the end.

He threw her one last burning look of rejection, then left the room. She made no further attempt to detain him. He stared straight ahead, as if the pictures on the walls down through which he passed were so many silent spectators. He was the last honorable man on the way to the scaffold. He had a great desire to cry; but nothing should wring tears from him in that house. And to cry out. As he came down to the hallway, the girl who had shown him up appeared from a room, holding a small child in her arms. She opened her mouth to speak. Charles's wild yet icy look silenced her. He left the house.

And at the gate, the future made present, found he did not know where to go. It was as if he found himself reborn, though with all his adult faculties and memories. But with the baby's helplessness—all to be recommenced, all to be learned again! He crossed the road obliquely, blindly, never once looking back, to the embankment. It was deserted; only, in the distance, a trotting landau, which had turned out of sight by the tune he reached the parapet.

Without knowing why he stared down at the gray river, now close, at high tide. It meant return to America; it meant thirty-four years of struggling upwards—all in vain, in vain, in vain, all height lost; it meant, of this he was sure, a celibacy of the heart as total as hers; it meant—and as all the things that it meant, both prospective and retrospective, be-gan to sweep down over him ha a black avalanche, he did at last turn and look back at the house he had left. At an open upstairs window a white net curtain seemed to fall back into place.

But it was indeed only a seeming, a mere idle movement of the May wind. For Sarah has remained in the studio, staring down at the garden below, at a child and a young woman, the child's mother perhaps, who sit on the grass engaged in making a daisy chain. There are tears in her eyes? She is too far away for me to tell; no more now, since the windowpanes catch the luminosity of the summer sky, than a shadow behind a light.

You may think, of course, that not to accept the offer implicit in that detaining hand was Charles's final foolishness; that it betrayed at least a certain weakness of purpose in Sarah's attitude. You may think that she was right: that her battle for territory was a legitimate uprising of the invaded against the perennial invader. But what you must not think is that this is a less plausible ending to their story.

For I have returned, albeit deviously, to my original principle: that there is no intervening god beyond whatever can be seen, in that way, in the first epigraph to this chapter; thus only life as we have, within our hazard-given abilities, made it ourselves, life as Marx defined it—the actions of men (and of women) in pursuit of their ends. The fundamental principle that should guide these actions, that I believe myself always guided Sarah's, I have set as the second epigraph. A modern existentialist would no doubt substitute "humanity" or "authenticity" for "piety"; but he would recognize Arnold's intent.

The river of life, of mysterious laws and mysterious choice, flows past a deserted embankment; and along that other deserted embankment Charles now begins to pace, a man behind the invisible gun carriage on which rests his own corpse. He walks towards an imminent, self-given death? I think not; for he has at last found an atom of faith in himself, a true uniqueness, on which to build; has already begun, though he would still bitterly deny it, though there are tears in his eyes to support his denial, to realize that life, however advantageously Sarah may in some ways seem to fit the role of Sphinx, is not a symbol, is not one riddle and one failure to guess it, is not to inhabit one face alone or to be given up after one losing throw of the dice; but is to be, however inadequately, emptily, hopelessly into the city's iron heart, endured. And out again, upon the unplumb'd, salt, estranging sea.

Ⅳ. Questions for Thinking

1. What is your attitude toward the book's different endings? What is Fowles trying to do? How does the structure of three endings contribute to the theme of the novel?
2. How does the first paragraph of chapter 13 relate to the broader idea of postmodernism?
3. Discuss the insertion of the novelist as a character in the novel.
4. What is Fowles saying about the novel as an art form? Does he practice what he preaches?
5. How does Fowles, as an author, confront the constraints of storytelling?
6. Why does Sarah allow herself to be called "the French lieutenant's whore" when in fact she never has sex with him? Why in fact does she start the rumor at all, since she was the one who first mentioned it to her employer, Mrs. Talbot?

7. Discuss the identity construction of Sarah.

8. What does the novel reveal about sexuality and sexual relations in the Victorian period? How does Victorian sexuality affect women?

9. How do you understand the influence of French Existentialism on this novel?

Ⅴ. Guidance for Appreciation

Since its publication, *The French Lieutenant's Woman* has been a great concern, arousing great repercussions among readers and critics. Its themes, characters, narrative techniques and other aspects have been thoroughly and deeply studied. The postmodernist elements in the novel have always been favored by scholars. Moreover, it is regarded as the first British post-modernist fiction and also a model of meta-fiction due to its tentative narrative techniques.

Postmodernism is a movement in the late 20th century, too broad to be defined in a simple way. Basically, it is characterized by broad skepticism, subjectivism, or relativism; a general suspicion of reason; and an acute sensitivity to the role of ideology in asserting and maintaining political and economic power. Postmodernism in literature emphasizes the deconstruction of the existing order, subversion of tradition, decentralization and uncertainty. Postmodernist literature experiments with narrative techniques, such as fragmentation, parody, intertextuality, collage, contradiction, permutation, discontinuity, randomness, etc. John Fowles, in his novel, has challenged the traditional novel composition in several ways.

From the very beginning, the novel is developed fully in the style of Victorian realism: the background, characters, themes, and narrative techniques, etc. But in the development of plot, Fowles adopts such postmodernism narrative techniques as parody, intertextuality, collage, open ending to fulfill certain purposes: subverting tradition, deconstructing the authenticity of the novel, conveying belief in freedom, and elaborating the process of historicizing fiction.

Fowles first deconstructs the reliability and authority of the narrator. In Chapter 13, the narrator admits that he is only an observer who "report, then, only the outward facts"(99). Fowles argues that the characters themselves must be allowed to behave as though they were free. The intrusion of the narrator, who enters a railway carriage with Charles, also lays bare the fictionality of novel. The novel's three endings in Chapters 44, 60 and 61 offer the reader choice and at the same time stress the artificial nature of fiction.

This technique of laying bare the artificial nature of fiction is termed as metafiction. In meta-fiction, the author often undertakes multiple identities, narrator, protagonist and author, gaining free access to the work and making comments on the characters, subjects and plots, etc. Traditional novels try to achieve a virtual reality through various narrative techniques, while meta-fiction has just broken the tradition, trying to convince the reader that the novel is fictional. Through parody and collage, Fowles restores the historical background of the Victorian period as much as possible and real events, real texts and real characters are cited to enhance its authenticity, while he deconstructs this authenticity through a variety of anti-traditional narrative techniques, blurring the boundaries between real and fictional, thus readers could appreciate the fictional nature of the novel. Moreover, open endings and reader' roles also illuminate Fowles' anti-tradition concepts, and presents his freedom belief in not only characters and text, but also in readers.

Another reading focus of many readers is laid on the enigmatic heroine, Sarah, the spokeswoman of freedom. In the novel, Sarah, the most salient character, is a woman of mystery and personality in an immoral society, also a new woman striving for freedom and independence in a male-dominated society. But why Sarah is rejected by the community as an outcast and fallen woman and diagnosed by the doctor as hysteria? How do we understand the awakening of Sarah's sexual awareness? What is the author's purpose of depicting a women with modern awareness in Victorian context?

John Fowles purposely sets the story in Victorian society to express his critique of Victorian sexual hypocrisy and female sexual oppression. Victorian society possesses the stringent sexual regulations, especially for women. The maintenance of virginity thus becomes the prominent duty in the sexual regulations of Victorian women. Women are educated to feel shameful about sex and repress their sexual instincts, which leads to woman's total ignorance of sex. According to the prevailing consensus at the time, women cannot physically enjoy sex. Ernestina will feel sinful when she observes her own body in the mirror. And she tries to resist the physical female implications of her body, sexual, menstrual, parturitional into her consciousness. Sex is considered ugly and violent.

There is a huge difference in how women and men view sex and are expected to engage or refrain from engaging in it. Men are allowed to gain knowledge about sex through experience and enjoy "carnal pleasure". The popularity of brothels in Victorian society explains the sexual hypocrisy.

Victorian society uses the dichotomy of virgin and whore as an instrument to classify women, and the image of whore is applied to a woman who is condemned for her sexual transgression. Sarah is condemned as a "whore" just for her lingering in the Cobb and forest and the rumor of her love story.

Moreover, Victorian women who cannot properly restrict the sexual desire are diagnosed as hysteria. Doctor's diagnosis on female hysteria manifests the fallacy of patriarchal version on female hysteria and phallocentric demonization of female sexuality. Such cognition strengthens the patriarchal domination over female sexual disciplines. This explains why Sarah is not only rejected as a fallen woman but also categorized as a madwoman.

However, Sarah in the novel does not fall victim. She is depicted as a woman who fights for her independent identity and subjectivity. Her construction of identity is realized in her rebellion against the conventions of the society.

Although Sarah is born humble, she receives some education, which makes her in an ambivalent state: "a noble and aspiring mind in a base-born frame confined". In this case, she must be an outsider in her age and environment to gain independence and freedom and to self-protect. The rumor she herself first starts destroys her chance of marriage and living a traditional life and playing the traditional roles. But at the same time, She ultimately liberates herself from the patriarchal sexual and social dominance over Victorian women who are fettered by the duty of sexual purity, the doctrines for being a feminine ideal and the virgin/ whore dichotomy. As being stigmatized as a French Lieutenant's Whore and being medically misconceived as a hysteric, Sarah possesses the freedom in choosing her identities, the materialization of Fowles's faith in freedom. Leaving Charles and pursuing her economic independence, Sarah transforms herself from a fallen woman to a New Woman.

Ⅵ. Further Reading

1. Aubrey, James. Filming John Fowles : Critical Essays on Motion Picture and

Television Adaptations[M]. North Carolina : McFarland & Company, Inc. , 2015.

2. Brooke, Lenz. John Fowles : Visionary and Voyeur[M]. Amsterdam : Rodopi, 2008.

3. Cooper, Pamela. The Fictions of John Fowles: Power, Creativity, Feminity [M]. Ottwa: University of Ottaw Press, 1991.

4. Mandal, Mahitosh. "Eyes a man could drown in": Phallic Myth and Femininity in John Fowles's *The French Lieutenant's Woman* [J]. Interdisciplinary Literary Studies, 2017,19(3): 274-298.

5. Wahida, Hasina. Interfacing Text and Paratexts: John Fowles' "The French Lieutenant's Woman"[M]. Munich: GRIN Publishing, 2012.

6. Warburton, Eileen. John Fowles : A Life in Two Worlds[M]. New York : Viking, 2004.

7. Wilson, Thomas M. The Recurrent Green Universe of John Fowles[M]. New York: Rodopi, 2006.

8. 梁晓晖. 叙述者的元小说操控:《法国中尉的女人》的认知诗学研究[M]. 北京: 北京大学出版社, 2012.

9. 张和龙. 后现代语境中的自我:约翰·福尔斯小说研究[M]. 上海:上海外语教育出版社, 2007.

10. 张晓华. 戏谑·操控·探寻:约翰·福尔斯作品女性人物研究[M]. 呼和浩特:内蒙古大学出版社, 2013.

Chapter 6

Dorris Lessing: *The Grass Is Singing*
Feminism and Postcolonialism

Ⅰ. Introduction to the Author

Doris Lessing (22 October 1919—17 November 2013), was a prestigious novelist and short story writer. In her career of literature, she has been awarded many prizes, including Somerset Maugham Award (1954), WH Smith Literary Award (1986), and S. T. Dupont Golden PEN Award (2002), etc. In 2007, she was awarded Nobel Prize for literature, being praised "that epicist of the female experience, who with scepticism, fire and visionary power has subjected a divided civilisation to scrutiny. " In 2001, Lessing was awarded the David Cohen Prize for a lifetime's achievement in British literature. In 2008, *The Times* ranked her fifth on a list of "The 50 greatest British writers since 1945".

Doris Lessing was born Doris May Tayler in Persia (now Iran) on October 22, 1919 to Alfred Cook Tayler and Emily Maud McVeigh. Her father Alfred Tayler was badly wounded and crippled when he served as a soldier in World War Ⅰ. Maud McVeigh was the nurse who looked after him in hospital. After the war, Afred Tayler got a position as a clerk in the Imperial Bank of Persia in Tehran. In 1925, Alfred Tayler decided to move the family to the British colony in Southern Rhodesia (now Zimbabwe), where he believed that he could obtain great wealth through maize farming. With a government loan, he bought three thousand acres of land, but it did not bring about the expected wealth.

Lessing has described her childhood as an uneven mix of some pleasure and much pain. In Lessing's view, her father acted on impulse, while her mother more practical. "This psychological division between the visionary and the ordinary, between two very different ways of seeing the world that Lessing continually ascribes to her parents in reminiscences, if destructive to actual family life, becomes a productive tension in much of her fiction" (Rowe, 4). Moreover, the rigid discipline and rules of her mother and then the convent school in the capital of Salisbury made her feel imprisoned. The natural world of Africa offered her one retreat from harsh reality.

Her school education ended when she was thirteen. After leaving school, Doris Lessing found a job at a telephone company. She then worked as a legal secretary. In 1939, Lessing married Frank Charles Wisdom, bore two children and divorced in 1943. During World War II, Lessing became interested in politics and joined the Left Book Club, a small Marxist group, where she met Gottfried Lessing. They married in 1945, bore a son in 1947, and divorced in 1949.

In 1949, she went to London, bringing her son and the manuscript of her first novel, *The Grass is Singing*. It was published in 1950 and was an immediate success. She began her career as a professional writer.

As a productive writer, Lessing has published more than 50 books, spanning several genres. Her important novels include, *The Grass Is Singing* (1950) , *Retreat to Innocence* (1956), *The Golden Notebook* (1962), *The Summer Before the Dark* (1973), *Memoirs of a Survivor* (1974), *The Good Terrorist* (1985), *The Fifth Child* (1988), *Love, Again* (1996), *Ben, in the World* (2000) , *The Cleft* (2007), *Martha Quest* (1952), *A Proper Marriage* (1954), *A Ripple from the Storm* (1958), *Landlocked* (1965), *The Four-Gated City* (1969), *Shikasta* (1979), *The Marriages Between Zones Three, Four and Five* (1980), *The Sirian Experiments* (1980), *The Making of the Representative for Planet* 8 (1982), and *The Sentimental Agents in the Volyen Empire* (1983). Short stories are collected in such collections as, *This Was the Old Chief's Country* (1951), *The Habit of Loving* (1957), *A Man and Two Women* (1963), *African Stories* (1964), *The Story of a Non-Marrying Man* (1972), *This Was the Old Chief's Country: Collected African Stories*, Vol. 1 (1973), *The Sun Between Their Feet: Collected African Stories*, Vol. 2 (1973), *To Room Nineteen: Collected Stories*, Vol. 1 (1978), *Through the Tunnel* (1990), *Spies I Have Known* (1995), *The Pit* (1996), and *The Grandmothers: Four Short Novels* (2003). Her writing also covers non-fiction, autobiography, poetry and drama.

II. Introduction to the Novel *The Grass is Singing*

The Grass is Singing is the first novel by Doris Lessing. Published in 1950, the novel was an instant success. Set in Rhodesia (then a British colony in southern Africa, now called Zimbabwe) in 1940s, when apartheid (institutionalized racism) was practiced, the novel explores themes relating to racial politics and gender politics.

The novel starts with a report in local newspaper on the murder of a white farmer's wife by her black houseboy. The news that Mary Turner is found dead on her own veranda spreads quickly and surprises the local white community. It is said that she was murdered by her black servant named Moses, which meets the expectations of local whites. Mary's husband, Dick has subsequently gone mad.

The novel then flashes back to Mary Turner's unhappy early life. In her memory of her childhood, she had an alcoholic and abusive father, a troubled mother and two older siblings who died during childhood. This is a family she wants to escape and she does as soon as she can. She finally finds a secretarial job in the city and lives a life that she believes is happy and fulfilled. As she gets older, she feels the pressure from people around her, especially from females. After overhearing an insulting remark at a party about her spinsterhood, she resolves to marry.

Mary marries Dick Turner in a haste, only after a brief courtship. She moves to his farm. Mary soon discovers that marriage is not what she has imagined. Dick is a white farmer struggling to make his farm profitable. However, his incompetence makes him fail in business ventures of raising pigs, turkeys, then rabbits. They have to struggle against poverty. She has to stay in the stuffy little house, endure the burning heat and bear lonesome. Because of poverty, Dick and Mary do not attend social events, living reclusively. They could not even afford to have a baby.

To make things even worse, Mary, as a racist, believing that whites should be masters over the native blacks, shows contempt for the natives and finds them disgusting and animal-like. The great tension between Mary and the black servants and workers is intensifying. She makes an attempt to leave the farm and return to her life in the city—only to find that it's moved on without her, and she's no longer welcome there. She has no choice but to return to her marriage.

Over the years Mary's spiritual condition steadily and deeply deteriorates. Mary often goes through spells of depression and hallucination. She finds herself depending more and more on Moses, a black servant. She even begins dreaming of Moses' body, which shocks her.

Charlie Slatter, the neighbour of Turners, decides to buy Turner's farm and hires Martson to run the farm. When Martson comes for a visit, he is surprised to see the intimacy between Mary and Moses when he helps Mary with her dress, which is considered taboo.

The novel ends with Mary's death at the hand of Moses. Moses waits for the arrival of the police and punishment.

Ⅲ. Excerpt

CHAPTER 1

Mary Turner, wife of Richard Turner, a farmer at Ngesi, was found murdered on the front verandah of their homestead yesterday morning. The houseboy, who has been arrested, has confessed to the crime. No motive has been discovered.

It is thought he was in search of valuables.

The newspaper did not say much. People all over the country must have glanced at the paragraph with its sensational heading and felt a little spurt of anger mingled with what was almost satisfaction, as if some belief had been confirmed, as if something had happened which could only have been expected. When natives steal, murder or rape, that is the feeling white people have.

And then they turned the page to something else.

But the people in 'the district' who knew the Turners, either by sight, or from gossiping about them for so many years, did not turn the page so quickly. Many must have snipped out the paragraph, put it among old letters, or between the pages of a book, keeping it perhaps as an omen or a warning, glancing at the yellowing piece of paper with closed, secretive faces. For they did not discuss the murder; that was the most extraordinary thing about it. It was as if they had a sixth sense which told them everything there was to be known, although the three people in a position to explain the facts said nothing. The murder was simply not discussed. 'A bad business,' someone would remark; and the faces of the people round about would put on that reserved and guarded look. 'A very bad business,' came the reply-and that was the end of it. There was, it seemed, a tacit agreement that the Turner case should not be given undue publicity by gossip. Yet it was a farming district, where those isolated white families met only very occasionally, hungry for contact with their own kind, to talk and discuss and pull to pieces, all speaking at once, making the most of an hour or so's companionship before returning to their farms where they saw only their own faces and the faces of their black servants for weeks on end. Normally that murder would have been discussed for months; people would have been positively grateful for something to talk about.

To an outsider it would seem perhaps as if the energetic Charlie Slatter had travelled from farm to farm over the district telling people to keep quiet; but that was something that would never have occurred to him. The steps he took (and he made not one mistake) were taken apparently instinctively and without conscious planning. The most interesting thing about the whole affair was this silent, unconscious agreement. Everyone behaved like a flock of birds who communicate-or so it seems-by means of a kind of telepathy.

Long before the murder marked them out, people spoke of the Turners in the hard, careless voices reserved for misfits, outlaws and the self-exiled. The Turners were disliked, though few of their neighbours had ever met them, or even seen them in the distance. Yet what was there to dislike? They simply 'kept themselves to themselves'; that was all. They were never seen at district dances, or fetes, or gymkhanas. They must have had something to be ashamed of; that was the feeling. It was not right to seclude themselves like that; it was a slap in the face of everyone else; what had they got to be so stuck-up about? What, indeed! Living the way they did! That little box of a house-it was forgivable as a temporary dwelling, but not to live in permanently. Why, some natives (though not many, thank heavens) had houses as good; and it would give them a bad impression to see white people living in such a way.

And then it was that someone used the phrase 'poor whites.' It caused disquiet. There was no great money- cleavage in those days (that was before the era of the tobacco barons), but there was certainly a race division. The small community of Afrikaners had their own lives, and the Britishers ignored them. 'Poor whites' were Afrikaners, never British. But the person who said the

Turners were poor whites stuck to it defiantly. What was the difference? What was a poor white? It was the way one lived, a question of standards. All the Turners needed were a drove of children to make them poor whites.

Though the arguments were unanswerable, people would still not think of them as poor whites. To do that would be letting the side down. The Turners were British, after all.

Thus the district handled the Turners, in accordance with that esprit de corps which is the first rule of South African society, but which the Turners themselvesignored. They apparently did not recognize the need for esprit de corps; that, really, was why they were hated.

The more one thinks about it, the more extraordinary the case becomes. Not the murder itself; but the way people felt about it, the way they pitied Dick Turner with a fine fierce indignation against Mary, as if she were something unpleasant and unclean, and it served her right to get murdered. But they did not ask questions.

For instance, they must have wondered who that 'Special Correspondent' was. Someone in the district sent in the news, for the paragraph was not in newspaper language. But who? Marston, the assistant, left the district immediately after the murder. Denham, the policeman, might have written to the paper in a personal capacity, but it was not likely. There remained Charlie Slatter, who knew more about the Turners than anyone else, and was there on the day of the murder. One could say that he practically controlled the handling of the case, even taking precedence over the Sergeant himself. And people felt that to be quite right and proper. Whom should it concern, if not the white farmers, that a silly woman got herself murdered by a native for reasons people might think about, but never, never mentioned? It was their livelihood, their wives and families, their way of living, at stake.

But to the outsider it is strange that Slatter should have been allowed to take charge of the affair, to arrange that everything should pass over without more than a ripple of comment.

For there could have been no planning: there simply wasn't time. Why, for instance, when Dick Turner's farm boys came to him with the news, did he sit down to write a note to the Sergeant at the police camp? He did not use the telephone.

. . .

CHAPTER 2

...

It had never occurred to her to think, for instance, that she, the daughter of a petty railway official and a woman whose life had been so unhappy because of economic pressure that she had literally pined to death, was living in much the same way as the daughters of the wealthiest in South Africa, could do as she pleasedcould marry, if she wished, anyone she wanted. These things did not enter her head. 'Class' is not a South African word; and its equivalent, 'race,' meant to her the office boy in the firm where she worked, other women's servants, and the amorphous mass of natives in the streets, whom she hardly noticed. She knew (the phrase was in the air) that the natives were getting 'cheeky.' But she had nothing to do with them really. They were outside her orbit.

Till she was twenty-five nothing happened to break the smooth and comfortable life she led. Then her father died. That removed the last link that bound her to a childhood she hated to remember. There was nothing left to connect her with the sordid little house on stilts, the screaming of trains, the dust, and the strife between her parents. Nothing at all! She was free. And when the funeral was over, and she had returned to the office, she looked forward to a life that would continue as it had so far been. She was very happy: that was perhaps her only positive quality, for there was nothing else distinctive about her, though at twenty-five she was at her prettiest. Sheer contentment put a bloom on her: she was a thin girl, who moved awkwardly, with a fashionable curtain of light-brown hair, serious blue eyes, and pretty clothes. Her friends would have described her as a slim blonde: she modelled herself on the more childish-looking film stars.

At thirty nothing had changed. On her thirtieth birthday she felt a vague surprise that did not even amount to discomfort—for she did not feel any different —that the years had gone past so quickly. Thirty! It sounded a great age. But it had nothing to do with her. At the same time she did not celebrate this birthday; she allowed it to be forgotten. She felt almost outraged that such a thing could happen to her, who was no different from the Mary of sixteen.

She was by now the personal secretary of her employer, and was earning good money. If she had wanted, she could have taken a flat and lived the smart sort of life. She was quite presentable. She had the undistinguished, dead-level appearance of South African white democracy. Her voice was one of thousands: flattened, a little sing-song, clipped. Anyone could have worn her clothes. There was nothing to prevent her living by herself, even running her own car, entertaining on a small scale. She could have become a person on her own account. But this was against her instinct.

She chose to live in a girls' club, which had been started, really, to help women who could not earn much money, but she had been there so long no one thought of asking her to leave. She chose it because it reminded her of school, and she had hated leaving school. She liked the crowds of girls, and eating in a big dining- room, and coming home after the pictures to find a friend in her room waiting for a little gossip. In the Club she was a person of some importance, out of the usual run. For one thing she was so much older than the others. She had come to have what was almost the role of a comfortable maiden aunt to whom one can tell one's troubles. For Mary was never shocked, never condemned, never told tales. She seemed impersonal, above the little worries. The stiffness of her manner, her shyness protected her from many spites and jealousies. She seemed immune. This was her strength, but also a weakness that she would not have considered a weakness: she felt disinclined, almost repelled, by the thought of intimacies and scenes and contacts. She moved among all those young women with a faint aloofness that said as clear as words: I will not be drawn in. And she was quite unconscious of it. She was very happy in the Club.

Outside the girls' club, and the office, where again she was a person of some importance, because of the many years she had worked there, she led a full and active life. Yet it was a passive one, in some respects, for it depended on other people entirely. She was not the kind of woman who initiates parties, or who is the centre of a crowd. She was still the girl who is 'taken out. '

Her life was really rather extraordinary: the conditions which produced it are passing now, and when the change is complete, women will look back on them as on a vanished Golden Age.

She got up late, in time for office (she was very punctual) but not in time for breakfast. She worked efficiently, but in a leisurely way, until lunch. She went back to the club for lunch. Two more hours' work in the afternoon and she was free. Then she played tennis, or hockey or swam. And always with a man, one of those innumerable men who 'took her out', treating her like a sister:

Mary was such a good pal! Just as she seemed to have a hundred women friends, but no particular friend, so she had (it seemed) a hundred men, who had taken her out, or were taking her out, or who had married and now asked her to their homes. She was friend to half the town. And in the evening she always went to sundowner parties that prolonged themselves till midnight, or danced, or went to the pictures. Sometimes she went to the pictures five nights a week. She was never in bed before twelve or later. And so it had gone on, day after day, week after week, year after year. South Africa is a wonderful place: for the unmarried white woman. But she was not playing her part, for she did not get married. The years went past; her friends got married; she had been bridesmaid a dozen times; other people's children were growing up; but she went on as companionable, as adaptable, as aloof and as heart-whole as ever, working as hard enjoying herself as she ever did in office, and never for one moment alone, except when she was asleep.

She seemed not to care for men. She would say to her girls, 'Men! They get all the fun.' Yet outside the office and the club her life was entirely dependent upon men, though she would have most indignantly repudiated the accusation. And perhaps she was not so dependent upon them really, for when she listened to other people's complaints and miseries she offered none of her own. Sometimes her friends felt a little put off, and let down. It was hardly fair, they felt obscurely, to listen, to advise, to act as a sort of universal shoulder for the world to weep on, and give back nothing of her own. The truth was she had no troubles. She heard other people's complicated stories with wonder, even a little fear. She shrank away from all that. She was a most rare phenomenon: a woman of thirty without love troubles, headaches, backaches, sleeplessness or neurosis. She did not know how rare she was.

And she was still 'one of the girls'. If a visiting cricket team came to town and partners were needed, the organizers would ring up Mary. That was the kind of thing she was good at: adapting herself sensibly and quietly to any occasion. She would sell tickets for a charity dance or act as a dancing partner for a visiting full-back with equal amiability.

And she still wore her hair little-girl fashion on her shoulders, and wore little-girl frocks in pastel colours, and kept her shy, naive manner. If she had been left alone she would have gone on, in her own way, enjoying herself thoroughly, until people found one day that she had turned imperceptibly into one of those women who have become old without ever having been middle-aged: a little withered, a little acid, hard as nails, sentimentally kindhearted, and addicted to religion or small dogs.

They would have been kind to her, because she had 'missed the best things of life'. But then there are so many people who don't want them: so many for whom the best things have been poisoned from the start. When Mary thought of 'home' she remembered a wooden box shaken by passing trains; when she thought of marriage she remembered her father coming home red-eyed and fuddled; when she thought of children she saw her mother's face at her children's funeral- anguished, but as dry and as hard as rock. Mary liked other people's children but shuddered at the thought of having any of her own. She felt sentimental at weddings, but she had a profound distaste for sex; there had been little privacy in her home and there were things she did not care to remember; she had taken good care to forget them years ago.

She certainly did feel, at times, a restlessness, a vague dissatisfaction that took the pleasure out of her activities for a while. She would be going to bed, for instance, contentedly, after the pictures, when the thought would strike her, 'Another day gone!' And then time would contract and it seemed to her only a breathing space since she left school and came into town to earn her own living; and she would feel a little panicky, as if an invisible support had been drawn away from underneath her. But then, being a sensible person, and firmly convinced that thinking about oneself was morbid, she would get into bed and turn out the lights. She might wonder, before drifting off to sleep, 'Is this all? When I get to be old will this be all I have to look back on?' But by morning she would have forgotten it, and the days went round, and she would be happy again. For she did not know what she wanted. Something bigger, she would think vaguely-a different kind of life. But the mood never lasted long. She was so satisfied with her work, where she felt sufficient and capable; with her friends, whom she relied on; with her life at the Club, which was as pleasant and as gregarious as being in a giant twittering aviary, where there was always the excitement of other people's engagements and weddings; and with her men friends, who treated her just like a good pal, with none of this silly sex business.

But all women become conscious, sooner or later, of that impalpable, but steel-strong pressure to get married, and Mary, who was not at all susceptible to atmosphere, or the things people imply, was brought face to face with it suddenly, and most unpleasantly.

She was in the house of a married friend, sitting on the verandah, with a lighted room behind her. She was alone; and heard people talking in low voices, and caught her own name. She rose to go inside and declare herself: it was typical of her that her first thought was, how unpleasant it would be for her friends to know she had overheard. Then she sank down again, and waited for a suitable moment to pretend she had just come in from the garden. This was the conversation she listened to, while her face burned and her hands went clammy.

'She's not fifteen any longer: it is ridiculous! Someone should tell her about her clothes.'

'How old is she?'

'Must be well over thirty. She has been going strong for years. She was working long before I began working, and that was a good twelve years ago.'

'Why doesn't she marry? She must have had plenty of chances.'

There was a dry chuckle. 'I don't think so. My husband was keen on her himself once, but he thinks she will never marry. She just isn't like that, isn't like that at all. Something missing somewhere.'

'Oh, I don't know.'

'She's gone off so much, in any case. The other day I caught sight of her in the street and hardly recognized her. It's a fact! The way she plays all those games, her skin is like sandpaper, and she's got so thin.'

'But she's such a nice girl.'

'She'll never set the rivers on fire, though.'

'She'd make someone a good wife. She's a good sort, Mary.'

'She should marry someone years older than herself. A man of fifty would suit her ... you'll see, she will marry someone old enough to be her father one of these days.'

'One never can tell!'

There was another chuckle, good-hearted enough, but it sounded cruelly malicious to Mary. She was stunned and outraged; but most of all deeply wounded that her friends could discuss her thus. She was so naive, so unconscious of herself in relation to other people, that it had never entered her head that people could discuss her behind her back. And the things they had said! She sat there writhing, twisting her hands. Then she composed herself and went back into the room to join her treacherous friends, who greeted her as cordially as if they had not just that moment driven knives into her heart and thrown her quite off balance; she could not recognize herself in the picture they had made of her!

That little incident, apparently so unimportant, which would have had no effect on a person who had the faintest idea of the kind of world she lived in, had a profound effect on Mary. She who had never had time to think of herself, took to sitting in her room for hours at a time, wondering: 'Why did they say those things? What is the matter with me? What did they mean when they said that I am not like that?' And she would look warily, appealingly, into the faces of friends to see if she could find there traces of their condemnation of her. And she was even more disturbed and unhappy because they seemed just as usual, treating her with their ordinary friendliness. She began to suspect double meanings where none were intended, to find maliciousness in the glance of a person who felt nothing but affection for her.

Turning over in her mind the words she had by accident listened to, she thought of ways to improve herself. She took the ribbon out of her hair, though with regret, because she thought she looked very pretty with a mass of curls round her rather long thin face; and bought herself tailor-made clothes, in which she felt ill at ease, because she felt truly herself in pinafore frocks and childish skirts. And for the first time in her life she was feeling uncomfortable with men. A small core of contempt for them, of which she was quite unconscious, and which had protected her from sex as surely as if she had been truly hideous, had melted, and she had lost her poise. And she began looking around for someone to marry. She did not put it to herself like that; but, after all, she was nothing if not a social being, though she had never thought of 'society,' the abstraction; and if her friends were thinking she should get married, then there might be something in it. If she had ever learned to put her feelings into words, that was perhaps how she would have expressed herself. And the first man she allowed to approach her was a widower of fifty-five with half-grown children. It was because she felt safer with him ... because she did not associate ardours and embraces with a middle-aged gentleman whose attitude towards her was almost fatherly.

He knew perfectly well what he wanted: a pleasant companion, a mother for his children and someone to run his house for him. He found Mary good company, and she was kind to the children. Nothing, really, could have been more suitable: since apparently she had to get married, this was the kind of marriage to suit her best. But things went wrong. He underestimated her experience; it seemed to him that a woman who had been on her own so long should know her own mind and understand what he was offering her. A relationship developed which was clear to both of them, until he proposed to her, was accepted, and began to make love to her. Then a violent revulsion overcame her and she ran away; they were in his comfortable drawing-room, and when he began to kiss her, she ran out of his house into the night and all the way home through the streets to the club. There she fell on the bed and wept. And his feeling for her was not one to be enhanced by this kind of foolishness, which a younger man, physically in love with her, might have found charming. Next morning, she was horrified at her behaviour. What a way to behave: she, who was always in command of herself, and who dreaded nothing more than scenes and ambiguity. She apologized to him, but that was the end of it. And now she was left at sea, not knowing what it was she needed. It seemed to her that she had run from him because he was 'an old man', that was how the affair arranged itself in her mind. She shuddered, and avoided men over thirty. She was over that age herself; but in spite of everything, she thought of herself as a girl still.

And all the time, unconsciously, without admitting it to herself, she was looking for a husband.

...

CHAPTER 5

With her own saved money Mary bought flowered materials, and covered cushions and made curtains; bought a little linen, crockery, and some dress lengths. The house gradually lost its air of bleak poverty, and put on an inexpensive prettiness, with bright hangings and some pictures. Mary worked hard, and looked for Dick's look of approval and surprise when he came back from work and noted every new change. A month after she had arrived she walked through the house, and saw there was nothing more to be done. Besides, there was no more money.

She had settled easily into the new rhythm. She found the change so embracing that it was as if she were an entirely new person. Every morning she woke with the clanging of the plough disc, and drank tea in bed with Dick. When he had gone down on the lands she put out groceries for the day. She was so conscientious that Samson found things had worsened rather than improved: even his understood one-third allowance had gone, and she wore the store keys tied to her belt. By breakfast time what work she had to do in the house was finished except for light cooking; but Samson was a better cook than she, and after a while she left it to him. She sewed all morning, till lunchtime; sewed after lunch, and went to bed immediately after supper, sleeping like a child all night.

In the first flush of energy and determination she really enjoyed the life, putting things to rights and making a little go a long way. She liked, particularly, the early mornings before the heat numbed and tired her; liked the new leisure; liked Dick's approval. For his pride and affectionate gratitude for what she was doing (he would never have believed that his forlorn house could look like this) overshadowed his patient disappointment. When she saw that puzzled hurt look on his face, she pushed away the thought of what he must be suffering, for it made her repulsive to him again.

Then, having done all she could to the house, she began on dress materials, finishing an inexpensive trousseau. A few months after her marriage she found there was nothing more to do. Suddenly, from one day to the next, she found herself unoccupied. Instinctively staving off idleness as something dangerous, she returned to her underwear, and embroidered everything that could possibly be embroidered. There she sat all day, sewing and stitching, hour after hour, as if fine embroidery would save her life. She was a good needlewoman, and the results were admirable. Dick praised her work and was amazed, for he had expected a difficult period while she was settling down, thinking she would take the lonely life hard at first. But she showed no signs of being lonely, she seemed perfectly satisfied to sew all day. And all this time he treated her like a brother, for he was a sensitive man, and was waiting for her to turn to him of her own accord. The relief she was unable to hide that his endearments were no more than affectionate, hurt him deeply, but he still thought: It will come right in the end.

There came an end to embroidery; again she was left empty-handed. Again she looked about for something to do. The walls, she decided, were filthy. She would whitewash them all, herself, to save money. So, for two weeks, Dick came back to the house to find furniture stacked in the middle of rooms and pails of thick white stuff standing on the floor. But she was very methodical. One room was finished before another was begun; and while he admired her for her capability and self- assurance, undertaking this work she had no experience or knowledge of, he was alarmed too. What was she going to do with all this energy and efficiency? It undermined his own self-assurance even further, seeing her like this, for he knew, deep down, that this quality was one he lacked. Soon, the walls were dazzling blue-white, every inch of them painted by Mary herself, standing on a rough ladder for days at a time.

And now she found she was tired. She found it pleasant to let go a little, and to spend her time sitting with her hands folded, on the big sofa. But not for long. She was restless, so restless she did not know what to do with herself. She unpacked the novels she had brought with her, and turned them over. These were the books she had collected over years from the mass that had come her way. She had read each one a dozen times, knowing it by heart, following the familiar tales as a child listens to his mother telling him a well-known fairy tale. It had been a drug, a soporific, in the past, reading them; now, as she turned them over listlessly, she wondered why they had lost their flavour. Her mind wandered as she determinedly turned the pages; and she realized, after she had been reading for perhaps an hour, that she had not taken in a word. She threw the book aside and tried another, but with the same result. For a few days the house was littered with books in faded dust covers. Dick was pleased: it flattered him to think he had married a woman who read books. One evening he picked up a book called 'The Fair Lady', and opened it in the middle.

'... The trekkers trekked North, towards the Land of Promise where never the cold grasping hand of the hated British could reach them. Like a cold snake through the hot landscape the column coiled. Prunella Van Koetzie skirmished lightly on her horse on the perimeter of the column, wearing a white kappie over her dainty sweat-pearled face and close clustering ringlets. Piet Van Friesland watched her, his heart throbbing in time to the great blood- stained heart of South Africa itself. Could he win her, the sweet Prunella, who bore herself like a queen among these burghers and mynheers and buxom fraus in their doeks and veldschoens? Could he?

He stared and stared. Tant' Anna, putting out the koekies and the biltong for the midday meal, in a red doek the colour of the kaffir-boom trees, shook her fat sides in laughter and said to herself, "That will be a match yet."

He put it down, and looked across at Mary, who was sitting with a book in her lap, staring up at the roof.

'Can't we have ceilings, Dick?' she asked fretfully.

'It would cost so much,' he said doubtfully. 'Perhaps next year, if we do well.'

In a few days Mary gathered up the books and put them away; they were not what she wanted. She took up the handbook on kitchen kaffir again, and spent all her time on it, practising on Samson in the kitchen, disconcerting him with her ungood-humoured criticisms, but behaving with a cold, dispassionate justice. Samson became more and more unhappy. He had been so used to Dick, and they understood each other very well. Dick swore at him often, but laughed with him afterwards. This woman never laughed. She put out, carefully, so much meal, and so much sugar; and watched the left-overs from their own food with an extraordinary, humiliating capacity for remembering every cold potato and every piece of bread, asking for them if they were missing.

Shaken out of his comparatively comfortable existence, he grew sulky. There were several rows in the kitchen, and once Dick found Mary in tears. She knew there had been enough raisins put out for the pudding, but when they came to eat it, there were hardly any. And the boy denied stealing them. ...

'Good heavens,' said Dick, amused, 'I thought there was something really wrong.'

'But I know he took them,' sobbed Mary.

'He probably did, but he's a good old swine on the whole.'

'I am going to take it out of his wages.'

Dick, puzzled at her emotional state, said: 'If you think it is really necessary.' He reflected that this was the first time he had seen her cry.

So Samson, who earned a pound a month, was docked two shillings. He accepted the information with a shut sullen face, saying nothing to her, but appealing to Dick, who told him that he was to take orders from Mary. Samson gave notice that evening, on the grounds that he was needed in his kraal. Mary began to question him closely as to why he was needed; but Dick touched her arm warningly and shook his head.

'Why shouldn't I ask him?' she demanded. 'He's lying, isn't he?'

'Of course he's lying,' said Dick irritably. 'Of course. That is not the point. You can't keep him against his will.'

'Why should I accept a lie?' said Mary. 'Why should I? Why can't he say straight out that he doesn't like working for me, instead of lying about his kraal?'

Dick shrugged, looking at her with impatience; he could not understand her unreasonable insistence; he knew how to get on with natives; dealing with them was a sometimes amusing, sometimes annoying game in which both sides followed certain unwritten rules.

'You would be angry if he did say so,' he remarked ruefully, but with affection still; he could not take her seriously, she seemed to him a child when she behaved like this. And he was genuinely grieved that this old native, who had worked for him all these years, was going now. 'Well,' he said at last, philosophically,'I should have expected it. I should have got a new boy right from the beginning. There's always trouble with a change of management. '

Mary watched the farewell scene, that took place on the back steps, from the doorway. She was filled with wonder, and even repulsion. Dick was really sorry to see the end of this nigger! She could not understand any white person feeling anything personal about a native; it made Dick seem really horrible to her. She heard him say,'When your work in the kraal is finished, you will come back and work for us again?' The native answered,'Yes, baas,' but he was already turned to go; and Dick came back into the house silent and glum. 'He won't come back,' he said.

'There are plenty of other munts, aren't there?' she asked snappily, disliking him.

'Yes,' he assented, 'oh yes. '

...

CHAPTER 7

...

She had to crush down violent repugnance to the idea of facing the farm natives herself. Even when she had called the dogs to her and stood on the verandah with the car keys in her hand, she turned back again to the kitchen for a glass of water; sitting in the car with her foot resting on the accelerator, she jumped out again, on an excuse that she needed a handkerchief. Coming out of the bedroom she noticed the long sambok that rested on two nails over the kitchen door, like an ornament; it was a long time since she had remembered its existence. Lifting it down, looping it over her wrist, she went to the car with more confidence. Because of it, she opened the back door of the car and let out the dogs; she hated the way they breathed down the back of her neck as she drove. She left them whining with disappointment outside the house, and drove herself down to the lands where the boys were supposed to be working. They knew of Dick's illness, and were not there, having dispersed, days before, to the compound. She took the car along the rough and rutted road as near as she could get to the compound, and then walked towards it along the native path that was trodden hard and smooth, but with a soft littering of glinting slippery grass over it, so that she had to move carefully to save herself from sliding. The long pale grass left sharp needles in her skirts, and the bushes shook red dust into her face.

The compound was built on a low rise above the vlei, about half a mile from the house. The system was that a new labourer presenting himself for work was given a day without pay to build a hut for himself and his family before taking his place with the workers. So there were always new huts, and always empty old ones that slowly collapsed and fell down unless somebody thought of burning them. The huts were closely clustered over an acre or two of ground. They looked like natural growths from the ground, rather than man-made dwellings. It was as though a giant black hand had reached down from the sky, picked up a handful of sticks and grass, and dropped them magically on the earth in the form of huts. They were grass-roofed, with pole walls plastered with mud, and single low doors, but no windows. The smoke from the fires inside percolated through the thatch or drifted in clouds from the doorways, so that each had the appearance of smouldering slowly from within. Between the huts were irregular patches of ill-cultivated mealies, and pumpkin vines trailed everywhere through plants and bushes and up over the walls and roofs, with the big amber-coloured pumpkins scattered among the leaves. Some of them were beginning to rot, subsiding into a sour festering ooze of pinky stuff, covered with flies. Flies were everywhere. They hummed round Mary's head in a cloud as she walked, and they were clustered round the eyes of the dozen small black children who were pot-bellied and mostly naked, staring at her as she picked her way through the vines and mealies past the huts. Thin native mongrels, their bones ridging through their hides, bared their teeth and cringed. Native women, draped in dirty store-stuff, and some naked above the waist with their slack black breasts hanging down, gazed at her from doorways with astonishment at her queer appearance, commenting on her among themselves, laughing, and making crude remarks. There were some men: glancing through doorways she could see bodies huddled asleep; some sat on their haunches on the ground in groups, talking. But she had no idea which were Dick's labourers, which were merely visiting here, or perhaps passing through the place on their way somewhere else. She stopped before one of them and told him to fetch the headboy, who soon came stooping out of one of the better huts that were ornamented on the walls with patterns of daubed red and yellow clay. His eyes were inflamed: she could see he had been drinking.

She said in kitchen kaffir: 'Get the boys on to the lands in ten minutes.'

'The boss is better?' he asked with hostile indifference.

She ignored the question, and said, 'You can tell them that I will take two and six off the ticket of every one of them that isn't at work in ten minutes.'She held out her wrist and pointed to the watch, showing him the time interval.

The man slouched and stooped in the sunshine, resenting her presence; the native women stared and laughed; the filthy, underfed children crowded around, whispering to each other; the starved dogs slunk in the background among the vines and mealies. She hated the place, which she had never entered before. 'Filthy savages!' she thought vindictively. She looked straight into the reddened, beer-clouded eyes of the headman, and repeated. 'Ten minutes.' Then she turned and walked off down the winding path through the trees, listening for the sounds of the natives turning out of the huts behind her.

She sat in the car waiting, beside the land where she knew they were supposed to be reaping maize. After half an hour a few stragglers arrived, the headboy among them. At the end of an hour not more than half of the labourers were present: some had gone visiting to neighbouring compounds without permission, some lay drunk in their huts. She called the headboy to her, and took down the names of those who were absent, writing them in her big awkward hand on a scrap of paper, spelling the unfamiliar names with difficulty. She remained there the whole morning, watching the straggling line of working boys, the sun glaring down through the old canvas hood on to her bare head. There was hardly any talking among them. They worked reluctantly, in a sullen silence; and she knew it was because they resented her, a woman, supervising them. When the gong rang for the lunch interval, she went up to the house and told Dick what had happened, but toning it down so that he would not worry. After lunch she drove down again, and curiously enough without repugnance for this work from which she had shrunk so long. She was exhilarated by the unfamiliar responsibility, the sensation of pitting her will against the farm.

Now she left the car standing on the road, as the gang of natives moved in to the middle of the field where the pale gold maize stood high above their heads, and where she could not see them from outside. They were tearing off the heavy cobs, and putting them into the half-sacks tied round their waists, while others followed, cutting down the pillaged stalks and leaning them in small pyramids that regularly dotted the field. She moved steadily along the land with them, standing in the cleared part among the rough stubble, and watched them ceaselessly. She still carried the long throng of leather looped round one wrist.

It gave her a feeling of authority, and braced her against the waves of hatred that she could feel coming from the gang of natives. As she walked steadily along beside them, with the hot yellow sunlight on her head and neck, making her shoulders ache, she began to understand how it was that Dick could stand it, day after day.

It was difficult to sit still in the car with the heat filtering through the roof; it was another thing to move along with the workers, in the rhythm of their movement, concentrated on the work they were doing. As the long afternoon passed, she watched, in a kind of alert stupor, the naked brown backs bend, steady and straighten, the ropes of muscle sliding under the dusty skin. Most of them wore pieces of faded stuff as loincloths; some, khaki shorts; but nearly all were naked above the waist. They were a short thin crowd of men, stunted by bad feeding, but muscular and tough. She was oblivious to anything outside of this field, the work to be done, the gang of natives. She forgot about the heat, the beating sun, the glare.

She watched the dark hands stripping cobs, and leaning the ragged gold stems together, and thought of nothing else. When one of the men paused for a moment in his work to rest, or to wipe the running sweat from his eyes, she waited one minute by her watch, and then called sharply to him to begin again. He would look slowly round at her, then bend back to the mealies, slowly, as if in protest. She did not know that Dick made a habit of calling a general rest of five minutes each hour; he had learned they worked better for it; it seemed to her an insolence directed against her authority over them when they stopped, without permission, to straighten their backs and wipe off the sweat. She kept them at it until sundown, and went back to the house satisfied with herself, not even tired.

She was exhilarated and light-limbed, and swung the sambok jauntily on her wrist.

CHAPTER 8

...

Dick, unable to stand the dirt and bad food any longer, said he would bring up one of the farm natives for training as a houseboy. When the man presented himself at the door, Mary recognized him as the one she had struck with the whip over the face two years before. She saw the scar on his cheek, a thin, darker weal across the black skin. She stood irresolute in the doorway, while he waited outside, his eyes bent down. But the thought of sending him back to the lands and waiting for somebody else to be sent up; even this postponement tired her. She told him to come in.

That morning, because of some inward prohibition she did not try to explain, she could not work with him as was usually her custom on these occasions. She left him alone in the kitchen; and when Dick came up, said, 'Isn't there another boy that will do?'

Dick, without looking at her, and eating as he always did these days, in great gulps, as if there was no time, said: 'He's the best I could find. Why?' He sounded hostile.

She had never told him about the incident of the whip, for fear of his anger. She said: 'He doesn't seem a very good type to me. ' As she spoke she saw that look of exasperation grow on his face, and added hastily, 'But he will do, I suppose. '

Dick said: 'He is clean and willing. He's one of the best boys I have ever had. What more do you want?' He spoke brusquely, almost with brutality. Without speaking again he went out. And so the native stayed.

She began on the usual routine of instruction, as cold- voiced and methodical as always, but with a difference. She was unable to treat this boy as she had treated all the others, for always, at the back of her mind, was that moment of fear she had known just after she had hithim and thought he would attack her. She felt uneasy in his presence. Yet his demeanour was the same as in all the others; there was nothing in his attitude to suggest that he remembered the incident. He was silent, dogged and patient under her stream of explanations and orders. His eyes he always kept lowered, as if afraid to look at her. But she

could not forget it, even if he had; and there was a subtle difference in the way
she spoke to him. She was as impersonal as she knew how to be; so impersonal
that her voice was free, for a while even of the usual undertone of irritation.

She used to sit quite still, watching him work. The powerful, broad-built
body fascinated her. She had given him white shorts and shirts to wear in the
house, that had been used by her former servants. They were too small for him;
as he swept or scrubbed or bent to the stove, his muscles bulged and filled out
the thin material of the sleeves until it seemed they would split. He appeared
even taller and broader than he was, because of the littleness of the house.

He was a good worker, one of the best she had had. She used to go round
after him trying to find things that he had left undone, but she seldom did. So,
after a while, she became used to him, and the memory of that whip slashing
across his face faded. She treated him as it was natural to her to treat natives,
and her voice grew sharp and irritated. But he did not answer back, and accepted
her often unjust rebukes without even lifting his eyes off the ground. He might
have made up his mind to be as neutral as he knew how.

And so they proceeded, with everything apparently as it should be, a good
routine established, that left her free to do nothing. But she was not quite as
indifferent as she had been.

By ten in the morning, after he had brought her tea, he would go off to the
back behind the chicken-runs under a big tree, carrying a tin of hot water; and
from the house she sometimes caught a glimpse of him bending over it, sluicing
himself, naked from the waist up. But she tried not to be around when it was
time for his bath. After this was over, he came back to the kitchen and remained
quite still, leaning against the back wall in the sun, apparently thinking of
nothing. He might have been asleep. Not until it was time to prepare lunch did
he start work again. It annoyed her to think of him standing idly there, immobile
and silent for hours, under the unshaded force of the sun which seemed not to
affect him. There was nothing she could do about it, though instead of sinking
into a dreary lethargy that was almost sleep, she would rack her brains to think
of work she could give him.

One morning she went out to the fowl-runs, which she often forgot to do
these days; and when she had finished a perfunctory inspection of the nesting-
boxes, and her basket was filled with eggs, she was arrested by the sight of the
native under the trees a few yards off. He was rubbing his thick neck with soap,

and the white lather was startlingly white against the black skin. He had his back to her. As she looked, he turned, by some chance, or because he sensed her presence, and saw her. She had forgotten it was his time to wash.

A white person may look at a native, who is no better than a dog. Therefore she was annoyed when he stopped and stood upright, waiting for her to go, his body expressing his resentment of her presence there. She was furious that perhaps he believed she was there on purpose; this thought, of course, was not conscious; it would be too much presumption, such unspeakable cheek for him to imagine such a thing, that she would not allow it to enter her mind; but the attitude of his still body as he watched her across the bushes between them, the expression on his face, filled her with anger. She felt the same impulse that had once made her bring down the lash across his face. Deliberately she turned away, loitered round the chicken-runs, and threw out handfuls of grain; and then slowly stooped out through the low wire door. She did not look at him again; but knew he was standing there, a dark shape, quite motionless, seen out of the corner of her eye. She went back to the house, for the first time in many months jerked clean out of her apathy, for the first time in months seeing the ground she walked over, and feeling the pressure of the sun against the back of her bare neck, the sharp hot stones pressing up under her soles.

She heard a strange angry muttering, and realized she was talking to herself, out aloud, as she walked. She clapped her hand over her mouth, and shook her head to clear it; but by the time that Moses had come back into the kitchen, and she heard his footsteps, she was sitting in the front room rigid with an hysterical emotion; when she remembered the dark resentful look of that native as he stood waiting for her to leave, she felt as if she had put her hand on a snake. Impelled by a violent nervous reaction she went to the kitchen, where he stood in clean clothes, putting away his washing things. Remembering that thick black neck with the lather frothing whitely on it, the powerful back stooping over the bucket, was like a goad to her. And she was beyond reflecting that her anger, her hysteria, was over nothing, nothing that she could explain. What had happened was that the formal pattern of black-and- white, mistress-and-servant, had been broken by the personal relation; and when a white man in Africa by accident looks into the eyes of a native and sees the human being (which it is his chief preoccupation to avoid), his sense of guilt, which he denies, fumes up in resentment and he brings down the whip. She felt that she must do something, and at once, to restore her poise. Her eyes happened to fall on a candle-box under the table, where the scrubbing brushes and soap were kept, and she said to the boy:'Scrub this floor.' She was shocked when she heard her own voice, for she had not known she was going to speak. As one feels when in an ordinary social conversation, kept tranquil by banalities, some person makes a remark that strikes below the surface, perhaps in error letting slip what he really thinks of you, and the shock sweeps one off one's balance, causing a nervous giggle or some stupid sentence that makes everyone present uncomfortable, so she felt: she had lost her balance; she had no control over her actions.

'I scrubbed it this morning,' said the native slowly, looking at her, his eyes smouldering.

She said,'I said scrub it. Do it at once.' Her voice rose on the last words. For a moment they stared at each other, exposing their hatred; then his eyes dropped, and she turned and went out, slamming the door behind her.

Soon she heard the sound of the wet brush over the floor. She collapsed on the sofa again, as weak as if she had been ill. She was familiar with her own storms of irrational anger, but she had never known one as devastating as this. She was shaking, the blood throbbed in her ears, her mouth was dry. After a while, more composed, she went to the bedroom to fetch herself some water; she did not want to face the native Moses.

Yet, later, she forced herself to rise and go to the kitchen; and, standing in the doorway, surveyed the wet streaked floor as if she had truly come to inspect it. He stood immobile just outside the door, as usual, gazing out to the clump of boulders where the euphorbia tree stuck out its grey-green, fleshy arms into vivid blue sky. She made a show of peering behind cupboards, and then said,'It is time to lay the table.'

He turned, and began laying out glass and linen, with slow and rather clumsy movements, his great black hands moving among the small instruments. Every movement he made irritated her. She sat tensed, wound up, her hands clenched. When he went out, she relaxed a little, as if a pressure had been taken off her. The table was finished. She went to inspect it; but everything was in its right place. But she picked up a glass and took it to the back room.

'Look at this glass, Moses,' she commanded.

He came across and looked at it politely: it was only an appearance of looking, for he had already taken it from her to wash it. There was a trace of

white fluff from the drying towel down one side. He filled the sink with water,
and whisked in soapsuds, just as she had taught him, and washed the glass while
she watched. When it was dry she took it from him and returned to the other
room.

　　She imagined him again standing silent at the door in the sun, looking at
nothing, and she could have screamed or thrown a glass across the room to smash
on the wall. But there was nothing, absolutely nothing, that she could give him
to do. She began a quiet prowl through the house: everything, though shabby
and faded, was clean and in its place. That bed, the great connubial bed which
she had always hated, was smooth and uncrumpled, the coverlets turned back at
the corners in a brave imitation of the inviting beds in modern catalogues. The
sight of it gritted on her, reminding her of the hated contact in the nights with
Dick's weary muscular body, to which she had never been able to accustom
herself. She turned from it, clenching her hands, and saw her face suddenly in
the mirror. Faded, tousled, her lips narrowed in anger, her eyes hot, her face
puffed and blotched with red, she hardly recognized herself. She gazed, shocked
and pitiful; and then she cried, weeping hysterically in great shuddering gasps,
trying to smother the sound for fear the native at the back might hear her. She
cried for some time; then, as she lifted her eyes to dry them, saw the clock. Dick
would be home soon. Fear of his seeing her in this state stilled her convulsing
muscles. She bathed her face, combed her hair, powdered the dark creased skin
round the eyes.

　　That meal was as silent as all their meals were, these days. He saw her
reddened, crumpled face, and her blood-suffused eyes, and knew what was
wrong. It was always because of rows with her servants that she cried. But he
was weary and disappointed; it had been quite a long time since the last fight,
and he had imagined she might be getting over her weakness. She ate nothing,
keeping her head bent down; and the native moved about the table through the
meal like an automaton, his body serving them because it must, his mind not
there. But the thought of this man's efficiency, and the sight of Mary's swollen
face, suddenly goaded Dick. He said, when the native was out of the room:
'Mary, you must keep this boy. He is the best we have ever had. ' She did not
look up, even then, but remained, quite still, apparently deaf. Dick saw that her
thin,sun-crinkled hand was shaking. He said again, after a silence, his voice
ugly with hostility: 'I can't stand any more changing of servants. I've had

enough. I'm warning you, Mary. ' And again she did not reply; she was weak
with the tears and anger of the morning, and afraid that if she opened her mouth
she might weep anew. He looked at her in some astonishment, for as a rule she
would have snapped back some complaint of theft, or bad behaviour. He had
been braced to meet it. Her continued silence, which was pure opposition, drove
him to insist on an assent from her. 'Mary,' he said, like a superior to a
subordinate,'did you hear what I said?' 'Yes,' she said at last sullenly, with
difficulty.

When he left, she went immediately to the bedroom so as to avoid the sight
of the native clearing the table, and slept away four hours of unendurable time.

CHAPTER 11

Mary awoke suddenly, as if some big elbow had nudged her. It was still
night. Dick lay asleep beside her. The window was creaking on its hinges, and
when she looked into the square of darkness, she could see stars moving and
flashing among the tree boughs. The sky was luminous; but there was an
undertone of cold grey; the stars were bright; but with a weak gleam. Inside the
room the furniture was growing into light. She could see a glimmer that was the
surface of the mirror. Then a cock crowed in the compound, and a dozen shrill
voices answered for the dawn. Daylight? Moonlight? Both. Both mingled
together, and it would be sunrise in half an hour. She yawned, settled back on
her lumpy pillows, and stretched out her limbs. She thought, that usually her
wakings were grey and struggling, a reluctant upheaval of her body from the
bed's refuge. To-day she was vastly peaceful and rested. Her mind was clear,
and her body comfortable. Cradled in ease she locked her hands behind her head
and stared at the darkness that held the familiar walls and furniture. Lazily she
created the room in imagination, placing each cupboard and chair; then moved
beyond the house, hollowing it out of the night in her mind as if her hand cupped
it. At last, from a height, she looked down on the building set among the bush-
and was filled with a regretful, peaceable tenderness. It seemed as if she were
holding that immensely pitiful thing, the farm with its inhabitants, in the hollow
of her hand, which curved round it to shut out the gaze of the cruelly critical
world. And she felt as if she must weep. She could feel the tears running down
her cheeks, which stung rawly, and she put up her fingers to touch the skin.
The contact of rough finger with roughened flesh restored her to herself. She

continued to cry, but hopelessly for herself, though still from a forgiving distance. Then Dick stirred and woke, sitting up with a jerk. She knew he was turning his head this way and that, in the dark, listening; and she lay quite still. She felt his hand touch her cheek diffidently. But that diffident, apologetic touch annoyed her, and she jerked her head back. 'What is the matter, Mary?'

'Nothing,' she replied.

'Are you sorry you are leaving?'

The question seemed to her ridiculous; nothing to do with her at all. And she did not want to think of Dick, except with that distant and impersonal pity. Could he not let her live in this last short moment of peace? 'Go to sleep,' she said. 'It's not morning yet. '

Her voice seemed to him normal; even her rejection of him was too familiar a thing to waken him thoroughly. In a minute he was asleep again, stretched out as if he had never stirred. But now she could not forget him: she knew he was lying there beside her, could feel his limbs sprawled against hers. She raised herself up, feeling bitter against him, who never left her in peace. Always he was there, a torturing reminder of what she had to forget in order to remain herself. She sat up straight, resting her head on locked hands, conscious again, as she had not been for a very long time, of that feeling of strain, as if she were stretched taut between two immovable poles. She rocked herself slowly back and forth, with a dim, mindless movement, trying to sink back into that region of her mind where Dick did not exist. For it had been a choice, if one could call such an inevitable thing a choice, between Dick and the other, and Dick was destroyed long ago. 'Poor Dick,' she said tranquilly, at last, from her recovered distance from him; and a flicker of terror touched her, an intimation of that terror which would later engulf her. She knew it: she felt transparent, clairvoyant, containing all things. But not Dick. No; she looked at him, a huddle under blankets, his face a pallid glimmer in the growing dawn. It crept in from the low square of window, and with it came a warm, airless breeze. 'Poor Dick,' she said, for the last time, and did not think of him again.

She got out of bed and stood by the window. The low sill cut across her thighs. If she bent forward and down, she could touch the ground, which seemed to rise up outside, stretching to the trees. The stars were gone. The sky was colourless and immense. The veld was dim. Everything was on the verge of colour. There was a hint of green in the curve of a leaf, a shine in the sky that was almost blue, and the clear starred outline of the poinsettia flowers suggested the hardness of scarlet.

Slowly, across the sky, spread a marvellous pink flush, and the trees lifted to meet it, becoming tinged with pink and bending out into the dawn she saw the world had put on the colour and shape. The night was over. When the sun rose, she thought, her moment would be over, this marvellous moment of peace and forgiveness granted her by a forgiving God. She crouched against the sill, cramped and motionless, clutching on to her last remnants of happiness, her mind as clear as the sky itself. But why, this last morning, had she woken peacefully from a good sleep, and not, as usually, from one of those ugly dreams that seemed to carry over into the day, so that there sometimes seemed no division between the horrors of the night and of the day? Why should she be standing there, watching the sunrise, as if the world were being created afresh for her, feeling this wonderful rooted joy? She was inside a bubble of fresh light and colour, of brilliant sound and birdsong. All around the trees were filled with shrilling birds, that sounded her own happiness and chorused it to the sky. As light as a blown feather she left the room and went outside to the verandah. It was so beautiful: so beautiful she could hardly bear the wonderful flushed sky, with red streaked and hazed against the intense blue; the beautiful still trees, with their load of singing birds; the vivid starry poinsettias cutting into the air with jagged scarlet.

The red spread out from the centre of the sky, seemed to tinge the smoke haze over the kopjes, and to light the trees with a hot sulphurous yellow. The world was a miracle of colour, and all for her, all for her! She could have wept with release and lighthearted joy. And then she heard it, that sound she could never bear, the first cicada beginning to shrill somewhere in the trees. It was the sound of the sun itself, and how she hated the sun! It was rising now; there was sullen red curve behind a black rock, and a beam of hot yellow light shot up into the blue. One after another the cicadas joined the steady shrilling noise, so that now there were no birds to be heard, and that insistent low screaming seemed to her to be the noise of the sun, whirling on its hot core, the sound of the harsh brazen light, the sound of thegathering heat. Her head was beginning to throb, her shoulders to ache. The dull red disc jerked suddenly up over the kopjes, and the colour ebbed from the sky; a lean, sunflattened landscape stretched before her, dun- coloured, brown and olive-green, and the smoke-haze was everywhere, lingering in the trees and obscuring the hills. The sky shut down over her, with thick yellowish walls of smoke growing up to meet it. The world was small, shut in a room of heat and haze and light.

Shuddering, she seemed to wake, looking about her, touching dry lips with her tongue. She was leaning pressed back against the thin brick wall, her hands extended, palms upwards, warding off the day's coming. She let them fall, moved away from the wall, and looked over her shoulder at where she had been crouching. 'There,' she said aloud, 'it will be there.' And the sound of her own voice, calm, prophetic, fatal, fell on her ears like a warning. She went indoors, pressing her hands to her head, to evade that evil verandah.

Dick was awake, just pulling on his trousers to go and beat the gong. She stood, waiting for the clanging noise. It came, and with it the terror. Somewhere he stood, listening for the gong that announced the last day. She could see him clearly. He was standing under a tree somewhere, leaning back against it, his eyes fixed on the house, waiting. She knew it. But not yet, she said to herself, it would not be quite yet; she had the day in front of her.

'Get dressed, Mary,' said Dick, in a quiet urgent voice. Repeated, it penetrated her brain, and she obediently went into the bedroom and began to put on her clothes. Fumbling for buttons she paused, went to the door, about to call for Moses, who would do up her clothes, hand her the brush, tie up her hair, and take the responsibility for her so that she need not think for herself. Through the curtain she saw Dick and that young man sitting at the table, eating a meal she had not prepared. She remembered that Moses had gone: relief flooded her. She would be alone, alone all day. She could concentrate on the one thing left that mattered to her now. She saw Dick rise, with a grieved face, pull across the curtain; she understood that she had been standing in the doorway in her underclothes, in the full sight of that young man. Shame flushed her; but before the saving resentment could countermand the shame, she forgot Dick and the young man. She finished dressing, slowly, slowly, with long pauses between each movement-for had she not all day? - and at last went outside. The table was littered with dishes; the men had gone off to work. A big dish was caked with thick white grease; she thought that they must have been gone some time.

Listlessly she stacked the plates, carried them into the kitchen, filled the sink with water, and then forgot what she was doing. Standing still, her hands hanging idly, she thought, 'somewhere outside, among the trees, he is waiting. ' She rushed about the house in a panic, shutting the doors, and all the windows, and collapsed at last on the sofa, like a hare crouching in a tuft of grass, watching the dogs come nearer. But it was no use waiting now: her mind told her she had all day, until the night came. Again, for a brief space, her brain cleared.

What was it all about? she wondered dully, pressing her fingers against her eyes so that they gushed jets of yellow light. I don't understand, she said, I don't understand. . . .

. . .

Ⅳ. Questions for Thinking

1. "When natives steal, murder or rape, that is the feeling white people have. " How does this statement reveal the relationship between the white and the black?

2. "She needed to think of Dick, the man to whom she was irrevocably married, as a person on his own account, a success from his own efforts. When she saw him weak and goal-less, and pitiful, she hated him, and the hate turned in on herself. She needed a man stronger than herself, and she was trying to create one out of Dick. "
   How does this quote explain the relationship between man and woman?

3. Mary Turner's tragedy lies to some extent in her failure of grasping her identity, as she reverses the social, racial and cultural orders of her society though unconsciously. Do you agree with this statement? Why?

4. Doris Lessing once said, "We, as a society, can't tolerate very much difference. " Explain your understanding of the point. Are Mary and Dick also difference that cannot be tolerated by the white community?

5. How does the novel support the dictum "the personal is the political"?

6. " Women have an extraordinary ability to withdraw from the sexual relationship, to immunize themselves against it, in such a way that their men can be left feeling let down and insulted without having anything tangible to complain of. " How does this quote explain women's understanding of their sexual power?

7. "Long before the murder marked them out, people spoke of the Turners in the hard, careless voices reserved for misfits, outlaws and the self-exiled. The

Turners were disliked, though few of their neighbors had ever met them, or even seen them in the distance. Yet what was there to dislike? They simply 'kept themselves to themselves'; that was all. "

Explain the reasons why the Turners are considered as misfits, outlaws and self-exiled.

8. List the possible causes to Mary's tragic ending.

9. "To live with the color bar in all its nuances and implications means closing one's mind to many things, if one intends to remain an accepted member of society. But, in the interval, there would be a few brief moments when he would see the thing clearly, and understand that it was "white civilization" fighting to defend itself that had been implicit in the attitude of Charlie Slatter and the Sergeant, 'white civilization' which will never, never admit that a white person, and most particularly, a white woman, can have a human relationship, whether for good or for evil, with a black person. For once it admits that, it crashes, and nothing can save it. "

Explain why white civilization can never admit the connection between a white woman and a black man.

10. "It is by the failures and misfits of a civilization that one can best judge its weaknesses. " How does Lessing reveal the weaknesses of the civilization?

V. Guidance for Appreciation

Since its publication, *The Grass is Singing* has attracted much attention from academic world. It is mainly studied from five perspectives: postcolonialism, feminism, psychoanalysis, ecocriticism, and Foucault's discourse theory. Since it is a story about being female in a conventional man's world and white in black Africa, we mainly discuss the novel from perspectives of feminism and postcolonialism.

The novel has been hailed for the commitment to antiracism for its revelation of the maltreatment of the black. It's critique of injustice and racism cannot be ignored.

The novel is set in Southern Rhodesia, which was colonized by the British colonizers. In a segregated society, the oppressed black majority, including Moses, are the colonized, while the white, including the Turners, are the colonizers and the latter treats the former as brutes. The white regarded themselves superior over the black who merely seems to be animals and tools to them. They make them work hard as animals regardless of hot sun or strong storm. The black may even be slashed if he stops for a while or complain a little, so black people have to be submissive.

Mary's attitudes toward the black servants reveals the power of colonial discourse. Discourse creates and upholds power structure and controls people by stipulating what is true and what should be knowledge. In a colonized society, the white colonizers control discourse. And they can define truth and knowledge. Mary's knowledge about the black is from the controlled discourse. Her distaste, hatred, and abuse for the black is based on her misunderstanding of the black personally and culturally.

But there are also independent black people, such as Moses, who are different from normal black people. He is as strong as other black people physically, but he differs from other black people spiritually. Even the Turners find that Moses should be so intelligent, rational and compassionate. The collapse of colonization needs people like Moses. To a great extent, we can see Doris Lessing's idea of anti-colonialism and Mary's death may be a proof of it.

Another point to discuss from the postcolonial perspective is the situation of the white. Racialism offers the white great superiority, but at the same time, it restricts how British colonizers are allowed to live. If they cannot shoulder the responsibility, they will be excluded from the white community. "The first law of white South Africa, which is: 'Thou shalt not let your fellow whites sink lower than a certain point; because if you do, the nigger will see he is as good as you are'" (210). As white colonizers, the Turners should be successful and dignified as power structure prescripts and they should live up to the expectation put on them. However, they lead a miserable and humble life almost as local black people. So other white colonizers naturally want to exclude them from their power structure so as to keep it strong. The novel reveals that "poorwhitedom" is for the Rhodesians a dangerous character flaw linked to degeneration and miscegenation.

The third point to discuss from the postcolonial perspective is interracial mixing between white women and black men, which is considered as a taboo in apartheid South Africa. Black men are regarded as "black peril". The tragedy of Mary is mainly caused by the connection between Mary and Moses which breaks the great taboo of the colour bar.

Many critics consider this novel as a novel of initiation, describing a young woman who has failed in discovering her own values in the geographical, social, economic, political, and psychological world. Examining her tragedy, we can find the reasons to her failure of achieving self-awareness and autonomy.

Born in family struggling for sheer economic survival, tired of her parents' endless quarrels and family violence, Mary grows up to be an emotional cripple, afraid of intimacy, preferring the "impersonality" of a solitary existence. She has no faith in marriage. Later, when she is able to have a stable job to be independent, she enjoys life as much as she can and pays no attention to love relationship. In her unconscious world, she doesn't believe in marriage, even avoid this kind of relationship. Unfortunately, she is badly hurt by her friends' malicious gossip. At this time, her friends' words represents rules, traditions and taboos of society. To be thirty and single in a white colonialist society is almost a form of heresy. Mary is forced into marriage by society.

Later, Mary has to marry someone because of the gossip. So Mary chooses a haste marriage with Dick to escape pressure from patriarchal society. But to her great disappointment, Dick cannot fulfill her dream physically and spiritually about a happy marriage life. Instead, Dick hopes that the can stop complaining and dreaming in order to play her role as a submissive wife. Though Mary tries to restore her past life several times, it is in vain. Dick, Slatter and Tony work as guardians of patriarchal society successively. Apart from men presenting themselves as defenders of patriarchy, women also act as keepers of it. To some extent, women work as accomplice to patriarchal society though they are victims at the same time. Patriarchy is so powerful and destructive that it even achieve "interior colonization" of women by men.

Their sexual relationship is a disaster from the beginning. None of them has the ability to share any intimacy. Dick unintentionally makes her a sexual object by idealizing her. Mary yields to him in a martyr-like way, with no feelings.

The economic difficulty makes their family life even more harsh. Mary finds herself lonely and bored. Because of poverty, Dick even denies to give her a baby. Reality of life is so tough that Mary is disillusioned by life step by step and her mental health also deteriorates gradually.

The appearance of Moses fulfills her need for warmth, care and communication which Dick has failed to provide. Moses' appearance lights her up and she is attracted by this intelligent native.

But she is afraid of the black due to the cultural training she receives. She clearly knows that this kind of relationship is forbidden. She experiences a conflict between sexual attraction and racial repulsion. While it is never explicitly stated, the novel suggests that Mary succumbs to Moses sexually just as her mental faculties begin to disintegrate.

To Lessing, the rivalry and conflict between men and women in marriage are not isolated psychological or sexual problems. They reflect complex economic, political, and philosophical relationships based on power and its effect on individuals and groups. Thus marriage is a microcosm of society.

Ⅵ. **Further Reading**

1. Aghazadeh, Sima. Sexual-Political Colonialism and Failure of Individuation in Doris Lessing's *The Grass is Singing*[J]. Journal of International Women's Studies. 2011, Vol. 12(1) :107-121.

2. Bloom, Horald. Doris Lessing[M]. Philadelphia: Chelsea House Publishers, 2003.

3. Brazil, Kevin, David Sergeant and Tom Sperlinger. Doris Lessing and the Forming of History[M]. Edinburgh: Edinburgh University Press, 2016.

4. Ridout, Alice and Susan Watkins. Doris Lessing: Border Crossings[M]. New York: Continuum, 2009.

5. Rowe, Margaret Moan. Women Writers: Doris Lessing[M]. Houndmills: The MacMillan Press Ltd, 1984.

6. 陈璟霞. 多丽丝·莱辛的殖民模糊性:对莱辛作品中的殖民比喻的研究[M]. 北京:中国人民大学出版社, 2007.

7. 胡勤. 审视分裂的文明:多丽丝·莱辛小说艺术研究[M]. 桂林:广西师范大学出版社, 2012.

8. 蒋花. 压抑的自我,异化的人生:多丽斯·莱辛非洲小说研究[M]. 上海:上海外语教育出版社, 2009.

9. 王丽丽. 多丽丝·莱辛的艺术和哲学思想研究[M]. 北京:社会科学文献出版社, 2007.

10. 杨颖,杨巍,唐霞. 多丽丝·莱辛作品家庭伦理思想研究[M]. 北京:中国文史出版社, 2014.

11. 张建春. 多丽丝·莱辛作品的生态女性主要批评研究[M]. 长春:吉林大学出版社, 2017.

Chapter 7

William Golding: *Lord of the Flies*
Sociopolitical Reading and Dystopia

I. Introduction to the Author

William Gerald Golding (19 September 1911—19 June 1993) was a British novelist, playwright, and poet. Best famous for his novel *Lord of the Flies*, he was awarded the Booker Prize for literature in 1980 for his novel *Rites of Passage*, the prestigious Nobel Prize in literature in 1983, and the James Tait Black Memorial Prize in 1979.

William Gerald Golding was born in Cornwall to Alec Golding and Mildred Golding. His father Alec was a science teacher and later became Senior Master at Marlborough Grammar School. His father's rationalist belief exerted overwhelming influence on him.

In 1930, Golding entered Brasenose College, Oxford where he switched to English Literature after two years study in science. At Oxford he wrote poetry and published some of them, which did not receive much attention. He graduated from Oxford with a Bachelor of Arts in English and a diploma in education.

After leaving Oxford in 1935, Golding moved to London, writing, acting and producing for a small and non-commercial theatre. In 1939, Golding took a teaching position at Bishop Wordsworth's School in Salisbury. The same year, he married Ann Brookfield, with whom he had two children.

Golding joined the Royal Navy in 1940, serving throughout the rest of the Second World War. He took part in the D-Day landings in Normandy, and rose to the rank of lieutenant. After the war, he returned to teach in Bishop Wordsworth's school. His reflection on his World War II experience brought out the novel *Lord of the Flies*, which was published by Faber &. Faber in 1954 after it had been rejected by twenty-one publishers. *The Inheritors* followed in 1955, *Pincher Martin* in 1956, and *Free Fall* in 1959.

Golding resigned from his position as a schoolmaster in 1961, devoting his most time to writing. In his life, he has published 13 novels, namely *Lord of the Flies* (1954), *The Inheritors* (1955), *Pincher Martin* (1956), *Free Fall* (1959), *The Spire* (1964), *The Pyramid* (1967), *The Scorpion God* (1971), *Darkness Visible* (1979), *The Paper Men* (1984), *Rites of Passage* (1980), *Close Quarters* (1987), *Fire Down Below* (1989), and *The Double Tongue* (posthumous publication 1995).

His three nonfiction collections, *The Hot Gates and Other Occasional Pieces* (1965), *A Moving Target* (1982), and *An Egyptian Journal* (1985) included his essays, nonfiction and travel notes. William Golding's works are popular in the world and so far have been translated into 35 languages. For his achievements in literature, he was elected a fellow of the Royal Society of Literature in 1955 and made a CBE (Commander of the British Empire) in 1966.

Golding's novels are rich in meaning and are broadly integrated into classical literature, mythology, Christian culture and symbolism. The theme of his work is generally related to the darkness of evil, but his novel also expresses a dim optimism. His first novel, *Lord of the Flies* (1954), highlighted the theme that he had been constantly discussing: the fighting between mankind's brutality and rationality. The Nobel Prize in Literature 1983 was awarded to William Golding "for his novels which, with the perspicuity of realistic narrative art and the diversity and universality of myth, illuminate the human condition in the world of today."

II. Introduction to *Lord of the Flies*

Lord of the Flies is the masterpiece of William Golding, Nobel Prize winner in 1983. It was written in 1954, in the atmosphere of the Cold War. It is a result of Golding's reflection on his experience of World War II and his concerns on the sociological and ideological problems.

The story happens in an imagined nuclear war. A group of British boys experience an airplane crash in a withdrawal and find themselves on a tropical island without an adult. The ages of the boys different from six to twelve. How to survive on the island is the first task before them. Ralph and Piggy find a conch shell on the beach and they use it as a horn to summon the other boys. In the first assembly of the boys, they elect Ralph as their leader. Some rules have been established including the right for speech, the obligation for sanitation and the maintenance of a signal fire. Ralph also makes a signal fire the group's great priority, hoping that a passing ship will see the smoke signal and rescue them. Jack is appointed to be in charge of the boys who will hunt food for the entire group.

The paradise-like island offers the boys abundant food. The boys succeed in getting fire through the lenses of Piggy's eyeglasses. Soon, without adult's guidance and supervision, the boys spend more time playing than fulfilling their duties. Problems and conflicts arise. The signal fire has burned out because of their negligence, which kills their chance of being saved when a ship passes by one day. Jack challenges Ralph's authority by leading a group of boys into hunting. Fears also spread among boys that there is some sort of beast or monster lurking on the island. Sam and Eric mistake the enormous silhouette of the parachute of a fallen pilot for the monster, which multiplies the fears.

The conflict between Ralph and Jack also reaches a point that they split into two opposing groups. Jack, together with his hunters, establishes another camp. Attracted by the protection Jack's ferocity seems to provide and the meat the hunters can get, more and more boys join Jack's group. The boys play the role of savages: putting on camouflaging face paint, hunting, and performing ritualistic tribal dances. Eventually, Jack's group actually kills a pig, puts the pig's head on a stick as an offering to the beast.

Only Simon has the courage to find out the mystery of the beast. When he climbs to the mountain top and finds that the monster is dead body of a pilot, he rushes down to bring the news to the other boys. However, the boys are in the wild and violent dance, celebrating the hunting. Simon is mistaken by the boys for the monster and killed with their bare hands and teeth.

The following morning when Ralph and Piggy are still mourning the death of Simon, Jack's followers attack them and steal Piggy's glasses. When Ralph and his small group goes to Jack's camp to get back the glasses. Roger rolls a boulder down the mountain, killing Piggy and shattering the conch shell. Jack even tries to kill Ralph, but Ralph escapes.

Jack orders his followers to round up Ralph. In order to get Ralph out of hiding, Jack even has the other boys ignite the forest. Ralph is forced out of the forest onto the beach, when suddenly he looks up and sees a British naval officer standing over him. Behind him, the paradise-like island has been turned into nothing less than purgatory.

The novel *Lord of the Flies* has been adapted into movies. A black and white version was made by Home Vision Cinema in 1963. A colored version came out in 1990 by Columbia Pictures.

Ⅲ. Excerpt

CHAPTER 4

. . .

A procession had appeared, far down among the pink stones that lay near the water's edge. Some of the boys wore black caps but otherwise they were almost naked. They lifted sticks in the air together whenever they came to an easy patch. They were chanting, something to do with the bundle that the errant twins carried so carefully. Ralph picked out Jack easily, even at that distance, tall, red-haired, and inevitably leading the procession.

Simon looked now, from Ralph to Jack, as he had looked from Ralph to the horizon, and what he saw seemed to make him afraid. Ralph said nothing more, but waited while the procession came nearer. The chant was audible but at that distance still wordless. Behind Jack walked the twins, carrying a great stake on their shoulders. The gutted carcass of a pig swung from the stake, swinging heavily as the twins toiled over the uneven ground. The pig's head hung down with gaping neck and seemed to search for something on the ground. At last the words of the chant floated up to them, across the bowl of blackened wood and ashes.

"Kill the pig. Cut her throat. Spill her blood. "

Yet as the words became audible, the procession reached the steepest part of the mountain, and in a minute or two the chant had died away. Piggy sniveled and Simon shushed him quickly as though he had spoken too loudly in church.

Jack, his face smeared with clays, reached the top first and hailed Ralph excitedly, with lifted spear.

"Look! We've killed a pig—we stole up on them—we got in a circle—"

Voices broke in from the hunters.

"We got in a circle—"

"We crept up—"

"The pig squealed—"

The twins stood with the pig swinging between them, dropping black gouts on the rock. They seemed to share one wide, ecstatic grin. Jack had too many things to tell Ralph at once. Instead, he danced a step or two, then remembered his dignity and stood still, grinning. He noticed blood on his hands and grimaced distastefully, looked for something on which to clean them, then wiped them on his shorts and laughed.

Ralph spoke.

"You let the fire go out."

Jack checked, vaguely irritated by this irrelevance but too happy to let it worry him.

"We can light the fire again. You should have been with us, Ralph. We had a smashing time. The twins got knocked over—"

"We hit the pig—"

"—I fell on top—"

"I cut the pig's throat," said Jack, proudly, and yet twitched as he said it. "Can I borrow yours, Ralph, to make a nick in the hilt?"

The boys chattered and danced. The twins continued to grin.

"There was lashings of blood," said Jack, laughing and shuddering, "you should have seen it!"

"We'll go hunting every day—"

Ralph spoke again, hoarsely. He had not moved.

"You let the fire go out."

This repetition made Jack uneasy. He looked at the twins and then back at Ralph.

"We had to have them in the hunt," he said, "or there wouldn't have been enough for a ring."

He flushed, conscious of a fault.

"The fire's only been out an hour or two. We can light up again—"

He noticed Ralph's scarred nakedness, and the sombre silence of all four of them. He sought, charitable in his happiness, to include them in the thing that had happened. His mind was crowded with memories; memories of the knowledge that had come to them when they closed in on the struggling pig, knowledge that they had outwitted a living thing, imposed their will upon it, taken away its life like a long satisfying drink.

He spread his arms wide.

"You should have seen the blood!"

The hunters were more silent now, but at this they buzzed again. Ralph flung back his hair. One arm pointed at the empty horizon. His voice was loud and savage, and struck them into silence.

"There was aship. "

Jack, faced at once with too many awful implications, ducked away from them. He laid a hand on the pig and drew his knife. Ralph brought his arm down, fist clenched, and his voice shook.

"There was a ship. Out there. You said you'd keep the fire going and you let it out!" He took a step toward Jack, who turned and faced him.

"They might have seen us. We might have gone home—"

This was too bitter for Piggy, who forgot his timidity in the agony of his loss. He began to cry out, shrilly:

"You and your blood, Jack Merridew! You and your hunting! We might have gone home—"

Ralph pushed Piggy to one side.

"I was chief, and you were going to do what I said. You talk. But you can' t even build huts—then you go off hunting and let out the fire—"

He turned away, silent for a moment. Then his voice came again on a peak of feeling.

"There was a ship—"

One of the smaller hunters began to wail. The dismal truth was filtering through to everybody. Jack went very red as he hacked and pulled at the pig.

"The job was too much. We needed everyone. "

Ralph turned.

"You could have had everyone when the shelters were finished. But you had to hunt—"

"We needed meat. "

Jack stood up as he said this, the bloodied knife in his hand. The two boys faced each other. There was the brilliant world of hunting, tactics, fierce exhilaration, skill; and there was the world of longing and baffled commonsense. Jack transferred the knife to his left hand and smudged blood over his forehead as he pushed down the plastered hair.

Piggy began again.

"You didn't ought to have let that fire out. You said you'd keep the smoke going—"

This from Piggy, and the wails of agreement from some of the hunters, drove Jack to violence. The bolting look came into his blue eyes. He took a step, and able at last to hit someone, stuck his fist into Piggy's stomach. Piggy sat down with a grunt. Jack stood over him. His voice was vicious with humiliation.

"You would, would you? Fatty!"

Ralph made a step forward and Jack smacked Piggy's head. Piggy's glasses flew off and tinkled on the rocks. Piggy cried out in terror:

"My specs!"

He went crouching and feeling over the rocks but Simon, who got there first, found them for him. Passions beat about Simon on the mountain-top with awful wings.

"One side's broken."

Piggy grabbed and put on the glasses. He looked malevolently at Jack.

"I got to have them specs. Now I only got one eye. Jus' you wait—"

Jack made a move toward Piggy who scrambled away till a great rock lay between them. He thrust his head over the top and glared at Jack through his one flashing glass.

"Now I only got one eye. Just you wait—"

Jack mimicked the whine and scramble.

"Jus' you wait—yah!"

Piggy and the parody were so funny that the hunters began to laugh. Jack felt encouraged. He went on scrambling and the laughter rose to a gale of hysteria. Unwillingly Ralph felt his lips twitch; he was angry with himself for giving way.

He muttered.

"That was a dirty trick."

Jack broke out of his gyration and stood facing Ralph. His words came in a shout.

"All right, all right!"

He looked at Piggy, at the hunters, at Ralph.

"I'm sorry. About the fire, I mean. There. I—"

He drew himself up.

"—I apologize."

The buzz from the hunters was one of admiration at this handsome behavior. Clearly they were of the opinion that Jack had done the decent thing, had put himself in the right by his generous apology and Ralph, obscurely, in the wrong. They waited for an appropriately decent answer.

Yet Ralph's throat refused to pass one. He resented, as an addition to Jack's misbehavior, this verbal trick. The fire was dead, the ship was gone. Could they not see? Anger instead of decency passed his throat.

"That was a dirty trick."

They were silent on the mountain-top while the opaque look appeared in Jack's eyes and passed away.

Ralph's final word was an ingracious mutter.

"All right. Light the fire."

With some positive action before them, a little of the tension died. Ralph said no more, did nothing, stood looking down at the ashes round his feet. Jack was loud and active. He gave orders, sang, whistled, threw remarks at the silent Ralph—remarks that did not need an answer, and therefore could not invite a snub; and still Ralph was silent. No one, not even Jack, would ask him to move and in the end they had to build the fire three yards away and in a place not really as convenient.

So Ralph asserted his chieftainship and could not have chosen a better way if he had thought for days. Against this weapon, so indefinable and so effective, Jack was powerless and raged without knowing why. By the time the pile was built, they were on different sides of a high barrier.

When they had dealt with the fire another crisis arose. Jack had no means of lighting it. Then to his surprise, Ralph went to Piggy and took the glasses from him. Not even Ralph knew how a link between him and Jack had been snapped and fastened elsewhere.

"I'll bring 'em back."

"I'll come too."

Piggy stood behind him, islanded in a sea of meaningless color, while Ralph knelt and focused the glossy spot. Instantly the fire was alight, Piggy held out his hands and grabbed the glasses back.

Before these fantastically attractive flowers of violet and red and yellow, unkindness melted away. They became a circle of boys round a camp fire and even Piggy and Ralph were half-drawn in. Soon some of the boys were rushing down the slope for more wood while Jack hacked the pig. They tried holding the whole carcass on a stake over the fire, but the stake burnt more quickly than the pig roasted. In the end they skewered bits of meat on branches and held them in the flames: and even then almost as much boy was roasted as meat.

Ralph's mouth watered. He meant to refuse meat, but his past diet of fruit and nuts, with an odd crab or fish, gave him too little resistance. He accepted a piece of halfraw meat and gnawed it like a wolf.

Piggy spoke, also dribbling.

"Aren't I having none?"

Jack had meant to leave him in doubt, as an assertion of power; but Piggy by advertising his omission made more cruelty necessary.

"You didn't hunt."

"No more did Ralph," said Piggy wetly, "nor Simon." He amplified. "There isn't more than a ha'porth of meat in a crab."

Ralph stirred uneasily. Simon, sitting between the twins and Piggy, wiped his mouth and shoved his piece of meat over the rocks to Piggy, who grabbed it. The twins giggled and Simon lowered his face in shame.

Then Jack leapt to his feet, slashed off a great hunk of meat, and flung it down at Simon's feet.

"Eat! Damn you!"

He glared at Simon.

"Take it!"

He spun on his heel, center of a bewildered circle of boys.

"I got you meat!"

Numberless and inexpressible frustrations combined to make his rage elemental and awe-inspiring.

"I painted my face—I stole up. Now you eat—all of you—and I—"

Slowly the silence on the mountain-top deepened till the click of the fire and the soft hiss of roasting meat could be heard clearly. Jack looked round for understanding but found only respect. Ralph stood among the ashes of the signal fire, his hands full of meat, saying nothing.

Then at last Maurice broke the silence. He changed the subject to the only one that could bring the majority of them together.

"Where did you find the pig?"

Roger pointed down the unfriendly side. "They were there—by the sea. "

Jack, recovering could not bear to have his story told. He broke in quickly.

"We spread round. I crept, on hands and knees. The spears fell out because they hadn't barbs on. The pig ran away and made an awful noise—"

"It turned back and ran into the circle, bleeding—"

All the boys were talking at once, relieved and excited.

"We closed in—"

The first blow had paralyzed its hind quarters, so then the circle could close in and beat and beat—

"I cut the pig's throat—"

The twins, still sharing their identical grin, jumped up and ran round each other. Then the rest joined in, making pig-dying noises and shouting.

"One for his nob!"

"Give him a fourpenny one!"

Then Maurice pretended to be the pig and ran squealing into the center, and the hunters, circling still, pretended to beat him. As they danced, they sang.

"Kill the pig. Cut her throat. Bash her in. "

Ralph watched them, envious and resentful. Not till they flagged and the chant died away, did he speak.

"I'm calling an assembly. "

One by one, they halted, and stood watching him.

"With the conch. I'm calling a meeting even if we have to go on into the dark. Down on the platform. When I blow it. Now. "

He turned away and walked off, down the mountain.

CHAPTER 8

Piggy looked up miserably from the dawn-pale beach to the dark mountain.

"Are you sure? Really sure, I mean?"

"I told you a dozen times now," said Ralph, "we saw it. "

"D'you think we're safe down here?"

"How the hell should I know?"

Ralph jerked away from him and walked a few paces along the beach. Jack was kneeling and drawing a circular pattern in the sand with his forefinger. Piggy's voice came to them, hushed.

"Are you sure? Really?"

"Go up and see," said Jack contemptuously, "and good riddance. "

"No fear. "

"The beast had teeth," said Ralph, "and big black eyes. "

He shuddered violently. Piggy took off his one round of glass and polished the surface.

"What we going to do?"

Ralph turned toward the platform. The conch glimmered among the trees, a white blob against the place where the sun would rise. He pushed back his mop.

"I don't know. "

He remembered the panic flight down the mountainside. "I don't think we'd ever fight a thing that size, honestly, you know. We'd talk but we wouldn't fight a tiger. We'd hide. Even Jack'ud hide. "

Jack still looked at the sand.

"What about my hunters?"

Simon came stealing out of the shadows by the shelters. Ralph ignored Jack's question. He pointed to the touch of yellow above the sea.

"As long as there's light we're brave enough. But then? And now that thing squats by the fire as though it didn't want us to be rescued—"

He was twisting his hands now, unconsciously. His voice rose.

"So we can't have a signal fire.... We're beaten. "

A point of gold appeared above the sea and at once all the sky lightened.

"What about my hunters?"

"Boys armed with sticks. "

Jack got to his feet. His face was red as he marched away. Piggy put on his one glass and looked at Ralph.

"Now you done it. You been rude about his hunters. "

"Oh shut up!"

The sound of the inexpertly blown conch interrupted them. As though he were serenading the rising sun, Jack went on blowing till the shelters were astir and the hunters crept to the platform and the littluns whimpered as now they so frequently did. Ralph rose obediently, and Piggy, and they went to the platform.

"Talk," said Ralph bitterly, "talk, talk, talk."

He took the conch from Jack.

"This meeting—"

Jack interrupted him.

"I called it."

"If you hadn't called it I should have. You just blew the conch."

"Well, isn't that calling it?"

"Oh, take it! Go on—talk!"

Ralph thrust the conch into Jack's arms and sat down on the trunk.

"I've called an assembly," said Jack, "because of a lot of things. First, you know now, we've seen the beast. We crawled up. We were only a few feet away. The beast sat up and looked at us. I don't know what it does. We don't even know what it is—"

"The beast comes out of the sea—"

"Out of the dark—"

"Trees—"

"Quiet!" shouted Jack. "You, listen. The beast is sitting up there, whatever it is—"

"Perhaps it's waiting—"

"Hunting—"

"Yes, hunting."

"Hunting," said Jack. He remembered his age-old tremors in the forest. "Yes. The beast is a hunter. Only—shut up! The next thing is that we couldn't kill it. And the next is that Ralph said my hunters are no good."

"I never said that!"

"I've got the conch. Ralph thinks you're cowards, running away from the boar and the beast. And that's not all."

There was a kind of sigh on the platform as if everyone knew what was coming. Jack's voice went up, tremulous yet determined, pushing against the uncooperative silence.

"He's like Piggy. He says things like Piggy. He isn't a proper chief."

Jack clutched the conch to him.

"He's a coward himself."

For a moment he paused and then went on.

"On top, when Roger and me went on—he stayed back."

"I went too!"

"After."

The two boys glared at each other through screens of hair.

"I went on too," said Ralph, "then I ran away. So did you."

"Call me a coward then."

Jack turned to the hunters.

"He's not a hunter. He'd never have got us meat. He isn't a prefect and we don't know anything about him. He just gives orders and expects people to obey for nothing. All this talk—"

"All this talk!" shouted Ralph. "Talk, talk! Who wanted it? Who called the meeting?"

Jack turned, red in the face, his chin sunk back. He glowered up under his eyebrows.

"All right then," he said in tones of deep meaning, and menace, "all right."

He held the conch against his chest with one hand and stabbed the air with his index finger.

"Who thinks Ralph oughtn't to be chief?"

He looked expectantly at the boys ranged round, who had frozen. Under the palms there was deadly silence.

"Hands up," said Jack strongly, "whoever wants Ralph not to be chief?"

The silence continued, breathless and heavy and full of shame. Slowly the red drained from Jack's cheeks, then came back with a painful rush. He licked his lips and turned his head at an angle, so that his gaze avoided the embarrassment of linking with another's eye.

"How many think—"

His voice tailed off. The hands that held the conch shook. He cleared his throat, and spoke loudly.

"All right then."

He laid the conch with great care in the grass at his feet. The humiliating tears were running from the corner of each eye.

"I'm not going to play any longer. Not with you."

Most of the boys were looking down now, at the grass or their feet. Jack cleared his throat again.

"I'm not going to be a part of Ralph's lot—"

He looked along the right-hand logs, numbering the hunters that had been a choir.

"I'm going off by myself. He can catch his own pigs. Anyone who wants to hunt when I do can come too. "

He blundered out of the triangle toward the drop to the white sand.

"Jack!"

Jack turned and looked back at Ralph. For a moment he paused and then cried out, high-pitched, enraged.

"—No!"

He leapt down from the platform and ran along the beach, paying no heed to the steady fall of his tears; and until he dived into the forest Ralph watched him.

. . .

CHAPTER 9

Evening was come, not with calm beauty but with the threat of violence.

Jack spoke.

"Give me a drink. "

Henry brought him a shell and he drank, watching Piggy and Ralph over the jagged rim. Power lay in the brown swell of his forearms: authority sat on his shoulder and chattered in his ear like an ape.

"All sit down. "

The boys ranged themselves in rows on the grass before him but Ralph and Piggy stayed a foot lower, standing on the soft sand. Jack ignored them for the moment, turned his mask down to the seated boys and pointed at them with the spear.

"Who's going to join my tribe?"

Ralph made a sudden movement that became a stumble. Some of the boys turned toward him.

"I gave you food," said Jack, "and my hunters will protect you from the beast. Who will join my tribe?"

"I'm chief," said Ralph, "because you chose me. And we were going to keep the fire going. Now you run after food—"

"You ran yourself!" shouted Jack. "Look at that bone in your hands!"

Ralph went crimson.

"I said you were hunters. That was your job. "

Jack ignored him again.

"Who'll join my tribe and have fun?"

"I'm chief," said Ralph tremulously. "And what about the fire? And I've got the conch—"

"You haven't got it with you," said Jack, sneering. "You left it behind. See, clever? And the conch doesn't count at this end of the island—"

All at once the thunder struck. Instead of the dull boom there was a point of impact in the explosion.

"The conch counts here too," said Ralph, "and all over the island."

"What are you going to do about it then?"

Ralph examined the ranks of boys. There was no help in them and he looked away, confused and sweating. Piggy whispered.

"The fire—rescue."

"Who'll join my tribe?"

"I will."

"Me."

"I will."

"I'll blow the conch," said Ralph breathlessly, "and call an assembly."

"We shan't hear it."

Piggy touched Ralph's wrist.

"Come away. There's going to be trouble. And we've had our meat."

There was a blink of bright light beyond the forest and the thunder exploded again so that a littlun started to whine. Big drops of rain fell among them making individual sounds when they struck.

"Going to be a storm," said Ralph, "and you'll have rain like when we dropped here. Who's clever now? Where are your shelters? What are you going to do about that?"

The hunters were looking uneasily at the sky, flinching from the stroke of the drops. A wave of restlessness set the boys swaying and moving aimlessly. The flickering light became brighter and the blows of the thunder were only just bearable. The littluns began to run about, screaming.

Jack leapt on to the sand.

"Do our dance! Come on! Dance!"

He ran stumbling through the thick sand to the open space of rock beyond the fire. Between the flashes of lightning the air was dark and terrible; and the boys followed him, clamorously. Roger became the pig, grunting and charging at

Jack, who side-stepped. The hunters took their spears, the cooks took spits, and the rest clubs of firewood. A circling movement developed and a chant. While Roger mimed the terror of the pig, the littluns ran and jumped on the outside of the circle. Piggy and Ralph, under the threat of the sky, found themselves eager to take a place in this demented but partly secure society. They were glad to touch the brown backs of the fence that hemmed in the terror and made it governable.

"Kill the beast! Cut his throat! Spill his blood!"

The movement became regular while the chant lost its first superficial excitement and began to beat like a steady pulse. Roger ceased to be a pig and became a hunter, so that the center of the ring yawned emptily. Some of the littluns started a ring on their own; and the complementary circles went round and round as though repetition would achieve safety of itself. There was the throb and stamp of a single organism.

The dark sky was shattered by a blue-white scar. An instant later the noise was on them like the blow of a gigantic whip. The chant rose a tone in agony.

"Kill the beast! Cut his throat! Spill his blood!"

Now out of the terror rose another desire, thick, urgent, blind.

"Kill the beast! Cut his throat! Spill his blood!"

Again the blue-white scar jagged above them and the sulphurous explosion beat down. The littluns screamed and blundered about, fleeing from the edge of the forest, and one of them broke the ring of biguns in his terror.

"Him! Him!"

The circle became a horseshoe. A thing was crawling out of the forest. It came darkly, uncertainly. The shrill screaming that rose before the beast was like a pain. The beast stumbled into the horseshoe.

"Kill the beast! Cut his throat! Spill his blood!"

The blue-white scar was constant, the noise unendurable. Simon was crying out something about a dead man on a hill.

"Kill the beast! Cut his throat! Spill his blood! Do him in!"

The sticks fell and the mouth of the new circle crunched and screamed. The beast was on its knees in the center, its arms folded over its face. It was crying out against the abominable noise something about a body on the hill. The beast struggled forward, broke the ring and fell over the steep edge of the rock to the sand by the water. At once the crowd surged after it, poured down the rock, leapt on to the beast, screamed, struck, bit, tore. There were no words, and no movements but the tearing of teeth and claws.

Then the clouds opened and let down the rain like a waterfall. The water bounded from the mountain-top, tore leaves and branches from the trees, poured like a cold shower over the struggling heap on the sand. Presently the heap broke up and figures staggered away. Only the beast lay still, a few yards from the sea. Even in the rain they could see how small a beast it was; and already its blood was staining the sand.

Now a great wind blew the rain sideways, cascading the water from the forest trees. On the mountain-top the parachute filled and moved; the figure slid, rose to its feet, spun, swayed down through a vastness of wet air and trod with ungainly feet the tops of the high trees; falling, still falling, it sank toward the beach and the boys rushed screaming into the darkness. The parachute took the figure forward, furrowing the lagoon, and bumped it over the reef and out to sea.

Toward midnight the rain ceased and the clouds drifted away, so that the sky was scattered once more with the incredible lamps of stars. Then the breeze died too and there was no noise save the drip and trickle of water that ran out of clefts and spilled down, leaf by leaf, to the brown earth of the island. The air was cool, moist, and clear; and presently even the sound of the water was still. The beast lay huddled on the pale beach and the stains spread, inch by inch.

The edge of the lagoon became a streak of phosphorescence which advanced minutely, as the great wave of the tide flowed. The clear water mirrored the clear sky and the angular bright constellations. The line of phosphorescence bulged about the sand grains and little pebbles; it held them each in a dimple of tension, then suddenly accepted them with an inaudible syllable and moved on.

Along the shoreward edge of the shallows the advancing clearness was full of strange, moonbeam-bodied creatures with fiery eyes. Here and there a larger pebble clung to its own air and was covered with a coat of pearls. The tide swelled in over the rain-pitted sand and smoothed everything with a layer of silver. Now it touched the first of the stains that seeped from the broken body and the creatures made a moving patch of light as they gathered at the edge. The water rose farther and dressed Simon's coarse hair with brightness. The line of his cheek silvered and the turn of his shoulder became sculptured marble. The strange attendant creatures, with their fiery eyes and trailing vapors, busied themselves round his head. The body lifted a fraction of an inch from the sand and a bubble of air escaped from the mouth with a wet plop. Then it turned gently in the water.

Somewhere over the darkened curve of the world the sun and moon were pulling, and the film of water on the earth planet was held, bulging slightly on one side while the solid core turned. The great wave of the tide moved farther along the island and the water lifted. Softly, surrounded by a fringe of inquisitive bright creatures, itself a silver shape beneath the steadfast constellations, Simon's dead body moved out toward the open sea.

CHAPTER 11

. . .

They set off along the beach in formation. Ralph went first, limping a little, his spear carried over one shoulder. He saw things partially, through the tremble of the heat haze over the flashing sands, and his own long hair and injuries. Behind him came the twins, worried now for a while but full of unquenchable vitality. They said little but trailed the butts of their wooden spears; for Piggy had found that, by looking down and shielding his tired sight from the sun, he could just see these moving along the sand. He walked between the trailing butts, therefore, the conch held carefully between his two hands. The boys made a compact little group that moved over the beach, four plate-like shadows dancing and mingling beneath them. There was no sign left of the storm, and the beach was swept clean like a blade that has been scoured. The sky and the mountain were at an immense distance, shimmering in the heat; and the reef was lifted by mirage, floating in a kind of silver pool halfway up the sky.

They passed the place where the tribe had danced. The charred sticks still lay on the rocks where the rain had quenched them but the sand by the water was smooth again. They passed this in silence. No one doubted that the tribe would be found at the Castle Rock and when they came in sight of it they stopped with one accord. The densest tangle on the island, a mass of twisted stems, black and green and impenetrable, lay on their left and tall grass swayed before them. Now Ralph went forward.

Here was the crushed grass where they had all lain when he had gone to prospect. There was the neck of land, the ledge skirting the rock, up there were the red pinnacles.

Sam touched his arm.

"Smoke. "

There was a tiny smudge of smoke wavering into the air on the other side of the rock.

"Some fire—I don't think. "

Ralph turned.

"What are we hiding for?"

He stepped through the screen of grass on to the little open space that led to the narrow neck.

"You two follow behind. I'll go first, then Piggy a pace behind me. Keep your spears ready. "

Piggy peered anxiously into the luminous veil that hung between him and the world.

"Is it safe? Ain't there a cliff? I can hear the sea. "

"You keep right close to me. "

Ralph moved forward on to the neck. He kicked a stone and it bounded into the water. Then the sea sucked down, revealing a red, weedy square forty feet beneath Ralph's left arm.

"Am I safe?" quavered Piggy. "I feel awful—"

High above them from the pinnacles came a sudden shout and then an imitation war-cry that was answered by a dozen voices from behind the rock.

"Give me the conch and stay still. "

"Halt! Who goes there?"

Ralph bent back his head and glimpsed Roger's dark face at the top.

"You can see who I am!" he shouted. "Stop being silly!"

He put the conch to his lips and began to blow. Savages appeared, painted out of recognition, edging round the ledge toward the neck. They carried spears and disposed themselves to defend the entrance. Ralph went on blowing and ignored Piggy's terrors.

Roger was shouting.

"You mind out—see?"

At length Ralph took his lips away and paused to get his breath back. His first words were a gasp, but audible.

"—calling an assembly. "

The savages guarding the neck muttered among themselves but made no motion. Ralph walked forwards a couple of steps. A voice whispered urgently behind him.

"Don't leave me, Ralph."

"You kneel down," said Ralph sideways, "and wait till I come back."

He stood halfway along the neck and gazed at the savages intently. Freed by the paint, they had tied their hair back and were more comfortable than he was. Ralph made a resolution to tie his own back afterwards. Indeed he felt like telling them to wait and doing it there and then; but that was impossible. The savages sniggered a bit and one gestured at Ralph with his spear. High above, Roger took his hands off the lever and leaned out to see what was going on. The boys on the neck stood in a pool of their own shadow, diminished to shaggy heads. Piggy crouched, his back shapeless as a sack.

"I'm calling an assembly."

Silence.

Roger took up a small stone and flung it between the twins, aiming to miss. They started and Sam only just kept his footing. Some source of power began to pulse in Roger's body.

Ralph spoke again, loudly.

"I'm calling an assembly."

He ran his eye over them.

"Where's Jack?"

The group of boys stirred and consulted. A painted face spoke with the voice of Robert.

"He's hunting. And he said we weren't to let you in."

"I've come to see about the fire," said Ralph, "and about Piggy's specs."

The group in front of him shifted and laughter shivered outwards from among them, light, excited laughter that went echoing among the tall rocks.

A voice spoke from behind Ralph.

"What do you want?"

The twins made a bolt past Ralph and got between him and the entry. He turned quickly. Jack, identifiable by personality and red hair, was advancing from the forest. A hunter crouched on either side. All three were masked in black and green. Behind them on the grass the headless and paunched body of a sow lay where they had dropped it.

Piggy wailed.

"Ralph! Don't leave me!"

With ludicrous care he embraced the rock, pressing himself to it above the sucking sea. The sniggering of the savages became a loud derisive jeer.

Jack shouted above the noise.

"You go away, Ralph. You keep to your end. This is my end and my tribe. You leave me alone."

The jeering died away.

"You pinched Piggy's specs," said Ralph, breathlessly. "You've got to give them back."

"Got to? Who says?"

Ralph's temper blazed out.

"I say! You voted for me for chief. Didn't you hear the conch? You played a dirty trick—we'd have given you fire if you'd asked for it—"

The blood was flowing in his cheeks and the bunged-up eye throbbed.

"You could have had fire whenever you wanted. But you didn't. You came sneaking up like a thief and stole Piggy's glasses!"

"Say that again!"

"Thief! Thief!"

Piggy screamed.

"Ralph! Mind me!"

Jack made a rush and stabbed at Ralph's chest with his spear. Ralph sensed the position of the weapon from the glimpse he caught of Jack's arm and put the thrust aside with his own butt. Then he brought the end round and caught Jack a stinger across the ear. They were chest to chest, breathing fiercely, pushing and glaring.

"Who's a thief?"

"You are!"

Jack wrenched free and swung at Ralph with his spear. By common consent they were using the spears as sabers now, no longer daring the lethal points. The blow struck Ralph's spear and slid down, to fall agonizingly on his fingers. Then they were apart once more, their positions reversed, Jack toward the Castle Rock and Ralph on the outside toward the island.

Both boys were breathing very heavily.

"Come on then—"

"Come on—"

Truculently they squared up to each other but kept just out of fighting distance.

"You come on and see what you get!"

"You come on—"

Piggy clutching the ground was trying to attract Ralph's attention. Ralph moved, bent down, kept a wary eye on Jack.

"Ralph—remember what we came for. The fire. My specs. "

Ralph nodded. He relaxed his fighting muscles, stood easily and grounded the butt of his spear. Jack watched him inscrutably through his paint. Ralph glanced up at the pinnacles, then toward the group of savages.

"Listen. We've come to say this. First you've got to give back Piggy's specs. If he hasn't got them he can't see. You aren't playing the game—"

The tribe of painted savages giggled and Ralph's mind faltered. He pushed his hair up and gazed at the green and black mask before him, trying to remember what Jack looked like.

Piggy whispered.

"And the fire. "

"Oh yes. Then about the fire. I say this again. I've been saying it ever since we dropped in. "

He held out his spear and pointed at the savages. "Your only hope is keeping a signal fire going as long as there's light to see. Then maybe a ship'll notice the smoke and come and rescue us and take us home. But without that smoke we've got to wait till some ship comes by accident. We might wait years; till we were old—"

The shivering, silvery, unreal laughter of the savages sprayed out and echoed away. A gust of rage shook Ralph. His voice cracked.

"Don't you understand, you painted fools? Sam, Eric, Piggy and me—we aren't enough. We tried to keep the fire going, but we couldn't. And then you, playing at hunting. . . . "

He pointed past them to where the trickle of smoke dispersed in the pearly air.

"Look at that! Call that a signal fire? That's a cooking fire. Now you'll eat and there'll be no smoke. Don't you understand? There may be a ship out there—"

He paused, defeated by the silence and the painted anonymity of the group guarding the entry. Jack opened a pink mouth and addressed Samneric, who were between him and his tribe.

"You two. Get back."

No one answered him. The twins, puzzled, looked at each other; while Piggy, reassured by the cessation of violence, stood up carefully. Jack glanced back at Ralph and then at the twins.

"Grab them!"

No one moved. Jack shouted angrily.

"I said'grab them'!"

The painted group moved round Samneric nervously and unhandily. Once more the silvery laughter scattered.

Samneric protested out of the heart of civilization.

"Oh, I say!"

"—honestly!"

Their spears were taken from them.

"Tie them up!"

Ralph cried out hopelessly against the black and green mask.

"Jack!"

"Go on. Tie them."

Now the painted group felt the otherness of Samneric, felt the power in their own hands. They felled the twins clumsily and excitedly. Jack was inspired. He knew that Ralph would attempt a rescue. He struck in a humming circle behind him and Ralph only just parried the blow. Beyond them the tribe and the twins were a loud and writhing heap. Piggy crouched again. Then the twins lay, astonished, and the tribe stood round them. Jack turned to Ralph and spoke between his teeth.

"See? They do what I want."

There was silence again. The twins lay, inexpertly tied up, and the tribe watched Ralph to see what he would do. He numbered them through his fringe, glimpsed the ineffectual smoke.

His temper broke. He screamed at Jack.

"You're a beast and a swine and a bloody, bloody thief!"

He charged.

Jack, knowing this was the crisis, charged too. They met with a jolt and bounced apart. Jack swung with his fist at Ralph and caught him on the ear.

Ralph hit Jack in the stomach and made him grunt. Then they were facing each other again, panting and furious, but unnerved by each other's ferocity. They became aware of the noise that was the background to this fight, the steady shrill cheering of the tribe behind them.

Piggy's voice penetrated to Ralph.

"Let me speak."

He was standing in the dust of the fight, and as the tribe saw his intention the shrill cheer changed to a steady booing.

Piggy held up the conch and the booing sagged a little, then came up again to strength.

"I got the conch!"

He shouted.

"I tell you, I got the conch!"

Surprisingly, there was silence now; the tribe were curious to hear what amusing thing he might have to say.

Silence and pause; but in the silence a curious air-noise, close by Ralph's head. He gave it half his attention—and there it was again; a faint "Zup!" Someone was throwing stones: Roger was dropping them, his one hand still on the lever. Below him, Ralph was a shock of hair and Piggy a bag of fat.

"I got this to say. You're acting like a crowd of kids." The booing rose and died again as Piggy lifted the white, magic shell.

"Which is better—to be a pack of painted Indians like you are, or to be sensible like Ralph is?"

A great clamor rose among the savages. Piggy shouted again.

"Which is better—to have rules and agree, or to hunt and kill?"

Again the clamor and again—"Zup!"

Ralph shouted against the noise.

"Which is better, law and rescue, or hunting and breaking things up?"

Now Jack was yelling too and Ralph could no longer make himself heard. Jack had backed right against the tribe and they were a solid mass of menace that bristled with spears. The intention of a charge was forming among them; they were working up to it and the neck would be swept clear. Ralph stood facing them, a little to one side, his spear ready. By him stood Piggy still holding out the talisman, the fragile, shining beauty of the shell. The storm of sound beat at them, an incantation of hatred. High overhead, Roger, with a sense of delirious abandonment, leaned all his weight on the lever.

Ralph heard the great rock before he saw it. He was aware of a jolt in the earth that came to him through the soles of his feet, and the breaking sound of stones at the top of the cliff. Then the monstrous red thing bounded across the neck and he flung himself flat while the tribe shrieked.

The rock struck Piggy a glancing blow from chin to knee; the conch exploded into a thousand white fragments and ceased to exist. Piggy, saying nothing, with no time for even a grunt, traveled through the air sideways from the rock, turning over as he went. The rock bounded twice and was lost in the forest. Piggy fell forty feet and landed on his back across the square red rock in the sea. His head opened and stuff came out and turned red. Piggy's arms and legs twitched a bit, like a pig's after it has been killed. Then the sea breathed again in a long, slow sigh, the water boiled white and pink over the rock; and when it went, sucking back again, the body of Piggy was gone.

This time the silence was complete. Ralph's lips formed a word but no sound came.

Suddenly Jack bounded out from the tribe and began screaming wildly.

"See? See? That's what you'll get! I meant that! There isn't a tribe for you any more! The conch is gone—"

He ran forward, stooping.

"I'm chief!"

Viciously, with full intention, he hurled his spear at Ralph. The point tore the skin and flesh over Ralph's ribs, then sheared off and fell in the water. Ralph stumbled, feeling not pain but panic, and the tribe, screaming now like the chief, began to advance. Another spear, a bent one that would not fly straight, went past his face and one fell from on high where Roger was. The twins lay hidden behind the tribe and the anonymous devils' faces swarmed across the neck. Ralph turned and ran. A great noise as of sea gulls rose behind him. He obeyed an instinct that he did not know he possessed and swerved over the open space so that the spears went wide. He saw the headless body of the sow and jumped in time. Then he was crashing through foliage and small boughs and was hidden by the forest.

The chief stopped by the pig, turned and held up his hands.

"Back! Back to the fort!"

Presently the tribe returned noisily to the neck where Roger joined them.

The chief spoke to him angrily.

"Why aren't you on watch?"

Roger looked at him gravely.

"I just came down—"

The hangman's horror clung round him. The chief said no more to him but looked down at Samneric.

"You got to join the tribe."

"You lemme go—"

"—and me."

The chief snatched one of the few spears that were left and poked Sam in the ribs.

"What d'you mean by it, eh?" said the chief fiercely. "What d'you mean by coming with spears? What d'you mean by not joining my tribe?"

The prodding became rhythmic. Sam yelled.

"That's not the way."

Roger edged past the chief, only just avoiding pushing him with his shoulder. The yelling ceased, and Samneric lay looking up in quiet terror. Roger advanced upon them as one wielding a nameless authority.

CHAPTER 12

Once more the invisible group sniggered. He heard a curious trickling sound and then a louder crepitation as if someone were unwrapping great sheets of cellophane. A stick snapped and he stifled a cough. Smoke was seeping through the branches in white and yellow wisps, the patch of blue sky overhead turned to the color of a storm cloud, and then the smoke billowed round him.

Someone laughed excitedly, and a voice shouted.

"Smoke!"

He wormed his way through the thicket toward the forest, keeping as far as possible beneath the smoke. Presently he saw open space, and the green leaves of the edge of the thicket. A smallish savage was standing between him and the rest of the forest, a savage striped red and white, and carrying a spear. He was coughing and smearing the paint about his eyes with the back of his hand as he tried to see through the increasing smoke. Ralph launched himself like a cat; stabbed, snarling, with the spear, and the savage doubled up. There was a shout from beyond the thicket and then Ralph was running with the swiftness of fear through the undergrowth. He came to a pig-run, followed it for perhaps a hundred yards, and then swerved off. Behind him the ululation swept across the island once more and a single voice shouted three times. He guessed that was the signal to advance and sped away again, till his chest was like fire. Then he flung himself down under a bush and waited for a moment till his breathing steadied. He passed his tongue tentatively over his teeth and lips and heard far off the ululation of the pursuers.

There were many things he could do. He could climb a tree; but that was putting all his eggs in one basket. If he were detected, they had nothing more difficult to do than wait.

If only one had time to think!

Another double cry at the same distance gave him a clue to their plan. Any savage balked in the forest would utter the double shout and hold up the line till he was free again. That way they might hope to keep the cordon unbroken right across the island. Ralph thought of the boar that had broken through them with such ease. If necessary, when the chase came too close, he could charge the cordon while it was still thin, burst through, and run back. But run back where? The cordon would turn and sweep again. Sooner or later he would have to sleep or eat—and then he would awaken with hands clawing at him; and the hunt would become a running down.

What was to be done, then? The tree? Burst the line like a boar? Either way the choice was terrible.

A single cry quickened his heart-beat and, leaping up, he dashed away toward the ocean side and the thick jungle till he was hung up among creepers; he stayed there for a moment with his calves quivering. If only one could have quiet, a long pause, a time to think!

And there again, shrill and inevitable, was the ululation sweeping across the island. At that sound he shied like a horse among the creepers and ran once more till he was panting. He flung himself down by some ferns. The tree, or the charge? He mastered his breathing for a moment, wiped his mouth, and told himself to be calm. Samneric were somewhere in that line, and hating it. Or were they? And supposing, instead of them, he met the chief, or Roger who carried death in his hands?

Ralph pushed back his tangled hair and wiped the sweat out of his best eye. He spoke aloud.

"Think."

What was the sensible thing to do?

There was no Piggy to talk sense. There was no solemn assembly for debate nor dignity of the conch.

"Think."

Most, he was beginning to dread the curtain that might waver in his brain, blacking out the sense of danger, making a simpleton of him.

A third idea would be to hide so well that the advancing line would pass without discovering him.

He jerked his head off the ground and listened. There was another noise to attend to now, a deep grumbling noise, as though the forest itself were angry with him, a somber noise across which the ululations were scribbled excruciatingly as on slate. He knew he had heard it before somewhere, but had no time to remember.

Break the line.

A tree.

Hide, and let them pass.

A nearer cry stood him on his feet and immediately he was away again, running fast among thorns and brambles. Suddenly he blundered into the open, found himself again in that open space—and there was the fathom-wide grin of the skull, no longer ridiculing a deep blue patch of sky but jeering up into a blanket of smoke. Then Ralph was running beneath trees, with the grumble of the forest explained. They had smoked him out and set the island on fire.

Hide was better than a tree because you had a chance of breaking the line if you were discovered.

Hide, then.

He wondered if a pig would agree, and grimaced at nothing. Find the deepest thicket, the darkest hole on the island, and creep in. Now, as he ran, he peered about him. Bars and splashes of sunlight flitted over him and sweat made glistening streaks on his dirty body. The cries were far now, and faint.

At last he found what seemed to him the right place, though the decision was desperate. Here, bushes and a wild tangle of creeper made a mat that kept out all the light of the sun. Beneath it was a space, perhaps a foot high, though it was pierced everywhere by parallel and rising stems. If you wormed into the middle of that you would be five yards from the edge, and hidden, unless the savage chose to lie down and look for you; and even then, you would be in darkness—and if the worst happened and he saw you, then you had a chance to burst out at him, fling the whole line out of step and double back.

Cautiously, his stick trailing behind him, Ralph wormed between the rising stems. When he reached the middle of the mat he lay and listened.

The fire was a big one and the drum-roll that he had thought was left so far behind was nearer. Couldn't a fire outrun a galloping horse? He could see the sun-splashed ground over an area of perhaps fifty yards from where he lay, and as he watched, the sunlight in every patch blinked at him. This was so like the curtain that flapped in his brain that for a moment he thought the blinking was inside him. But then the patches blinked more rapidly, dulled and went out, so that he saw that a great heaviness of smoke lay between the island and the sun.

If anyone peered under the bushes and chanced to glimpse human flesh it might be Samneric who would pretend not to see and say nothing. He laid his cheek against the chocolate-colored earth, licked his dry lips and closed his eyes. Under the thicket, the earth was vibrating very slightly; or perhaps there was a sound beneath the obvious thunder of the fire and scribbled ululations that was too low to hear.

Someone cried out. Ralph jerked his cheek off the earth and looked into the dulled light. They must be near now, he thought, and his chest began to thump. Hide, break the line, climb a tree—which was the best after all?

The trouble was you only had one chance.

Now the fire was nearer; those volleying shots were great limbs, trunks even, bursting. The fools! The fools! The fire must be almost at the fruit trees—what would they eat tomorrow?

Ralph stirred restlessly in his narrow bed. One chanced nothing! What could they do? Beat him? So what? Kill him? A stick sharpened at both ends.

The cries, suddenly nearer, jerked him up. He could see a striped savage moving hastily out of a green tangle, and coming toward the mat where he hid, a savage who carried a spear. Ralph gripped his fingers into the earth. Be ready now, in case.

Ralph fumbled to hold his spear so that it was point foremost; and now he saw that the stick was sharpened at both ends.

The savage stopped fifteen yards away and uttered his cry.

Perhaps he can hear my heart over the noises of the fire. Don't scream. Get ready.

The savage moved forward so that you could only see him from the waist down. That was the butt of his spear. Now you could see him from the knee down. Don't scream.

A herd of pigs came squealing out of the greenery behind the savage and rushed away into the forest. Birds were screaming, mice shrieking, and a little hopping thing came under the mat and cowered.

Five yards away the savage stopped, standing right by the thicket, and cried out. Ralph drew his feet up and crouched. The stake was in his hands, the stake sharpened at both ends, the stake that vibrated so wildly, that grew long, short, light, heavy, light again.

The ululation spread from shore to shore. The savage knelt down by the edge of the thicket, and there were lights flickering in the forest behind him. You could see a knee disturb the mold. Now the other. Two hands. A spear.

A face.

The savage peered into the obscurity beneath the thicket. You could tell that he saw light on this side and on that, but not in the middle—there. In the middle was a blob of dark and the savage wrinkled up his face, trying to decipher the darkness.

The seconds lengthened. Ralph was looking straight into the savage's eyes.

Don't scream.

You'll get back.

Now he's seen you. He's making sure. A stick sharpened.

Ralph screamed, a scream of fright and anger and desperation. His legs straightened, the screams became continuous and foaming. He shot forward, burst the thicket, was in the open, screaming, snarling, bloody. He swung the stake and the savage tumbled over; but there were others coming toward him, crying out. He swerved as a spear flew past and then was silent, running. All at once the lights flickering ahead of him merged together, the roar of the forest rose to thunder and a tall bush directly in his path burst into a great fan-shaped flame. He swung to the right, running desperately fast, with the heat beating on his left side and the fire racing forward like a tide. The ululation rose behind him and spread along, a series of short sharp cries, the sighting call. A brown figure showed up at his right and fell away. They were all running, all crying out madly. He could hear them crashing in the undergrowth and on the left was the hot, bright thunder of the fire. He forgot his wounds, his hunger and thirst, and became fear; hopeless fear on flying feet, rushing through the forest toward the open beach. Spots jumped before his eyes and turned into red circles that expanded quickly till they passed out of sight. Below him someone's legs were getting tired and the desperate ululation advanced like a jagged fringe of menace and was almost overhead.

He stumbled over a root and the cry that pursued him rose even higher. He saw a shelter burst into flames and the fire flapped at his right shoulder and there was the glitter of water. Then he was down, rolling over and over in the warm sand, crouching with arm to ward off, trying to cry for mercy.

He staggered to his feet, tensed for more terrors, and looked up at a huge peaked cap. It was a white-topped cap, and above the green shade of the peak was a crown, an anchor, gold foliage. He saw white drill, epaulettes, a revolver, a row of gilt buttons down the front of a uniform.

A naval officer stood on the sand, looking down at Ralph in wary astonishment. On the beach behind him was a cutter, her bows hauled up and held by two ratings. In the stern-sheets another rating held a sub-machine gun.

The ululation faltered and died away.

The officer looked at Ralph doubtfully for a moment, then took his hand away from the butt of the revolver.

"Hullo."

Squirming a little, conscious of his filthy appearance, Ralph answered shyly.

"Hullo."

The officer nodded, as if a question had been answered.

"Are there any adults—any grownups with you?"

Dumbly, Ralph shook his head. He turned a halfpace on the sand. A semicircle of little boys, their bodies streaked with colored clay, sharp sticks in their hands, were standing on the beach making no noise at all.

"Fun and games," said the officer.

The fire reached the coconut palms by the beach and swallowed them noisily. A flame, seemingly detached, swung like an acrobat and licked up the palm heads on the platform. The sky was black.

The officer grinned cheerfully at Ralph.

"We saw your smoke. What have you been doing? Having a war or something?"

Ralph nodded.

The officer inspected the little scarecrow in front of him. The kid needed a bath, a haircut, a nose-wipe and a good deal of ointment.

"Nobody killed, I hope? Any dead bodies?"

"Only two. And they've gone."

The officer leaned down and looked closely at Ralph.

"Two? Killed?"

Ralph nodded again. Behind him, the whole island was shuddering with flame. The officer knew, as a rule, when people were telling the truth. He whistled softly.

Other boys were appearing now, tiny tots some of them, brown, with the distended bellies of small savages. One of them came close to the officer and looked up.

"I'm, I'm—"

But there was no more to come. Percival Wemys Madison sought in his head for an incantation that had faded clean away.

The officer turned back to Ralph.

"We'll take you off. How many of you are there?"

Ralph shook his head. The officer looked past him to the group of painted boys.

"Who's boss here?"

"I am," said Ralph loudly.

A little boy who wore the remains of an extraordinary black cap on his red hair and who carried the remains of a pair of spectacles at his waist, started forward, then changed his mind and stood still.

"We saw your smoke. And you don't know how many of you there are?"

"No, sir."

"I should have thought," said the officer as he visualized the search before him, "I should have thought that a pack of British boys—you're all British, aren't you? —would have been able to put up a better show than that—I mean—"

"It was like that at first," said Ralph, "before things—"

He stopped.

"We were together then—"

The officer nodded helpfully.

"I know. Jolly good show. Like the Coral Island."

Ralph looked at him dumbly. For a moment he had a fleeting picture of the strange glamour that had once invested the beaches. But the island was scorched up like dead wood—Simon was dead—and Jack had. . . . The tears began to flow and sobs shook him. He gave himself up to them now for the first time on the island; great, shuddering spasms of grief that seemed to wrench his whole body. His voice rose under the black smoke before the burning wreckage of the island; and infected by that emotion, the other little boys began to shake and sob too. And in the middle of them, with filthy body, matted hair, and unwiped nose, Ralph wept for the end of innocence, the darkness of man's heart, and the fall through the air of the true, wise friend called Piggy.

The officer, surrounded by these noises, was moved and a little embarrassed. He turned away to give them time to pull themselves together; and waited, allowing his eyes to rest on the trim cruiser in the distance.

Ⅳ. Questions for Thinking

1. What causes the change of the island from a paradise to hell? Discuss the deterioration of the "society" on the island. What circumstances, events, and psychological forces cause this deterioration?

2. In Chapter 3, Piggy asks the boys "How can you expect to be rescued if you don't put first things first and act proper?" What does Piggy mean by "act proper?" Why does he feel acting properly will make them be rescued? What is the author's design that the rescue ship is brought by the damaging fire?

3. Why does it matter that these are kids? Would adults in the same situation act any differently?

4. What Parellel is there between what has been going on in the adult world and what has occured on the island?

5. Only one female voice is mentioned in this novel, that of Piggy's aunt. Is this a story about the capacity of humans for violence, or is it a story about the male capacity for violence?

6. Compare Ralph and Jack as two leaders and their leadership? What makes Ralph be left alone though he possess many good qualities?

7. What do you think about the rules of civilization? Do they free us and enable

us to rise to our best selves? Or do the rules constrain our bad nature that lie at the heart of ourselves?

8. Golding's boys are real boys, but they are more than that. Discuss.

9. How could this novel be described as an allegory? If it is an allegory, what message does Golding seem to want to get across to his readers? What allegorical roles are the characters playing?

10. Discuss the deterioration of the "society" on the island. What circumstances, events, and psychological forces cause this deterioration?

V. Guidance for Appreciation

William Golding once talked about the theme of the novel *Lord of the Files*, "The theme is an attempt to trace the defects of society back to the defects of human nature. The moral is that the shape of a society must depend on the ethical nature of the individual and not on any political system.... The whole book is symbolic in nature." This statement guides us to interpret the novel at different levels: individuals, society, ethics, and politics.

First, at the level of individuals, the most common interpretation in depth is that readers will find human evil reflected in children. Unlike other novels about isolating adults on an island, this novel chooses only children as characters. However, these children are not innocent. The children's selfishness, narrowness, indulgence, evasion of responsibility, ignorance and preference for violence are revealed in the development of plot. In the preface of *Lord of the Flies*, Golding said, "The brutal nuclear war brought the children to the isolated island, but the children reproduce the whole process of making them fall into this situation. It is not a foreign from outer space but the people themselves that turn the paradise into a slaughterhouse." What is clearly stressed is that the evil of children makes the original paradise of the coral island into a bloody battleground.

Second, at the level of macro social and historical context, this novel attempts to reveal the defects of society. The process of the boy's efforts of constucting a society, the split of society into two, the war between two societies, is a miniature of the world situation of WWII and cold war. The process of turning the original Eden-like beautiful world into a bloody and brutal world is actually an allegorical expression of the development of human society.

So the novel can be perceived as the author's indirect criticism over western democracy, science, rationality and violence during the early 20th century. It could also be understood as an allegory of western civilization.

This novel is special not only in its use of the technique of diminution, which reduces the adult world to the world of children to reveal the intrinsic evil of human nature, but also in its exclusion of women in the novel. The absence of women in *Lord of The Flies* is a key to William Golding studies. It is closely related to Golding's view on male and female characterization and serves as a key to the study of the narrative structure of his novel.

First, the absence of women is the tradition of the British desert island literature. In *Robinson Crusoe*, *Gulliver's Travels*, *Coral Island* and other desert island literary classics, female roles have always been a dispensable part, and *Lord of the Flies* just follows the tradition.

Moreover, the absence of women offers a perfect climate for the boys to get rid of social restraints and cultural constraints to the greatest extent, liberate themselves and to return to their nature. Then the evils and violence in their nature can be fully displayed.

At political level, the novel can be read as an allegory of world politics. The novel was composed in 1954, after WWⅡ. The dreadful effects of one war after another not only extended to adults but also to children. Ralph represents democracy and Jack totalitarianism. L. L. Dickson identifies the novel as political allegory, referring to World War II atrocities, particularly those inflicted upon the Jews. Jack's gang is regarded as "fascist coup", and Jack "Hitler".

Another perspective to interpret this novel is to read it as a dystopia novel. The word of dystopia is derived from two Greek words, dus and topos, meaning a diseased, bad, faulty, or unfavourable place. Dystopia is defined as "the antithesis of Utopia. A hellish state brought about by attempts to construct unrealizable ideal systems." Mainly three forms of dystopia are discussed, the political dystopia, the environmental dystopia, and the technological dystopia. Gregory Claeys points out that "the relation between utopia and dystopia may be more intimate still... Like the snake in the Garden of Eden, dystopian elements seem to lurk within Utopia"(6). When they first come to this unkown island, the boys attempts to build a utopia world. Great efforts have been made to ensure that everyone has the food, shelter. Everyone should shoulder his responsibility. Democracy is enforced through voting and assembly. Ralph, as the leader, hopes to lead the boys to establish a free, democratic and just society. The affluent food, agreeable climate make this place an Eden-like utopia. However, with the development of the plot, the latent dystopia elements start to appear. Inner monstrosity is released. Intrinsic violence is unleashed. The rescue fire is finally turned into the hellish fire. Pig-hunting is developed into man-hunting. Democracy is taken by totalitarianism. "In the novel, Jack, by ways of food temptation and totalitarianism, establishes a negative community" (Xiao Mingwen, 131). The Eden-like utopia is turned into hellish dystopia.

Ⅵ. Further Reading

1. Claeys, Gregory. Dystopia: A Natural History—A Study of Modern Despotism, Its Antecedents, and Its Literary Diffractions [M]. Oxford: Oxford University Press, 2017.

2. Crawford, Paul. Politics and History in William Golding: The World Turned Upside Down[M]. Columbia: University of Missouri Press, 2002.

3. Golding, Judy. The Children of Lovers: a Memoir of William Golding by His Daughter[M]. London: Faber & Faber, 2011.

4. McCarron, Kevin. William Golding [M]. Tavistock: Northcote House Publishers, 2004.

5. Olsen, Kirstin. Understanding Lord of the Flies: a Student Casebook to Issues, Sources, and Historical Documents [M]. Westport: Greenwood Press, 2000.

6. Tiger, Virginia. William Golding: The Unmoved Target [M]. London: Marion Boyars Publishers Ltd, 2003.

7. Tomoiaga, Ligia, Minodora Barbul, and Ramona Demarcsek. From Francis Bacon to William Golding: Utopia and Dystopia of Today and of Yore. Newcastle: Cambridge Scholars Publishing, 2012.

8. Wilson, Raymond. Lord of the Flies by William Golding[M]. Hampshire: MacMillan Education Ltd, 1986.

9. 沈雁. 威廉·戈尔丁小说研究[M]. 苏州:苏州大学出版社,2014.

10. 肖明文. 乌托邦与恶托邦:《蝇王》中的饮食冲突[J]. 外国文学,2018(3):124-132.

Chapter 8

Angela Carter: The Company of Wolves
Deconstructionism and Feminism

I. Introduction to the Author

Angela Carter is mainly known as an author of novels, short stories, nonfiction essays, plays, and children's books. She is also a translator. In 2008, The *Times* ranked Carter tenth in their list of "The 50 greatest British writers since 1945".

Angela Carter was born on 7 May, 1940, in Eastbourne, Sussex to Hugh Alexander Stalker and Olive Farthing Stalker. Her father was a journalist. Angela Olive Stalker grew up in South London where she attended a local grammar school. After leaving school, she worked as a reporter on a London local newspaper, *The Croydon Advertiser*.

She married Paul Carter in 1960. After marriage, she returned to school and in 1962 she got enrolled at the University of Bristol, specializing in medieval literature. During this time, she read wildly medieval romances and fables. She also started her first novel *Shadow Dance*, which was published in 1966 after her graduation in 1965. Since then, Angela Carter devoted to her professional writing career. Carter's second novel *The Magic Toyshop* was published in 1967 and was awarded John Lewellyn Rhys Memorial Prize of 1967. Her third novel *Several Perceptions* won the Somerset Maugham Award.

In 1969, Angela Carter went to Japan under the auspices of a Somerset Maugham Travel Award. She returned there in 1970 and stayed for two years. She wrote about her experiences there in a collection of short stories, *Fireworks: Nine Profane Pieces* (1974).

In 1972, Angela Carter divorced her husband and settled down in London in 1976. During the following years, she divided her time among writing, teaching and traveling around the world. Between 1976 and 1978 she was the Arts Council of Great Britain Fellow in Creative Writing at Sheffield University. In 1977 her translation of *The Fairy Tales of Charles Perrault* and a novel, *The Passion of New Eve*, were published. In 1979 she published her second collection of short stories, *The Bloody Chamber and Other Stories*, which won the Cheltenham Festival of Literature Award. From 1980 through 1988, she was a visiting professor first in Brown University, then at the University of Adelaide, the University of Texas at Austin, the Iowa Writers' Workshop in Iowa City and the State University of New York at Albany.

In the 1980s, Carter settled in South London with her partner, Mark Pearce and gave birth to her son, Alexander Pearce. In 1991 Carter was diagnosed with lung cancer. She died at her home on 16 February 1992.

Angela Carter has completed nine novels, *Shadow Dance* (1966), *The Magic Toyshop* (1967), *Several Perceptions* (1968), *Heroes and Villains* (1969), *Love* (1971), *The Infernal Desire Machine of Doctor Hoffman* (1972), *The Passion of New Eve* (1977), *Nights at the Circus* (1984), and *Wise Children* (1991). Her collections of short stories include, *Fireworks: Nine Profane Pieces* (1974), *The Bloody Chamber* (1979), *The Bridegroom* (1983), *Black Venus* (1985), *American Ghosts and Old World Wonders* (1993), and *Burning Your Boats* (1995). In addition to her novels and short story collections, she also published 4 non-fiction, *The Sadeian Woman and the Ideology of Pornography* (1979), *Nothing Sacred: Selected Writings* (1982), *Expletives Deleted: Selected Writings* (1992), *Shaking a Leg: Collected Journalism and Writing* (1997). Angela Carter is also a children's book writer and translator. Her children's books include, *The Donkey Prince* (1970), *Miss Z, the Dark Young Lady* (1970), *Comic and Curious Cats* (1979), *Moonshadow* (1982)　, and *Sea-Cat and Dragon King* (2000). she has translated and published *The Fairy Tales of Charles Perrault* (1977) and *Sleeping Beauty and Other Favourite Fairy Tales* (1982).

Ⅱ. Introduction to the Short Story

The Company of Wolves is one of Angela Carter's short stories published in the collection *The Bloody Chamber and Other Stories* in 1979. It won the Cheltenham Festival Literary Prize in the same year.

The collection includes 10 stories, respectively, "The Bloody Chamber", "The Courtship of Mr. Lyon", "The Tiger's Bride", "Puss-in-Boots", "The Erl-King", "The Snow Child", "The Lady of the House of Love", "The Werewolf", "The Company of Wolves", and "Wolf-Alice". All these ten stories are closely based upon fairytales or folk tales.

The collection includes Carter's wolf trilogy—"The Werewolf", "The Company of Wolves", and "Wolf-Alice". "The Company of Wolves" is an adaption of the world-known fairy tale "Little Red Riding Hood".

The short story "The Company of Wolves" is composed of two parts. The first part begins with the description of wolf, a forest assassin. Some incidents about werewolves are introduced. In one incident, a witch turns a whole wedding party into wolves. In another incident, a young woman's husband vanishes on the wedding night. Years later, he returns and turns into a wolf who tries to attack the woman's husband and children. He is hacked to death and turns back into a man.

The second part of the story is like "Little Red Riding Hood". The Little Red Hood sets off to visit her grandmother. Though the forest is similarly dangerous, this little girl is confident, believing that "the wild beasts cannot harm her". On the way, she meets a man in the woods. The man tricks the girl into a bet to see who would get to her grandmother's house first. If she loses she has to kiss him. The man hurries and arrives early at the grandmother's house. He tricks his way into the house by pretending to be the granddaughter and murders the grandmother. The ending of the story is greatly different from Charles Perrault's version of "Little Red Riding Hood" and Jacob and Wilhelm Grimm's "Little Redcape". Instead of being eaten by the wolf, The Little Red Hood, "sweet and sound she sleeps in granny's bed, between the paws of the tender wolf".

Ⅲ. Excerpt

The Company of Wolves

One beast and only one howls in the woods by night.

The wolf is carnivore incarnate and he's as cunning as he is ferocious; once he's had a taste of flesh then nothing else will do.

At night, the eyes of wolves shine like candle flames, yellowish, reddish, but that is because the pupils of their eyes fatten on darkness and catch the light from your lantern to flash it back to you —red for danger; if a wolf's eyes reflect only moonlight, then they gleam a cold and unnatural green, a mineral, a piercing colour. If the benighted traveller spies those luminous, terrible sequins stitched suddenly on the black thickets, then he knows he must run, if fear has not struck him stock-still.

But those eyes are all you will be able to glimpse of the forest assassins as they cluster invisibly round your smell of meat as you go through the wood unwisely late. They will be like shadows, they will be like wraiths, grey members of a congregation of nightmare; hark! his long, wavering howl... an aria of fear made audible.

The wolfsong is the sound of the rending you will suffer, in itself a murdering.

It is winter and cold weather. In this region of mountain and forest, there is now nothing for the wolves to eat. Goats and sheep are locked up in the byre, the deer departed for the remaining pasturage on the southern slopes —wolves grow lean and famished. There is so little flesh on them that you could count the starveling ribs through their pelts, if they gave you time before they pounced. Those slavering jaws; the lolling tongue; the rime of saliva on the grizzled chops —of all the teeming perils of the night and the forest, ghosts, hobgoblins, ogres that grill babies upon gridirons, witches that fatten their captives in cages for cannibal tables, the wolf is worst for he cannot listen to reason.

You are always in danger in the forest, where no people are. Step between the portals of the great pines where the shaggy branches tangle about you, trapping the unwary traveller in nets as if the vegetation itself were in a plot with the wolves who live there, as though the wicked trees go fishing on behalf of their friends —step between the gateposts of the forest with the greatest trepidation and infinite precautions, for if you stray from the path for one instant, the wolves will eat you. They are grey as famine, they are as unkind as plague.

The grave-eyed children of the sparse villages always carry knives with them when they go to tend the little flocks of goats that provide the homesteads with acrid milk and rank, maggoty cheese. Their knives are half as big as they are, the blades are sharpened daily.

But the wolves have ways of arriving at your own hearthside. We try and try but sometimes we cannot keep them out. There is no winter's night the cottager does not fear to see a lean, grey, famished snout questing under the door, and there was a woman once bitten in her own kitchen as she was straining the macaroni.

Fear and flee the wolf; for, worst of all, the wolf may be more than he seems.

There was a hunter once, near here, that trapped a wolf in a pit. This wolf had massacred the sheep and goats; eaten up a mad old man who used to live by himself in a hut halfway up the mountain and sing to Jesus all day; pounced on a girl looking after the sheep, but she made such a commotion that men came with rifles and scared him away and tried to track him to the forest but he was cunning and easily gave them the slip. So this hunter dug a pit and put a duck in it, for bait, all alive —oh; and he covered the pit with straw smeared with wolf dung. Quack, quack! went the duck and a wolf came slinking out of the forest, a big one, a heavy one, he weighed as much as a grown man and the straw gave way beneath him —into the pit he tumbled. The hunter jumped down after him, slit his throat, cut off all his paws for a trophy.

And then no wolf at all lay in front of the hunter but the bloody trunk of a man, headless, footless, dying, dead.

A witch from up the valley once turned an entire wedding party into wolves because the groom had settled on another girl. She use to order them to visit her, at night, from spite, and they would sit and howl around her cottage for her, serenading her with their misery.

Not so very long ago, a young woman in our village married a man who vanished clean away on her wedding night. The bed was made with new sheets and the bride lay down in it; the groom said, he was going out to relieve himself, insisted on it, for the sake of decency, and she drew the coverlet up to her chin and she lay there. And she waited and she waited and then she waited again — surely he's been gone a long time? Until she jumps up in bed and shrieks to hear a howling, coming on the wind from the forest.

That long-drawn, wavering howl has, for all its fearful resonance, some inherent sadness in it, as if the beasts would love to be less beastly if only they knew how and never cease to mourn their own condition. There is a vast melancholy in the canticles of the wolves, melancholy infinite as the forest, endless as these long nights of winter and yet that ghastly sadness, that mourning for their own, irremediable appetites, can never move the heart for not one phrase in it hints at the possibility of redemption; grace could not come to the wolf from its own despair, only through some external mediator, so that, sometimes, the beast will look as if he half welcomes the knife that dispatches him.

The young woman's brothers searched the outhouses and the haystacks but never found any remains so the sensible girl dried her eyes and found herself another husband not too shy to piss into a pot who spent the nights indoors. She gave him a pair of bonny babies and all went right as a trivet until, one freezing night, the night of the solstice, the hinge of the year when things do not fit together as well as they should, the longest night, her first good man came home again.

A great thump on the door announced him as she was stirring the soup for the father of her children and she knew him the moment she lifted the latch to him although it was years since she'd worn black for him and now he was in rags and his hair hung down his back and never saw a comb, alive with lice.

"Here I am again, missus," he said. "Get me my bowl of cabbage and be quick about it."

Then her second husband came in with wood for the fire and when the first one saw she'd slept with another man and, worse, clapped his red eyes on her little children who'd crept into the kitchen to see what all the din was about, he shouted: "I wish I were a wolf again, to teach this whore a lesson!" So a wolf he instantly became and tore off the eldest boy's left foot before he was chopped up with the hatchet they used for chopping logs. But when the wolf lay bleeding and gasping its last, the pelt peeled off again and he was just as he had been, years ago, when he ran away from his marriage bed, so that she wept and her second husband beat her.

They say there's an ointment the Devil gives you that turns you into a wolf the minute you rub it on. Or, that he was born feet first and had a wolf for his father and his torso is a man's but his legs and genitals are a wolf's. And he has a wolf's heart.

Seven years is a werewolf's natural span but if you burn his human clothes you condemn him to wolfishness for the rest of his life, so old wives hereabouts think it some protection to throw a hat or an apron at the werewolf, as if clothes made the man. Yet by the eyes, those phosphorescent eyes, you know him in all his shapes; the eyes alone unchanged by metamorphosis.

Before he can become a wolf, the lycanthrope strips stark naked. If you spy a naked man among the pines, you must run as if the Devil were after you.

It is midwinter and the robin, the friend of man, sits on the handle of the gardener's spade and sings. It is the worst time in all the year for wolves but this strong-minded child insists she will go off through the wood. She is quite sure the wild beasts cannot harm her although, well-warned, she lays a carving knife in the basket her mother has packed with cheeses. There is a bottle of harsh liquor distilled from brambles; a batch of flat oatcakes baked on the heathstone; a pot or two of jam. The flaxen-haired girl will take these delicious gifts to a reclusive grandmother so old the burden of her years is crushing her to death. Granny lives two hours' trudge through the winter woods; the child wraps herself up in her thick shawl, draws it over her head. She steps into her stout wooden shoes; she is dressed and ready and it is Christmas Eve. The malign door of the solstice still swings upon its hinges but she has been too much loved ever to feel scared.

Children do not stay young for long in this savage country. There are no toys for them to play with so they work hard and grow wise but this one, so pretty and the youngest of her family, a little late-comer, had been indulged by her mother and the grandmother who'd knitted her the red shawl that, today, has the ominous if brilliant look of blood on snow. Her breasts have just begun to swell; her hair is like lint, so fair it hardly makes a shadow on her pale forehead; her cheeks are an emblematic scarlet and white and she has just started her woman's bleeding, the clock inside her that will strike, henceforward, once a month.

She stands and moves within the invisible pentacle of her own virginity. She is an unbroken egg; she is a sealed vessel; she has inside her a magic space the entrance to which is shut tight with a plug of membrane; she is a closed system; she does not know how to shiver. She has her knife and she is afraid of nothing.

Her father might forbid her, if he were home, but he is away in the forest, gathering wood, and her mother cannot deny her.

The forest closed upon her like a pair of jaws.

There is always something to look at in the forest, even in the middle of winter —the huddled mounds of birds, succumbed to the lethargy of the season, heaped on the creaking boughs and too forlorn to sing; the bright frills of the winter fungi on the blotched trunks of the trees; the cuneiform slots of rabbits and deer, the herringbone tracks of the birds, a hare as lean as a rasher of bacon streaking across the path where the thin sunlight dapples the russet brakes of last year's bracken.

When she heard the freezing howl of a distant wolf, her practised hand sprang to the handle of her knife, but she saw no sign of a wolf at all, nor of a naked man, neither, but then she heard a clattering among the brushwood and there sprang on to the path a fully clothed one, a very handsome young one, in the green coat and wideawake hat of a hunter, laden with carcasses of game birds. She had her hand on her knife at the first rustle of twigs but he laughed with a flash of white teeth when he saw her and made her a comic yet flattering little bow; she'd never seen such a fine fellow before, not among the rustic clowns of her native village. So on they went together, through the thickening light of the afternoon.

Soon they were laughing and joking like old friends. When he offered to carry her basket, she gave it to him although her knife was in it because he told her his rifle would protect them. As the day darkened, it began to snow again; she felt the first flakes settle on her eyelashes but now there was only half a mile to go and there would be a fire, and hot tea, and a welcome, a warm one, surely, for the dashing huntsman as well as for herself.

This young man had a remarkable object in his pocket. It was a compass. She looked at the little round glassface in the palm of his hand and watched the wavering needle with a vague wonder. He assured her this compass had taken him safely through the wood on his hunting trip because the needle always told him with perfect accuracy where the north was. She did not believe it; she knew she should never leave the path on the way through the wood or else she would be lost instantly. He laughed at her again; gleaming trails of spittle clung to his teeth. He said, if he plunged off the path into the forest that surrounded them, he 'ould guarantee to arrive at her grandmother's house a good quarter of an hour before she did, plotting his way through the undergrowth with his compass, while she trudged the long way, along the winding path.

I don't believe you. Besides, aren't you afraid of the wolves?

He only tapped the gleaming butt of his rifle and grinned.

Is it a bet? he asked her. Shall we make a game of it? What will you give me if I get to your grandmother's house before you?

What would you like? she asked disingenuously.

A kiss.

Commonplaces of a rustic seduction; she lowered her eyes and blushed.

He went through the undergrowth and took her basket with him but she forgot to be afraid of the beasts, although now the moon was rising, for she wanted to dawdle on her way to make sure the handsome gentleman would win his wager.

Grandmother's house stood by itself a little way out of the village. The freshly falling snow blew in eddies about the kitchen garden and the young man stepped delicately up the snowy path to the door as if he were reluctant to get his feet wet, swinging his bundle of game and the girl's basket and humming a little tune to himself.

There is a faint trace of blood on his chin; he has been snacking on his catch.

He rapped upon the panels with his knuckles.

Aged and frail, granny is three-quarters succumbed to the mortality the ache in her bones promises her and almost ready to give in entirely. A boy came out from the village to build up her hearth for the night an hour ago and the kitchen crackles with busy firelight. She has her Bible for company, she is a pious old woman. She is propped up on several pillows in the bed set into the wall peasant-fashion, wrapped up in the patchwork quilt she made before she was married, more years ago than she cares to remember. Two china spaniels with liver-coloured blotches on their coats and black noses sit on either side of the fireplace. There is a bright rug of woven rags on the pantiles. The grandfather clock ticks away her eroding time.

We keep the wolves outside by living well.

He rapped upon the panels with his hairy knuckles.

It is your granddaughter, he mimicked in a high soprano:

Lift up the latch and walk in, my darling.

You can tell them by their eyes, eyes of a beast of prey, nocturnal, devastating eyes as red as a wound; you can hurl your Bible at him and your apron after, granny, you thought that was a sure prophylactic against these infernal vermin... now call on Christ and his mother and all the angels in heaven to protect you but it won't do you any good.

His feral muzzle is sharp as a knife; he drops his golden burden of gnawed pheasant on the table and puts down your dear girl's basket, too. Oh, my God, what have you done with her?

Off with his disguise, that coat of forest-coloured cloth, the hat with the feather tucked into the ribbon; his matted hair streams down his white shirt and she can see the lice moving in it. The sticks in the hearth shift and hiss; night and the forest has come into the kitchen with darkness tangled in its hair.

He strips off his shirt. His skin is the colour and texture of vellum. A crisp stripe of hair runs down his belly, his nipples are ripe and dark as poison fruit but he's so thin you could count the ribs under his skin if only he gave you the time. He strips off his trousers and she can see how hairy his legs are. His genitals, huge. Ah! huge.

The last thing the old lady saw in all this world was a young man, eyes like cinders, naked as a stone, approaching her bed.

The wolf is carnivore incarnate.

When he had finished with her, he licked his chops and quickly dressed himself again, until he was just as he had been when he came through her door. He burned the inedible hair in the fireplace and wrapped the bones up in a napkin that he hid away under the bed in the wooden chest in which he found a clean pair of sheets. These he carefully put on the bed instead of the tell-tale stained ones he stowed away in the laundry basket. He plumped up the pillows and shook out the patchwork quilt, he picked up the Bible from the floor, closed it and laid it on the table. All was as it had been before except that grandmother was gone. The sticks twitched in the grate, the clock ticked and the young man sat patiently, deceitfully beside the bed in granny's nightcap.

Rat-a-tap-tap.

Who's there, he quavers in granny's antique falsetto.

Only your granddaughter.

So she came in, bringing with her a flurry of snow that melted in tears on the tiles, and perhaps she was a little disappointed to see only her grandmother sitting beside the fire. But then he flung off the blanket and sprang to the door, pressing his back against it so that she could not get out again.

The girl looked round the room and saw there was not even the indentation of a head on the smooth cheek of the pillow and how, for the first time she'd seen it so, the Bible lay closed on the table. The tick of the clock cracked like a whip. She wanted her knife from her basket but she did not dare to reach for it because his eyes were fixed upon her —huge eyes that now seemed to shine with a unique, interior light, eyes the size of saucers, saucers full of Greek fire, diabolic phosphorescence.

What big eyes you have.

All the better to see you with.

No trace at all of the old woman except for a tuft of white hair that had caught in the bark of an unburned log. When the girl saw that, she knew she was in danger of death.

Where is my grandmother?

There's nobody here but we two, my darling.

Now a great howling rose up all around them, near, very near, as close as the kitchen garden, the howling of a multitude of wolves; she knew the worst wolves are hairy on the inside and she shivered, in spite of the scarlet shawl she pulled more closely round herself as if it could protect her although it was as red as the blood she must spill.

Who has come to sing us carols, she said.

Those are the voices of my brothers, darling; I love the company of wolves. Look out of the window and you'll see them.

Snow half-caked the lattice and she opened it to look into the garden. It was a white night of moon and snow; the blizzard whirled round the gaunt, grey beasts who squatted on their haunches among the rows of winter cabbage, pointing their sharp snouts to the moon and howling as if their hearts would break. Ten wolves; twenty wolves —so many wolves she could not count them, howling in concert as if demented or deranged. Their eyes reflected the light from the kitchen and shone like a hundred candles.

It is very cold, poor things, she said; no wonder they howl so.

She closed the window on the wolves' threnody and took off her scarlet shawl, the colour of poppies, the colour of sacrifices, the colour of her menses, and, since her fear did her no good, she ceased to be afraid.

What shall I do with my shawl?

Throw it on the fire, dear one. You won't need it again.

She bundled up her shawl and threw it on the blaze, which instantly consumed it. Then she drew her blouse over her head; her small breasts gleamed as if the snow had invaded the room.

What shall I do with my blouse?

Into the fire with it, too, my pet.

The thin muslin went flaring up the chimney like a magic bird and now off came her skirt, her woollen stockings, her shoes, and on to the fire they went, too, and were gone for good. The firelight shone through the edges of her skin; now she was clothed only in her untouched integument of flesh. This dazzling, naked she combed out her hair with her fingers; her hair looked white as the snow outside. Then went directly to the man with red eyes in whose unkempt mane the lice moved; she stood up on tiptoe and unbuttoned the collar of his shirt.

What big arms you have.

All the better to hug you with.

Every wolf in the world now howled a prothalamion outside the window as she freely gave him the kiss she owed him.

What big teeth you have!

She saw how his jaw began to slaver and the room was full of the clamour of the forest's Liebestod but the wise child never flinched, even when he answered:

All the better to eat you with.

The girl burst out laughing; she knew she was nobody's meat. She laughed at him full in the face, she ripped off his shirt for him and flung it into the fire, in the fiery wake of her own discarded clothing. The flames danced like dead souls on Walpursignacht and the old bones under the bed set up a terrible clattering but she did not pay them any heed.

Carnivore incarnate, only immaculate flesh appeases him.

She will lay his fearful head on her lap and she will pick out the lice from his pelt and perhaps she will put the lice into her mouth and eat them, as he will bid her, as she would do in a savage marriage ceremony.

The blizzard will die down.

The blizzard died down, leaving the mountains as randomly covered with snow as if a blind woman had thrown a sheet over them, the upper branches of the forest pines limed, creaking, swollen with the fall.

Snowlight, moonlight, a confusion of paw-prints.

All silent, all still.

Midnight; and the clock strikes. It is Christmas day, the werewolves' birthday, the door of the solstice stands wide open; let them all sink through.

See! sweet and sound she sleeps in granny's bed, between the paws of the tender wolf.

Ⅳ. Questions for Thinking

1. "The Company of Wolves" is based on the fairy tale "Little Red Riding Hood". In which ways, it departs from and deconstructs the original story? And why?

2. Fairy tales play an important role in helping small girls learn about the world and their future gender roles. Carter once said what she has done is to debunk myth. By retelling those famous fairy tales, Carter aims at exploring the gender identities. What key elements does Carter want to establish in the new gender identities?

3. How does Carter describe the heroine in the story? How is this heroine different from the traditional girls in fairy tales, such as "Little Red Riding Hood"?

4. How does Carter portray virginity in her stories? What are the strengths and weaknesses that accompany being a virgin? How do we understand the ending of the short story when the girl sleeps in granny's bed, between the paws of the tender wolf?

5. When the wolf says he will eat her, she laughs because "she [knows] that she [is] nobody's meat." How do you understand it?

6. The ending of this story is radically different from traditional fairy tales. Why did Carter choose to end this story the way she did?

7. Explore the meaning of clothing in several stories. What is significant about the acts of dressing and undressing?

8. In the collection The Bloody Chamber, the last three stories, namely "The Werewolf", "The Company of Wolves", and "Wolf-Alice", all feature wolves. Read these stories and compare the images of wolves. What or whom does the wolf represent? What purpose does the wolf serve in the heroine's development? Make sure to examine the differences, as well as the similarities, between the wolves in the three stories. Bidisha points out that

these tales use wolves to explore sexual and gender politics, social violence and the possibility of liberation. Do you agree with her? State your reasons.

9. Examine the figure of the wolf in "The Werewolf," "The Company of Wolves," and "Wolf-Alice." Explore the meaning of clothing in several stories. What is significant about the acts of dressing and undressing? Some stories to consider: "The Bloody Chamber," "Puss-in-Boots," "The Snow Child," "The Tiger's Bride," "The Company of Wolves," and "Wolf-Alice."

V. Guidance for Appreciation

Angela Carter developed her interest and research into fairy tales when she translated Perrault's collection from French into English. When she started her own versions of fairy tales, she declared that "I am all for putting new wine in old bottles, especially if the pressure of the new wine makes the old bottles explode", which fully displayed her purpose of deconstructing those fairy tales.

The Company of Wolves is based on the fairy tale *Little Red Ridding Hood*. It deconstructs the original story both in the structure of the story and the images of the main characters.

First, Angela Carter deconstructs the structure of fairy tales by blending fairytale with pornography, two genres hostile to each other in traditional view. "Carter had always played with other 'genres' - the Gothic, science fiction... but they don't afford the formal distance of the fairy tale, which has longer and larger history (Sage, 55). Her creation of "adult tales" breaks the wall between the two genres.

Carter also deconstructs the structure of the original fairy tales the Red Riding Hood story, by introducing in the first part stories within the main story. These stories are by no means irrelevant. Instead, they are used to reveal the brutal nature of wolves.

Second person narration is also a technique used by Carter to deconstruct the traditional fairy tale writing. Instead of the authorial storytelling voice, Carter gets the reader involved by a dialogic mode. It is also a way to deconstruct the traditional male authority in fairy tale writing and challenge the expression of dominant ideologies.

More important, Carter deconstructs the image of the heroine. Carter frees Red Riding Hood and turns her into a strong, independent, courageous, witty and self-reliant girl. She is by no means a helpless victim of wolf or someone waiting passively to be saved. Instead, she is her own savior. First, she is strong. She is stronger than her grandmother, and definitely stronger than the girls in traditional fairy tales. Her strength gives her the confidence that "she knew she was nobody's meat". Her confidence not only comes from her strength, but also from the inner strength provided by happiness and emotional security: "she has been too much loved ever to feel scared". Second, this heroine is depicted as an independent woman who can make decision and choices in her life. Although she is told the danger of the woods, this girl is confident and "quite sure the wild beasts cannot harm her". Carter gives the reader a Red Riding Hood that can defend herself without a man's help. Angela Carter, in this way, deconstructs the traditional image of girls as a saved and males as saviors.

She is courageous and alert when she is aware of the danger of wolves in the forest. "She is quite sure the wild bests cannot harm her although, well-warned, she lays a carving knife in the basket her mother has packed with cheeses." When the young girl discovers the traces of a distant wolf, she holds her knife firmly and prepares herself to fight with the beast bravely.

All of these extraordinary behaviors are sharply different from that in the traditional version. Compared with the conventional image of a naive, ignorant little girl waiting for others' help, the girl in Carter's story comes to her own rescue with her vigilance, courage and wisdom.

Another important difference between Carter's image of Little Riding Hood and the one in the traditional fairy tale is her growing awareness of her sexuality and the power of sexuality. "Her breasts have begun to swell; her hair is like lint, so fair it hardly makes a shadow on her pale forehead; her cheeks are an emblematic scarlet and white and she has just started her woman's bleeding, the clock inside her that will strike, henceforward, once a month." In order to win the kiss from the handsome young man, she deliberately loses the bet with him.

What's more, by using erotic tales, Carter aims to lay bare the cultural fetisization and sexualization of young women. According to Sandra Gilbert and Susan Gubar's observation, "most Western literary genres including fairy tales are … essentially male-devised by male authors to tell male stories" (Gilbert and Gubar 2000: 76). So Carter's new fairy tales intend to reconstruct female sexuality by describing women as subjects rather than objects. In *The Company of Wolves*, Little

Red Ridding Hood is a sexually precocious girl, but she is not so much a desired object of patriarchal projection as an autonomous desiring subject.

The ending of the story that the girl sleeps "sweet and sound" in granny's bed, between the paws of the tender wolf, reveals the girl's choice of this sexual relationship voluntarily not passively. It is her decision to give up her virginity, not any man's decision. In this way, Carter challenges the traditional view of virginity and passivity of women. Red Riding Hood is updated to be a woman who considers her body her own to do with what she pleases.

The fairy tale makes the reader reconsider the sexual relationship and power politics of the gender relationship.

Ⅵ. Further Reading

1. Andermahr, Sonya & Lawrence Phillips. Angela Carter: New Critical Readings[M]. London: Continuum International Publishing Group, 2012.

2. Gordon, Edmund. The Invention of Angela Carter[M]. Oxford: Oxford University Press, 2017.

3. Munford, Rebecca. Re-visiting Angela Carter: Texts, Contexts, Intertexts [M]. Hampshire: Palgrave MacMillan, 2006.

4. Pitchford, Nicola. Tactical Readings: Feminist Postmodernism in the Novels of Kathy Acker and Angela Carter[M]. London: Associated University Presses, 2002.

5. Sage, Lorna. Angela Carter: The Fairy Tale[J]. Marvels & Tales, Vol. 12 (1): 52-69.

6. Tucker, Lindsey. Critical Essays on Angela Carter[M]. New York: G. K. Hall &Co. 1998.

7. Warner described From the Beast to the Blonde : On Fairy Tales and Their Tellers (1994.

8. 潘纯琳. 英美童话重写与童话批评(1970—2010)[M]. 成都: 四川辞书出版社, 2015.

9. 庞燕宁. 安吉拉·卡特诗学问题[M]. 北京: 中国社会科学出版社, 2017.

10. 邱小轻. 叙事策略与女性成长: 安吉拉·卡特作品研究[M]. 北京: 人民出版社, 2015.

11. 曾雪梅. 安吉拉·卡特的小说对表现论的颠覆[M]. 北京: 中国社会科学出版社, 2014.